13 · 9 · 2011

SPITE &

To Sandra
Hope you enjoy.
the authoress is
a friend of mine

Penelope Lye.

2nd Edition
published in 2011 by

Woodfield Publishing Ltd
Bognor Regis PO21 5EL England
www.woodfieldpublishing.co.uk

ISBN 1-84683-111-3

The characters and situations portrayed in this book
are entirely fictional; any resemblance to actual
events or to persons either living or dead is entirely
coincidental.

Printed and bound in England

Cover design by Mike Rowland

Spite & Malice

*A Tale of Sibling Rivalry,
Murder and Revenge*

PENELOPE LYE

Woodfield

Woodfield Publishing Ltd

Bognor Regis ~ West Sussex ~ England ~ PO21 5EL
tel 01243 821234 ~ **e/m** info@woodfieldpublishing.co.uk

Interesting and informative books on a variety of subjects

For full details of all our published titles, visit our website at
www.woodfieldpublishing.co.uk

Dedicated to my adored husband,
who spoils me rotten and keeps me going
with cups of tea and bacon sarnies!

Acknowledgements

My thanks to all the friends who read the manuscript
and came back with great reports on it, especially
Emma, who was my proof-reader
and Sue, for her encouragement.

My thanks too to Woodfield Publishing Ltd
for their help and encouragement.

~ CONTENTS ~

The Author

Penny Lye was born in the lovely town of Richmond, in the beautiful Dales of the North Riding of Yorkshire and spent many happy holidays in Redmire, near Leyburn. Married for the second time in 1999, she has four daughters by her first marriage, who are all married with children of their own, a boy and a girl each. She started writing in her off-duty times when working night shifts in the nursing profession. She and her husband now live in Cyprus. While there, she came across her old manuscripts and notes and decided to do something with them. She says, "You can't sunbathe all the time, it gets boring!"

Penny Lye in 2010.

I. 1942–1952

I have clear memories of my babyhood. I won't bore you with them all; I shall just recall two incidents. I remember being pushed in my pram, a lovely Silver Cross, by my very beautiful mother. We were going down a steep hill, it was a breezy day and the light wind kept blowing the fringes on my pram cover up onto the top of the blanket. I would bend forward and brush them off. My mother gently laughed at me. 'They won't stay down, Lucy darling; the wind will just blow them up on top again.' And just to prove her point, the wind did just that. 'See?' she said. I still bent forward to brush them off again. I don't remember arriving home. I guess I was asleep. The whole purpose of the walk, I expect.

The other memory I will recall is of being held by my father to have our photographs taken by his sister, Auntie Betty, with her Box Brownie camera. My cousin, Elena, older than me by one and a half years, was screaming because she didn't want to have her photograph taken and I remember thinking what a baby she was for crying. Auntie Betty said, 'Watch the birdie.' The camera clicked and then I burst into tears, because I had looked but had seen no birdie! Childhood memories are, of course, far more and just as clear. My sister, Jo-Ann, older than me by two and a half years, had a friend called Gill. She was the devil incarnate to me. She once accused me of stealing her mother's fairy wings! She opened the drawers in her mother's dressing table, shouting, 'Do you see them?' Of course I hadn't – and said so. She'd snap the drawer shut prior to opening another one and repeating the same question. Having gone through all the drawers, she yelled, 'Do you see them? No, because you've stolen them!' She hit me hard across the face, then, grabbing Jo-Ann's hand, they both ran out of the bedroom, laughing their heads off.

It was Gill who made me eat laburnum seeds, deadly poisonous, on the assumption that if they didn't kill me, they would be all right for her to eat. It was Jo-Ann who rushed inside to tell my mother what I had done that saved my life – which is odd, as twice after that she tried to smother me. My poor mother dragged my old pushchair out of the garage and with me in it, ran all the way to the nearest hospital, slapping me as she went to stop me from going to sleep. I have no memory of reaching the hospital but I do remember coming round after having the contents of my stomach pumped out and finding myself in a cot. I was really cross about that, as I was no baby.

Jo-Ann was terribly jealous when I was chosen to be a bridesmaid at Auntie Elsie's wedding. She was Mother's sister-in-law. I found out years later that I was chosen because I was more of a Stevens, my mother's maiden name, than a Bradley, my father's surname. Jo-Ann was all Bradley and Auntie Elsie didn't like my father very much. She said, even then, that Jo-Ann had a sulky look. I had a lovely time chasing the pigs on her parents' farm while waiting for the wedding cars to turn up. Then, at the reception, I got all the men, young and old, to smell my pretty posy, then I sat on their knees. I was four at the time!

It must have been about then that I realised that my father would take Jo-Ann away for the first two weeks of her school summer holidays. This did not worry me in the slightest, nor did I know where they were going; it simply meant that I had my mother all to myself and we would do all sorts of exciting things in that first week. She had a favourite café in West Hartlepool, where I was born, that I would be taken to as a treat, or she would take me on a picnic or to see a matinee performance at the local cinema. The following week would be my favourite time. We would take a train ride to the borders of Scotland and stay with my Uncle Teddy and Auntie Barbara. They had a large farm and reared Highland cattle – huge, shaggy beasts with very long horns.

Uncle Teddy would take me on his shoulders, introduce me to the animals and tell me not to be afraid of them. I'd grab handfuls of grass and put my hands through the fence. Uncle Teddy said I must hold my hands flat and the cattle would take it from me with their gentle but whiskery mouths. Or he would take me by the hand and we'd go round the big farm sheds to see the calves and I was allowed to collect our breakfast eggs in the morning from the hen house. I carried a little basket to put the eggs in that I would carry very carefully. At other times, Auntie Barbara would chase me round the garden and when she caught me she would take a leg and an arm and twirl me round, then she would gently drop me on the ground and stagger all over the place saying she was dizzy. She used to make me laugh so much. We would go for walks in their woods and pick armfuls of bluebells and if we kept very, very quiet, we might see some deer. I did, just the once and I was enchanted.

They had two daughters, Sadie and Judith. They were much older than I was and each had their own horse. When they had been out for a ride, Judith, the older one, would collect me and let me ride on her horse, back to the stables. I was, at once, terrified and delighted. I had a wonderful time and was sad when it was time to leave and go back home.

It was Gill, again, who called me 'a baby' because I wouldn't climb a haystack in the farmer's field and then slide down. To show her and Jo-Ann that I was no baby, I did it, landed badly and broke my leg. As playing on the haystacks was absolutely forbidden, they dragged me to the gate into the field, hoisted me onto the top bar, shook the gate until I fell off, then placed my broken leg against a stone. This completed to their satisfaction, they ran off to tell Dad. He was supposed to be looking after us that afternoon, as Mum was at the tennis club, playing in a championship game. They claimed that we were all sitting on the gate 'minding our own business' when the wind shook the gate and I fell off. It was years later that my parents learned the truth. But all that pain and discomfort had its own bonus – I never saw Gill again.

It was when we moved to a little village in North Yorkshire, Gales, near Richmond, that I began to feel that I was not the favoured one. Jo-Ann was a beautiful child, with flaming red hair and big green eyes. It wasn't that I was plain; I just wasn't a child of beauty, or so I thought. Going by my photographs, though, I was a blonde, blue-eyed cutie.

It was my turn to wash up after Sunday dinner and for Jo-Ann to dry the dishes. Both jobs were hated but washing up was the better option. Jo-Ann made such a fuss that I changed jobs with her. It wasn't that I wanted to gain Brownie points but because I knew that if I didn't do what she wanted me to, she would wreak her revenge sometime later in our shared bedroom. I dried the plates and dishes, getting my own back by rejecting a few things I didn't think were clean enough. I stacked the dishes by the edge of the table, as I would be expected to put them away as well. They were kept in a top cupboard, on the top shelf. They were not our usual plates; these were better quality and very pretty. We always used them for Sunday dinner and on special occasions. The floor of the kitchen was slate and slightly uneven. I stood on a chair to put the plates back into their rightful place. The chair wobbled and the four plates I was about to put away shot out of my hand and landed on the floor right at Father's feet. They were smashed to smithereens.

For a second there was complete silence. I remained standing on the chair, shaking. Mother's hand flew to her mouth to stop the scream as she saw her lovely plates broken beyond repair. Jo-Ann, shocked out of her usual apathy, stared at me with huge eyes. My father came towards me, yanked me off the chair by my right arm, hauled me into the dining room, shook me, smacked me and shouted. The more he yelled and shook me, the more I screamed. Eventually he hit me across the face. He had a signet ring on his little finger that caught me on my right cheek. Even seeing the blood didn't stop him; it just seemed to enrage him more. My mother came into the room as his hand was coming down for another smack.

'Ray that's enough!' she shouted, appalled and pulled him away. 'For goodness sake, it was an accident.' His excuse for hitting me was because I was getting hysterical.

'Go to your room!' he roared at me. I crept upstairs and into the bathroom to wash my face, then, holding a towel against my cheek I went into my bedroom, lay on my bed and cried and cried.

No one came near me for the whole of the afternoon. Teatime came and went. Shortly before Jo-Ann came to bed, my mother came upstairs with a glass of milk and some bread and butter. No squashy cake for me that Sunday. When Jo-Ann got herself ready for bed, she totally ignored me, just as though I wasn't there.

Once when Jo-Ann and my father had returned from their usual holiday and Mum and I were back from our visit to Uncle Teddy and Auntie Barbara, we all went on holiday together. It was just for a week and it was at a farmhouse in the deepest part of Yorkshire, in a little place called Osmotherly. Within two days of being there, Jo-Ann became very ill and was rushed to hospital. She was diagnosed with pleurisy and pneumonia. It must have been a very worrying time. Both Mother and Father would drive to the hospital and spend the whole day with her and I was left to fend for myself. I was six at the time. Children were not allowed in hospitals to visit their relatives. The place we were staying at was on a dinner, bed and breakfast basis and had to be vacated during the day. I'd wander the hills during the day, waiting for my parents to return from their bedside vigil. If I wanted to go to the toilet, I would have to go behind a hedge. By the time they got home, I would be ravenously hungry and so tired I would sleep the sleep of the dead, only to go through the same thing again the next day.

When my parents and I returned home from our week away, I was passed into the care of my grandparents and Auntie Peggy, Mum's mother, father and sister, whom I adored. Dad had to return to his job at the bank and Mum headed straight back to be with my sister, who was still too ill to be moved into a hospital nearer home. I was still on my summer holiday but, even so, Auntie Peggy would sit me down during the morning and do simple sums with me and would also read me stories. In the afternoons we'd make cards for Jo-Ann, or, if the weather was holding out, we would all go to the park located opposite to where my grandparents lived and I'd feed the ducks. I felt very guilty, as I was having a lovely time, but all good things must come to an end and, two weeks later, Jo-Ann was well enough to be moved to a hospital nearer home.

I returned to school and life returned almost to normal.

When Jo-Ann came home, I must say she looked awful. She had no colour to her face and was very thin. I was allowed into her room to play with her. She had been moved to a room downstairs so that Mum didn't have to keep going up and down stairs to see to her needs. Jo-Ann would get tired very quickly so, more often than not, I'd be playing by myself, which I didn't mind, as I had our shared bedroom to myself.

Father would come home in the evenings and enter her bedroom, saying, 'And how is my beautiful girl today?'

He ignored me but I didn't mind that either. As long as he was with Jo-Ann, I would be left alone. She loved the attention she got from everybody, with neighbours popping in to see her and asking her how she was and after, when she was up and about, they would say how well she had done and how bonny she was looking again.

Jo-Ann never went on holiday again with Dad and didn't seem unduly worried but I never got to see Uncle Teddy or Auntie Barbara again for years and was bitterly disappointed. Dad thought Jo-Ann must have picked up a germ on her holiday with him and that was his reasoning for them not going again.

It was a year after her illness that she tried to smother me for the second time. It was summertime and all my friends and Jo-Ann were out somewhere in the village. At times, I got tired of playing on my own and it was better to play with Jo-Ann, even though she could be so mean to me. I set out to find her. She was playing on waste ground that lay at the bottom of the third street. There were only three streets in the entire village. Each had just five or six houses and petered out onto moorland. We lived in the middle street. Jo-Ann was playing with Sue, a mutual friend and they had six boys in attendance. She would just have had her 10th birthday. Having her younger sister turn up wasn't what she wanted. Nor, it seemed, did the boys. As one the boys turned on me, they hit the back of my knees with a stick. As my knees buckled, they shoved another piece of wood behind them, then forced my arms behind the stick, so the inside of my elbows were facing the wood. One of the boys just happened to have some string on him, so they tried to tie my wrists together but my arms weren't long enough to get them together no matter how hard they pulled. In that position I couldn't move. They then all ran off laughing, including my sister, who shouted, 'get out of that you fat toad!' I yelled at them to come back but it just made them laugh all the more. The only thing I could do was fall over sideways and hope to somehow dislodge the wood. It took all the courage a seven-and-a-half year old could muster. I knew it was going to hurt, as the wasteland I was on was quite gravelly. I took a deep breath, leaned sideways and fell. The wood was the first thing that hit the ground, the second thing was my face. I had to wriggle about a bit to dislodge the wood, it took some time but it came away eventually. I was free.

I lay where I was for a few seconds, then I got up shakily and started to run home. I still had my wrists tied, as I hadn't been able to undo the knots. I went home by the road that joined the three streets together and hoped I wouldn't meet Jo-Ann or the boys again. I don't know who it was but suddenly a huge clod of earth flew through the air and hit the left side of my face. Unfortunately, the sod of earth had rather a large stone in it. Up to that time, I hadn't been crying, although tears were threatening to fall but this assault caught me completely by surprise and I burst into tears and ran as fast as my sore and bloody little legs could go.

My mother saw the full effect of my injuries and was furious. Firstly, the string was cut from my wrists, which were red and raw. My hands were also turning blue. Next, I had my face gently bathed, then my legs and arms, which were both heavily grazed. She had to apply iodine, the only disinfectant we had at that time and it stung like mad and made me cry even more. My legs were bandaged, as the bad grazing wouldn't stop bleeding, as were my elbows. Large plasters were put on the cut on my face. I looked a fright. What wasn't covered with bandages or plasters was covered in yellow iodine. My mother got Mrs Bridges from across the road to sit with me while she went out to look for Jo-Ann.

She didn't have to look far. The boys and Jo-Ann were playing in the field behind Mrs Bridges' house. Sue wasn't with them. My mother yelled at the boys, who scuttled home quickly and then dragged Jo-Ann home. She was marched into the sitting room, where I had been settled on the sofa, to look at me and see what damage had been done. I think she was quite shocked at the sight of me covered with bandages, plasters and iodine, with my left eye going black. She was sent to her room and went without her tea.

My mother then went round to the boys' houses and complained to their mothers about their behaviour towards me, especially as they were all older than I was. If their fathers found out, some of them would get a belt taken to their backsides. Sue always claimed that she went back to untie me but I had gone. My father came back from the bank to find my mother sewing up my dress, which had caught on the stick and torn. He walked into the sitting room to see me, said nothing but simply walked out again and started up the stairs to see Jo-Ann. My mother stopped him. She called from the bottom of the stairs, which were just outside the sitting room door.

'Where are you going?' She demanded.

'To see Jo-Ann, of course.'

'Don't you dare, she is in disgrace.'

'I was going to tell her off.'

'A likely story. Come down please, I want to talk to you.'

He did as she asked. I think he could see that Mum was still very angry. They must have gone into the kitchen to have this 'talk', as I heard nothing else.

Jo-Ann didn't like to be ignored. She had loved the fuss people made of her after she was ill. Suddenly things changed and the villagers were asking her how I was and she didn't like that, not one little bit. And that's when she decided to smother me. I truly believe that she meant to carry it out to the end. The only reason I'm alive is because Mum came up to our bedroom to see what we were doing, because we were too quiet, to find Jo-Ann sitting on a pillow that was over my face. I was hardly breathing and unable to move. Mum pulled Jo-Ann off the bed and bent over me to see if I was still breathing. I had never seen Mum so angry with Jo-Ann. She actually smacked her across the face.

After that incident and that day, she moved us into separate bedrooms. Jo-Ann had our shared room to herself and I was put into the small back room. I didn't mind because it was MINE. To the left of the bed was a small door that led into the eaves of the house. It was boarded over and used for storage but it was a great place to hold tea parties with my dolls and teddies. Jo-Ann didn't know what she was missing and I made sure she never did. I loved my little room and it became my sanctuary. Years later, another bedroom was to become my sanctuary as well.

Then came a day when I was more frightened than I have ever been in my entire life...

Behind our house was a very big field, it was in a sort of sloping Y shape and very steep. The corn had been cut, so we were allowed to walk on it. At the top end of the field, a path led down to the first street of our village. My friend Belinda lived there and it was the quickest route to go and call on her. At the top of the field it went into a wide clearway. If a fire were to start in the right hand wood, the clearway would stop it spreading over to the left, where there was a much bigger forest. I heard voices in the wood on the left and went to investigate. There was a little brook to cross and the well-used bridge was made of an old wooden door set solidly into each bank. I crossed this and walked into the wood. I came to a clearing where my sister was with Sue and Ann, her friends and the three Davidson boys, my main tormentors. The oldest, Michael, was about 14 and went by the name of Spike. The other two were twins of 12, Peter and John (called Podge and Pie respectively). They were both rather plump.

They were standing in a tight ring and chanting something. They raised their clasped right hands and yelled, 'All for one and one for all!' I had the feeling that I shouldn't be there. Unfortunately, Jo-Ann saw me. She pointed to me and yelled 'Kill the fat toad!'

They all ran over and encircled me.

'You have seen something you shouldn't have seen, so we will have to kill you,' Jo-Ann said. Podge and Pie looked a bit uncomfortable.

'Come on Jo-Ann, that's not fair,' Podge said.

'You dare defy me, Podge, when we have just sworn our allegiance to each other?'

'She's only a silly kid,' he protested.

Jo-Ann looked at me. 'I'll count to ten to give you a chance to run away, you nasty fat toad. Go on. Go!'

I ran out of the wood and to the stream. No way was I going to make it over the clearway to the other forest, my only plan was to hide in there before they caught up with me but they had their bikes with them.

Somehow, I slipped and fell into the brook, just as I heard them all shout, 'Ten... We are coming to get you!'

I swam to the bridge and hid under it. The door was only just above water level. I pushed myself into the reeds at one end and, by holding onto a cross-member of the door, I managed to keep afloat. It was very cold and deep. I heard their banshee shrieks as they raced out of the wood. I felt the door sink slightly as they raced across it. I couldn't possibly be seen and knew that but I still shook with fear or cold, I'm not sure which, both probably.

I don't know how long I stayed there but eventually they must have lost interest in looking for me because their shrieks diminished as they moved further away. I slipped out of my hiding place and peered over the bank. I could see no-one. I crawled further out and saw them half way down the field; their feet off the pedals as they freewheeled down the hill. I ran, still shivering with cold, across the clearway and into the opposite forest. I ran as fast as I could, hampered by my wet dress flapping around my legs. Once in the wood, I followed a well-worn track. I had to stop once or twice to get my breath and ease the stitch in my side. I came to a part of the forest that had been cut back. I had to leave the path and go deeper into the wood. I could hear their voices. They were on the right stroke of the Y now, preparing to race their bikes down that hill, which was steeper than the other was. I hid from sight again, by a large tree and a bramble bush. My heart was thumping so hard and loudly I thought they surely must hear it. At last, they moved off, shrieking again with glee as they raced away down the hill. After my enforced rest, I started to run again. I had to turn right to land up somewhere near home. I would have to climb Mrs Wilson's wall, to get to safety. I liked her, Mum and I used to help her pick her produce. The Wilson's were very wealthy but she loved garden-ing and could grow anything. The wood here was very overgrown and my arms and legs got very scratched, as did my face.

I suddenly realized I could hear pounding feet behind me. I looked back and there they were. Jo-Ann, Sue, Ann, Spike and the twins I was so near and yet so far to safety but they had fooled me into thinking that they had become bored with the idea of killing me. I lost my footing and fell headlong into some bushes and then they were on me. They kicked and punched me. Spike had some string in his pockets. This was tied round my neck and I was hauled to my feet. First Jo-Ann spat at me, then they all followed suit. I was crying by now and terrified.

'String her up from a tree!' Jo-Ann yelled.

Spike threw one end of his ball of string up into a branch of a nearby tree, it went deftly over the branch and he caught it as it came down the other side.

'Prepare to meet thy doom!' screamed Jo-Ann.

Spike gathered up the ends of the string and started to pull.

'What in hell is going on here?' It was Mrs Wilson. 'Let that child go immediately! Are you alright dear?' she asked me. 'I don't believe what I'm seeing. Here's Barbara's child being attacked by some village kids and her sister is here too, who seems to be the main perpetrator,' Mrs Wilson said, in shocked tones.

Mr Wilson climbed his wall and stomped towards us. 'What have you got to say for yourselves?' he bellowed.

The boys backed away. 'Nothing sir, just playing.'

'Playing indeed. I don't call trying to string a young girl up *playing*.' He undid the string from my neck, then lifted me up and passed me over the wall to Mrs Wilson, who was still standing in her garden. She put me gently on the ground and sat down with me.

'My dear girl, whatever were they doing?'

Through my tears and sobs, I managed to say, 'They were trying to kill me. They said they would.'

'But why?'

'I saw them in the other wood and because I saw them they said they were going to kill me.' I was still shaking and I was also very cold.

'You're soaking wet and scratched to bits.'

'I hid under the bridge over the stream. It was very cold and deep.'

'I'm surprised you weren't swept away. It run's high just there, because it's so narrow. I'll clean you up a bit, though, before I take you home, your mother has to hear about this. Anyway, dry your tears and come with me.' Mr Wilson had climbed back over the wall by then.

'Upon my soul, I wouldn't have believed it if I hadn't seen it with my own eyes. Disgraceful! Disgusting! Let's see if we can find little Lucy a treat of some sort.'

Mr Wilson led the way and, with my hand in Mrs Wilson's, we followed. Mrs Wilson wrapped me in a blanket first, then bathed my legs, arms and face and sat me down in their big, warm kitchen and handed me a plate with a generous slice of chocolate cake on it. It was delicious. When I had finished it, Mrs Wilson escorted me home. The gate to our house was all of 20 yards from theirs. The three Davidson boys were still hanging around. Mrs Wilson told them to go away but, before they went, they had one thing more they wanted to do to me.

One of them had a catapult. The stone hit me in the middle of my back. It made me cry again. Mrs Wilson turned round and told them that they were nothing but bullies and the village idiots and if they didn't look out they were all going to come to sticky ends. I found out years later that Spike did a stretch in prison for rape and for drug trafficking. Knowing that and looking back, I think Spike had given them all some sort of drug, their behaviour that day was so awful and even for Jo-Ann it was unusual.

My mother was appalled at what had happened and could barely believe the story Mrs Wilson told her.

'Mr Wilson saw as well Barbara. I really do think you should go round to Mrs Davidson and complain. God only knows what would have happened to Lucy if I hadn't been at the bottom of the garden. I heard Jo-Ann scream "String her up from a tree!" and "Prepare to meet thy doom!" I have cleaned her up a bit but it may be better if Lucy has a bath, she does feel dreadfully cold.'

Jo-Ann was sent to bed without tea and grounded for two weeks. My mother was furious with her. Jo-Ann never apologised and had a mutinous look on her face for days after.

The Davidson boys had a thrashing from their father and Sue and Ann were banned from our house. Dad never believed that Jo-Ann could have been so nasty and if anything, his behaviour towards me got worse. Anything that happened that was bad, was blamed on me. Even when it was found to be Jo-Ann's fault, she would just get a mild rebuke, while I would be sent to my room without supper. I was always blamed for the untidiness of our shared room. Only when we had separate bedrooms did Dad finally see that Jo-Ann was the really untidy one. It wasn't that I was much tidier but my room was just so small I had to keep it neat and clean, although I did have that secret extra space in the eaves that I used to my advantage.

No one could get into my room when I was in the eaves, as to get the little door open I had to push my bed in front of my bedroom door. If Mum wanted to come in, I would say I was just dusting the skirting board and so that it wasn't a lie, I kept a duster in my room for just that purpose. Having dusted the skirting boards, I would then move my bed back into its rightful place, so that Mum could come in. Jo-Ann and I were forbidden to go into each other's rooms; even so, some of my little treasures disappeared, to be found years later.

I was eight when my best friend arrived – in the shape of a Labrador puppy. She was called Honey because she was that colour. She really belonged to my father. I had to admire him in his training of Honey. She was intelligent and learned quickly. She always stuck by your side and never needed her lead on. She was very obedient and when told to 'go' would take off and run like the wind. I adored her. Honey and I would walk miles, although never again did I walk in the woods to the left of our house. I'd climb up to the high moors or 'the top of the world', as I called it. It was a big area of craggy moorland. I would arrive there panting almost as much as Honey. To start with, I could only do that when Dad was working and Jo-Ann and I were on holiday from school or at weekends but, as with all things, Dad got bored with the walking, so I was given it as one of my many small jobs. Honey was allowed upstairs and would come into my bedroom and I would allow her into my inner sanctum, under the eaves. She would be quite happy until it neared my father's time to return from work. Honey would look at me and whine just the once. I would let her out of my room and she would trot downstairs and wait for Dad by the front door. She was so loyal.

Jo-Ann didn't bother with her much. When Mum suggested that Jo-Ann come for a walk with Honey and me, I'd hold my breath and hope she'd say she didn't want to, which she always did. I'd let my breath out slowly, pleased that she didn't want to come. We could be gone for a couple of hours and Mum didn't seem to be worried that we were gone so long. We'd go left out of the house, fork right into a field that was usually full of young, inquisitive bullocks that used to get uncomfortably close to me. Honey must have felt my unease, because she would round them up, away from me, until I reached the style at the other side of the field, then chase after me and jump the style. Now on the moor itself, I'd let her run off, chasing rabbits that she never caught.

When I was ten, my beloved Grandmother died. It was not unexpected; she had been ill for a long time. Even so, my mother was devastated when it happened and I cried for days. Jo-Ann seemed unmoved but at least she didn't tease me about crying so much, as she didn't know. In my room, I would cuddle into a pillow and weep buckets. Honey would be with me, worried because she didn't understand what was going on. She would put her front paws onto my bed and lick whatever part of my face or hand she could reach. Her devotion helped pull me through that awful time, I'm sure of that.

II.   1953-1957

When I was 11 years old, we moved down south. My father wanted to run his own hotel business. We had to leave our Labrador dog, Honey, behind. We had all gone up to Redmire to say goodbye to Grandad, Auntie Peggy and hand over Honey. Dad with Jo-Ann had driven the car to the edge of the village to wait for us, as we wanted to walk from Crofters Cottage, where Grandad and Auntie Peggy now lived, to the car, as a last short walk with Honey.

There was just Mum, Grandad, Auntie Peggy and me. Grandad was holding Honey, who was on a lead, I hadn't understood that then, I just thought that, as she was so good and wouldn't have run away, her lead wasn't necessary.

None of us was saying anything. All had been said that was going to be said. Mum looked upset, as did Auntie Peggy, Grandad didn't look too happy either and I was openly crying.

Once at the car, Dad and Jo-Ann got out to say their final goodbyes. I gave Grandad and Auntie Peggy a final kiss and a cuddle then bent down to say goodbye to Honey and couldn't let go. I buried my head in her fur and sobbed. A sharp kick on my rump got me to stand up. It was the only time I knew Honey growl at Dad.

'There was no need for that Ray,' Grandad said sharply.

'She can be very difficult at times,' Dad replied.

I heard what he said but I was already upset, so made no comment.

The four of us got into the car. I knelt on the back seat to wave to Grandad and Auntie Peggy and Honey. I now understood why Honey was on a lead. She was straining on it, trying to follow the car. Her front legs were up as she clawed the air to get away. Her family were leaving her behind. It is a picture that haunts me still. It took Grandad and Auntie Peggy all their combined strength to hold her back. It was harrowing to watch. I curled myself up in the corner of the back seat and sobbed my heart out.

Dad had been in a terrible temper for ages before our move. Even Jo-Ann behaved herself. Years later, I was to learn that he had been passed over for promotion to Bank Manager at the branch of the bank where he had worked since he'd left school. A younger man had been given the position; he was furious. It had given him much pleasure to hand in his notice, especially when they asked him to stay on.

Southern people, I found to be cold and unfriendly. No one seemed to smile. They looked at me as though I was odd, because I smiled at everyone. I missed Yorkshire in so many ways, especially Auntie Peggy, Grandad and Honey, the rolling moors and the beautiful dales, the people and the village of Redmire and Crofters Cottage. I vowed to myself that one day I would go back and remain for good.

Jo-Ann and I had to share a room again and it was my job to keep it clean and tidy, as well as our private sitting room. I learned to do whatever my father told me to do, without question.

In the evenings after school and at weekends I was expected to work in the hotel. I helped with the early morning teas, with another member of staff: Sandra, Irene or Betty. I helped Mrs Crow, our housekeeper, make beds or cleaned with Pearl or Gladys. I learned to make cakes, scones and little fancy pastries in the afternoon and serve them up for afternoon tea. My sister was not expected to do anything too strenuous; she would pass on to me whatever job she didn't want to do, her reason being that she was too fragile. She played on her illness for years.

I was very unhappy during this time, as I had to contend with the chef, who had a terrible temper (it was nothing for him to throw a freshly made cake at me) and my father, whose attitude towards me just got worse.

The idea of sending me to boarding school came about when I was 13. The school was in Darlington, County Durham. My grandmother (my father's mother) had taught elocution there, many years ago. Auntie Betty went there as, in turn, did her daughter. I was taken to Temple Meads Station in Bristol by my tearful mother and my smirking sister. Mother went off to get me a magazine.

'I wouldn't be sent away to boarding school,' Jo-Ann boasted.

'Obviously not,' I replied, in a very calm voice. 'You're just not clever enough for them to bother.'

'I shall be glad to get rid of you,' she spat back furiously.

'Well, now that I'm not going to be around for a while, you're going to have to work for a change. Won't that be a pleasure for you?'

Jo-Ann looked quite shocked. She obviously hadn't thought of that.

'Whatever,' she said carelessly, and turned away.

Just them Mum came back and tucked the magazine into my carrier bag. I waved goodbye to my crying mother and went on waving until I could see her no more.

I can't say I actually enjoyed my three years at boarding school but it had three wonderful redeeming features. It took me away from my father's increasing antipathy toward and me, Jo-Ann's open hostility. Best of all, it was just a three-hour bus journey from Redmire, my Auntie Peggy and Grandad and I would get to see Honey again in the half-term holidays.

The cottage only had two bedrooms. Auntie Peggy's room was the whole width of the cottage and she had two beds in it. The cottage had no bathroom, just a three-seat privy in the back yard. Personal washing was done in the cold scullery. Once a week we would troop next door to the pub and have a bath. Things were a bit primitive but I didn't care. I loved it there.

I would make my own way to the bus station in Darlington and get in the correct queue to wait for the bus to take me to Richmond. That would take just under two hours, as the bus would stop at every hamlet and village on the way. Once there, I would wander around the picturesque old town, which had a huge cobbled square with shops arranged around all four sides, and look in the windows. These were the same shops that Mum would have done her shopping in. Little had changed in the shops themselves. The butcher's still had sawdust on the floor and the sweet shop on the corner had old-fashioned glass jars arranged on the counter and behind on shelves, rows and rows of them. It had a sweet, sugary, fudgy smell, which brought back memories of waiting in the queue with my ration coupons clutched in my hand and being very indecisive as to what to have.

Then the Leyburn bus arrived and rumbled over the cobbles to the waiting line of people and I'd run to join it.

Leyburn was much the same as Richmond but perhaps even more quaint. I didn't know which town I loved more. It used to have a market every Friday and does still. If I were staying with Grandad and Auntie Peggy at the time, I'd get up early with Grandad, go with him and help carry his groceries home.

In Leyburn, with mounting excitement, I'd catch the bus to Redmire and turn my head this way and that to take in the beautiful views, knowing I was nearly there when Penhill came into view.

I'd alight at Redmire and, with my travel case bouncing against my side, I'd run to Crofters Cottage and fall into my aunt's arms, almost crying with pleasure at being there. Grandad would come out of the sitting room, I'd kiss his old, sweet face and he'd ruffle my hair, his only show of affection, but his smile of welcome told me that he loved me as much as I loved him.

My welcome from Honey was something else. She would wag her tail, dance on the spot and give little squeaks of pleasure at seeing me again.

In the morning, I'd walk to the River Ure. It was Grandad's and my favourite walk. Honey would trot between us. In the afternoon Grandad would go into the sitting room for his nap, Auntie Peggy would get out her old paint box and we'd sit painting and chatting all afternoon. Sometimes she would make her mouth-watering doughnuts with jam inside. Many times I burned my mouth on the hot jam because I couldn't wait for the jam to cool. With no television to watch, we'd play cards in the evening or just sit and chat or read, Grandad, Auntie Peggy and me. Although conditions were not ideal, I loved my time with them and it broke my heart when I had to return to school. Many times I nearly didn't go, for neither Auntie Peggy or Grandad would have made me return. But visions of my father's anger always drove me back.

In the long summer, Christmas and Easter holidays, I'd always return home. My mother was always pleased to see me and would meet me at Bristol Temple Meads train station. We'd fling our arms around each other and kiss each cheek. Jo-Ann's 'Hello, nice to see you' lacked in sincerity and my father showed complete indifference on my return. No change there then!

Once home, it was back to the old routine. At least I had been given a room to myself but it was back to work. There was no holiday for me. There was not even time for me to do my holiday homework, never mind anything I actually *wanted* to do.

In my last summer holiday before I left school for good, my father found me in our private sitting room, sitting down (God forbid!) and doing my homework. To all intents and purposes, it looked as though I was just reading.

'What do you think you are doing?' he demanded.

'Homework,' I answered, shortly.

'Oh yes?'

'Yes, I have to learn Hamlet's soliloquy – 'To be or not to be...' that one. Then re-write it in modern language to show that I understand it.'

He walked over to me and snatched the book away.

Boarding school makes you stand on your own two feet if nothing else, so I said, with a note of sarcasm in my voice.

'Checking to see if I'm telling the truth?'

'Say it then.'

'Ha! Funny. How can I possibly do that? Just today have I had the time to open the book and start to learn it and with just three weeks to go before I return to school, with the work I've had to do and probably will continue to do, I shall be lucky if I get another chance to open the book, never mind learn anything.'

He threw the book back at me; it landed on the floor by my feet.

I bent to pick it up. 'It's the school's book, not mine. They won't be best pleased if it gets damaged.'

'Learn it. I'll test you on it before you go back to school.'

'Oh, I wouldn't bother to do that. They'll do that at school, then you won't have to spend more time with me than you have to.' I looked up at him and he was staring at me. I think in that moment we understood each other's antipathy towards the other.

'You are so right,' he said, in a uncaring tone and walked out.

It was almost a relief to get back to school.

My 16th birthday was in November. My father rang the school to say that, as my mother was ill, I would be leaving the school for good when we broke up for Christmas.

I was given a weekend's leave to say a very sad and tearful goodbye to Grandad, Auntie Peggy and Honey. I didn't know when I would see them again.

My mother, as usual, met me at Temple Meads train station. It was good to see her but she looked pale and tired.

'Dad said you were ill,' I ventured but continued with, 'but here you are to meet me.'

'Did he? Well, I did have a bad dose of flu. But he said he found you learning Hamlet's soliloquy. He said that it was certainly not going to help you to learn something that bore no relation to modern living and if all the school was going to do was get you to learn long speeches, you may as well leave. Anyway, I missed you and I readily agreed that you should come home.'

'I see,' I murmured. And I did. They needed the workhorse back to do the work that Mum could no longer do and Jo-Ann refused to do.

Once again, I had no time to myself. I was not even given a whole day to settle in. The next morning Sandra tapped on my door at 6.00.am. I opened the door to her.

'I'm so sorry to bother you,' she whispered, 'but I can't rouse Jo-Ann. She's down to help with the early morning teas.'

I sighed, donned my dressing gown and went to her room. I didn't knock, I just went in and shook her.

'Wake up. You are supposed to be working,' I snapped.

She merely mumbled 'Go to hell,' turned over and went back to sleep again.

I turned to Sandra. 'Give me five minutes and I'll be down.'

'I'd be ever so grateful,' she replied and ran lightly down the stairs.

I was with her a few minutes later. While waiting for the big urn to boil to make the tea, I asked Sandra if Jo-Ann ever made it down for her turn of duty. Sandra blushed and looked away.

'That says it all,' I said. 'Not often, I guess.'

'No, I usually have to wake Betty but it's her day off today. Failing that, I have to ask your mother to help. I can't ask Irene, as she lives too far away.'

'So that's how it is,' I replied. 'It's not fair.'

'I'm sorry I had to ask, only I didn't know what else to do. Your Mum looks so tired sometimes when she comes downstairs to help. I know you've only just come back too.'

'Yesterday at 4 pm. I'd rather do it than have Mum disturbed, though.'

'That's what I thought.'

The urn started to hiss and steam and stopped all conversation, as we were busy running to and fro with trays of tea.

I'd had exams at the end of term. When my results came through in late December my father went berserk.

'I knew I should have sent you to a school for the mentally handicapped, you cretin, you dumb idiot!'

I gaped at him. I certainly wasn't going to take that remark lying down. 'What a nasty thing to say. I bet you 10 quid that those results are better than anything Jo-Ann did.' The wonderful Jo-Ann's results had always been a well-guarded secret. 'And,' I continued, 'if you think a mentally handicapped child could get the results I've got,' I took two steps towards him, 'then you are more stupid than I gave you credit for. But you are only saying that to needle, hurt and humiliate me. Well you have succeeded – but no more. I'm not taking that from you or anybody. I got 90% for art and nothing under 69% including an 80% for history and I think I've done pretty well.'

He stared at me in shocked surprise. 'How dare you speak to me like that? Get out!' he roared.

'Gladly,' I shot back and walked out of our private sitting room and up to my bedroom on the fourth floor. I locked my door, once I was inside and stood there shaking, then burst into tears.

III.   1958

Two events were to take place that made me decide that enough was enough. The first happened when I went into the stillroom to prepare the afternoon tea. My sister and Mrs Crow were in there, chatting. I lit the gas under the boiler and started to prepare the two trolleys with cups, saucers, hot water jugs, teapots, sugar bowls, milk jugs and small plates. I put doilies on larger plates, cut up the cakes I had made that afternoon and set them out on to the doilied plates, plus a selection of tiny sandwiches I had also made that afternoon. Jo-Ann and Mrs Crow were still talking (I had always got on well with Mrs Crow). I hadn't spoken a word up to that point, having always been told that it was rude to interrupt people when they are talking.

Jo-Ann, looking directly at me said, 'She is such a snob. Obviously we aren't good enough for her to speak to us.'

To say I was surprised by this outburst is an understatement. I must have had a startled expression on my face. 'Don't be so ridiculous. You were talking.' I managed to say.

'Just 'cause we were talking doesn't mean you can't join in,' she retorted, standing in front of me, with her beautiful face a foot away from mine.

'And if I had joined in while you were talking, that would have been wrong as well,' I said. 'I can't win with you.'

'You can't win with me anyway, you nasty fat toad,' was her reply.

Stung, I said tiredly, 'Whatever, Jo-Ann. And how childish of you to use a name that you used to call me when we were little. I assume you're not in the stillroom to help, so maybe you'd both like to vacate it and let me get on with it.'

'Help you! You must be joking. Why should I help you?'

'Because I did your early morning tea round this morning and because you don't seem to do anything in this hotel. You swan around like Lady Muck, thinking that your beauty is all you need to get by on.'

'It is,' she spat at me, her face inches from mine.

'Then beware,' I said. 'Beauty fades and then what have you got? You certainly have no brains.'

She looked daggers at me and stormed out, with Mrs Crow in her wake. Two minutes later, my father strode in.

'What's going on?' he demanded. 'Jo-Ann tells me that you have just been very rude to Mrs Crow.'

'How pathetic. I merely asked them both to move out of the stillroom, unless Jo-Ann was there to help. I am trying to get tea ready.'

'Why should Jo-Ann help anyway?' He grunted.

'Because I have been up this morning from 6.30 doing her early morning tea shift, with Betty. After that, I helped Mrs Crow make beds, then I baked this afternoon and now I am doing the afternoon teas. What, I would like to know, has Jo-Ann done? Well, I will tell you. Precisely nothing.'

He lied by saying she had been helping him with the accounts.

'No, she hasn't,' I ventured bravely. 'She's been out. I know that because that's what she was talking to Mrs Crow about.'

Caught out, he changed tack. 'You didn't do the early morning teas; Jo-Ann is down for that.'

'Well, tell *her* that. Betty couldn't rouse her this morning. So, as usual, she had to call on me to help. Perhaps if Jo-Ann hadn't come in so late last night she would be able to do her share of the work. She earns more than I do and for what? Doing nothing. Fat chance of me being able to do that.'

'How do you know how much she earns? Been sneaking around?'

'I don't need to 'sneak around', as you put it, she brags about it.' I shot back. 'Now perhaps you would like to go, unless of course, you're going to help.'

'Don't you get cheeky with me, my girl and get on with the tea, it's late.'

'And whose fault is that? Certainly not mine.'

He gave me a filthy look and walked out of the stillroom.

Once he had gone, I held tightly onto the trolley handle to try to calm myself down and stop shaking. After I'd taken a few deep breaths, I resumed my task.

In the large sitting room, there is a big sideboard. I rolled one of the trolleys in and unloaded it onto that, then brought the other trolley in with all the cakes and sandwiches on and laid all that onto the sideboard as well. 'Just help yourselves, please. If any more is needed I'm just across the hall.' I had got into the habit of laying a small tray with a cup of tea, a slice of cake and a couple of sandwiches on a plate for Mum or my father, whichever one was in the little office at the time. It's just along the hall from the stillroom, in the main reception area. My father was there so I just passed him the tray through the hatch. If Mum had been there, I would have gone in and sat with her for a while. My father said nothing, not even a mumbled 'thanks'.

'Sorry,' I said. 'What did you say?'

'I didn't say anything,' he snapped.

'Oh, I thought I heard a "thank you". Obviously I was mistaken.'

He called me back as I was walking away. 'For that cheek you can take a tray to Jo-Ann, she's downstairs in our sitting room.'

I looked at him. 'I certainly will not. She knows tea is served up here. She can get off her fat arse and come and get her own tea. I'm not here to wait on her. I have enough to do without that.'

He wasn't pleased with my answer. 'She has a headache.'

'Oh shame,' I said sarcastically. 'Been working too hard has she?'

'Stop it. And do as you're told.'

I stood my ground. 'Sorry, I'm not doing that. That's starting down a very slippery slope that I'm not going to go down.'

I was saved from any more unpleasantness by a man coming out of the sitting room.

'We would like some more hot water, please Miss,' he said.

'Certainly Sir, just coming,' I replied and was able to escape what could have turned into an even more horrible scene.

It always took about one and a half hours for tea to be over. I'd usually sit on a stool in the stillroom, having a well-earned rest and a refreshing cup of tea and a couple of little sandwiches before going into the sitting room once again with the trolleys to clear away the tea things.

A guest, Mr Adams, walked up to me. He came rather too close and said, 'You always seem to be working. You should sit down and I could give you a nice relaxing massage. We could get to know each other better.'

'Sorry,' I said, giving him an icy look. 'I don't fraternize with the guests.' He stepped back, almost as though I had hit him.

'Well, your beautiful sister is quite happy to.'

'That's up to her,' I said. 'Since she does nothing, she has more time than I do. But I would imagine she wouldn't want one of your massages either. She has a lot of younger men after her.'

Stung, he backed away and waved a hand at me as if to dismiss me before walking away.

I cleared away quickly and escaped to the stillroom to do the washing up. I put the cakes away in airtight tins then was crouched down putting the tins away. It's an awkward cupboard, as the door doesn't open fully, the tall cupboard that holds all the teapots, water jugs, etc, stands proud of the base units I was putting the cake tins away in. So I have no idea who came into the stillroom and kicked me viciously in the back. I could only guess it was Jo-Ann; it would be her revenge for not bringing her a cup of tea earlier. I crashed forward, catching my head on the cake cupboard door and hinge. I then collapsed backwards, lying in an undignified heap on the stillroom floor. I always put the cakes away first, so the two trolleys were still full of crockery, etc and one got pushed against the other as I fell and two cups crashed to the floor. I wasn't knocked unconscious but I certainly felt disorientated. My back and head were really hurting.

My mother was either just passing, or coming in for a cup of tea, she heard the crash and came running in to see what was going on and found me on the floor. She helped me into a sitting position.

'Whatever happened?' Mum asked. I told her of my exchange of words with Jo-Ann, then Dad and Mr Adams in the sitting room. It all came tumbling out and my suspicions that it was Jo-Ann who had kicked me.

'But surely Jo-Ann wouldn't do a thing like that?' Mum was holding a wet tea towel against my head to try and stop the swelling.

'I'm sick of it Mum, you and Dad always side with Jo-Ann. If it wasn't her, who else would do that? Dad or maybe Mrs Crow?'

She had no answer.

'She is lazy but is allowed to do what she wants, when she wants. Because she came in so late and drunk last night and Betty couldn't rouse her, I had to do her early morning tea round. But does she come and thank me?' I answered my own question, 'Of course not. She'd never do that. It's not the first time Betty or Sandra have had to get me up to help them. Yet she gets paid more than I do. I know that because she boasts about it. She does practically nothing and gets paid for it.'

'Well, she'll have to help in the dining room tonight, as Irene's just rung in sick.'

'She won't help, I bet. She will come up with some excuse and not do it.' My head was pounding and I winced when I stood up.

'Well you certainly can't help. Just look at yourself.'

She reached up above the sink and took down a small mirror. I looked at my reflection. I had a bump on my forehead as big as the rock of Gibraltar with a deep 'V' shape just under it where my forehead had connected with the hinge. It was oozing blood and both eyes were going black. My right eye was bloodshot as well.

'God I look a sight!' I said.

'I think you deserve a few days off, starting from now. Go upstairs and lie down on your bed for a while. Call if you feel sick and leave Jo-Ann and your father to me and I'll make sure that your wages are increased.'

'I have the washing up to do.'

'No, no. I know someone who would just *love* to do it.' Mum winked at me. 'Go on, up you go.'

I made my weary way up to my room and did what Mum had advised. It was a relief simply to lie down.

I remained in my room for two days. I had some reading to do and I wanted to write to Auntie Pegs and Grandad. Otherwise, I slept. I only went downstairs for my meals and had lovely hot baths that I could take my time over. I don't know what my mother said to Jo-Ann or my father but I do know it was Mum who helped in the dining room that night, not Jo-Ann. My father had tapped on my bedroom door later on that same evening.

'Come in,' I called. My father opened the door and stood in the doorway just looking at me. 'You can come in, you know.'

He shook his head and mumbled, 'Just called to see that you're alright.' He looked so uneasy standing there, that a nasty thought entered my head. Surely no. Not him...? He wouldn't, would he? He didn't like me but surely even he wouldn't stoop so low as to kick me. It was too preposterous to think but the kick had been so vicious. I tried to put the thought to the back of my mind but it just wouldn't go away.

'I assume it was Jo-Ann who kicked me in the back?'

I watched him intently but he gave nothing away.

'She will be... dealt with,' he said.

'Oh yeah, I'm sure she will be,' I said, with all the sarcasm I could muster. 'Sent to bed without her tea?'

He gazed at me a little more, turned away and closed the door. I still wasn't sure it had been him or Jo-Ann. But it had to be one or other of them.

The other occasion was more serious and it wasn't until years later that it was solved. I was helping Mrs Graham, our daily chambermaid. She was quite old but had wanted a job to earn money to help eke out her pension. She was quite sweet, I liked her. We were making beds in the west wing. The large trolley of linen was getting low on sheets and pillowslips. Nancy Graham asked me to pop downstairs to the linen room to get some more. 'You've younger legs than I have,' she said. 'You'll be quicker than me.' I ran down the two flights of stairs and entered the laundry room. To the left is another door that leads into the boiler room. In those days, the boilers were fired by coal. Stan Hadley, a slightly handicapped 63-year-old, was in charge of both boilers. There was another one in the basement of the east wing. He kept the coalscuttles full and kept the fires going in the drawing room, lounge, TV room, library, our private sitting room and the staff room. He checked on the boilers every two hours. There was a large cupboard to the left of the boiler.

I moved the steps over to the cupboard, opened it, then went up the steps and reached in to get a load of sheets. Maybe I took too many, because as I came down the steps (there were only three) I lost my balance, fell off the remaining two and hit my head on the cast iron fender that surrounds the boiler. I was knocked out cold. It was the heat from the boiler that eventually brought me round. I felt so hot that I thought I was burning up. I tried to sit up and move away. Blood was everywhere from the deep gash in the back of my head. I couldn't sit up, so I crawled on my hands and knees into the laundry room. It was blessedly cooler in there. I made slow and unsteady progress but could only manage to get just beyond the boiler room door. The two washing machines were not working yet and an ironing board hindered my progress, as did a washing basket full of clean towels. I reached for a towel and held it to my head. I was beginning to feel sick and dizzy. I slid down onto my right side and slipped into unconsciousness again. When I next came round, both washing machines were working, the ironing board had been folded up and was leaning against the wall and the towels had gone from the washing basket. So who had come in and ignored a 16-year-old girl in desperate need of help? Surely even Jo-Ann wouldn't do that? Neither would any member of staff. Did someone hate me so much?

It was poor old Stan, doing his two hourly check, who found me. He nearly had a heart attack, he told me later.

'Lucy? Miss Lucy! What are you...? Oh, my God! What happened? Wait there (Bless him, was I going anywhere?) while I go and get your Mummy.' And he trotted off.

In a surprisingly short time, my mother arrived. I was awake but terribly groggy. I had managed to sit up and lean against the wall. I had a splitting headache and still had the blood-stained towel in my hand but hadn't been able to hold it against my head any longer.

'Dear God! Don't talk, darling,' she said when she saw me. 'Stan stay with her, I need to phone for an ambulance.' And out she went at a run. After that, things were too hazy to say what went on.

They kept me in hospital for seven days. I had 10 stitches put into my head, both eyes were black (again) and I looked very odd, as they had had to shave some of my hair off to get to the wound to put the stitches in. The hospital staff told me to get lots of rest when they let me go home. *Fat chance of that*, I thought.

But Mum would not let me do anything for two whole weeks and then insisted that I take it slowly for another two weeks. My father informed me that some of that time off would be taken as my holiday entitlement. I was furious but said nothing, because in those weeks off I had formulated my plan of action.

It wasn't that I felt that my life was in danger but someone had come into the laundry room, found me injured and had done nothing to help. I suspected Jo-Ann but the laundry room was hardly her domain. She entered it only to drop off her washing. I wasn't even sure if she knew how to switch on the washing machines and putting away a basket of towels was just not her style. As for Mrs Graham, she had sat down to await my return with the clean linen and had fallen asleep. She was found by our house-keeper, Mrs Crow, and was immediately dismissed.

IV.   1958

I had two days off a week, nearly always mid-week. The luxury of a weekend off was very rare indeed. I would rise late, laze around and catch up on some reading, or write a letter to Auntie Pegs and Grandad but if I stayed in the hotel I would often be called upon to do extra hours, so I put a stop to that by going out.

I had an old school friend called Wendy. I had known her since before going to boarding school. She was tall, had fair hair and was rather plain in her bottle-bottom glasses, but she was very sweet, good-natured and a loyal friend. She worked at the hotel to supplement her income. She was doing a shorthand and typing course at a college in Bristol. She went three times a week. I would tell her everything. I told her about my father's mental cruelty (for that's what I thought it was and still do) to me, the vicious kick in the back and being left on the floor in the laundry room, badly injured. She was appalled.

I started to go off to Bristol on my days off. If Wendy was at college that day, we would meet up in College Green, go off together to have a bite to eat, then do a bit of retail therapy and have a really good time. Often we would take in a film. We had a lot of laughs, Wendy and me. My father knew of our friendship and would put Wendy on duty on my days off.

My next visit to Bristol, I did on my own. I brought a holdall and a few items of underclothes. I then took a bus into Temple Meads railway station and hired a locker. You could do that then; I don't know if you still can. I put my new clothes inside the holdall and put that into the locker. On my second day off, the next day, I packed two carrier bags with some good clothes. I hoped I wouldn't bump into Mum or my father, as they would be bound to ask what I was carrying *before* I went shopping. I was out of luck. My father was in the office in the main reception hall. 'Off to Bristol again?' he asked, in his usual surly manner when talking to me.

'Yes,' was my only reply.

'Full carrier bags before you go shopping?' He snapped.

'Just a few things to take to a charity shop,' I lied.

'Must be paying you too much if you have clothes to give away.'

'Talking of pay, you didn't pay me yesterday when you paid everyone else. Why is it I always have to ask for mine? It's as though you think I don't deserve it.'

He said nothing but chucked my pay packet on the hatch shelf.

'Thanks,' I said and stuffed it into my handbag.

'Not going to check it?' he sneered, 'to make sure I haven't diddled you out of a few pennies?'

I heaved a sigh. The bus would be arriving soon. I put everything down, opened my bag, rummaged around inside, located my pay packet, took it out, tore it open and counted it out. It contained what it said on the outside of the envelope.

'This is not fair!' I burst out. 'All those extra hours I have done. I don't know how you can do this to me. This is almost insulting!'

My father looked surprise that I dared to complain.

'Just be grateful that you got anything,' he grated out.

I didn't have time to argue about it. Unless the bus was late, I had missed it. I simply gave him an angry look, gathered my things together and left to see the bus sailing down the road. *Oh well*, I thought, *I'll walk. I've done it many times before and I will save on a few coppers on the fare.* I walked to Six Ways, called that as six roads converge at a roundabout. I caught the Bristol bus from there and arrived in Bristol about an hour and a half later. I changed buses at the main bus station and got another to Temple Meads Train Station. I packed my holdall again with the contents of the two carrier bags. I had a good look through to see what I should bring next time. I would need to bring my winter coat; I'd need that later in the year. With the money I had been given that morning, I brought a reserved ticket for next week.

During dinner that night, I said that in future I was only going to work the hours I was paid for. It caused a stir, of course, but what did I care? I was leaving next week. 'Jo-Ann gets more for doing almost nothing and it isn't fair. I should get more than her, as I work and work hard.'

I could see my father going red in the face but even he wouldn't shout at me in the crowded main dining room. We always ate our meals there; it was good for the paying public to see we ate what they did.

My mother asked me what I'd had in my last pay packet. When I told her, she looked at my father.

'Ray,' she chided gently. 'Come on love, that's not right. She sometimes works from 6.30 am to 9.00 at night, sometimes even later.'

'I don't care how many hours she works. She is paid on a weekly basis,' he snapped.

'Well,' she continued, 'she should get more than that for all the work she does.'

Between clenched teeth he said, 'This is no place to talk,' he jabbed his fingers at me, 'about her pay.'

There was a lot of talking going on in the dining room at the time, so our conversation went unheard but my father's angry, blotchy red face had caught people's attention and it had grown suddenly quiet. 'We'll talk later,' he said, and got up from the table.

After dinner we all went into our private sitting room. Once George, our headwaiter, had served us our coffees and gone, my father started on me. He paced up and down, ranting and raving.

'You ungrateful brat!' he roared. He called me all the names under the sun. Selfish, pig-headed, rude, stupid, cheeky, ill mannered, impertinent and insolent, to name just a few. I think outwardly I appeared calm but my heart was bumping violently against my ribcage. He eventually stopped his pacing and put his angry, flushed face near mine. 'I pay you what you're worth.'

'No you don't,' I found myself saying. 'Tell me,' I said, in an ordinary voice, 'if I wasn't here, how much would you have to pay someone else to do all the work I do? Well, I'll tell you but I'm sure you will tell me if, in your opinion I'm wrong. *Nobody* would do the work I do and then accept the pittance I get. I start at 6.30 in the morning sometimes. Then work through the morning in a chambermaid's capacity, work all afternoon making cakes, scones, pastries and sandwiches to serve for tea, which I also do most afternoons, with all its accompanying work, then, if we are short staffed, I sometimes do waiting at the tables in the evening. I fall into bed sometimes at 11.30, to start again the following morning. You would need two full timers at £4.50 per week, that's £9 extra in wages you would need to find. Jo-Ann, who I heard coming upstairs last night, drunk again, going by the fact that she kept falling over, would never put up with that ... and what's more, she wouldn't be asked to.'

'She very nearly died!' he bellowed.

'Yes, *ten years ago!* I was six and left to fend for myself during the day, while you and Mum went to see Jo-Ann. I would have thought that since both of you could drive, you could have taken it in turns to visit Jo-Ann. Then someone would have been there to see to *my* needs.'

'We paid Mrs Spalding extra money to look after you during the day and give you lunch.'

I got up from my chair. I suddenly had no fear of my father. He was nothing but a lying bully. I went right up to him.

'You're lying,' I retorted. 'Once you and Mum had gone, I was shooed out of the farmhouse and had to fend for myself until you came back. I had to hide behind a hedge to go to the loo. So don't give me that one. Nobody cared for me and my feelings or how I felt – and nobody cares now.'

I really thought he was going to hit me. If he had been angry before, he was now more furious than I had ever seen him.

Mum stood up at this point. 'That's enough. That's enough from both of you,' she said, crossly. 'We have got off the point of Lucy's pay. She should get far more than she does for the hours she puts in. Jo-Ann was terribly ill but it was 10 years ago and she can't hide behind that all her life. It certainly doesn't stop her from staying out late nearly every night. So enough of this. I'm saying Lucy should get at least what Jo-Ann gets.'

'That's £1.50 extra!' my father shouted (remember this was 1958 when an extra £1.50 meant something).

I thought I'd try my luck once more and said, 'Back paid. For all the hours I've put in that I haven't been paid for.'

Dad was rooted to the spot. Before he could say anything Mum said, 'Yes, I think that's right. You should be.'

'Thank you Mum.' I was really grateful.

My father just looked at me as though I was something low and horrid that the cat had brought in. He stormed out of the room, slamming the door behind him. Jo-Ann looked mutinous.

Mum smiled at me and said, 'Don't worry. I'll make sure you get it.' Then she followed my father out.

Jo-Ann opened her mouth to speak. I looked at her, pointed a finger and said. 'You tired-looking hag. Don't you say anything?' Shocked, she closed her mouth and stood up to examine her face in the mirror above the fireplace. I left her to it. I walked slowly up to my bedroom and lay on my bed.

I'd sorted through all the clothes that I wanted to take with me, not that I had that much, the rest I had given to a charity shop. I wanted to leave nothing behind. It wasn't packed; I couldn't do that until my last evening, so that if someone were to go into my room, they would not be suspicious. It was just an extra precaution because I kept my bedroom door locked and carried the key with me at all times. My reserved train ticket and my locker key were hidden and could only be got to by moving my bed and feeling under the carpet in the furthest corner, even so, I checked every night, just to make sure they were still there. I had just one more week to go...

The following week was dreadful. My feet barely touched the ground. If I was to get that extra £1.50 then I was going to have to work for it. My father had me running from one side of the hotel to the other. I went up and down stairs dozens of times. As each day went by, I'd cross it off a calendar that I had in my bedroom. It may be wicked to say it but by then, I hated my father.

When my two days off finally came I was shattered and over-slept. I just made it to the bank before it closed to get all my money out. I left one penny in it, just to keep my account open. In the afternoon, I went to see Wendy. She was the only one who knew of my plans. We said a very tearful goodbye. She offered to see me off at the station, which was so like her. She'd said she would be going to Bristol anyway, to go to college but I said no, as her college was in a totally different area. We promised to write and keep in touch. I'd said that as soon as I was settled she would have to come and see me. We keep in touch to this day.

That evening at table, I vowed to say nothing that would aggra-vate. I didn't want to antagonise anyone. My mother asked me if I had enjoyed my first day off.

'Yes very much, thank you. I went to see Wendy,' was all I said but Mum wanted to talk.

'She is such a nice girl, so polite and a good worker too.'

'Yes, she's always been such a good friend to me.'

'So plain,' Jo-Ann said.

'Well, we can't all be beautiful Jo-Ann,' Mum chided her. She turned back to me.

'Off to Bristol tomorrow?' she asked.

'Yes, I thought I'd go. I might take in a film, so I could be late.' I hated lying to Mum.

'Can I come with you?' Jo-Ann asked.

'I thought you would be working. Silly me, you don't do that do you? Anyway no. I'm meeting someone.'

'Oh yes, got a boyfriend have we?' she sneered.

'No, SHE is just a friend.'

Father, who had said nothing up to then said, 'Well, you can't have your day off tomorrow. You're needed here.'

I knew it! Trust my father to put a spanner in the works. I looked at him and bile rose in my throat.

'Ray!' My mother said, crossly. 'Come on, she deserves her days off.'

Again, I looked at him. 'You have run me ragged this week, making sure I earn my £1.50 extra. I worked hard, so I am taking my day off. I need it to re-charge my batteries for next week's onslaught... and the week after that. Get Jo-Ann to do something for a change. I can't do it all.'

He couldn't shout at me, as we were in the main dining room. He said through gritted teeth, 'Don't speak to me in that tone of voice. You are working tomorrow and that's the end of it.' He got up and strode out of the dining room.

Once more I appealed to Mum. 'I must have that day off tomorrow. I have arranged something and I can't let my friend down. She has no phone. There is no way I can let her know.'

'And what arrangement would *that* be?' Jo-Ann asked, adding, 'not that I'm interested.'

'So why ask?' I said mildly. 'Sometimes you say the most stupid of things.' I turned back to my mother.

'I don't see any reason why you can't have your day off tomorrow. I really can't. You go and I'll square it with your father.'

'Thank you Mum, I'm really grateful.'

I got off my chair, gave her a kiss on her cheek and went off to my room. I finished packing, sat at my table and wrote my note to Mum.

Dearest Mum,

I would not hurt you for the world but I know by my actions that I am doing just that. For this I will be forever sorry. Things have not been easy for me. I am used badly and I can no longer tolerate it. It seems that he won't be satisfied until I am dead. I am dead on my feet most nights, anyway. I can no longer remain here and be continually so abused.

I love you and I always will and I will miss you so much.

I will of course let you know where I am, please don't worry.

All my love,

Lucy xx

I put it in an envelope and just wrote 'Mum' on the front. There is a post box in the main hall for our guests to put their mail in. It is emptied every day at 2.30 by Jo-Ann (I believe this to be her only set job. She likes doing it as she gets to read all the postcards to see what people say about her. I know this is true, she told me). She walks down to a post box on the corner of our road and pops them in the mail to catch the 3.30 collection. This is where I'd post my letter tomorrow, knowing that it would be found when Jo-Ann opened the box in the hall to get the post out. By then I would be long gone.

I hid my letter, money, train ticket and locker key in its usual place and put my packed case under my bed. It's where it's usually kept anyway. Jo-Ann would be in her room getting herself ready to go out. I took the opportunity to venture downstairs to see Mum. My father would be in the bar. She was working in the office, in the main hall. I leant on the hatch sill and asked for my pay packet.

'Didn't you get it yesterday with the other staff?'

'No Mum. Dad always makes me ask for mine. I really need it,' I added gently.

'Then, you must have it,' she said, brightly. She looked into the safe. 'Lucy dear, it's not here.'

I sighed. 'Mum, why does he do it? I expect he hasn't even put it aside for me. Why does he hate me so? What have I ever done to hurt him?'

She looked uncomfortable. 'I don't know Lucy and I'm sure he doesn't hate you.'

'Tell *him* that.'

'I know what I shall do; I'll take it out of the petty cash.' She opened the little cash box, took out £15.00 and handed it to me. 'I would suspect he hasn't paid you your overtime, has he?' I simply shook my head. She sighed. 'I just don't know what he's thinking of. That's this weeks' wages and some past overtime. Do you feel that's enough?'

'Dad is going to be furious.'

'No Lucy dear, not with me and I'm sure he doesn't hate you.'

I wasn't going to argue. She fiddled in her bag, drew out £4.00 of her own money and put it together with my £15. It was almost my undoing.

'Mum, you mustn't, you can't afford it.'

'Take it lass, you deserve it,' she smiled rather sadly. 'I'll get it back, don't you worry on that score. I've had a word with your Dad about tomorrow's day off. He's relented to a certain extent. You can have the morning off but he wants you back in the evening to help wait at tables. I'm sorry, I did my best.' But she couldn't look at me.

'I'm so sorry Mum,' I said, rather unsteadily. I had my first misgivings about going.

'Whatever for?' she asked.

'I seem to cause trouble. The money, maybe you shouldn't have given it to me. He will take it as underhand of me in asking you for it.'

'You've worked for it Lucy. It's yours.'

I opened the counter flap, stood behind my mother and put my arms round her shoulders. I kissed her cheek and laid mine next to hers just for a second. 'Goodnight Mum,' I said, feeling so guilty. But I knew I had to get away, my life in the hotel had not been a happy one. I hoped that maybe one day she would understand.

During the evening, once Jo-Ann had gone out, I walked into her bedroom. She never locked her door, except when she was inside her room. I wanted to collect my personal belongings that she had taken from my room over the years. They were presents received for Christmas and birthdays when I had lived at Gales and things that had gone missing when they, Mum and Jo-Ann, had cleared out our shared room and put my clothes and personal effects into the bedroom I now had. They had done that while I was at boarding school and Jo-Ann had helped herself to some of my most prized possessions. Her room was in a frightful mess. Clothes had been dropped where she had stood to take them off, her wastepaper basket was overflowing and her make-up and cosmetics were scattered all over her dressing table; some had been spilled and never cleaned up. Tea rings were on every flat surface and I came across several half-empty teacups.

It was going to take me some time to find my things. Most were ornaments that I had loved. I found my little blue fawn with big ears that I had been given by a commercial traveller. He said it was his good luck charm. It hadn't given me much luck but it was very pretty. I found that first and slipped it into my pocket. Next, I found my china dog that was curled up on a red cushion. My white pig moneybox with a big blue flower on its back was under a pair of her discarded knickers on her bedside table. My Auntie Sally (a godmother, now deceased) had given me a little girl ornament dressed in winter woollies; it was really sweet. She had said the little child looked just like me. One of my favourite pieces was another pig but he was standing on his hind legs, dressed in dungarees and holding a pitchfork. I'd been given a delightful hedgehog, standing underneath a large leaf sheltering from the rain; a large raindrop was hanging from one edge. A beautiful heart shaped stone that Wendy had found and had had it highly polished, to show off all its beautiful colours, she had given it to me as a friendship stone. Two cream ducks with flapping wings, I had bought myself with pocket money I had saved up. But my favourite piece was a crystal ballerina, standing on her points, her arms bent elegantly in front of her, a look of concentration on her pretty face. She was dressed in a loose-fitting shift. Every tiny detail, even her eyebrows were there, you could see every finger and the ribbons on her shoes. The work involved with this ornament was outstanding. Jo-Ann wouldn't have seen that, she just wanted it because it was mine.

'What the hell do you think you are doing?' It made me jump. My father was standing at the door. Having got over the shock of seeing him there I answered truthfully.

'I am collecting the stuff that over the years Jo-Ann has stolen from me. This seemed an ideal opportunity to get them back.'

'A likely story,' he said angrily.

'Oh, I can assure you, these ornaments are all mine.'

'Couldn't you have just asked for them back?'

'Oh funny ... and be told to go to hell? I would never have been given them back.'

'Come out onto the landing and show me what you've taken.' He marched out of Jo-Ann's room. I had no option but to follow.

There is a chest on the landing; it stands against the banister rail just outside my mother and father's bedroom. It holds Mum's personal bed linen. It's the same height as the banister rail.

I carefully put my ornaments down on the chest. I lifted each one up and told him who had given each piece to me. I came to the ducks.

'These I saved up my pocket money for. See the mark on this one's neck,' and I pointed to the one standing on the right, 'you mended it for me when it got broken.

The little dog on the cushion, you and Mum gave me about three or four years ago.'

I picked up the ballerina. 'And this Uncle Teddy and Auntie Barbara gave me.'

'I don't believe you,' he said. 'I don't remember giving you such good things; those ornaments must have cost a fortune.'

'But you wouldn't know. Mum does all the Christmas shopping and present buying – and for birthdays too.' I still had the ballerina clutched in my hands. I liked the feel of the crystal.

My father then did something so unexpected that it shook me to my very core. He swept his arm across the chest top and all my ornaments went tumbling over the rail and down the stairs. The pretty stone hurtled down from that (the third) floor to the hall. It made quite a thud when it landed.

I stared at my father in shocked horror.

'What did you do that for?' I asked, on the verge of tears.

'Because a girl as plain as you doesn't deserve pretty things.'

I recoiled from him. My desire to go, now, this minute was very strong. The only thing that stopped me was that I heard my mother coming up the stairs and to get to my bedroom. I would have to push past him.

'What is going on?' she said, when she was halfway up the last set of stairs, 'and what's all this broken china lying on the floor?'

I could say nothing.

'I found her in Jo-Ann's bedroom, stealing some of Jo-Ann's things.'

'Ray stop. Jo-Ann never had ornaments, she always had clothes. The ballerina Lucy has in her hand is hers. What have you done?' She surveyed all the broken things scattered on the stairs.

'He broke them all,' I muttered, almost in tears. 'Here,' I said, putting the ballerina down on the chest. 'Perhaps you want to destroy her as well, as you have almost destroyed me.'

'Ray, no don't. Lucy, I don't know what to say,' my mother said in shocked tones.

I stared at my father and said, 'Just once, I would like to have heard you say, I love you Lucy. But you can't because you don't and never have. Let me assure you that I hate you with all my heart.' I picked up the ballerina again.

'Well, for that, your glass ornament is too good for you. I think Jo-Ann should have it, as it was in her bedroom.'

My mother said, 'No Ray, it's Lucy's. It was never intended for Jo-Ann.' My father's hand came towards me to take the ballerina from my icy fingers. I turned away from him and then I threw, with all my strength, the ballerina against the far wall. She broke into thousands of pieces that glittered as they fell.

'Lucy, Lucy, my dear girl, what have you done?' My mother sounded appalled.

'She, Jo-Ann, has tainted them all with her evilness. I've decided that I don't want any of them. They aren't important.' The little blue fawn though, remained snug in my pocket. 'I certainly don't want her to have my beautiful ballerina.'

I brushed past my father, who stood rooted to the spot in shocked surprise. 'I'll bid you both goodnight.' I said, then escaped into my room and locked my door against them both.

V.   1958

The following morning, very early with my winter coat on, my case and my last few belongings in a carrier bag, my handbag, now filled with money, my locker key and my train ticket, I stole out. I carefully locked my bedroom door as quietly as I could. I could hear my father snoring in my parents' bedroom just along the hall. Then I spotted it, Wendy's friendship stone, in the middle of the chest, the only survivor of my treasured ornaments that my father had so cruelly smashed last night. Yes, I had thrown my lovely ballerina against the far wall but I'd rather have it broken than Jo-Ann be given it. I picked the stone up and slipped it into my pocket. I'd pack it into my case along with my pretty blue fawn once I got to Bristol Temple Meads train station. I would never forgive my father for what he did but what he said was far more damaging.

I crept quietly down the stairs. Once in the main hall, I put my bedroom key into my mother's letter and dropped it into the mail box; it rattled alarmingly. I stood listening but nothing seemed to move. I went to the front door and opened it, then picked up my worldly possessions and stepped outside. It was still dark, with just a tiny lightening of the sky in the east. I was glad I wore my winter coat, as it was chilly at that time of the morning. I closed the door as quietly as I could but the final click sounded loud in the quiet of the morning. I looked around and realized that I would probably never see the hotel again. And I never did. It gave me a frisson of pleasure. With resentment and hate in my heart, I went on my way.

My parents' bedroom and Jo-Ann's room were at the back of the hotel, facing the sea but even so I kept looking up in case I saw someone at the window as I hurried up the short drive, clutching my belongings to me.

Clevedon, where I lived, had a little train station, just one line connecting it to Bristol Temple Meads. It was quite a walk. I was puffing a bit by the time I reached the station and my case felt as though I'd filled it with lead. The station wasn't even open. I put my belongings down and sat on a wooden seat to wait. The clock in the square chimed six o'clock. A yawning Station Master came round the corner and jumped when he saw me. 'My, you're early,' he said.

'Yes, I am a bit. What time does the first train go to Bristol?' I asked.

He scratched his head. 'Well now, let's see. There is the really early goods train. They do take a few passengers but it's not very comfortable.'

'I wouldn't mind that.'

'It should be here by 6.30. Why not pop over to yon caff and have a cup of tea while you're waiting. Better than hanging around here. I'll mind your case for you.'

I thanked him very much and, picking up the carrier bag and my handbag, I wandered over the road to the Greasy Spoon Café. It wasn't called that, but we had christened it that years ago. It looked what it was, a grubby 'transport caff'. However, the tea was hot, sweet and very strong. Twenty minutes later, I paid for the tea and walked back across the road to the station. I paid the stationmaster the fare, he gave me my luggage back and, with a cheery wave, he walked off, whistling, to see to his other duties.

'Hello dearie.'

Oh God, that's all I need, I thought. It was the 'town crier' of Clevedon, Mrs Thompson.

'Off to town for the day?'

'No,' I replied, rather sharper than I meant to. 'I'm off on holiday.'

'Somewhere nice, Dearie?'

'South Cornwall way,' I lied.

'Not on your own?'

'Travelling on my own but staying with friends.' Almost true.

'Courting yet?' She asked, raising an eyebrow.

'No. Boys don't really interest me as yet. Anyway, Dad keeps me working so hard that I don't get the time to go out and enjoy myself and by the evening I'm too tired to bother.'

'Saw your beautiful sister the other day. She should be in filums. You don't look a bit alike.'

'Thanks,' I said. 'I know I'm the frumpy one.'

'Don't say that!' she laughed. She thought I was having a joke. 'You're pretty in your own way.' She paused for breath, then said, 'I always get this early train, it's cheaper and I can always get back in good time to make Bert's tea before I go to bingo. Have you ever been?'

'No. As I said, I rarely get out.'

The train rattled in just then, cutting off her incessant chat. The last coach had wooden seats and was uncomfortable. The conductor sat with us and was the quiet type. Mrs Thompson made up for that by continuing her chatting.

What was bothering me was losing her at Bristol Temple Meads Station. She would wait with me, thinking it was her duty to see that I got the right train. She would think it very odd that I caught the northbound train when I said I was going to Cornwall.

Then I thought, *What does it matter what she thinks?* It was unlikely that she'd ring my family, as she would assume that they knew of my whereabouts. She chatted on, telling me of all the shops she was going to visit and which shop had the best bargains. I lost interest when she started to tell me about Bert's haemorrhoids. I don't think the conductor was that interested either. As I shifted my position, I wondered if Bert had ever ridden on that uncomfortable early train. In Bristol, I said. 'You may as well go, Mrs Thompson, if you want to get back in time to go to bingo tonight. My train doesn't go until nine.'

'You started early,' she said, 'and I have a few minutes to spare.'

Getting rid of her was not going to be easy.

Truthfully, I said, 'I didn't sleep too well last night, so as I was awake I thought I'd get going. And as you are going to visit so many shops, I think you should go and not bother to wait with me, although it's very kind of you.'

'Alright dearie, I'll go, as I don't want to be late back, but I can spare a minute or two.'

I tried again. 'I wouldn't if I was you. I have to go out of the station to get my ticket, then pay to get back into the station again, (all lies, as I had my ticket) and find out what platform I need to wait on, where I need to change trains, if I need to, get a few magazines and generally get myself organised...'

She looked a bit put out but shrugged and said, 'Cheerio then dearie, enjoy your holiday.' She turned and walked away but turned a couple of times to wave. I waved back and watched her go out of the station. She wasn't a bad old stick, just a bit of a busybody. Picking up my case and bags, I walked to where the lockers were located. Using my key, I retrieved my holdall and went into the ladies. I changed into my one and only good blue matching jacket and skirt, put on one of my new blouses, a cream one, and changed my shoes from sensible (for walking) to high-heeled. I managed to squeeze the contents of the carrier bag into the holdall and felt in my pocket for Wendy's stone and put that in my case near to the little blue fawn. I applied some make up and came out of the ladies looking rather different to the schoolgirl who went in. I carried my suitcase, holdall and handbag with my coat over my arm and went to the nearest kiosk to get my magazines.

I then sat in the ladies waiting room and ... waited.

I got through a whole magazine before my train came in. It had labels on the windows so it was easy to get into the right compartment. The last three carriages would be unhooked at Crewe and put onto another engine, which is why I had to change trains there. I had done all this before when I had gone off to boarding school. I went off to get another magazine.

In those days, there were porters to carry your luggage. It would mean a tip but it would save me looking into every compartment to find my reserved seat. Each compartment would hold from six to eight people and each compartment had its own door onto the platform, as well as a corridor to wander to the buffet carriage or visit the toilets.

The porter found my seat in no time and hefted my case and holdall onto the overhead luggage racks. I vaguely wondered how I was going to get them down again at Crewe when I got off to get my connection as I gave him a sixpence tip (two and a half pence now but it was plenty then). He doffed his cap, said 'Thank you, Miss', then went off to help someone else. We seemed to wait for ages before we got going. It was then that I was hit by a fit of nerves, or was it guilt? Not about the coming journey, I was looking forward to that, but I did think a lot of my mother and any action of mine that caused her worry or unhappiness was the cause of my guilt. I bit on my lip, surely she would understand in time. And anyway I'd ring her tomorrow and explain.

The train shuddered and the loudspeaker crackled into life. No one really heard what was said but from experience the announcer would be rattling off the names of the stations we would be stopping at. It shuddered again and with a lot of banging of doors and the guards whistle blowing, we were off. I held a magazine in front of my face just in case someone I knew was waving a friend or relative off on the same train.

The guard came round half an hour into our journey, saying that breakfasts were being served. I had been looking forward to this. I'd always eaten a good breakfast in the hotel, as it was often evening before I ate again, apart from the two little sandwiches I would eat in the stillroom at 4.00. I never had time for lunch.

I wandered off to the restaurant car right away. I was hungry, having been up since five. The dining car was one carriage long. Tables were set at each side of the carriage, with white linen and napkins. The waiters dressed exactly the same as in hotels and looked very smart. As soon as I was settled at one of the tables, one of the waiters came over and offered me the menu. I declined it and asked for a full English breakfast, a pot of tea and lots of toast. The breakfasts then were out of this world. There would be bacon and egg, tomato, sausage, a few chopped kidneys, half a slice of fried bread, mushrooms and tiny fried potatoes. I then had four halves of toast, butter and marmalade. *That will keep me going until tonight*, I thought. I ate slowly, savouring the taste. I thoroughly enjoyed it. Eventually I finished, paid my bill and wandered back to my seat. I found there was a young man in my compartment, who, as I walked in, stared at me, then gave me a charming smile. I returned the smile, sat down and started to read my magazine again.

Much later, we stopped at a station for longer than usual. I had my jacket off and was fanning myself with one of my magazines. It was August, after all, and the sun was streaming in the windows.

The young man said. 'My name is Mathew Howard; people call me Matt. I was wondering if you would like an ice cream?' He pointed outside to a man walking our way with a tray of ice creams.

'That would be very nice indeed,' I replied. He opened the compartment door and stepped out. He went just out of my view and he seemed to be gone for ages. He came back into the carriage. 'Whew. By the time I got to him, there was quite a queue. I thought I was going to miss the train.' He gave me my ice cream.

'Thank you,' I said, and took my first lick. 'Oh, that's lovely. So refreshing. It's ages since I had an ice cream.'

'I eat them all the time, even in the coldest of winters,' he confessed.

Soon the train rattled off again and Matt and I chatted all the time; it was as if we had known each other for ages.

At Crewe, he got my luggage down for me. I thanked him and also for the ice cream. 'It was the best,' I said. His train went off before mine. I had half an hour to wait, so I stood talking to him on the platform and waved him off when the train went on its way. He shouted something to me that sounded like, 'Until we meet again...' but that was silly. I didn't know where he was going and he only knew I was going to Darlington. Perhaps I was mistaken and he'd said something else. Little did I know that Mathew Howard was going to mean a lot to me in a few years' time. But we both had a lot of growing up to do in the meantime.

I made my way to Platform 3 to get my connection.

VI.   1958

The second leg of my train trip took two hours. I must have gone to sleep, because suddenly we were at Darlington Station. It must have been the squealing of the brakes that woke me up. I caught the eye of a porter who ran with the train until it stopped altogether; he hefted my luggage down for me and took them onto the platform. He asked me where I was going.

'To the bus station,' was my reply.

'Just down the hill,' he said helpfully.

'Yes, I know the way, thank you,' I said. I gave him sixpence for his trouble.

'Ta, Miss.' He doffed his cap and went away whistling.

I carried my belongings out but had to put it all down again to give the guard my ticket. I picked it all up once more and started down the hill. My case seemed to get heavier as I went. I found the right queue (it brought back memories of my boarding school days and how excited I would be waiting for the bus, just as I was now). I put my luggage down with relief, upturned my case on one end and sat down on it.

It took two hours to get to Richmond. Once past Scotch Corner (now a very busy main road) the bus took a right turn and stopped at every little village and hamlet on the way. Again, I must have slept, as the two hours seemed to pass quickly.

I alighted in Richmond, almost my hometown. I'd come back another day to wander round and visit old haunts but, impeded as I was by my luggage, I just sat on the steps of the war memorial and feasted my eyes on the view. It's a huge square, still cobbled, with shops all the way round the outside. Snatches of the Yorkshire dialect assailed my ears and I loved it. This is where Mum would do her weekly 'big shop' when we lived in Gales, about 7 miles away. If I had had the time, I would have called in at the little café where Mum would always have a refreshing cup of tea after shopping and Jo-Ann and I would have an orange squash each and maybe, if we had been extra good, a piece of cake or homemade shortbread.

It was quaint still, Richmond. It had been cleaned up a bit and a tarmac road went straight from one side to the other but it still had its olde-worlde charm and atmosphere.

The Leyburn bus trundled in, rumbling over the cobbles. The queue was quite long. Many hands helped me in with my luggage.

'Goin' on yer holidays lovie?'

'No,' I said, 'I'm going home.'

'Aye, nowt like it lass,' someone called from the back of the bus. ''ome sweet 'ome.'

I smiled. *Yes*, I thought, *I'm going home.*

I sat right at the front of the bus. I wanted to see everything. Richmond to Leyburn is only twenty-five minutes by car but an hour by bus. Again, it stopped at every tiny village and hamlet. Leyburn, like Richmond has another huge cobbled square and it also has shops ranged round the side. In the months since I had last seen it, it had tarmac roads going off in different directions.

But if I loved Richmond, I adored Leyburn. It's a typical north Yorkshire market town. Every shop you could think of and would ever want it had, along with at least four pubs. It did me good just seeing it. At the very top of the square was a lane that petered out onto the moors I loved so much.

I didn't have long to wait for the Redmire bus and the last leg of my journey. Again, people helped me on with my bags. The men couldn't let a 'wee slip of a lass' lug in her own cases, they would be letting themselves down if they didn't help. This bus stopped everywhere, certainly not at designated places. Sometimes it stopped and waited for villages who were running late. They'd come puffing up saying, 'Sorry ducks for being late; got 'eld up.'

'Aye, don' you worry love. I've got all the time in the world for 'e.' There would be a cackle of laughter.

'Silly bugger,' said the woman, in good humour.

The beautiful views, I remembered so well. Penhill, a huge craggy hill on my left, with the last of the sun touching its side. I was wide awake for the whole of the journey, just looking out of the window and drinking in the countryside. How I loved this place. Soon we were going down the steep hill that leads into the village, then follow the left bend, under the railway bridge, then the right bend and there was Redmire, spread out in front of me. I waited by the door for the bus to stop – 200 yards, 100 yards, then stop. The driver hopped out of his cab and came round to help me with my cases. 'Bye' someone yelled, I shouted back 'Bye' and waved as the bus trundled off. I walked as quickly as I could down the road to Crofters Cottage, my aunt's and Grandad's house. I knocked on the door and only seconds passed before it was opened by a very surprised Auntie Peggy. I almost fell into her arms and burst into tears.

'I knew it, I knew it,' she crooned to me, as her arms enfolded me. 'I knew you'd come back someday.' Grandad came out of the sitting room to see what the noise was about. He wasn't used to crying women and hastened back in again. But later, much later, when I had calmed down, he came into the kitchen and ruffled my hair.

'Lovely to see you Lucy.' He was a man of few words but the ruffling of my hair said it all. I knew he was pleased to see me.

I hiccupped my way through what had led me here. Honey, who had given me such a welcome, sat at my feet with her head on my lap. She didn't understand but knew something was wrong. Auntie Pegs sat and listened. Occasionally she nodded or shook her head and two or three times her eyes opened wide as though she couldn't believe what she was hearing.

When I had finished my tale of woe, I said, 'Anyway Auntie Peggy, I'm here to stay for as long as you'll have me.' She bent forward and took both my hands in hers. 'For as long as you like, lovie, your Grandad and I will just love to have you.'

'I hoped you'd say that.' I opened my bag and took out my purse. I smiled at my aunt.

'Don't argue about this 'cause you'll need it if I'm to stay.' I pushed over the £25 I had brought with me. Not much now but a King's ransom then, when £1.25 fed a family of four for a week.

'I have to say,' My aunt said, 'I would love to say, "no, put it away" but we only live on Dad's pension and although we don't go without, we have to be careful. So what I would like you to do is put 10 shillings (now 50p) into a pot on a weekly basis; that should cover your food and maybe an extra 2 shillings to go towards the electric and heating.'

I divided the money up into 16 piles of 12 shillings and put it on the mantelpiece above the old range. The change, nearly £6, I put back into my purse. I would keep that for my personal needs.

'That should keep us going for about 16 weeks,' I said. 'But before that goes, I shall have to get a job.'

'That's not going to go down well with your Grandad.'

'No. I guessed that. I shall have to talk to him.'

'In the meantime,' my aunt said, 'I'm baking cakes, scones, tea breads and little individual meat pies and ginger cakes. The local shop takes anything I can bake. Walkers and bird watchers buy them for their picnics. Those few shillings make all the difference. We loved your letters, so full of news. You said that you make cakes and things, so perhaps you could help?'

I was very uncertain about this, as I eyed the old kitchen range. 'I shall certainly try. What a great idea, a little cottage industry in the making.'

My aunt's eyes sparkled; she looked so pleased and happy.

'What fun we shall have. This is going to be grand.' She rose from her seat. 'Stay here lovie, I'm off to air and make up your bed, then when I come downstairs, you can have one of my freshly made meat pies for your supper. How about that?'

I got up to and went to hug her. 'Oh, Auntie Pegs, you have no idea how good it is to be here.' My eyes welled up again but I took a few deep breaths. *No more crying*, I vowed to myself.

'You go and ring your Mum and let her know where you are.'

'I'll do that tomorrow. I left her a note in our post box; she should have it by now. I told her why I was going but not where. I think she will assume I'm here. And if my father comes to take me back, I'm not going.'

'We'll face that if it happens,' My aunt said, and she went out of the kitchen, smiling.

For me, it was the happiest time of my life. I'd walk with Grandad in the morning, with Honey, down to the river, our favourite walk. In the afternoon, I'd bake and cook with Auntie Pegs. I slept the sleep of the dead. No longer was I rushing around helping to run a hotel. I had been very run down and tired when I'd arrived but after a couple of weeks of rest and good, hearty, tasty meals, I put on a little weight and felt tons better. When the weight increased some more, I simply took Honey out for another walk in the evenings on my own. At the top end of the village was a railway line that carried large amounts of coal to all places north of Redmire. Above that were the rolling hills of North Yorkshire I loved so much. Honey and I would go up there. When we got to the moor I'd give her the command to go and off she would run. It was like when I was a child again. I loved my walks, as did Honey.

When I called for her she'd come at once and we would walk back together, she to go to sleep at Grandad's feet and me with a reviving cup of tea with Auntie Pegs. The extra weight soon came off again but Honey expected that walk every evening after that.

The only fly in the ointment occurred the first week I was there. I'd rung Mum on the second evening to tell her that I was all right and not to worry. My poor mother said she'd been worried to death. She had even spoken to the police about my supposed disappearance but they wouldn't do anything for 48 hours. I couldn't understand it. 'Surely you found my note? I posted it in the post box in the main hall.'

'Jo-Ann never said she'd found it,' my mother said.

'That answers it. She found it alright and wanted me to look bad in your eyes.'

'Lucy, that's not fair. She may have just grabbed the letters in a bundle and just not seen yours.'

'Not Jo-Ann, she is far too nosy. She posts the letters one by one and reads all the postcards. Grill her, or better still, go to her room and look for it. It will be there somewhere and the key to my room was in the envelope as well. She never gets rid of any evidence. I doubt that she even realises that all my china has gone, as her room is in such a mess. So you'll find it. Never getting rid of evidence will get her into big trouble one day.'

I spoke those words not realising that one day evidence against her was going to get her into very deep trouble indeed.

It turned out I was right. Jo-Ann had merely torn my letter to Mum in half and put it into her wastepaper basket.

Auntie Peggy said she would like to have a word with Mum. I handed her the phone and went out of the phone box to wait outside for her. I heard just a smattering of what she said.

'I'm shocked and disgusted at the treatment of Lucy. When she got here she was in a terrible state and very near to collapse. Did you never notice how thin she was?' I heard no more as I moved away from the phone box. I rang Mum every week after that, always at the same time. I never got to speak to Jo-Ann or my father. The first few weeks I was a little nervous about ringing. If my father had answered the phone, doubtless I would have got an ear bashing. Mum must have made sure that she was in the office or nearby when I was due to call. It was lovely to speak to her. It was good to know that they'd had to employ more staff to fill in for me and Wendy was given as many hours as she could manage. Mum said she was doing less. She never mentioned Jo-Ann or my father and I never asked after them.

VII.   1958-1959

Friday is market day in Leyburn. I'd get up early with Grandad and we would catch the 7.30 bus. By the time we got there the market, traders had their makeshift awnings up and already selling their wares. I followed Grandad around and he introduced me to each market trader he visited. We went to the cheese stall first. The array of chesses was amazing. Some I had never ever seen before, never mind tasted. I'm not a cheese lover but I was allowed to taste as many cheeses as I wanted to. Grandad got a good slice of cheddar, Edam and some delightful creamy-white, crumbly Wensleydale. Then it was the turn of the fruit and veg man. Again, fruits I had never seen before. He got some Bramley apples for Auntie Peg's pies and three Granny Smith apples, green and sharp, three bananas and three oranges. This was our week's supply of fruit, after that he got a selection of vegetables. The market traders put it all in a box for us and we left it there to collect later when we'd finished our shopping. We visited the fish man and the meat trader. Our last port of call was the grocer's for packets of different things and canned goods and a sack of flour. I carried some of his bags and we managed between us to carry the box of fruit and veg as far as the bus that would take us home.

One Friday we met David Ashby, my married cousin and his cross-eyed wife, Shirley (I never knew which eye to look at when I spoke to her). They had two of the sweetest children with them. Michael must have been about seven and a shy little girl called Sylvia, who was five. Grandad asked them down to tea on Sunday; David accepted quite happily, Shirley was not so sure.

David said, 'Oh come on, it's ages since I saw Lucy. We have a lot of catching up to do.'

'It will be fun and Auntie Peggy would love to meet the children,' I put in.

It was arranged but still I could tell that Shirley wasn't keen.

Sunday dawned bright and sunny. Auntie Peggy and I baked all day. Cakes, biscuits and we made sandwiches and I made a jelly, all children seem to like jelly.

They arrived on time and the children, dressed in their Sunday best, behaved impeccably, almost uncannily so. Shirley seemed to rule the roost. She never shouted at the children in our presence but one look from her and they quailed under her gaze. I felt sorry for them both.

Auntie Peggy, who liked children, asked if we could take them for a picnic next weekend. We seemed to be enjoying an Indian summer and it was a pity not to grab a chance of enjoying the weather.

Shirley wasn't keen at all. David said. 'Let them go, Shirl, They'll be fine. They'll be in responsible hands.' I didn't dare look at Auntie Pegs. Us responsible!

In the end, with much wheedling on David's part, she gave in. 'You two, just behave yourselves this week'. I was stung to reply. 'Well, they have behaved beautifully this tea time.'

'I do like children who know their manners.' Auntie Peggy chipped in.

And so it was arranged.

David dropped them down the next Saturday. It was late September and the weather held for us. We had our picnic already packed up. They said 'Good afternoon, Sir' to Grandad and Michael did a little bow and Sylvia did a little curtsy. I was very impressed. Grandad, I think, was quite touched.

They were totally unsuitably dressed. Sylvia had a pretty dress, white socks and white sandals. Michael had what looked like his school uniform, plus his tie, for goodness sake.

We went down to Redmire River (the Ouse) for our picnic.

Try as we could, we could not get them to kick off their shoes and go for a paddle, nor even get Michael to remove his tie! There was something not quite right here.

I sat with Michael on the grass. 'What is wrong Michael?' I asked gently, 'Surely you can take your tie off.' He just shook his head.

'Do you want to go home?'

A 'no' came out very quickly.

'What is it then? You're supposed to be enjoying yourself.'

'Mummy gets cross if we get dirty or look untidy. She whips us if we don't behave.'

'She what?' I gasped. 'Does Daddy know this?'

He looked worried.

'It's alright; I won't repeat what you have said about your mother.' He looked relieved. 'She doesn't do it when Dad's around.'

I laid my hand on his arm. 'If ever you need someone, Auntie Peggy or me will always be there for you and Sylvia, to talk to or help however we can.'

Just then, Auntie Peggy came back with Sylvia; she was carrying some wild flowers.

'We've been picking these for Sylvia to take home to Mummy, haven't we lovie?' Sylvia nodded shyly. We unpacked our picnic and ate it sitting on the grass.

After that, Auntie Peggy and I took it upon ourselves to get these kids to relax, have some fun and enjoy themselves. We even went to a jumble sale to get them kitted out with clothes more suitable for climbing trees and roughing it. They'd change out of their good things and wear the old stuff. A pair of shorts for both of them, a shirt for Michael and a blouse for Sylvia, then change back into their good things before going home. When winter kicked in, we got long trousers for each of them and thick woolly jumpers, again from jumble sales, where you can pick up things like that for pennies. We arranged with David that we would have them every other Saturday. During the winter, they had tea at Crofters Cottage and we'd play cards or board games.

David made them a sleigh and we would use it on the hills that led to the river. I with Sylvia and Auntie Peggy went down with Michael until they were confident to go by themselves and *they had some fun*. They squealed with delight, shouted encouragement to one another and come home ravenously hungry and a bit wet. But dried and back into the clothes they had come in, they once more looked clean, tidy and rosy cheeked with health. Shirley surely couldn't find fault with that but she did, she didn't like it and unfortunately stopped them from coming.

Before this, though I had to get a job. It wasn't that I was bored. I'd had a good long rest and needed to work. The little piles of money on the mantelpiece in the kitchen were dwindling fast. I'd pour over situations vacant in the paper but there didn't seem anything suitable for me to do.

I rang David from the phone box in the village and asked him if he knew of any jobs going, or could he tip me the wink if he heard of one.

David said that the Red Lion would be looking for staff shortly as the pub owner had built a big hotel just behind the Inn. But did I want hotel work again; it was the only thing I knew how to do.

'Is the hotel up and running?' I asked

'Hell no. It will be another two months, before it's decorated and furnished. I'm doing the decorating with my team. We built the hotel.'

'You're not just a pretty face then.' I taunted him.

'Cheeky. I can put in a good word for you if you like. What can you do?'

'Anything to do with a hotel really.'

'He's going up market. His pub already has three bedrooms and living space upstairs and they are booked from one year to the next. It's that, that gave him the idea of building a hotel in the first place.'

'Well, I have four years' experience of working in a hotel.'

'He's not going to buy that when he sees how young you are.'

'Except that it's true. My parents have a hotel down south. They had me working in it from the time I was 13. Admittedly, the first couple of years were in the school holidays. But work I definitely did.' He didn't ask questions but said, 'I'll see what I can do for you.'

True to his word, he came to Redmire a few days later to see me, to say could I go for an interview next Wednesday. I was highly excited but nervous too.

Grandad said. 'What's this about you working?'

'Grandad, I need to work. It's what girls of my age do.'

'I'm not having my granddaughter working in a public house.'

'Mr Stephens,' said David. 'I understand your view but it isn't in the pub. It's in the new hotel down the lane and round the back. Lucy would fit in there a treat. She would bring a bit of class into the place. Reg is no fool he isn't going to employ just anyone. Lucy has been working in her parents hotel since she was thirteen.'

'Aye, I know. And a lot of good it did her.'

'Lucy can't stay on here doing absolutely nothing.'

'And why not?'

'Because, all girls work for a living; it's not just the village kids anymore. It gives girls and boys a sense of pride to be able to hold down a job and a hell of a kick when they get their first pay packet. Would you withhold that pleasure from Lucy? Miss Henshaw, her father is Sir Leonard Henshaw, she works as does Lady Christina Taylor and neither family is short of a bob or two.'

I kept quiet. This was far better than any argument I could put forward to get Grandad to change his mind about me working. I don't say it changed his mind completely but it certainly helped my cause.

When it came to my interview the following week, David came to collect me. Which I thought was very nice of him. My aunt gave me a kiss, wished me good luck and crossed her fingers. Grandad didn't exactly do the same but he did come to the front door to wave me off. 'Nervous?' Asked David.

'I've never had an interview before. It was just assumed I'd work in my parents place.

So, yes, I am nervous, very.'

'So what happened to bring you down here?' He asked.

'Not now, David, sorry, another time maybe.'

He changed the subject. 'Reg is a bit grumpy most of the time. He doesn't suffer fools gladly. He's big and loud. A true Yorkshire man and calls a spade a spade. Just be yourself and don't be cowed down by him, he hates 'yes' men.'

'David! You haven't helped me one bit. I'm even more nervous than I was before.' To change the subject, I said, 'you must move in high circles to know Miss Henshaw and Lady Christina Taylor. Where do they work?'

'I haven't a clue. A pure figment of my imagination.'

'David! I'm shocked, you lied to Grandad.'

'It helped you get a job, are you going to tell him?' He grinned, 'I thought not.' He said as I shook my head. 'Anyway, there are people like them who do work. Granted, it may just be voluntary but it's still work.'

He'd made me laugh and I felt better.

I became a bit anxious when I arrived, as Reg couldn't be located. I was shown into his office by the foreman, so he told me. 'Take a seat, lady. Don't know where he is right now. He'll be along.'

Carpenters and painters were everywhere. I was offered a chair but declined the invitation to sit, as it was very dusty. I had on my blue wool jacket and skirt that I had travelled down in and the cream coat that I had carried. It was bitterly cold. I tied my coat more firmly round me and waited a good hour. After a time I grabbed a cloth from one of the workman, I wiped the seat and sat down and continued to wait.

Eventually Reg came in, red faced and blustering. I stood up.

'Mr Reg.' And then realized that David hadn't told me his surname.

'That's me. What do you want? I'm busy'

If I was frightened of the chef in my parent's hotel, then this man terrified me! But I needed a job, so held firm and said rather quietly. 'You asked me to come for a job interview.'

'Speak up girl, I can't hear you.'

I cleared my throat and repeated what I'd said.

'Job interview! What job? The place is nowhere near finished.'

'David Ashby, my cousin, set it up for me. He said you'd soon be advertising for staff for your hotel.'

'Did he now? I know Davis.' He sniffed as in disapproval . 'As you can see, hotel's not ready.' He bellowed. 'It's supposed to be. Aye, by God it is.'

'*David*,' I said loudly, 'Not *Davis*.'

'What? oh, David then.'

'So there is no job?' Part of me was relieved but I still wanted a job.

'Where you from?'

'Redmire. I live with my aunt and grandfather.'

'No.' He scowled. 'Where you from? Not from these parts with that posh voice.'

'I come from the southwest of England, Somerset.'

'Um, well. What can you do?'

'Reception work, cleaning, cooking, making beds. Anything to do with running a hotel.'

'Jack of all trades' He quoted, 'Master of none. Aye.'

'No Mr Reginald. I've worked in my parent's hotel since I was 13. Granted, at that age I did it in the evenings, at weekends and in the holidays but work I did. I did it all, from the bottom almost to the top.'

'So why did you leave? Sacked?' He grinned at his own joke.

'I wanted to spread my wings. I wanted a change, if you like, and to broaden my outlook.'

'Well nowt's ready.'

'May I look around?' I asked, surprised at my own bravery.

'Come on then and mind where you're walking.' And he marched out. I followed as best I could. I had to do little running step occasionally to keep up with him.

The place seemed in a terrible mess. The dividing walls were up and most of the windows were in but no doors. I guessed during my walk around that there were maybe 26 rooms to let. The large dining room was almost completed and the imposing large lounge. The kitchen area, I didn't go into. I just stood in the doorway.

Five men were having an argument and the air was blue. They saw me and stopped their arguing and stared. Reg roared, 'Never seen a girl before? Get on with your work!' They resumed their argument. 'If they didn't bloody argue so much, they might get some work done,' he grumbled.

'What do you think of it?' He asked, once my conducted tour was over and we were back to his untidy office.

'I liked what I saw,' I answered truthfully.

'What do you see yourself doing?'

I thought about my answer. 'I see myself welcoming your guests, checking them in, having already seen that their rooms are ready, answering the phone, dealing with inquiries, preparing their bills and trying to make their stay a happy one. I'm good at organising.'

He gave me a funny look. 'Don't think you can organise *me*.'

'No.' I smiled. 'I'll keep that in mind. But all you need is someone to go behind these men and clean up after them, it would look so much better. Have you organised the carpets, curtains and other furniture, the cutlery, crockery, the pots and pans for the kitchen besides all the linen? We had to almost restock the hotel when we took it over.'

He gave me a quizzical look and raised an eyebrow. Maybe he was a bit surprised.

'It's all in hand. If I need your help, I'll ask for it.' But it wasn't said in his usual bellow. 'Anyhow, bit busy so go home and I'll be in touch. I'll speak to Davis.'

'David.' I prompted.

'Um. Yes, David.'

I felt deflated but fixed a smile on my face. 'I'll wait to hear from you.' I shook his hand and walked out.

David had to go on an errand for Reg so he couldn't take me home. I walked across the road and waited for the Redmire bus.

Auntie Pegs was agog for news.

'I really can't tell you if I have the job or not.' I said. 'He's a big man, all bluster and maybe a bit of a bully. But I think his bark is worse than his bite, as the old saying goes. He showed me round and seemed quite proud of what he has achieved. It is a lovely hotel and I can see myself working there but whether he can, is a different thing.'

'How disappointing. I was so sure you'd get the job.'

'I'm not keeping my hopes up too high, he may get in touch, he may not.' Trouble was, I *was* keeping my hopes up high. I really wanted that job.

VIII.   1959

As it happened, I did get the job, and it was as a receptionist, but to begin with I was cleaner, bed maker and general factotum. The hotel wasn't ready to open until Easter.

The few guests Reg had in were in the bedrooms in the pub. The heating costs of keeping the big hotel open through the winter with no bookings at all, just depending on passing trade, he thought would cost him more than it was worth.

We had a lovely Christmas; Auntie Pegs, Grandad and I. For me it was a new experience not to be working over Christmas. Money was tight but we didn't stint on our festivities. It was quiet, as there were just the three of us, but I loved it. It was just so homely. We had a tiny tree in the corner of the sitting room and long forgotten Christmas decorations I found in the junk room 'the black hole of Calcutta', as Auntie Pegs and I called it. It was in a long passageway that led to the scullery; it had once been a workroom of some sort. It's where Honey slept. We made paper chains – just coloured paper cut into strips and glued together – even Grandad lent a hand. My only moment of unhappiness was ringing Mum on Christmas Day. I missed her such a lot in those early days. I didn't, as usual, get to speak to my father or to Jo-Ann.

Lean times were had in the New Year, as all the money from the mantelpiece above the old grange had gone. And, on top of that, I got a bad dose of flu. Poor Auntie Pegs was run off her feet because she was still cooking in the afternoons to keep up with her orders. Everything she made she sold and people were missing out the shop and coming straight to the cottage and giving her orders for certain items. She was able to make ends meet but it wasn't easy for her. Grandad was forbidden to enter my room. It wouldn't do for him to get it. How Auntie Peggy didn't come down with the flu is a miracle.

In February I visited a doctor in Leyburn to get a tonic, as I needed to be fit for when I started work. It was with a certain amount of relief that I actually started to work in early March. I was on half pay to begin with. There were no guests to deal with; we were just sorting out and making final preparations for opening day. I got the reception area organised quickly, as it was the first place people would see when they entered the hotel, and I spoke to Reg about the ordering of the stationery. He just said, 'Sort it out,' so I did. Then he complained about the money I had spent on it!

We were going to have a big opening party. I was organising it. Reg had said, 'You said you can organise, so organise it.'

It was a roaring success; every business, no matter how small, was asked and local bigwigs were invited too. We must have had over 200 people turn up. Reg and I were exhausted by the end of the day.

One other thing that changed is that during the week I stayed at the hotel, as often Redmire would get cut off by the snow. It was odd being in this big hotel on my own until guests started to arrive.

I went to Redmire for my two days off, if the bus I caught could get through the snow. I worked six days then had two days off. Eventually, as my days off moved through the week, I'd occasionally get a weekend off. Bliss! They became very treasured.

As spring came, I moved back into Crofters Cottage. Grandad had got into the habit of calling in on a Friday after his market trips, if I was working. Reg would make himself available whenever he called in. He said of Grandad, 'A true Yorkshireman and a true gent.' Grandad and I would sit in the reception area together and have coffee 'on the house' with a few biscuits thrown in. I was working, so we would often get interrupted. But it was good to see him. I think it was his way of telling me that he accepted that I needed to work.

Sometimes in the afternoon, Auntie Peggy would get a bus into Leyburn and come to see me. I would order afternoon tea to be sent up to reception. There was a little table set up in the corner, with two chairs. The table had magazines and newspapers on it for our visitors, which I would move off on to my work counter and we would sit there drinking our tea and just chat all the time. It was a change for her and Grandpa didn't mind, as he would be asleep anyway.

The other person who enjoyed her visits was Reg. Sometimes, if I was about to go, she would wait for me and we would travel back home together. I was extremely happy. I loved my job and my time with Grandad and Auntie Peggy. I felt very lucky to have the perfect job and a happy family life. I was doing all the hours I could to help Reg out. He was such a nice person to work for and very fair. He mentioned my wages and then asked if I was happy with that or did I feel I should have more? I said as long as I was paid overtime, what he had mentioned seemed fair enough to me (£4 a week). He was big and loud but beneath that tough shell was a shy and quiet gentleman who I came to like and trust.

It was never my intention to spend the rest of my life with Grandad and Auntie Peggy but I did not want to hurt the two people I loved most in the world, so I had to broach the subject of me moving out with great care. I was coming home so late, grabbing my evening meal, then going to bed early, only to get up in good time to go back to work the next day. It just would be easier all round if I had a place of my own in Leyburn. I sat down with them one evening and explained it all as gently as I could to them. Grandpa wasn't keen that I was to live alone in Leyburn. Auntie Peggy said she would miss me but did understand. Whatever hours I did, I had to add another hour to that for travelling time and I was getting tired. I said I wouldn't be leaving for good, as I would like to come back on my days off. This brought a smile to Auntie Peggy's face and she agreed that it would probably be better for me to live in Leyburn. We scoured the papers but nothing seemed available. I got Auntie Peggy to come with me, so she could give me her input, but the places I could afford were damp, dingy and dirty whereas any half-decent, I couldn't afford.

One day after work, I wandered up to Hope Farm. There was talk that the owners were thinking of opening up a farm produce shop and I was curious. It was a beautiful evening. I'd been cooped up all day in the hotel and I wanted to stretch my legs. Hope Farm was at the end of a lane that started at the very top of the market square. There was a house facing the square, then at right angles facing the lane was what appeared to be a barn, half converted, I guessed, because an enormous window, floor to ceiling had just been put in. I passed the half-glassed front door and saw a 'for sale' notice stuck to the glass. My pulse quickened. It said to call next door for a viewing. All interest in Hope Farm's produce shop went out of my head. I called next door. A Mrs Wright answered my knock. She called over her shoulder to someone, 'I'm off for a minute, lovie. Look after the little ones for me. I won't be but a few minutes.' No answer came from whoever was inside. She took a key from just inside her front door, giving me a half smile as we walked past her front room window, past another window and then to the barn door. She inserted her key in the lock and opened it.

I stepped inside and fell in love with the cottage as soon as I saw it. It wasn't so much a cottage at the time but one very long room. The owner, who showed me around, said that it had had a new roof last year, the floor to ceiling window in the front and the four windows in the back wall were all new. The thing that struck me as odd was the door in the middle of the right hand wall, which, if opened would lead directly into the next door house. I asked if it could be removed. She said that under no circumstances could it be taken out. I had met the woman before, who showed me round but I just couldn't place her. As soon as I met her son, who slouched in later, saying he wanted to go out and didn't want to mind the kids anymore, I remembered where I had seen her.

After my really bad dose of flu, the after affects, being lethargic and permanently tired, had remained with me for ages. I had visited the doctor in the hope that he would be able to give me a tonic or something to buck me up. I sat in the waiting room; the owner of the barn was there too. She had a tiny boy on her knee; he was about six months old and looked very ill indeed. A little girl with bright blue eyes and a curly mop of fair hair, she would be no more than three, leant against her mother's arm. Her elder son, approximately 14 years old, was standing in front of her, absently kicking the leg of the chair she was sitting on. Three times she asked him to stop but she may as well have saved her breath, as he took not a blind bit of notice. Eventually he stopped out of boredom, slung himself into the chair next to hers and started to kick the front leg of his chair with the heel of his shoe.

It was their turn next to see the doctor; when the surgery door shut behind them, it was a relief. The only other person waiting his turn was an old man with a hacking cough.

He said, 'er be 'avin' a lot o' problems wi' 'e. Nasty piece 'e be goin' t' be when e's growed. 'is stepdad is so good to 'im too. 'Tis my opinion 'e needs a dam good beltin'. That would sort 'is kind out.'

I am no child-beater but I was inclined to agree.

'Spoilt rotten 'e were when 'e were livin' wi' just 'is Mam. But once she married again an' 'ad they kiddies 'e became a right 'andful an' no mistake. Aye, ah should knows 'cause they do live next door to I. 'Er be married to the local policeman.'

'What happened to his real dad?' I asked tentatively.

"He were killed in yon farm.' He waved his hand in the general direction of Hope Farm, the farm up the road from the place I now wanted to buy.

After that, the old man was taken by a fit of coughing and remained quiet after the attack was over. He didn't offer up on how the farm worker had died.

But back to the cottage... It had no garden, which was fine by me, as I am no gardener. Nor did it have any electricity or water. It had plumbing of sorts, which was two pieces of piping sticking out from the concrete floor where the bathroom and kitchen would be. I could see this barn in my mind's eye, finished, completed, decorated and furnished. I loved the huge window in what would be my sitting room area. I fancied myself sitting in an armchair and taking in the view. The window would have fine netting across it so that nobody could look in but I could look out. It faced the lane but across from there I had uninterrupted views to die for, of the rolling hills and moors of North Yorkshire, the place I loved.

I was able to get a small mortgage, although, annoyingly Grandpa had to stand surety for me because of my age. David, my married cousin, offered to do the work needed to make it habitable at cost but although I knew that would mean only working in the evenings and at weekends, I readily agreed.

He was quick and efficient, so that six months later, just before Christmas, I was able to move in. There was just a bit of decorating left to do that I could do myself.

To the right of the front door, just 14 feet away from that silly door in the middle of the right wall, were two steps that led up to my bedroom on the right and the bathroom on the left. On the left of the front door was a vast area that I wanted left as open plan. The kitchen was opposite the front door and that left plenty of room for a sitting room area and a dining room. I was thrilled with it all. When washing up I had a lovely view of the back garden. It was beautifully taken care of. It all belonged to Old Man Randal (the man who had spoken to me at the doctor's a year ago). It had become too much for him to take care of and the policeman, who lived between us, had taken it over on the understanding that any produce the policeman grew was shared with Mr Randall. His passion, though, was flowers and they were outstanding.

Mr Randall's house was in a terrible state. The roof sagged and it looked very damp and some of the upstairs windows were either broken or cracked. The ramshackle outbuildings that stood at right angles to the lane were in the same condition. One seemed to be a small cowshed but with no cows. Next door to that was what appeared to be a tack room or workshop; this is where he kept his chickens and tacked onto the end of that, was a tumbledown pigsty. Beyond that, to the high boundary back wall, was where the policeman grew his vegetables. The gates to the yard hung on rusty hinges and leant drunkenly against each other. They would not open or close but a gap remained between the two gates, Mr Randall used as his exit and entrance. The front door to his house was never opened.

It was not unusual to see Mr Randall shepherding his hens in off the lane. It wasn't a busy track, just farm machinery, the early morning milk lorry to collect Hope Farm's milk churns and the policeman's car. The policeman had a porch outside his house that protruded into the lane. It opened facing down the road. To give him his due, he parked the car as near to his front door as possible, so that his car's bonnet didn't pass my bedroom window.

In the summer, walkers and bird-watchers used to pass by, booted up and carrying walking sticks, with their binoculars hanging round their necks. Beyond Mr Randall's smallholding was a stile that led to 'The Shawl' – a stretch of common ground that eventually led to the next village, called Scarfell, about 7 miles away, a good walk if you could do it.

I was as happy as Larry in my little house for just two years, before things started to go horribly wrong...

IX. 1959

I'd haunted auction rooms to get the furniture for my little barn conversion. Reg gave me a double bed. He said he was slinging it out as it was broken and I would be doing him a favour if I took it off his hands. David brought it up in his truck and we spent an exhausting couple of hours putting it together. David put two new legs on it, which seemed to be the only broken parts; a comfortable bed it was too. The carpet, tall cupboard and dressing table (not matching) I got very cheaply. I was told no-one wanted big furniture anymore. My dining table and four chairs were being sold by David's neighbour. David told me that if I wanted them he could pick them up for me and I'd have them for 'nowt', as his neighbours just wanted to get rid of them. I said 'yes please' to them. My sitting room furniture was a bit tatty; from the same auction rooms I got a job lot of material. It was in long, wide strips. I tucked these in and around the sofa and easy chairs and they looked really good. A large kitchen cupboard, another smaller table, a sideboard and two more chairs comprised my kitchen furniture, not forgetting an oven. It had seen better days but it worked and that was all I needed. I picked up other niceties during my two happy years there.

I asked Reg if Auntie Peggy and Grandad could have their Christmas lunch at the hotel. He readily agreed. I told him to take the money for their lunch from my wages. He never did and I forgot to mention it.

It didn't snow so much that year and there was a skeleton bus service, so they were able to get themselves to the hotel. Reg offered to take them back after tea.

Auntie Peggy was so excited. Grandpa, I'm sure, would have preferred to stay at home. I think he had agreed to go because of Auntie Peggy. He realised, I feel sure, that she didn't have much of a life and didn't enjoy the niceties of life as did other women her age, like having her hair done, buying nice clothes and going on spending sprees. I could sit with them over Christmas dinner, some of the time but we were busy and I was working, after all. Reg had done a big advertising drive beforehand about being open during the winter and the response had proved well worth the expense. We were nearly always full at lunchtime.

Every Friday, market day, Grandpa and Auntie Peggy would both come over to Leyburn to go shopping and call in to my place afterwards. If I was working they'd call in at the hotel to collect my key, go home to my little barn, both have a bath and Auntie Pegs would make something for us to have for supper after I returned home.

Grandad could still have his nap, lying on my sofa. Honey would be quite content to snooze the afternoon away until I came home and Auntie Pegs could relax and read to her heart's content. She loved reading and could read a book in a day.

They did seem to make themselves at home and that is what I wanted them to do. It was better if I had the Saturday off, then we could all return to Crofters Cottage together on Friday night and I'd be able to help carry the groceries home. If I stayed with them, as I did for all my weekends off, I always made sure that I left some money on the mantelpiece over the old range.

What a pleasure I had on my two weeks off to have Wendy come and stay with me. I met her at Darlington Station. We must have talked non-stop the entire three-hour journey back home. She was charmed by my house. I offered her my bed, saying that I would be quite happy on the sofa. She said as long as I hadn't turned gay, why didn't we share the bed, it was a double after all. The trouble was, we talked all night. I took her everywhere and introduced her to Auntie Peggy, Grandad and Reg. Reg terrified the life out of her. I said he was a pussycat really but she didn't believe me!

We did the walk down to the river and bathed above the falls where the water is deeper. We went into Richmond on a shopping spree. We went to the little café to have our lunch where Mum used to go after her shopping trips. I took her to Gales, where we used to live and Aysgarth Falls, beyond Redmire. We took a picnic with us that day and ate it sitting on the grass by the main falls. We really did have a good time and lots of laughs. When it was time for her to go, David kindly took us to Darlington train station and I waved her off. She promised to come again, as she had enjoyed herself so much. I did miss her but threw myself back into work with renewed vigour. She did come the following year, as promised, when we did a few coach trips to go further afield but she still wanted to bathe in the river and see Aysgarth again. She was such a laugh and a good friend to me. I see her still.

It was shortly after she went the second time that things started to go wrong... I knew as soon as I entered my cottage that something was wrong. I wandered around. Nothing seemed amiss but did I leave my easy chair so near the coffee table? I walked into the bedroom to put my slippers on; my feet were aching, I'd been on them all day. Wearing such high heels didn't help. I looked around. Had I left my eiderdown so crumpled? And that smell again, what was it? Was it cigarettes? I tutted to myself. Maybe I was imagining it but still I checked, as I had never had to do before, that my front door was locked and bolted, before heading for bed.

There was a new block of flats on the opposite side of the road. They didn't completely block my lovely view of the hills and moors beyond Leyburn. I could still sit and drink in the view.

On my next two days off I completely did my bedroom out and changed the linen on my bed. The middle door led to next door. As it was recessed back into their house, David had put bolts on my side of the door and had removed the spindle and door knob and made it into a cupboard to hold my spare sheets, pillowcases, blankets and pillows. I had acquired an old washing machine that I got on the go and went to the cupboard to get the clean linen to find the bolts shot back and not forward, as they should be. I was sure I had not left them back; why would I want to move them? I looked stupidly at the bolts as if they could tell me something. With the spindle gone, the door couldn't be opened, even if the bolts were not in their correct position and, anyway, next door wouldn't want to come in, why would they? I shot the bolts forward again, finished my washing, hung it out on my wooden clothes-horse and left them in the sun by the big windows to dry. I packed an overnight case and, making sure I locked the door behind me, went off to spend the weekend with Auntie Pegs and Grandad. I didn't mention about the bolts to them; I didn't want to worry them.

I mentioned it to Reg though when I next went to work. He laid my fears to rest by saying the hotel had been extra busy and that I was probably a bit tired and I was imagining it. I thought, maybe he was right. And I put it to the back of my mind. But that evening when I walked into the house cigarette smoke was heavy in the air and my eiderdown was rumpled again and once more the bolts were shot back. I began not to sleep well. I'd jump at every creak and rattle as the house settled itself down for the night.

I didn't know the people over the road. It was a block of nine flats, three storeys high, built in an 'E' shape without the middle stroke. So I was surprised at the knock on my door, just after returning from work one day. I opened it to find a pleasant young lad standing there. He was about 17. He shyly said that he lived over the road with his mother in their first storey flat and that she would like to meet me. I said I would love to meet her too, then I realised that he meant now, this minute. I locked my door and was escorted across the lane and entered the building. There was a lift but I said I'd prefer to walk up the stairs as I didn't like lifts. I hated the confined space. We entered a spacious flat. His mother introduced herself to me as Carol and her son as Tommy. She must have once been very pretty but she was suffering from MS and the ravages of it were showing on her face. Tommy was caring for her. He went off to make a pot of tea for us all, then he went to his bedroom to get on with his homework.

She started off by saying, 'I know you will think I'm an interfering old biddy with nothing else to do but stir up trouble but did you know that the boy next door uses your house? Or, is it alright and you know about it?'

My jaw must have hit the floor.

'Oh, I see,' she continued. 'I'm so sorry, you obviously didn't know.'

'I knew it!' I exploded, hitting my fist into my hand. 'I knew it. Things are not quite how I would leave them in the mornings.' Then another thought hit me. 'Oh, my God, he's has been using my bed, because it's always sort of crumpled. This is awful! How often have you seen him go into my house?' Carol thought for a moment.

'At least 5 or 6 times. The thing is, I rarely see him come out again. I thought you must have another door... Are you alright, dear? You've gone rather pale. Tommy, get Lucy some water.' As he came in with a tumbler, she said to him, 'Did you hear that, Tommy? She didn't know. I'm so sorry to bring you this bad news. He's not a nice boy, not nice at all.'

I took a sip of water. 'That bloody door...' I muttered.

I apologised for swearing, then told her what I knew of the family and about buying the barn, having it converted and about Mrs Wright's refusal to remove 'that bloody door'.

'And you think it's that door he goes out of?' She asked.

'It has to be; that's why I keep finding the bolts drawn back. He must have got a spindle from somewhere and a doorknob. That's certainly the reason you don't see him come out. Does, he bring girls in with him?'

'Only his six-year-old sister and their little brother. Mrs Wright works, you see, once or twice a week, depending if she is needed. She works at The Magpie Guest House. Lately she seems to be working rather a lot. And since the older boy doesn't appear to do anything, she gets him to babysit. He's about 17 and looks a real ruffian. What are you going to do about it?' Carol asked, tentatively.

'Face him with the accusation. Tell him he's been seen. Say I know he's doing it.'

Carol cast her eyes downwards. 'Lucy, I'm so sorry but I can't become involved. I'm really not fit enough for a lot of trouble. As I said, he's not a nice boy.'

'Can I inform the police but not mention your name?' I asked.

'That would probably be a good idea.'

'There is just one thing. How does he get in to start with?' I mused.

'He seems to have a key.'

'Of course! Mrs Wright said she would bring the spare key round but never did and I forgot about it. I think I might mention this to my cousin David and see what he has to say.'

'I'd change the locks. That's easily done. My ex was a locksmith. He used to say there wasn't a lock he couldn't open.'

She said nothing more about her ex and I didn't like to ask questions about him.

'Yes, I'll get him to do that as well. I won't involve you, I promise.'

The next day, in my dinner-hour, I rang David. I had to leave a message with Shirley that I wanted to see him urgently.

As I entered the house, again I caught the smell of cigarette smoke and my bed was crumpled. David called even before he went home.

'What's up kid? Shirley said you sounded in a bit of a state... My, I didn't know you smoked, this place stinks of it.'

I told David what I knew.

'Right, come on, no time like the present. We'll go round and face the little sod.'

'That's the problem. We can't. He's sure to work out who has seen him. It's Carol and we can't involve her, she has MS.'

'Tomorrow then, I'll change your locks. Is that stupid door locked?'

We looked and the bolts were not in place and my spare sheets and pillowcases were on the wrong shelves.

'He's getting sloppy.' I put the linen in their rightful places and bolted the door again.

'I'll make it so he can't get in by your front door, by changing the locks. Not being able to get in to drawer the bolts back, will stop him using that stupid middle door as his own private exit.'

I told Carol in the evening of the following day. She had been in bed all day, so hadn't seen David change the locks.

'Look Carol, if there is anything I can do for you, you only have to ask. Anything, shopping, washing, please don't hesitate.'

'We manage.' Tommy said from the door. He was carrying a tray in his hands. It had a soup bowl on it and a plate of bread and butter. 'Don't we Mum?'

Carol smiled weakly. 'My son, we most certainly do. You are just wonderful.'

'Oh, get off!' Tommy said, embarrassed. He put the tray on his mother's lap. 'Eat it up, all of it mind. It's your favourite, tomato soup.' He left us to it.

'He does his very best for me and I am so blessed with such a good and wonderful son. But I feel so guilty. I feel that I have robbed him of his childhood. He seems to have no friends, he goes out once a week, he's a railway enthusiast and goes to their meetings in the town. He does all the cleaning, washing, cooking... everything.'

'You get on with your soup before it gets cold and I get into Tommy's bad books. But I am just over the road, call me if you should ever need me.' I jotted down my phone number on a spare leaf in my diary, tore it out and left it by her bed.

It was a very prophetic thing to say, at that time, because call me she did.

Carol kept vigil by her sitting room window and reported back that Robert had tried my front door the following day but with the locks changed he couldn't get in. 'He looked up at my window,' she reported, 'but I don't think he saw me. Anyway, he gave the door a vicious kick, I heard it from here. I thought he was going to break the glass in your door.'

'David said we should just go next door and confront him.'

'So why don't you?' Carol asked.

'He'd deny it, wouldn't he? They would believe him. What I need is solid proof. I'm not going to involve you but tomorrow I'm going to the police to see if they can do anything or have any suggestions.'

Constable Plod was most unhelpful. 'What proof do you have that this youth has been entering your property.'

'He's been seen.' I replied.

'Well, that's helpful. Who has seen him?'

I hesitated. 'I can't tell you. The person who saw him is ill and doesn't want to be involved. There have been no repercussions as yet but it could be just a matter of time.'

'Has anything gone missing?' Constable Plod asked.

This wasn't going well.

'Well, no. But things have been moved and I think he has been on my bed as my eiderdown is not as straight as I would leave it and it seems crumpled.'

The constable bit the end of his stub of pencil, then shook his head. 'There's nowt to go on. Until he is either found inside your property or something has gone missing, then we can't do anything.'

'He's too clever for that.'

'Who is he, anyroad?'

'Robert Wright, he lives next door.'

The policeman's eyebrows shot up to his hairline in surprise.

'You're joking me. He's the Sergeant's stepson.'

'I know that!' I snapped back. 'I'm fully aware of that fact.'

He gave me a sharp look. 'Now look, lass. There is no need to take that attitude. If the lady...'

'Who said anything about a lady?'

'Well, it's obvious. Mrs Carol Grafton, she lives opposite and would see what was going on. I know she is unwell, too. But if she won't come forward...' He shrugged. 'We can't do anything.'

'Thanks for your help,' I said, sarcasm heavy in my voice and walked out.

David and I went next door that evening after we had both finished work and accused Robert in front of his parents about what he had been doing. There was a huge row. Of course, Robert denied it, saying he had never been near the house.

'I have had the locks changed but then you know that, don't you? I know that it's you who has been in as you have been seen. Also, you take your little sister and brother in with you sometimes.'

The Sergeant said, 'Get Rosie down here, Margery and we'll see what she says.'

Rosie looked tiny and frightened. She was in her dressing gown and slippers. When she was asked if she had been next door with her brothers she looked directly at Robert, with big tears rolling down her cheeks and slowly shook her head.

'This is a serious charge you have laid at my stepson's door and I'm not happy about it,' the Sergeant said.

I stepped nearer him and said angrily. 'You're dead right. I'm not happy about it either. But he has been going in and not coming out again, as he has been using the connecting door. I want that door taken out and a proper wall put up in its place.'

'Well, you'll have to go on wanting,' said Margery Wright indignantly, 'because it's staying.'

'My house stinks of cigarette smoke and there is a scratch on my new coffee table.' I looked directly at Robert. 'I want it stopping Robert; I know it's you.'

He looked daggers at me but said nothing. His mother was saying it for him. 'Stop it! Stop it!' She yelled at me. 'It can't be Robert; he doesn't smoke.' As if that was proof enough that it couldn't be her darling son.

'Have you searched his pockets, smelt his breath or seen his yellowing teeth. There are no fags in my house, as I don't smoke.'

'Miss Bradley, just go now and we will forget this stupid accusation against Robert.

We are confident that it is not him that is entering your house unlawfully, so just go,' the Sergeant said sharply.

We turned to go we could see that we weren't going to get anywhere. Somehow, if he continued to get into my house, though I couldn't see how, I would get my proof.

Their hall was tiny. To get out David was going to have to go first and open the front door, there wasn't room for the Sergeant or Mrs Wright to do it for us. David seemed to trip, the front door stopped him from falling, he put his arm in his coat as if he had hurt it. In the Wrights porch I asked David if he was alright.

'Twisted my arm, I think, trying not to fall.'

'Well, I hope you've really hurt yourself,' Mrs Wright said waspishly. 'Goodnight.' And she slammed her front door on us.

Once inside my house, I fumed, 'Well, that was a waste of time. Robert doesn't smoke, what a joke. We'll just have to do something to prove he's been in my house.'

David said in a placid manner, 'I just might have it.'

'What do you mean?' I asked, shrugging off my coat.

He pulled his arm out of his jacket. And like a conjurer, he was holding up a toy rabbit.

'It was no fall. It was hanging on the front door handle and I couldn't resist it.'

'David!' I gasped. 'From a policeman's house! You must be mad.'

'Look, in a few days' time, you can go next door with this toy. Say you were spring cleaning and you found this stuffed down the side of a chair.'

'David, I don't know whether to congratulate you on a brilliant idea or be cross with you for taking such a risk.'

'There was no risk. You were behind me. Mrs Wright was behind you and their hall is so small, she couldn't have seen anything other than see me stumble. You'll have to leave it for a while or they may put two and two together. At least you know he can't get in any-more.'

Oh no?

Carol had informed me that Robert had come round to my house with a load of keys. He spent ages trying them out but none of them could have fitted and he went home looking very angry.

'So he didn't get in?' I asked.

'No, definitely not,' she said vehemently.

'Well, I feel fairly confident that with all my cousin has done, he won't get in again. It will be breaking and entering if he does.'

'What a relief for you.'

'Yes,' I breathed. 'Thank goodness!'

X.   1960

A few days later, after a very busy day at the hotel, I strolled back home. I got my front door key out of my bag, my hand went to the lock and I froze. In one of the small panes near the lock was a jagged hole. Using my own key, I hesitatingly opened the door and entered. The familiar smell of smoke assailed my nose. I walked into my bedroom and my eiderdown was ruffled and not on straight. There was another smell that I didn't recognise at all.

I sighed and made my way back into the living room. I walked over to my settee and felt down the side to retrieve the rabbit. I had stuffed it down the sofa merely as a double precaution. One reason was that Robert seemed to prefer to sit on an easy chair, so was unlikely to see the rabbit and the second was, I couldn't just leave it lying around, on the slim chance that he would get in again, see it and take it home.

But he had gone too far now, by breaking and entering.

I went next door and rang the bell.

The sergeant himself answered the door. 'Yes... what now?'

'I want to speak to Robert. This time he has gone too far as he has broken a pane of glass to get into my house.' Sergeant Wright was going to say something. I took the toy out of my pocket and held it up. 'I found this stuffed down the side of my sofa.'

He looked at it, recognised it and said. 'You'd better come in.' I stepped inside. He walked ahead. I closed the front door behind me and followed the sergeant into their sitting room. Robert was sprawled on the sofa. Mrs Wright was in the kitchen, she came in saying, 'Who is it love?' She saw me and said rudely, 'Oh it's you. What do you want?' I said nothing but held the rabbit up.

'My Thumper,' Rosie cried excitedly, getting up from the floor where she had been sitting, doing a jigsaw puzzle.

'It was down the side of my sofa.' I looked at Robert as I spoke. 'Now tell me you don't go next door to my house. I'd like to know, what for? Why? And what on earth do you do on my bed?' Robert said nothing. 'I'm waiting for some explanation.' I dangled the rabbit in front of his eyes. He went to grab it but I was expecting that and was quicker than he was. Then I saw a plaster on the back of his hand. 'I see you have cut yourself. On the pane of glass you smashed in my door, I presume.'

'No, no,' Mrs Wright said, very agitated, 'He wouldn't have, he wouldn't...'

'How, then, Mrs Wright, has your daughter's toy rabbit got into my house? By magic, do you think? Like a conjurer?' She said nothing.

'It's breaking and entering this time. There is a small pane of glass that needs mending. I want it replaced and something sorted out.' I was so angry. With that, I gave the rabbit back to Rosie and stalked out.

I rang David. 'He's been in again – by breaking a pane of glass in my front door.'

'I don't believe it. I just don't believe it. The sly little bugger. What are you going to do?'

'I've already done it. I went next door with the rabbit. Rosie said 'My Thumper.' I've told them I want that pane of glass replacing and Robert sorting out'.

I heard David sigh. 'That poor kid is going to get it from Robert. I wouldn't like to be in her shoes the next time he's left to babysit.'

I agreed. 'Now I feel guilty because I have heard Rosie crying. I was just so cross, I didn't think.'

'Don't be, Lucy. It needed sorting. What did Robert do?'

'He remained slouched on the sofa. His mother still doesn't believe it's him. I told Sergeant Wright that I want Robert sorted out. I dangled the rabbit in front of Robert's eyes, he tried to grab it. I saw he had cut himself.'

'Cut his wrists, I hope.'

'David!' I gave a snort of a laugh. 'That's a horrid thing to say.'

'So you have a hole in your door. I'll be up after I've had my tea and put some wood over the crack. I'll re-glaze it for you. But it won't be till the weekend. He's a bugger, isn't he?'

'I'm hoping Sergeant Wright will pay for that.'

'Well, if he does, it's like admitting that Robert is guilty. Still, I'll drop the bill in their letterbox when the job's done and see what happens.'

'Thanks David. You're a star.'

I found the pane of glass replaced when I came back from work the following day. I rang David to thank him but he said that he hadn't done it, as he wouldn't have had the time as he was so busy. I assumed that it must have been the Sergeant himself, or had arranged for someone to do it. I also assumed he'd used the hole to open the door, as the glass and any rubbish had been taken out from inside the house.

I certainly wasn't going to go next door to thank him, not after my reception of the day before.

Everything calmed down after that for a while, which was a relief. I got back to sleeping well and I didn't see Robert for quite some time.

One night, just as I was going to sleep, I heard the sound of running feet, they went past my house to the Sergeant's. I heard their door slam, my immediate thought was that Robert was back, as only he would slam the door like that. I was on the verge of sleep again when I heard my phone ringing. I tottered out of bed to answer it. It was Carol in an awful state.

'I'm so sorry to ring so late, Lucy but Tommy is missing. He came back after school, made us our meal and went out again to his Railway Enthusiasts Club. He's never this late, he's usually back by, between, 9.30 or 10.00 at the latest and if he is going to be late, he would always ring.' It *was* late. It was close to midnight. 'I've rung the club secretary and he said the meeting finished at 9.45. And he remembers saying goodnight to Tommy. Lucy, I don't know what to do.'

I did the only thing I could do. 'I'll go and look for him. Don't worry.' It was stupid to say that, as that is exactly what she was going to do, until and if I located him. I had an uneasy feeling in the pit of my stomach. I hurriedly dressed, then I rang David.

'David I'm so sorry I wouldn't ring so late but Carol has been on the phone. She says Tommy hasn't come back from his club and that he is usually home at 9.30 to 10.00. She's rung the secretary of the club and he says the meeting finished at 9.45. And David... Robert's back.'

'Meet me at the bottom of your road and bring your torch. Give me five minutes.'

I waited for David to pick me up. It was cold and drizzling with rain. David arrived a few minutes later and, with a torch each, we drove slowly around town but saw nothing of Tommy. Reluctantly, we decided that we would have to get out of the car and look in the narrower streets that the car couldn't go down. The drizzle had turned into heavy rain; we were going to get soaked. I had told David about the running feet and the slammed door.

'I wouldn't think Robert could run,' David said sardonically.

'I think, if you've done something bad, you want to get away from the scene as quickly as possible in case you're seen.'

'Am I being overly suspicious? Are we looking for a body here?'

'I have a feeling we could be. It wouldn't have taken much thinking for Robert to reach the conclusion that if he was seen going into my house, it could only have been by Carol. All the other occupants of the flats work during the day, only Carol is in.

She can see my house from her flat, even though my place is up the road a little from hers.'

'Are you saying that you think Tommy's disappearance is linked to Robert's return?'

'Well, I may be wrong but have you got a better reason for Tommy's disappearance?'

'Er, no but you said, whoever it was you heard was really running and Robert doesn't run, he slouches.'

'Very true but have you noticed how fit he seems? He's no couch potato. He may seem that to us but I think he does some fitness training.'

'But you can't be sure it was Robert you heard.'

'David. Would the Sergeant run and bang the door?'

'Er, no.'

'I'll er no you in a minute. I just have this horrible gut feeling that it's connected. I'm assuming, I know. Call it sixth sense if you like.'

'Well, can you get that sixth sense of yours to tell us where the hell he is. I'm wet and cold.'

'I wish.' I said.

We poked into corners and went down alleyways, narrow roads and paths, shining our torches into every nook and cranny.

It was David who found him. What at first he thought was just a bundle of old rags was, on closer inspection, Tommy – beaten to a pulp. David called me over, as I was going down the same alley but looking on the opposite side.

'Oh, my God.' I whispered. 'Is he... dead?'

David was feeling for a pulse. 'No, I don't think so. Go home and call for an ambulance, you'd better tell Carol, although what you can tell her, God only knows.'

I ran all the way back to my house, called for an ambulance, then went over to see Carol. She was still up. I played Tommy injuries down, although in truth I didn't really know what they were, other than he was unconscious. Carol was really upset.

'I feel so helpless and useless,' she wept. I offered to stay with her but she wanted me to hurry back and go with Tommy in the ambulance to the hospital. I raced back to see the paramedics in the process of easing Tommy into a head and neck brace and then onto a stretcher.

'His mother wants me to go with him. She has MS and can't come.' I said to the paramedic.

'Hop in then love. Talk to him if you know him, he may hear you, he may not.'

David said. 'I'll follow in the car as you will need to get back.'

'That's kind of you David. But you're working tomorrow.'

'So are you and you need to get home sometime tonight.'

That was true and there was no time to argue, as the ambulance was ready to go.

Tommy was seriously injured. He had 3 broken ribs and was kicked so badly round the back that the doctors thought he might lose a kidney. The rest of his body was black and blue. His left cheekbone was fractured and his eyes were so swollen that if he had not been unconscious, he would not have been able to open them. He had 17 stitches put into his face. I was allowed to see him before I went home. He was still unconscious and, poor lad, he looked at death's door. What wasn't black and blue was deathly white. He was hooked up to all sorts of medical paraphernalia. I wasn't sure he was going to make it. What could I tell Carol?

David drove me home. He was wide awake, he'd gone to sleep on a hospital chair but neither of us felt like talking. I was dropping but didn't think I'd sleep anyway.

Once home, I saw Carol's light still on and went over to her flat. She had left her door unlocked so that I could get in. She was dozing in her chair but was instantly awake after my knock and walking in.

'What's happened to my son? Is he alright?' She sounded near to tears.

'He looks bad, Carol.' I felt that I had to be honest with her this time. She was going to find out anyway and I'd rather she heard it from me than from some clinical voice on the phone. I told her about his injuries.

'They are doing what they can Carol. He's in the best place.' A terrible, hackneyed phrase but true nevertheless.

'Did he say what had happened or who did it?' Her voice was shaking.

I drew up a chair and sat opposite her and took her hands in mine.

'Carol, he's unconscious,' I said, as gently as I could.

'Oh my God.' She was sobbing now. 'It's that horrid, evil Robert, I know it is.'

I agreed with her and felt somehow to blame. 'Let me make you a hot drink Carol.

You must try and relax and get some sleep.' I did what I could for her and got her into bed. I left her sipping some hot milk, promising to call in after work the next day and suggested that maybe she should call her doctor. She nodded her head too distraught to speak.

My alarm woke me the next morning. I felt groggy and tired that a hot bath didn't dispel.

Reg said when I got to work, 'my, have you had a night on the tiles or what? You look a fright.'

'Thanks Reg, that makes me feel heaps better.' I said sarcastically, then I told him what has transpired 'Jesus. That poor kid. Who would do a thing like that?'

I told him of my suspicions. He said almost the same as David. 'You can't just assume it's Robert, Lucy.'

'You haven't met him and you know the trouble I've been having?'

'Have you ever gone home at odd times?'

'Yes in my lunch hour but that's not often. This is not a complaint Reg but I don't often have a proper break for lunch. It's usually just a sandwich while working. David has a key and goes in at odd times too but we have never found him there. But the smell of cigarettes is there, it's sometimes quite strong, at other times not so bad. It got so bad David thought I had taken up smoking. Robert knows that it is Tommy's mother, who has seen him and reported him to me, this is his revenge.'

'Put like that,' Reg said, 'it makes sense.'

XI.   1960

Tommy improved but very slowly. Carol had to be admitted to hospital, she had made herself ill with worry and anyway couldn't look after herself. She went to the same hospital as Tommy was in. Whenever someone was free, they would take her to his room to see him, she would sit by his bed and just hold his hand.

When he was taken out of intensive care, they put them together in a side ward so that they could remain together. I visited as often as I could but would only stay for about half an hour, as I didn't want to tire them out.

Auntie Pegs was harassed to death over Robert's behaviour, even though I had tried to play it down. I hadn't told her everything but she guessed something was wrong, she said she would worry less if she knew what it was that was troubling me. She was horrified when I eventually told her.

'Surely, though, now that communicating door is bolted and you have a new lock on your front door, the problem must be solved.'

It's what we all thought. But the day came when that familiar cigarette smell was back and my eiderdown was crumpled. I had no idea how he was getting in.

It was David who helped solve the problem. He knew a lot of people in and around Leyburn and further afield. He'd built up a good portfolio of useful people to know and had lots of contacts.

A friend of a friend (!) let me have his video cameras (very new at the time and not perfected). He came over one day to discuss it and fix them up.

My sofa and easy chairs were grouped around the big picture window, as the view was so spectacular. Behind them was my dining area with a table and four chairs. Auntie Peggy had given me her corner cupboard. She had always said it just wasn't big enough for her needs, as each shelf would only hold four of anything. It was antique and I was enormously proud of it. On the top of it and from each side there were sweeping scrolls that met in the middle where there was a small aperture. He got one camera positioned behind this aperture. He was unsure if it would work as it faced the window. The bedroom was a bit easier, the big old cupboard I had moved, so that it was crossways over a corner, the window was to the side of it. The second camera was put on top of that and hidden behind a vase of dried flowers.

He said to David. 'When your man comes into the room the cameras will automatically switch on.'

David said sharply. 'Norman, speak to the lady, I did say it was her house and not mine.'

'Oh. Sorry. You have to press this switch on your remote control that you do by pointing it towards the hidden camera. We'll see a bit of you each time you switch it on and you'll know it's working as this red light will come on.' He stood too near me and I didn't like him much but I suppose I had to be shown what to do and what buttons to press. Anyway, I was prepared to put up with that to get the 'Robert problem' solved. 'Once you go out it will stop recording. When your intruder calls, it will start to record again. I can only let you have it for three days. I'll come back with my video and show you what's on the films. Any Questions?'

'Yes. Do I take the remotes with me when I go out?'

'No, you have to leave them here, inside the house.'

'That's difficult as I think he goes through my drawers when he's here.'

'Get a chair and leave them next to the cameras. Of course we will see your retreating back and you moving the chair away but maybe you won't mind that.'

'No, as long as we get this evil boy caught and have proof that he comes into my house, as his parents don't believe that he does.'

'It should certainly do that. We'll have to hope it all works okay. Any problems, ring me.' He passed me his business card. It said *Norman Prowser. Private Investigator. General enquiries. Anything checked out. No result, no fee.* His telephone number was on the bottom right hand corner.

'About the fee...' I started to say.

Norman looked across at David, who said. 'Don't worry, I'm calling in a favour.'

'Remember you can only have it for three days.' Norman reminded me.

Three days was long enough.

Norman called again one evening three days later. David arrived again and plonked himself down on one of my easy chairs. 'Just thought you might need me.' He said offhandedly. I thought that was nice of him. Knowing I didn't like Norman much was the reason for his coming up to be with me, I thought. While Norman got his camera up, collected the tapes and loaded the camera I made us all a cup of coffee. He didn't need a screen, I removed a couple of pictures from the left hand wall and he could show the film on that. I closed my curtains.

He was right about the film in the sitting room. You saw my back as I walked away from the sitting room area. Next Robert appeared in the picture. He sat himself down in the chair David was now sitting in. He opened a bottle of beer, lit a cigarette and placed his feet on my coffee table. He drank two bottles of beer and had two fags while he was there. But in truth it could be almost anyone. With the camera facing the big picture window, you really just saw someone's silhouette. Except that I knew it was Robert, as did David.

'I don't expect you want to see if he comes in another day?' Norman asked. 'No, not really,' I said, 'it seems a bit pointless.'

'Okay we'll see the bedroom tape. That should be a lot clearer as the light is on the camera's right.' As he said this, he was changing the tapes over.

The bedroom tape started. David had moved and was now leaning against the back of my chair. I was totally unprepared for what I was about to see. I was absolutely disgusted and open mouthed in disbelief at what I saw. It showed Robert coming into my bedroom. He took his trousers off, then his underpants, knelt on my bed facing the headboard. He started to masturbate and continued, with all the accompanying noises, until he ejaculated all over my pillows. I stood up, white and shaking. David, I think was embarrassed, Norman seemed unmoved but then he had probably seen that, or something similar, loads of times. Neither of them said anything. I raced for the bathroom and was violently sick. I looked at this white shocked face staring back at me in the bathroom mirror and was sick again. I said to myself, you stupid, naïve, idiot. Thinking he was just lying on your bed and maybe going through your drawers. *You fool*, I castigated myself.

'You all right, Lucy? I thought as much, which is why I'm here. I didn't think he was just lying on your bed.' David was standing in the bathroom doorway; I hadn't even had time to close the door. He looked anxiously at me, 'I hoped I was wrong.' He gave a sort of helpless shrug.

'To think I was lying on those same pillows.' I sat heavily down on the bathroom chair. 'It's so disgusting.' With that, I burst into tears. David came right into the bathroom then and gave me a bear hug.

'Come on Lucy, be brave. We have to go next door with this evidence.'

'Oh God it's so awful. It's going to be such a shock for them. No wonder you insisted on me having a camera in my bedroom. Where is Norman now?' David popped his head round the door. 'Packing his equipment away.'

'Would he take it next door to show them?' I asked.

'It's all part of the deal, to show the evidence.' David said.

'Give me a minute then.' I said, still shaking David went out of the bathroom and closed the door behind him.

I cleaned my teeth and washed my face in cold water. I really wanted to have a bath. I felt so dirty, sullied and *so* angry too. Which was what was going to carry me through the next couple of hours.

Norman was quite prepared to go next door; he said it was part of the deal too. I looked out of my bedroom window; the Sergeant's car was parked outside their house, so at least he was home. Armed with the tapes, camera, etc, we trooped next door.

It was Sergeant Wright, himself who answered the door when I rang the bell.

'What do you want?' He asked gruffly.

'To see you, Sergeant, Mrs Wright and Robert,' I replied, sounding ultra-polite.

'And who are these people?' He asked.

'You've met my cousin David and this gentleman is a private investigator.'

Sergeant Wright gave me a startled look, then looked hard at Norman. 'I've seen you somewhere before.'

'Yes sir, you probably have.' Norman didn't say any more.

'You'd better come in.' Sergeant Wright sighed. He led us into the sitting room on the left of the front door.

'Make yourselves comfortable. I'll just go and get my wife and Robert.' He strode out of the room.

Once he had gone, Norman started to set up his equipment.

Mrs Wright bustled in.

'What's going on here?' She demanded.

'It's just my proof, once and for all, that your son is breaking and entering my house, Mrs Wright.'

'Oh no, not that again. I've told you he doesn't.' She glared at me. I glared back and said, 'Well, you're going to have to eat your words any second now.'

Norman coughed to attract attention, we all looked at him. He spoke to Mrs Wright. 'I need to remove a couple of pictures on your far wall, I hope you don't mind that Madam.'

'You don't have my permission to move anything,' she said crossly.

'We can just as easily see it over the pictures, it just distorts the picture slightly,' Norman answered, totally unfazed.

'We want Robert here. He might enjoy seeing himself on camera,' David said.

I butted in with, 'But not Rosie or the little boy.'

'I'm sure it's all just harmless fun,' Mrs Wright said.

'So you admit that he goes into my house?' I snapped.

She simply stared at me and said nothing, knowing she had been caught out.

Sergeant Wright came in just then, almost dragging Robert with him.

'Ted! Don't be so rough with the boy.'

'He's nearly 18, Margery, he's hardly a boy.' Sergeant Wright snapped.

Mrs Wright moved to one end of the sofa, patted the cushion next to her and said to Robert, 'Sit by me pet.' Robert sat but at the other end of the sofa.

Sergeant Wright stood behind him. I walked to where I could watch them, especially Robert. David stood a few feet away from me, whilst Norman fiddled with his equipment, getting it sorted.

'Where are Rosie and Jamie?' asked Mrs Wright.

'I suggested they play in their bedrooms.' The Sergeant remarked.

'I'll go and get them. They might like to watch their brother on film.' Mrs Wright started to rise from her seat.

'Margery,' the Sergeant grated out. 'Leave them be. Sit and *listen*! Watch and *learn*.'

'Are we ready?' Asked Norman politely. 'Could you close the curtains please Lucy, as you are the nearest to them?'

I did as I was bid. We were plunged into near darkness. Norman pressed buttons and the film started on the back wall. He fast-forwarded my tiny part. I watched avidly, the three faces almost opposite me.

The first film was of Robert making himself comfortable on one of my easy chairs. He opened a bottle of beer, lit up a cigarette and put his feet up on the coffee table.

'That could be anyone,' scoffed Mrs Wright.

'Margery! Enough. Listen and take it in.' The Sergeant said sharply.

The date and time was across the bottom of the film. Once we had seen about five minutes of this, Norman switched his machine off. 'There is, of course, far more but it is all of the same thing. Could I have the light on, please?' Sergeant Wright turned smartly and switched on the light. Norman changed the tapes over and I was beginning to feel sick, as I knew what would be seen next. Norman asked the Sergeant to switch the lights off again. Once more Norman fast-forwarded until Robert was on the screen once more. I concentrated hard on watching their faces. Going by the grunts and groans coming from the sound system, I knew what part of the film they were watching. Mrs Wright's hand went to her mouth. Robert sat watching himself with what appeared to be a grin on his face. I really wanted to hit him. The Sergeant watched the film with total horror and disgust written on his face. Mrs Wright stifled a sob, got up from the sofa and fled from the room.

Norman stopped the film. 'There is more but we have probably seen enough... Lucy, the curtains.' I pulled the curtains back, flooding the room with sunlight. There was complete silence in the room. All but Norman stood staring at Robert. The Sergeant looked directly at me, then, shifted his gaze to Robert.

'You dirty, lying, deceitful little bastard... have you nothing to say for yourself?' He roared.

Robert got up from his seat and rounded on his stepfather.

'It's your fault!' He shouted. 'Everything was alright until you came along. I hate you! I hate you! Mum promised me that room when I turned 18 and I *want* it.'

'You won't get anything at all now. Nothing but a spell in Borstal,' the Sergeant grated out. Robert looked at me and there was such hatred in his eyes. I quailed but made myself stare back.

'You disgust me,' I said. 'It must please you to know I was sleeping on pillows spattered with your semen. Did you get off on that as well? I don't find your excuse of...' and here I put on a whiney voice. *"Mum promised me that room"* good enough for what you have done in my bedroom.' He moved with such suddenness and speed, he caught everyone unawares. He ran at me at full tilt and head butted me, catching me on my chin and upper chest, it all but knocked me out and I fell to the floor. His foot would have caught me too if David hadn't pulled him away.

'Don't confound your felony, you stupid boy, by attacking Miss Bradley. That doesn't help your cause at all.' His stepfather roared.

Mrs Wright came in just then to see what the noise was about. She was red eyed and hiccupping.

'I've decided...'

She stopped, seeing me lying on the floor and her husband holding tightly onto Robert. We will never know what she had decided as the Sergeant said. 'Face up to it Margery, he's an evil bastard.'

'No, no!' she wept, 'I can't believe it.'

'You saw it on film, for goodness sake. Wake up Margery!' Sergeant Wright was shouting at her.

David bent down and helped me into a chair. 'Are you alright?'

Clearly, I was not.

Rosie and Jamie came in just then.

'What's happening?' Rosie asked. She saw her father holding tightly onto Robert and added, 'Daddy, what's Robert done?'

'Something nasty in Miss Bradley's house. Rosie, now the truth, have you been in the house next door?'

Rosie started to cry.

'Sergeant Wright, please, it doesn't matter. I don't want Rosie and Jamie involved.' I was able to say.

'Keep out of this, Miss Bradley. This is my family and I don't want my two children tainted by this evil, disgusting boy. So answer me Rosie.' She clung to her mother's skirt, sobbing and shaking.

Jamie, who was then four years old, said, 'We've been in Miss Bradley's house two times.' And he held up two, grubby, stubby fingers.

'No!' Screamed Rosie, 'Don't tell them. Robert will...'

There was silence in the room. 'Robert will, *what* Rosie?'

'Nothing Daddy, nothing,' she sobbed.

'May I have a word?' I asked. I was feeling decidedly groggy. No one answered me. I looked at Rosie and said gently 'Come over here.' I bent forward, although it gave me a frightful headache and held out my hand. 'Please, Rosie...' She looked at me and was undecided. 'A pretty please,' I cajoled. She sort of smiled through her tears, let go of her mother's skirts and walked to within a metre of me. I stretched forward, took her hand and drew her to me. 'Tell me, did Robert say, "Don't tell Mummy or Daddy"?' He did, didn't he?' She nodded her head, tears filling her eyes again. 'Well you can tell me what he said because he didn't say "Don't tell Miss Bradley," now did he?' She thought about this and the logic made sense to her because she shook her head.

I asked quietly. 'So what would he do?' She looked back at Robert. 'Don't look at him and don't be afraid,' I said, 'because he will be going away for a long time.'

'To where?' She asked in a timid little voice.

'To prison, I hope, for hurting little girls. I know he does 'cause I've head you crying.

He didn't hurt Jamie though did he?'

'No, he didn't,' she replied, shaking her head.

'If it makes it any easier, whisper to me what he used to say to you.'

'I've heard enough of this. Putting words into her head,' Mrs Wright said angrily.

'Be quiet, Margery,' ground out the Sergeant. 'At least Miss Bradley is getting answers, which is more then you and I have managed to do.' Mrs Wright scowled at her husband but remained quiet. 'Answer her Rosie,' her father said, using a far softer voice.

Rosie bent forward and put her lips to my ear. 'He'd say he'd kill me if I told,' she whispered.

I put my lips to her ear and said, 'But did he hurt you?' Tears were pouring down her face again, I cuddled her to me, I'd been down this road with my sister.

'Yes.' She finally got out on a sob.

'Rosie, Rosie,' I groaned. If only I had acted on my instincts when I heard her crying.

'Now I want you to go to Mummy and with Jamie go into the kitchen. Maybe she can get a biscuit for you for being so brave.' She hopped off my lap and went to her mother. Mrs Wright opened her mouth to say something but one look from her husband stopped her in her tracks. She swept out, taking the younger children with her.

I looked at Robert. 'You fucking bastard. You vicious, contemptible, corrupt, depraved bastard.' I was *so* angry.

'What's he done?' ground out Sergeant Wright.

' I suggest, Sergeant, that if you have never bathed your children, then do it tonight and see all the bruises and little scars on Rosie's body. I'm guessing that they are there, if they are, they will have been inflicted by *him*.' I pointed at Robert.

'She's very clumsy. ' He stopped as realization swept over him. He turned to Robert. 'You... I took you and your mother under my wing, fed you, clothed you and gave you mostly what you wanted. You don't deserve to live in the same house as a small, defenceless child. I'll make sure you are locked up for this.'

Robert looked unsure of himself all of a sudden. He was a young man, found out doing dreadful deeds and not liking the consequences.

'Please... Dad.'

'Oh! It's *Dad* now is it? When usually you can't even be civil to me. Oh no, you're no son of mine.'

Someone, I suspect David, had rung for an ambulance for me and the police for Robert.

Everything is pretty hazy after that. I was very groggy and felt sick again.

They kept me in hospital for two nights. The doctors said I was suffering from delayed shock, had cracked an upper rib, had a hairline fracture of the jaw and concussion. The police interviewed me in hospital. I could only tell them what had happened and answer their questions as best as I could. I was in the same hospital as Carol and Tommy, so on my last morning I slipped along to visit them.

Carol looked loads better, obviously the rest had done her good and to be with her son was a godsend. Tommy was propped up in bed, leaning against a load of pillows. The black was going from around his eyes and the swelling was going down, he was wrapped in an amazing amount of bandages but still didn't look too well.

'Hiya folks!' I said as I walked in, in my matching hospital gown. "Snap"!'

'Oh my God! What are you doing here?'

'Got jealous,' I joked, 'of you two being in here, so I thought I would join you.'

'Sit down,' said Carol, laughing. 'What are you doing here?'

I told them most of what had happened, from the time Norman came to fix up the cameras. I didn't go into too much detail about what we saw on the film but Carol wasn't stupid; she could fill in the gaps as I told the story. She wrinkled her nose up in distaste. 'How disgusting. How could he? That's just awful'

'How about Tommy? Have the police been in to interview him?'

'Yes. The trouble is, Tommy knows who did it, because he spoke. He said, 'This is for your noisy effing mother.' But it's Tommy's word against Robert's.'

'I don't think you'll have a problem there, not after what he did to me. He's certainly capable of it.'

'If we can get him for GBH, it gets a horrible boy off the streets.' 'David said that after I'd gone, Robert broke down and cried like a baby. His mother was hysterical, saying she couldn't believe anything and her Robert wouldn't do such a thing. David helped Norman pack his equipment away and stayed on in case the Sergeant needed help with Robert. When Robert was led away in handcuffs, David left, leaving the Sergeant to deal with his wife.'

'Are you pressing charges?' Carol asked.

'I think so. It's unlawful entering and he did attack me. I'll have to think about it. It's his little sister I feel sorry for; she is so sweet and she was terrified of her brother.'

'When do you go home?' Asked Carol.

'Later today, David is collecting me.'

'He is such a nice man. I need to thank him for going out on that dreadful night to search for Tommy.'

'I'll tell him, when I see him. I can't imagine what you are going through Tommy, my one cracked rib is bad enough, to say nothing of my aching jaw. What about you? When will you be going home?'

'Tommy gets out of bed in the afternoons. When he can stand and is up for a full day, then we will be allowed home.'

'It's nothing to do with me, I know, but how will you manage?' I asked tentatively.

Carol smiled. 'We'll manage fine. Social Services will call in twice a day, until such times, as we can manage on our own.'

'That's marvellous news.' I enthused.

'Tommy won't be able to do anything for ages but it will be just nice to get back home.'

Tommy's eyes were dropping, I didn't want to tire them out, so I said goodbye to them both and went back to my own ward.

When David arrived to take me home, he'd said he'd had a talk with Auntie Peggy and had told her some of the details. She had been disgusted and wanted me to come home to them for a while.

I thanked him for all he had done and gave him Carol's message of thanks too.

'Anybody would do the same,' he'd said, quite embarrassed.

He said Shirley (surprisingly) had made the same offer for me to stay with them. I'd said I needed to get back to my little place or I would never want to return. He understood totally, as he would have acted in the same way and had explained that to Auntie Peggy.'

'But on your first night back you shouldn't be left on your own. It was a hell of a wallop Robert gave you, so I am staying the night. I'll sleep fine on your sofa.'

'There is no need for you to babysit me.'

'Aye, well you say that but you never know. And it's settled, so don't argue.'

Secretly, I was quite pleased about this. It had worried me at odd moments about sleeping on my own again. Robert had knocked my confidence a bit.

'Shirley and I have changed your sheets, we've turned the mattress, thrown your pillows away...' I did an involuntary shiver '...and used your spare ones. I hope we did right.'

'Yes, thank you. You've both been so good. Thank Shirley for me will you.'

'No need, she's there now preparing a simple meal for you. Tomato soup, I seem to remember is your favourite. With your fractured jaw, you won't be able to eat anything hard, or crisp. So it's slops for you and steak for me!' I tried hard not to laugh.

'David, don't, you're so funny,' I said weakly, 'but don't make me laugh.'

His cross-eyed wife welcomed me back. She'd set the table for just the three of us.

'Where are the children?' I asked.

'I thought they would be too much for you, so I have left them next door. I'll collect them later when I get home. It won't hurt them for once to have their tea late.'

'But they are so good,' I protested.

She was adamant. 'No, they will be fine.'

After our simple supper, she suggested that she help me get to bed. I said I could really manage on my own, if I took it slowly.

'Well, I think you should go to bed before I go, just in case.'

I felt like a child again, being told to go to bed. However, I did and was grateful for her suggestion. I was really shattered. I took my painkillers, like the good little girl I am! I intended to get out of bed once she had gone and spend a convivial evening with David but it wasn't to be, as I fell asleep!

The following week was really uncomfortable for me. My jaw ached intolerably. I couldn't even eat my cereals in the morning.

On that first morning, David popped out and came back with some porridge oats, luckily I like that and it was simple to eat. My rib was killing me. I could only get up if I put my hand on the rib and press gently.

Reg came to see me. David had called on him to say I wouldn't be in for work and said I probably wouldn't be in for at least a couple of weeks. I filled Reg in on the finer details. He was appalled.

By Friday, I'd had enough, I felt so low. I called David (again) Shirley helped me to pack and he took me, driving slowly, down to Crofters Cottage. Auntie Pegs felt so sorry for me. She gave me a gentle hug and took David and me into the kitchen and gave us each a cup of tea, shortly after David had a word with Grandad and left. We had home-made soup for the evening meal. I couldn't do anything for myself without feeling intense pain. I was off work for four weeks.

XII.   1961

Reg came to see me once I was settled into Crofters Cottage. He seemed to spend most of his time talking to Auntie Peggy. It started to dawn on me that he fancied her! I teased her after he had taken up her offer to stay for supper. Whilst she busied herself in the kitchen, Reg had gone into the sitting room and was having an animated conversation with Grandad. Auntie Peggy took my teasing quite happily and said she found him good company and he made her laugh.

I remained there for two weeks. The first week I did a lot of sleeping and could still only have soup or mashed potato and vegetables in gravy. My jaw remained painful for a long time and I moved with care. I felt better in myself after my two weeks there. I have always said that Crofters Cottage had healing properties.

I spent another two weeks off at my own house. I felt okay about being there on my own and relief, in a way, I could have a hot bath and try and soak the aches away.

Carol and Tommy were back from hospital. I had been over to see them a couple of times. Their home help from Social Services seemed a nice enough woman and they were happy to be back in their own place, as I was in mine.

I'd been pottering around, I had some washing on the go and I was doing some dusting when the front door bell went. When I opened the door, Ted Wright was standing there.

'May I come in or would you rather I didn't?' I hesitated but only for a second. I stepped back to let him in.

'I won't take up much of your time. I just thought I'd tell you what's going on. My wife is staying with her sister in Richmond. That way Rosie can continue at infants' school and we have just started Jamie at kindergarten. Robert is on remand and remains in prison. I refused to bail him. He's been done for cruelty to children and two counts of GBH – his unprovoked attack on Tommy and his attack on you.

Margery simply can't take it in about what he has done. So he remains in prison, because if he wasn't, he would be with Rosie and I can't take that risk. You have my word that you won't see Robert again.'

'I'm pleased to hear that Sergeant.'

'You know I bent over backwards for that boy. Perhaps that's where I went wrong, letting him have his head, so to speak. I was harder on my own children, so that he wouldn't think I favoured them. His mother will stand by him but I won't. I've told her she thinks too much of him. Hiding Rosie's 'little accidents' from me is unforgivable. I really thought she was just clumsy. The children will be staying with me, next door, on my days off.' He smiled somewhat sadly. 'Rosie has taken quite a shine to you.'

'I found her very appealing but I find myself feeling guilty. I heard her crying so often, that I feel I should have gone to her aid. But if I had gone next door and said something, I would not have been believed and probably told to mind my own business.'

'A very strong possibility, I think,' the Sergeant said. 'Even now Margery can't believe that it's Robert on that film. It's as if she has blanked it out. Anyway, I have put in for a transfer down South. I have recently put the house up for sale, as it is mine. I'm at liberty to keep my job in Richmond until such time I can take up my new post. I wonder if your cousin would be interested in removing that door. I just don't have the time to do it myself. I have no idea why Margery insisted on keeping it there.'

'That would certainly be a relief. I will ask David and let you know. I gather that at the moment he is very busy, so it could take time to organise it but as long as Robert's not around, I don't have too much of a problem with it.'

'I'm just so terribly sorry about everything. How are you?'

'Mending,' I said. 'It seems a slow progress. The mental scars remain, though; I don't think they will ever go away. The invasion of my property and Robert's obscene behaviour in my bedroom, I have nightmares even now. But my physical injuries will go eventually.'

He was looking at his hat that he was absently turning in his hand. Perhaps he was embarrassed at my mentioning Robert's misdeeds. I changed the subject.

'I start work on Monday. It will stop me from going mad with boredom. I still have to take it easy though, until I'm in no pain at all. A girl from Harmby has taken on my job and has caused a few howlers; she does her best, as she knows not to get on the wrong side of Mr Boulting. I get on with him very well, for underneath all that bluster and yelling, beats a heart of gold.'

Again, there was a pause in the conversation. I said to break the silence.

'There are two things I would like to know, how did he get into my house again when I had changed the locks? And when I went home, even at unexpected times, I never found him in the house.'

'We have a mountain of keys in our house, one will nearly always fit another house lock, that, or he simple picked the lock I'm not sure which option he took. Your other point I can answer, he stationed Rosie in our front porch. We can see a long way down into the square, nearly to the hotel, where you work, as soon as she spotted you coming home, she would run in and tell Robert. She knew it was wrong to do that but she didn't feel she had a choice.'

'Poor little girl.' I sympathised.

I'd had enough now and I really wanted him to go, almost as though he read my thoughts, he said,

'I'll leave you in peace. Thank you for your kindness to Rosie, I appreciate that. She has nightmares too. I can't ever forgive Robert'.

I edge towards the front door.

'Perhaps Rosie would like to come round for tea one day when she is down here with you, Jamie too if he wants to.'

'That's kind, I'm sure they would love to.'

I opened the front door, he took his leave and went.

After my first full day at work, I felt exhausted at the end of the day. All I had done was write three letters confirming accommodation and ordering a list of food from the wholesalers. My back, shoulders, injured rib and my jaw ached intolerably. Once home, I drank a cup of soup, had a long hot bath and crawled into bed. I must have gone to sleep as soon as my head touched the pillow; even so, I arrived 10 minutes late the following day. 'What's up lass?' Reg asked.

'Just ache all over.' I replied as I sat behind the typewriter, getting ready to do battle with his dreadful handwriting.

'Can't abide lateness, as you know,' (This from a man who was always late) 'but you looked exhausted yesterday, so I'll let it go today. But I can't be seen to favour you.'

'Sorry Reg,' I said, 'it won't happen again.' He stomped out of the office, leaving me to get on with the work.

It took 8 weeks altogether to be completely free of pain; even then, if I got overtired or did too much, I'd feel a dull ache in my rib and jaw.

At last, my doctor pronounced me fit enough to resume my normal duties. Reg seemed relieved to have me back behind the reception desk and what a mess I found.

For two weeks I didn't know, who was going, who was coming, what rooms had been booked, by whom and more importantly, who had paid and who hadn't.

Two men had booked in with the same surname and the same letter to their Christian names. The temp thought they were the same man. All we had left was the Bridal Suite with its four-poster bed.

I found out by chatting to the guests that a Mr and Mrs Paul Andrews were celebrating their 40th wedding anniversary. We moved them into the Bridal Suite, as a surprise for them and thereby getting us out of a sticky problem. They were thrilled when I told them what we had done for them, with a bottle of champagne, two champagne glasses, a box of chocolates and a huge bouquet of flowers left in their room, they were delighted. No one knew of the mix up.

We hurriedly cleaned the room and put clean sheets on the bed for Mr Adam Savoury and Mr Andrew Savoury had the original booked room.

I explained it all to Reg when he'd asked what we had done about it, he just harrumphed, said 'that dratted girl' and walked off into his office. 'That dratted girl' and I looked at each other, raised our eyes heavenwards, sighed with relief and she was able to go off duty, a good hour late but in a happier frame of mind.

Auntie Elsie, a cousin of Auntie Peggy's appeared in my life again. Elsie had been married to a Michael Robbins. I was their bridesmaid when I was four. Michael had died suddenly about five years ago. They'd had one son, Julian, an absolute drip of a boy. I had always liked her. She was very beautiful and vivacious. She'd had to give up the farm, as Julian had shown no interest or inclination to run it. He was a struggling accountant. She worked as a receptionist in a big hotel in Sutton Bridge, about 30 miles away and thoroughly enjoyed it. People adored her. She just appeared one day at Auntie Peggy's. I happened to be there as it was my first day off from my usual two.

'I'd heard you were here,' she said. Mum must have told her, that I now lived up North. 'I had to come and see if you were still the sweet little girl who was my bridesmaid all those years ago.' She looked me up and down in fun and said. 'Umm, you've grown some but still as sweet.' I was delighted to see her although I thought Auntie Peggy's reception of her was a little cool but Grandad was very pleased to see her. So pleased that he asked her to stay for tea. Auntie Peggy didn't seem too keen, however. She shooed us out, saying she could manage on her own. Grandad had just got over a nasty cold, so I suggested we go for a walk with Honey the dog. She was now 12 years old and didn't walk so far as she used to, we just wandered about the village, chatting all the time. I admired Auntie Elsie's little car that she had driven down in, a little 1,000cc Morris Minor in blue.

Maybe I shouldn't have done, it wasn't my place to do so, but I apologised for Auntie Peggy's coolness towards her.

'She has never forgiven me,' Auntie Elsie said sadly.

'About what?' I asked.

'She said I had 'stolen' her boyfriend.'

'And did you?'

She sighed. 'It's true to say that he had gone out with her on a couple of occasions. He told me she was merely a passing fancy but according to your aunt they were engaged to be married, although there was no official announcement of it, nor was it in the papers and there was certainly no engagement ring. If there had been, I wouldn't have gone out with him. When we broke up, he didn't return to Peggy. Anyway, he was killed in the war.'

I remained quiet and then said, 'It hurts me to think that she believed she had found her man. Auntie Peggy was made for marriage and babies; she loves children. She has been so wonderful to me and Grandad has too. I couldn't have managed without them.'

'In what way?'

I told her my story of what it was that had driven me up north, not in the same detail as I had told Auntie Peggy and Grandad but she was still horrified.

'You poor dear, you have been through it. I maybe shouldn't tell you this but your father once made a pass at me and that, I certainly hadn't encouraged.'

I must have looked stunned.

'I sorry, I shouldn't have said anything,' she added.

'Was he married to Mum at the time?'

'Oh yes, he was.'

'Well,' I managed at last. 'It just makes me, if it's possible, hate him even more.'

We walked on in silence for a while. I sighed and let it go. I couldn't worry about something that had happened so long ago.

I told her the problems I had had with Robert. She was disgusted and wrinkled her nose in distaste.

'Ugh! The disgusting boy. So your Sergeant Wright says this Robert will remain in prison until his trial?'

'I believe so.'

'A good thing too.'

We turned for home.

'I'd love to see your little cottage,' Auntie Elsie said.

'Well, if we can tie up our days off, you can come over to see it,' I said.

'Why not tonight? I have to go through Leyburn to get home.'

'Okay,' I said, 'let's do that.'

The tea was lovely and the talk was lively, although Auntie Elsie did most of the talking. She told us very amusing stories about her hotel life. After tea, I helped with the washing up and broached the subject of going into Leyburn, as Auntie Elsie wanted to see my place. I asked Auntie Pegs to come with us, then we could catch the last bus home together, and to my delight she said she would.

We piled into Auntie Elsie's car. Grandad didn't come; he said he would prefer to stay at home. It was a jolly little threesome that went to Leyburn. I pointed out the hotel where I worked and Auntie Elsie was charmed with my cottage. She explored every nook and cranny and pronounced it 'grand'. Auntie Pegs said she wished she'd thought of bringing her washing things, so she could have a bath. I gave her a towel of mine and pushed her into the bathroom. After that I made us all some coffee and we sat and chatted. It was Auntie Elsie who suggested that she stay in my cottage overnight and go back early tomorrow. She wasn't keen on driving far in the dark as she said her lights were playing up. That seemed a good suggestion to me. I loaned her a nightgown.

She said, 'I'm sure you're not dirty, so don't change the sheets.' I told her, 'I did them this morning before going to Auntie Pegs and Grandad's for my two days off.'

Auntie Peggy and I had to run to catch the last bus. I had thoroughly enjoyed my day and hoped Auntie Pegs had as well.

Auntie Elsie and I didn't meet up as much as I would have liked to have done, as our days off didn't often match up, but even when I was working she'd come over to visit me, stay the night and we'd have a great gossip. She said she would have liked to come over more often and teach me to drive. I mentioned this to Reg.

'Far better for me to teach you to drive,' he said. 'You'll pick up all her bad habits.'

'And you haven't got any, I suppose,' I teased.

After I'd finished work, if he wasn't too busy – and we weren't, as autumn had crept in and it was beginning to get cold – he'd take me out for an hour. All I paid for was the petrol I used. He bullied me into having a couple of lessons with B.S.M. (British School of Motoring), as they could organise my test, which I passed on my second attempt. That first time was really just nerves. Reg made me put in for my second test almost immediately. I was thrilled when I passed.

David called on Sergeant Wright to organise a date for the removal of the middle door and told him he would need entry into his house to do the job. It could be done from my side but he would need to remove the architrave and plaster up on his side. The Sergeant was quite amenable and wanted it done as soon as possible. David took down two pictures from each side of the door; he didn't want them to fall off with the vibration from him taking the door and its surrounds down and the glass breaking. That's when he found a spy-hole into my bedroom. The walls were two feet thick but with some small piping and a tiny magnifying glass pushed through to the end, Robert would have got a good view into my bedroom. Sergeant Wright was as shocked as David was.

'No wonder Robert wouldn't have that picture moved by me. It's a picture of his real Dad. So as not to upset him, I never touched it.' He sat heavily on the arm of the sofa. 'I'm just so sorry.'

David said, when he was telling me later, that the Sergeant sounded quite broken and bowed down by the past few months' events. David had said to him, 'I think you have a very sick stepson.'

David removed the piping and the magnifying glass, stopped up the hole and had a job finding it on my side of the wall, as I had quite busy wallpaper on the dividing wall my bed head stood against. Again, I was appalled and somewhat sickened at this new discovery – but at least I'd never have to face the bastard again.

Wrong.

With David's help I redecorated my bedroom. He took down the dividing wall between my bedroom and the passageway that had led to the middle door; it made my bedroom much bigger. I was thrilled. I brought a load of new linen, pillows and towels and gave my little abused cottage a good clean. I had just cleaned my big sitting room window inside and was debating whether to do the outside as well. The Sergeant had just come back from somewhere, I heard a door or two slam but hadn't looked out. I carried my long steps outside, I knew I wasn't going to settle until they were done, so I told myself that I may as well get on with it.

They sparkled in the early autumn sun when I had finished them and I was very pleased with the result and thought it well worth the effort too. I carried my steps inside again. I went out once more to survey my handiwork. I moved towards the window to rub at a smudge I could see. I still had my duster in my hand. I heard a knocking on a window; it would be Carol trying to catch my attention. I looked left and up at her window. She was waving franticly at me. She looked frightened and was pointing to my right. I looked and saw Robert behind the wheel of his father's car. It was freewheeling straight towards me. The car was just feet away from me. I ran the few yards to the end of my house. The house that was at right angles to mine, that looked directly onto the square was not flush with mine, there was a foot gap that I pressed myself into and looked up at Carol. Her eyes were huge and her hands were pressed to her mouth. The next moment there was what sounded like a massive explosion. The sound was as loud as it was shocking. I closed my eyes tight shut and had my hands over my ears. I could guess what Robert had done, he had not been successful in running me down, so had swung the wheel of his stepfather's car straight into my beautiful windows.

There was a terrible grinding sound and splinters of glass flew in all directions. When a deafening hush descended, I ventured to peep out. Sergeant Wright had just emerged from his house to see what the noise was about. He looked as appalled as Carol, who was still standing at her window. Robert remained in the car. I started to shake and couldn't move from my corner. All I could think of at that moment was that I had just cleaned the windows!

Sergeant Wright walked slowly to his car but he couldn't open the driver's door to get Robert out because of the distortion of the impact. He looked at me over the roof of his car as I emerged from my corner.

'Is he...? 'I started, in a shaking voice.

'I think he's just in shock but the steering wheel is hard up against his chest and his legs might be trapped.'

I walked slowly and shakily across the road, leaned heavily on Carol's garden wall and surveyed my damaged house.

'He's done a good job of that,' I said, rather obtusely, looking at my smashed windows.

The wooden surrounds were broken beyond repair. Pieces of glass where hanging at odd angles. What wasn't still hanging was in the road in millions of glittering pieces. The window frame was half hanging out. The wooden cross members were broken also beyond repair. The stone lintel above had moved slightly causing a crack down the front wall.

Stupidly, I said, 'He's won. I can't live in my little cottage any more. It holds too many bad memories.'

The police were called, as was an ambulance and the fire brigade. Robert had to be cut out of the car. As he was lifted into the ambulance he gave me a sly, satisfied grin. It said, "I can't have it, so you can't either." The car, a big Ford Zephyr had fared better than my house but probably would still be a right off.

Statements were taken from Carol – who had seen the whole thing – and myself.

The only good thing in this awful state of affairs, was that Robert pleaded guilty on the grounds of diminished responsibility, so there would be no trial. As he had other convictions he was eventually given 15 years. His legs had taken a battering but he would walk again. He had many broken ribs where the steering wheel had gone into his chest and minor grazes on his face.

The Sergeant was still standing outside his house, watching Robert being driven away in the ambulance.

'So I won't see him again, huh?' I said scathingly.

'Well, you won't see him now,' he said, as I walked into my ruined house.

I rang David. When I heard his friendly voice answer the phone I burst into tears.

'Whatever... Lucy is that you?'

I couldn't answer. I just sobbed into the phone. Eventually I managed to splutter 'Oh, David!' Sobs took control of me again and I could say nothing else.

'Give me five minutes kid and I'll be with you.' Then he was gone.

The police had closed the lane. The rear of the Sergeant's car was sticking out of my window and with so much glass around it was too dangerous to drive over even if they could pass the car. David had to park his car at the top of the square. I saw him pass what remained of my windows and skirt round the car and stop to stare in horror.

'What the hell has been going on?' he snapped at the Sergeant as he passed in front of him to come into my ruined cottage.

'Whatever, in God's name, has happened?'

I was a bit more in control of my emotions and told him as best I could what had occurred.

'Did you know Robert was back?' David asked. 'I thought he was in prison.'

'I had no idea,' I said, shaking my head. 'I didn't suspect anything was different next door. I didn't know he was out of prison either.'

David went out of the house to speak to the Sergeant, who was still outside, speaking to the police. I went with him. Apparently his wife was in hospital undergoing a hysterectomy and her sister was looking after Rosie and Jamie but had refused to have Robert in the house. The reason he was back was because Mrs Wright had got the money together and got him bailed by borrowing the full amount from the bank 'I had no option but to bring him here. With the door gone and also his filthy spy hole, I just didn't expect any trouble. I didn't think he would do this terrible thing. I am *so* very sorry.'

There was nothing I could say because 'sorry' hardly covered it. I couldn't bring myself to even look at him.

'Well, you can't stay here, with the windows as they are,' David said.

'I'm not living here anymore, David,' I said. 'I can't.'

Once more I went back to Auntie Peggy and Grandad's house. I was distraught.

XIII.   1961-1962

I never went into my little cottage again on my own. Auntie Peggy and I spent a morning there getting my personal items and clothes out. The car had been removed from my sitting room window and David had boarded it up the day after it had been destroyed. He said he could do the work to put it right but couldn't just then as he was busy and anyway we had to have the insurance assessors to come and see the damage. I wanted to see the Sergeant to tell him I wanted him to pay for the damage.

I didn't see why I should lose my no claims bonus, through no fault of mine. But when Auntie Peggy and I were there, of Sergeant Wright and Robert there was no sign. I left a note in his letterbox to that effect and would he get in touch with me via the hotel and left. I never returned to it. Whenever I went to see Carol, I simply averted my eyes from the cottage. She was very upset for me, I said I wouldn't lose contact with her and tried to see her once a week.

I came near enough to having a nervous breakdown, without actually having one. Reg would come into the office and find me in tears but when he asked me what the problem was, I couldn't tell him, because I didn't know myself. We were not very busy at the hotel, so he gave me a week off to see if I could get myself together again. The calming effect of Crofters Cottage, my daily walks with Grandad and Honey and Auntie Peggy's cooking seemed to work some kind of magic, so that when I returned to work a week later, I returned feeling a lot better and with renewed vigour.

David eventually re-stationed the lintel, replaced the window and sorted the crack out on the front wall of my little cottage. Sergeant Wright did pay for everything. He sold his house and moved away to his new job down South. The last I heard of him and Mrs Wright, is that they were divorced and I never saw Robert again. The sergeant got his promotion to inspector and must have got some clout behind him, because he got custody of Rosie and Jamie. It's unusual, even now, for a man to get custody of his own small children. I could only assume that Mrs Wright still couldn't believe that her Robert was the evil bastard that he was and was still going to 'stand by him.'

I was able to rent my little house out on a long-term basis. One of Reg's customers, a retired couple, often came up to Yorkshire on walking holidays. They had been talking to Reg about wanting to rent somewhere full time for themselves and their family's for holidays. Reg had mentioned my place. David showed them around and they were charmed with the place. They loved the big windows! I met them in the hotel one evening; I was just going off duty. They said it all hinged on whether I would allow them to make the dining area into another bedroom. I agreed with that quite happily, I just wanted to be shot of the place. They signed a rental agreement that night and we came to an amicable settlement on the rent. As long as I could pay my mortgage with a bit over, that was okay by me. I could even give them a name of a man who could do the alteration for them! David said he should give me an introductory fee for all the work I had put his way over the past three years!

One day, it must have been a Friday, Grandad was no longer doing the shopping on market days, he was nearing 80 after all. Auntie Peggy had taken on the job and, as always, before catching the bus home she would pop into the hotel to have a late morning cup of coffee. Reg was always around and would sometimes join us. I'd sit with her but always got interrupted by telephone calls or guests asking for directions to somewhere, bringing back their keys, paying their bills or wanting their money out of the safe. Friday was always a busy day, anyway. The pub was heaving but Reg could always spare time for Auntie Peggy. His bar staff would just have to manage without him.

I was at my desk, going through someone's bill, then went into the office to the safe to collect the money they had left as part settlement of their bill. They had to sign a chitty to say they had received their money back, only for them to return it to me, with the full amount if they were checking out. It all took about half an hour. I looked over to Auntie Peggy and Reg; their heads were close together, then Auntie Pegs threw hers back and was laughing at something he said. It hit me like a thunderbolt. They were in love.

Stupid question, maybe, but did they know it? Selfishly, I had a stab of jealousy. Here was Auntie Peggy, at 48, with a boyfriend and here was I, 20 next birthday, without one. I shoved that thought to the back of my mind and went to join them again.

Reg said he would take Auntie Pegs home. He said he'd be no longer than an hour. I wouldn't have thought he could spare the time, going by the noise coming from the pub. They were doing a roaring trade. He was gone for an hour and a half!

I came home one day and knew Auntie Peggy had been crying. I put my arms round her and asked her what the problem was.

'Lucy,' she sniffed, dabbing at her eyes, 'I don't know what to do. Reg has asked me to marry him.'

'But that's absolutely fantastic,' I said, enthusiastically.

'No, no. I had to decline. I can't leave Dad on his own.'

Unfortunately, that was true. Like my mother, he could be very stubborn. He'd say he could manage when we knew that he couldn't. 'I can't move Dad now and get him to live out the rest of his life in Reg's flat. He'd hate that.'

'No, I see that you are right, of course. I'm not here all the time, so I would be no help. Surely there must be an answer?'

'We've been through every equation imaginable. Dad would never accept someone coming in here to 'do' for him and make him his meals, he'd hate it.'

'So what are you going to do?' I asked.

'Reg said he'd wait,' she answered with a sob.

'Life is so unfair, Auntie Peggy. Your chance of happiness taken away from you.'

'No Lucy, don't say that. I've had a good life. I could never say I wasn't happy. Dad and me rub along quite well, you know.' There was a note of rebuke in her voice.

'I didn't mean you hadn't been happy but what an adventure to be married to Reg!'

She gave a sort of laugh. 'You romantic old thing.'

'So how has it been left?'

'I said to forget it altogether.'

My mouth fell open.

'Lucy, I'm not looking forward to Dad dying. He could go on for another ten years and I hope he does. By then I'd been nearing 60 and far too set in my ways to want to change but we'll remain friends.'

She got up and went from the kitchen. I heard the door at the bottom of the stairs open, the third stair squeak and her going up the rest of the stairs and into her bedroom, I heard her bedroom door close and then muffled sobs.

I left her on her own; she didn't want me just then. I'd be there for her later when she might need me.

But it was sooner rather than later and I was hopeless.

It was a hard winter. We'd had a snow free Christmas but on Boxing Day, it started and just never let up. I had to stay at the hotel on a permanent basis. Reg gave me a room, as I couldn't get home. The roads became blocked. Sometimes it was days before buses could get to Redmire, they'd stop at the top of the hill going down to the village and people would have to walk from there. But there were days when the buses couldn't even get that far. On top of that, influenza was rife. Everyone was going down with it.

I did a lot of overtime, Mavis, my trainee, couldn't get in, she lived at Harmby (halfway between Leyburn and Redmire) then she succumbed to the 'flu 'as well. Reg and I could just about manage as long as neither of us went down with the dreaded bug. We somehow got through the worst without either of us getting it but we both had heavy colds.

I got to know Reg very well in that time. I dared to mention that I knew he had asked Auntie Pegs to marry him. He looked at me 'You know then lass?'

'Auntie Peggy and I are very close. We talk woman to woman and I love her and I don't want to see her hurting.'

'Aye, well, that makes the two of us. We talk all the time when we are together. We have nowt in common but my, we can talk. She told me about you and why you're down here.' There was a pause. 'After all you've been through kid, you're alright.' Praise indeed from Reg.

'I guessed one day on market day when she was visiting us. I wondered at the time if you both realized what had happened.'

'Aye, it was about that time that I tumbled to the fact that I had been caught good and proper. The roads are too bad so I can't get down to see her. She has no phone, so I can't ring her either. I just want to know that she is all right and that she's coping. By but I miss her.'

'That makes the two of us,' I said, copying his phrase. 'I also admit that I felt a stab of envy. Here was Auntie Pegs at her age with a boyfriend and here I was without one. I also felt bereft as Crofters Cottage would go and I'd be homeless.'

'Aye, lass no, no. The Red Lion has three bedrooms. You would never be homeless.'

I suddenly had a horrible thought. 'It wasn't me who stopped her from marrying you? Please say it wasn't.'

'No, no. You came into the conversation, of course you did, you're her family. She stated that you would always have a home with us, as long as you wanted it.' He whistled softly to himself, then he beamed, 'I've got it. We could keep Crofters Cottage as our holiday retreat. Living 'over the shop' so to speak I never feel off duty.

So you could go on living there if you wanted to but you would have us popping down occasionally but when we are there you would probably be working.'

'My, my, you have got it all worked out but what a brilliant idea.' I laughed at him, which started a fit of coughing. When I'd stopped, Reg said 'I'll wait for ever if I had to.' I was quite touched by his words. He continued with, 'She thinks we can remain friends, that is what I have agreed to but I didn't mean it.' He grinned at me wickedly, 'But I can't see that friends can't become lovers at a later date.'

'Reg...' I stopped. What on earth was I doing to mention sex to my boss? But too late...

'Go on,' he said. 'What?'

I took a deep breath. 'Reg...' I started again. 'Have you ever thought that Auntie Pegs might know nothing about what being married means?' I couldn't say it more vaguely but he understood.

'You mean sex?'

I blushed. 'Yes. I know she has had a boyfriend but he was killed in the war.' I'd got this from Auntie Elsie. 'She said that she loved him but I don't think as a relationship it had got very far.'

'Woman to woman, you said, you'll have to tell her.'

I gasped. 'I can't do that. I know the mechanics of a union but I have never even had a close boyfriend, so what would I know?'

'Probably more than me, I expect,' he continued, 'so, I'll have fun in teaching her.'

'As long as she finds it fun as well,' I said quietly.

He shot me a look and said, 'Aye lass, aye.' The subject was dropped and was never spoken of again.

The following day, the last day of February it was, it came to our ears that the road to Redmire was open.

I went shopping in my lunch hour and got essentials, as I didn't know if the delivery vans had got through. Reg was determined to go and see Auntie Peggy and wanted me to go with him. Reg collected Mavis to fill in for me. She was much better, although had lost some weight, it was suggested that she bring her nightclothes just in case we couldn't get back as more snow was on the way. There was little for her to do, everything was up to date, she just had to sit in reception and keep warm and see to the few guests that we had in. She said she would remain until I returned.

Reg passed me his car keys. 'I don't think this is a good idea, Reg, for me to drive in this snow.'

'Well, it's time you started.' He said unsympathetically, 'Just take it slowly'

I managed fairly well until we got to the steep hill just outside Redmire. I turned to Reg and said, 'I really don't want to do this hill. You'll manage better than me.'

'Well lass, that remains to be seen but you have done well, so far.'

It was a relief to change places.

Reg took it slowly and managed the hill and the sharp turn at the bottom. High snowdrifts were everywhere. It was even more of a relief to get to Crofters Cottage. I knocked on the door while Reg got the box of provisions out of the boot of the car.

My aunt opened the door; she looked dreadful.

'Lucy! Reg! Oh thank goodness, come in, come in.'

We stepped inside, it was bitterly cold in the cottage

'What's going on?' Reg asked aghast.

'We ran out of coal a few days ago. I've been up to the shop to get some bundles of wood but that's all gone as well. The coalman should have called but he failed to show up.'

'Where's Grandad?' I asked.

'He's not at all well. He's in bed. It was a battle to make him go. He's warmer in bed.

I've used all the hot water bottles I have, to pack his bed with.'

I ran up the stairs, knocked on his bedroom door and went in

'Hello Pet.' He said in a croaky voice. He looked really ill.

'Have you seen the doctor yet?' I asked, as I bent over him to kiss his hot, dry cheek.

'Your aunt sent for him but it's nothing but a cold.' I knew it was more serious than that, I'd heard his chest rattle horribly.

'I'll get you a cup of tea and something to eat.'

'Just tea would be lovely.' He seemed to sink further into his pillows and closed his eyes. I raced down stairs and started to put my outdoor things on again.

'Where are you going?' asked Auntie Pegs.

'To ring for the doctor. He's a dreadful colour and as I bent over him to give him a kiss, I heard a terrible rattle in his chest. He'd like a cup of tea by the way.'

'I've tried to contact Doctor James and left messages with his dreadful housekeeper but he seems to be permanently out. I hope you have better luck than I have had.' Auntie Peggy said unhappily.

'I know, I'll go to his house,' I said, as I went to the front door.

On a journey that should have taken all of 10 minutes, it must have been more than half an hour before I got to the doctor's house. High snowdrifts were everywhere but his driveway was clear. I half slid and half ran to his front door.

His housekeeper, a sour-looking woman, opened the door to my knock.

'The poor man has only just come in,' she snapped.

'Who is it Marion?' The doctor said, as he walked out of his office.

'It's about Mr Stevens, doctor.' Marion said.

He sighed heavily. 'I'll come as soon as I can. It's Crofters Cottage isn't it?'

'Yes, doctor. I'll wait for you,' I said breathlessly.

'No. Run along. I really will come as soon as possible.' The housekeeper almost shut the door in my face. I slithered home slower than I had come and it had started to snow again.

Reg had somehow got the fires going in the sitting room and kitchen. He was black though.

'An old trick,' he said, when I asked him how he had done it. 'Dampened coal dust in paper cones. Very economical and they last for ages and give out a good heat. Now you're back, I'm going to go back to Leyburn to see if I can get some coal. You stay with your aunt. Is the doctor coming?'

'Yes, he said soon.'

'Peggy is with her father but she's exhausted.'

'If you can do without me, I'll willingly stay.'

Just then the doctor arrived. I showed him up to Grandad's room. Auntie Peggy went downstairs to get warm by the fire. I stayed in Auntie Peggy's room to be on hand when the doctor had finished his examination. A little while later, Grandad's door opened and the doctor came out. I escorted him downstairs. Reg was rubbing Auntie Peggy's hands to try and warm them up. The doctor approached my aunt.

'Miss Stephens, your father is very ill. I would really like him to go to hospital but I don't think an ambulance will make it from Richmond to here. Keep him warm and comfortable and give him plenty of fluids. He will need careful monitoring through the night. What I will do is ring for an ambulance and see if I can get one to call. But it's doubtful, as it is snowing again. If one turns up, all well and good but if one doesn't...' He left his words hanging in the air. I think I knew then that if an ambulance didn't turn up, Grandad wouldn't last the night.

It was dark and terribly cold out. Reg never made it into Leyburn to get some coal. He got as far as the steep hill and, try as he might, he couldn't get up it. His wheels just spun on the icy road and landed him in a snowdrift. He left his car there and walked back to the Cottage. I was downstairs warming myself by the fire when he arrived back.

'My but it's parky out there,' he said, as he stood by the fire.

'They're not coming are they?' I meant the ambulance wouldn't arrive but he knew what I meant.

'No, lass. Me car is stuck at the bottom of the hill in a snowdrift. Nowt is going to get down that hill this night. I passed a telephone kiosk, so rang Mavis and told her to use one of the bedrooms as we wouldn't be back the night. Where's Peggy?'

'Sitting with Grandad. I said I'd sit with him but she said she wanted to.'

'Should I go and sit with her?' He asked.

'Have a warm up first, Reg you look frozen.' He held his hands towards the fire. I noticed he kept his overcoat on for some time. We didn't speak, there was no need, we both knew the outcome of this night. After a while he took his coat off and threw it on to the back of a chair, walked to the bottom of the stairs and gave me a sort of sad, hopeless look and clumped up them.

I leaned back in the chair I was sitting in and gazed into the fire. I must have dozed off, because, the next thing I remember is being shaken awake by Reg.

'He wants to speak to you.' He said.

Auntie Peggy was sitting on the right of the bed. The dear old man was awake. He gave me a weak smile as I came in. It almost broke my heart to see him so. I sat on a chair brought in from Auntie Peggy's room and leaned forward. 'Grandad.' I whispered.

One old, knarled hand came out of the bedclothes and gripped mine. It was warm and dry but so thin.

'Look after Peggy,' was all he said. He made three attempts at saying it but in essence that is what he meant.

'I'll do anything I can for her. I am so grateful to you both for taking me in when I needed a home.'

I felt the pressure of his hand in mine as he gently squeezed it. He said nothing else but seemed to fall asleep quickly. I collected two blankets from the bedroom next door and draped Auntie Peggy in one, upped the temperature on the electric heater and covered myself in the other.

We said nothing, Auntie Peggy and I, we just watched the old man fade away.

XIV.   1962-1963

The grief shared by Auntie Peggy and I was palpable. It was Reg who made all the arrangements for Grandad's funeral. It was him who called the doctor out again, to sign the death certificates. Auntie Peggy and I just went to pieces. I had loved that old man so much. The little cottage seemed so empty without his presence.

Reg had got to Leyburn the next day and had come back with coal and more provisions. He also came with the name and telephone number of an undertaker and he was there when the undertaker came to take Grandad away. Auntie Peggy and I clung together, sobbing our hearts out.

His funeral was held in the little parish church that is two miles down an unmade track. The snow had at long last stopped but it was a bitterly cold day. There were a lot of people there that I didn't know and also many of the villagers who came to pay their respects. A buffet was laid on at the Crofters Cottage, the food was done by the chef at the Red Lion Hotel. He also attended, as he had met Grandad on a number of occasions.

Mum came, as did Jo-Ann, who drifted around looking beautiful and devastated at the same time. She may well have been upset by Grandad's death but I never believed that she really cared.

'That's the famous Jo-Ann is it?' Whispered Reg, as he spotted her amongst the mourners.

I sighed and simply said, 'Yes, that's her.'

It was good to see Mum again but I was quite shocked by her appearance; she looked pale and tired. I pleaded with her to stay longer than a week but she insisted that she had to get back. I think Jo-Ann had lent on her. There was no man there she could flirt with, or could admire her and she didn't like being ogled at by the village lads. She wanted to get back to the place where she was known and adored. She had refused to stay at the cottage; it was far too basic for her tastes. She stayed at the pub next door.

Grandad's will was read the next day. He had left everything to Auntie Peggy and his magnificent desk to Mum. For reasons unknown, he left his wedding ring to me. I got a long gold chain to thread it on to and wore it round my neck for years.

Jo-Ann collared me in the passage leading to the scullery, where I had been washing up.

'I bet you're disappointed at not being left anything of value,' she said.

'I shall treasure his ring, Jo-Ann, that's worth so much more to me than its monetary value. But you wouldn't understand that. I can tell that you are cross at getting nothing, though.'

'Don't be so stupid, toad face, there is nothing of value here that I would want.'

'Well, there you are then, that's probably why he didn't leave you anything, knowing you wouldn't value it.' She stalked off. I called after her, 'Give up the devastated look, it fools no-one.'

Jo-Ann came back and said, 'And I suppose you are?'

'Yes, Jo-Ann,' I said quietly, 'I am. His priceless gifts to me are my memories of him, something you will never have. I adored him.' I turned away to resume my task of washing up. She hadn't changed, why had I thought she would.

I was more upset than I thought I would be when Mum went back. Reg got me to drive them to Darlington Train Station. Saying goodbye on a cold and draughty station was more than I could cope with. I clung to my mother; I was going to miss her so much. Jo-Ann had already got onto the train, she hadn't even bothered to say goodbye to me.

I drove back to Redmire, crying the whole way; not just for Mum, I was still very raw over Grandad.

I had a further week off to be whatever help I could be to Auntie Peggy, except I was pretty hopeless. We were still both so upset. We seemed unable to do the simplest of things without it becoming a drama. I assume we ate, went to bed, washed up but I don't remember doing any of it.

My first week back was very difficult. The staff, in trying to be kind, made it worse. I spent a lot of that first week cooped up in Reg's office crying, or trying to calm myself down after another bout of tears.

By the following week I was more in control of my emotions, which was just as well, as we had a wedding and a conference to organise. Some of the wedding guests were staying over and the conference was a three day event, starting on Friday and finishing on Monday afternoon.

It was a shock to get through a day when I hadn't thought of Grandad at all, the guilt was awful. But time does heal and there came a time, too, when I could think of him without dissolving into tears. And later I could talk of him to Auntie Peggy, like recounting a funny story concerning him and she didn't cry. Reg had been our rock; he was there for both of us and never made me feel that his only concern was for Auntie Peggy's welfare. I don't think that I was any help to her at all.

It had been a particularly cold and dreary day at the beginning of May and I had just used the outside privy! I seated myself in the kitchen to have a warm up by the old range and announced to

Auntie Peggy that we should think about installing a bathroom. She looked at me in amazement. 'I can't afford that, Lucy.'

'Auntie Pegs, the money I get from renting my little house, once the mortgage is paid, there is money left over and it is lying untouched in the bank. What is more, I'm making more money now than I have ever done. It would be a pleasure for me and a kind of thanks for putting up with me for all this time.'

'I have loved having you. You are the only person that I care for. Your presence after Dad died and Reg's help is what got me through it all. I don't need paying.'

'Auntie Peggy!' I said sounding shocked. 'What a thing to say! Payment indeed. It would be so much more comfortable for both of us. But I don't want you to feel that I am trying to take over, it is your cottage.'

'It would be lovely, of course it would. But what I make in cakes and pies will never cover the cost.'

'Could I just do a costing and get David to do the work? What then?'

'Well, you can certainly do that. It would be exciting, wouldn't it?'

It was the first glimmer of interest I had got from her since Grandad had died. It was a start and I felt better in myself. I noticed, too, that Reg came into her conversation at odd times. Reg had said this, Reg had said that, Reg thought... Reg and Reg again. Reg had obviously been down to see her more often then I realised. I hide a smile. Thinking of it, I remembered that he had sometimes disappeared. I'd assumed he'd gone to his private flat to have a kip, or put his feet up, when, some of the time he must have been with Auntie Pegs.

We got our bathroom. Reg, I think, had had a hand in paying for it. I had thought that I would need a small loan from the bank but I found that that wasn't necessary. The bathroom made a huge difference to our lives. 'The Black Hole of Calcutta' had always been the name of a room between the sitting room and the scullery. It had once been someone's workroom. It was transformed into a spacious bathroom with storage cupboards down one side. Coloured sanitary ware was all the range at the time but we chose white, as it was cheaper. We cleaned the privy out and made it into a garden shed and put flowerpots all over the back yard until it was a pleasure to sit out there.

The bathroom didn't just materialise, of course, it took weeks of planning, costing and major work for David to undertake. He also helped us decorate the house. Nothing fancy, no wallpaper, just matt paint on all the walls and gloss on all the woodwork. He couldn't start until the summer, as he was so busy.

It was late autumn by the time he had finished. Auntie Peggy and I were thrilled to bits with it. Auntie Peggy had a bath first and was so pleased she couldn't stop grinning.

It was a year and a half since Grandad had died that I caught her in the pretty backyard in a pensive mood when I took out a tray of tea. It was one of my treasured weekends off.

'A penny for them, Auntie Pegs?'

She blushed but said, 'I was thinking about Reg.'

So what's new, I thought, hiding my smile. 'What about him?' I wanted to know.

'I... He wanted to marry me, you know.'

'Yes,' I smiled. 'I remember.'

'Do you think he still wants to?'

'Good heavens, yes, of course he does,' I said, surprised at her question.

'He hasn't mentioned it, not even hinted at it since before Dad died.'

'Perhaps he's judging when he thinks the time is right. Maybe you could give him some encouragement.'

'Like what?'

'Ask him down for a meal. If he's here, I'll certainly be at the hotel, so I won't be a gooseberry.'

Auntie Peggy laughed. 'You're daft, you are.'

'Do a special meal that you're so good at and have candles on the table.'

'He'd think the electricity was off.'

It was my turn to laugh. 'Yes, you're right, he probably would. Wear a pretty dress; that blue one is lovely.'

'It's not very fashionable.'

'He's not coming down for a fashion show,' I countered. 'Use your best table ware, put the dining table in the sitting room, so that it's different.

'Kitchen table,' she corrected

'Yes but he won't know once a nice tablecloth's on it. On the other hand, just ask him to marry you.'

'Oh my goodness! I couldn't do that.' She sounded very shocked at my suggestion.

'Why not? You've known him for about four years now. If he fights shy and runs a mile then you know he's not for you.'

'Oh but he is,' she said wistfully. 'I adore him. We couldn't have managed without him when Dad died.'

'Don't I know it. I was no help to you at all.'

'I didn't mean it like that. You were there and, more to the point, you loved the old man.'

'Then some,' I murmured.

'Can I ask you something?' Auntie Peggy asked.

'Of course, anything.' But what she asked me shook me to the core.

'Jo-Ann said that you were boasting to her that when I pop my clogs, you would get the house.'

I gasped and must have looked shaken. 'And you believed her? The thought had never entered my head. Surely you believe that?'

'I had to ask. She's so plausible.'

'She is an evil cow and would do, has done, has said, anything to put me in a bad light. Has that been bugging you since the funeral?'

'Oh no, not really, just on and off, at odd times. I saw you talking to her in the passageway and she said as she reached me, something like, "it would serve her right if you left the house to me instead of her".' Then she linked arms with me and was as nice as pie to me for the rest of the time she was here. I couldn't fault her. When she left she gave me a kiss and a cuddle and said, "remember what I said about the house." Auntie Peggy looked at me with a troubled expression on her face.

'On my honour, on Grandad's life, I swear, I never said, at any time, anything about the cottage to her. I was far, far, too upset to give it a single thought. As far as the house goes, you must leave it to whomever you like. I haven't given it a single thought at any time.' I was very hurt by her question.

She sighed. 'I had to ask, just to be absolutely sure. I have made a will and I have left it all to you. It's you who badgered me to have a bathroom put in, decorate the house and have me move into Dad's old room and I'm sure you and Reg paid for it all to be done. It's so much more comfortable. I love this little house.' She was now smiling and I knew she believed I was telling the truth. 'I have one further comment,' I waited with bated breath. Then she grinned and said, 'I think we should redesign the scullery.'

I breathed a sigh of relief and laughed.

'Wow, what a great idea!' I enthused.

'Nothing too expensive mind.'

'What is it you have in that mind of yours?'

She put her head on one side. 'I wouldn't mind a couple of floor units and I'm sick of looking at those rafters.'

We thought, we planned and we sketched ideas and designs. It was one of the best weekends we'd had since Grandad had died.

Again, we got David in to do the work. I'm almost sure Reg dipped his hand in his pocket once more – or it turned out to be less expensive than I thought it would be. As David said, it was a much easier job than the bathroom had been. He was busy, as usual but he gave up two weekends to get the job done, so that we wouldn't have to wait too long. David certainly gave no hint that Reg had helped to pay for the work, it was just a feeling I had.

Auntie Peggy must have thought about my idea of getting Reg into a romantic frame of mind, as two weeks later she asked me if I minded going out for the evening. I said I thought Reg would probably ask me to stay on if he was going to be away. Which is what happened. He said he'd run me home when he came back. I said don't worry about that as I would be happy to stay the night in the hotel. He nodded his approval of that idea.

I told Auntie Peggy what had been arranged between Reg and I.

'It doesn't seem right asking you to stay away from your home,' she fretted.

'Don't worry about it, I'm only too happy to oblige. After all, it won't be too long before I'll be staying there for the odd night.

Winter's just round the corner and if the weather is anything like last year, I could be staying there for weeks'.

She gave me a cuddle. 'Whatever happens, Lucy, our relationship will never change.'

'That's good to hear. Maybe just your perception will change. After all, you may be a married woman.'

She playfully pushed me away. 'Go on, away with you.'

On the appointed day, I packed an overnight case, kissed her goodbye and good luck for the evening and went off to catch the bus.

The day seemed long and everlasting. I was clock watching wondering what Auntie Pegs was doing.

Reg presented himself at the reception desk a few minutes before he was due to go. He was in a right tis-was.

'You're not nervous, are you?' I asked. 'But why? You've had dinner with her before?"

He sidled up to my desk and fished out of his pocket a little box. He lifted the lid.

'Look,' he said, and sparkling on a blue velvet cloth, lay a beautiful diamond ring.

'Reg!' I gasped, feeling quite choked, 'it's absolutely beautiful.'

'I'm going to ask her again, tonight.'

'On your knee, I hope.' I teased. 'And can I say, you wash up well. She will be bowled over by you tonight.... I assume,' and I kept my face straight 'that we are talking about the same woman?'

'What? Oh, you stupid girl! Who else but your aunt? There is no-one, nor ever could be anyone, I think more of in the whole world than your aunt. I've waited patiently, haven't I Lucy? It's a year and eight months since your Grandad died. I've been patient, haven't I?' He asked again.

'You, who is not a patient man, have waited long enough. And you'd better get going or you will be late and that won't do at all. She will be on tenterhooks. If you're late she'll think you're not coming.'

He looked at his watch. 'Hell, yes, I'd better get going. Wish me luck...'

'Believe me, you don't need it.' But I said it to the air as he'd gone, in a mad rush.

I raised my eyes heavenwards and said to myself. 'Grandad, please make it alright for her.'

XV.   1964

It must have been two in the morning when I was woken by Auntie Peggy shaking me gently and saying, 'Wake up, Lucy, wake up!'

I slowly opened my eyes. She put on my bedside light.

'Auntie Peggy,' I said drowsily. 'What's going on?' I shielded my eyes for a moment against the sudden light. Her eyes were sparkling. She held her left hand in front of me. 'Look, Lucy, look... I'm engaged!' Her excitement was catching. I sat up and threw my arms around her neck. 'Auntie Pegs, congratulations! Oh, I'm so pleased for you. Let's see...' I grabbed her left hand to have a closer look. The diamond ring that Reg had shown me earlier sat prettily on her finger. It just seemed to suit her. I didn't tell her I had seen it before.

'We wanted you to be the first one to know. Reg is just outside your bedroom door. He had to show me which room you would be sleeping in. Reggie (Reggie now, whatever next?!) you can come in now.' Auntie Pegs drew the covers up around my neck, very conscious that all I wore was a flimsy nightgown. It may have been the swinging 60s – anything goes and let it all hang out – but it hadn't quite reached the far North of England! Reg came in, looking as pleased as Punch and grinning from ear to ear. He came over to my bed and gave me a kiss on my cheek and said, 'And don't you dare call me Uncle Reg!' We laughed. 'This deserves some champagne.' And off he went to get it and three glasses.

There we sat, in the early hours of Saturday morning, drinking bubbly, a happy threesome, all talking at once.

The wedding was set for 8 months' time, on September 11th 1964. Auntie Pegs wanted an autumn wedding, as she loved the autumnal colours. 'We'll have to get cracking with the arrangements,' I said at breakfast in Reg's flat, the following day. Auntie Pegs had stayed the night. I don't know where she slept but I do know she would have been given her own room.

'Don't get too carried away,' Auntie Peggy said. 'I want a small private wedding. Just you, your Mum ... and, I suppose, Jo-Ann.'

'Then there's Reg's brother and sister-in-law and David, you can't miss him out after all the work he's done for us, and Shirley and the two children. Reg must have other relations...'

'Hang on,' said Reg, 'small and private, remember?'

'That's only 11 people coming counting us,' I grumbled.

'We'll stick on that,' said Reg. 'My so-called drinking pals really wouldn't be interested.'

'Presumably the reception will be held here?' I queried.

'Probably not,' said Reg. 'Because our nearest Registry Office is in Darlington.'

'Why not in the little church in Redmire?' I wanted to know.

There was dead silence, an uncomfortable one.

'What's the matter? What have I said?' I asked anxiously.

'Slight problem there, Lucy,' said Reg. 'I've been married before, so we can't.'

It was just as well that I was sitting down and about to bite into my toast. My mouth stayed open.

'I'm divorced. My first wife did a runner with a friend and I'd close my mouth if I was you, it makes you look half-baked.'

'Well, that's nice. But Reg, you never said...'

'I'd marry Reg in Alcatraz if it was the only place where I could marry him,' Auntie Peggy said.

'Oh, Auntie Peggy, of course you would. Please, I'm not disapproving. I was just surprised. I'm really sorry if I have put my foot in it.'

'Ah, well lass. It was a long time ago and I never thought I'd marry again, that is, until I met your Aunt Pegs and now I'm just chuffed to bits.'

'So we will be married in Darlington Registry Office and love it,' said Auntie Peggy.

'That we will,' Reg said, in fine form.

'We most certainly will,' I echoed – but I felt disappointed for Auntie Pegs, as I was sure she would love to have been married in the little church in Redmire. But I put a smile on my face and said, 'What about asking Betty? She's your friend in the village. Surely she would love to come?'

'What! With her mouthy brood of kids and that drunken husband of hers? I don't think so.' Was Auntie Peggy's reply.

'I thought, at one time she was your best friend. I remember having tea with her, oh, ages ago and one of her kids stuck chewing gum on my back and I'd cried as Mum tried to get it off.'

'That caused a huge row, as it happens. She said it wasn't her kids, they wouldn't do a thing like that – as if – and I said it must have been as you and Jo-Ann weren't allowed chewing gum.'

'So she is off the list.'

'Most definitely.'

'It could mend a rift.'

'No, it's over, long gone.'

'I don't think you're going to win this one, Lucy,' Reg said, laughter in his voice.

'Eleven people it is then. That's quite respectable.' Auntie Peggy was happy with that and that was all that mattered in the end.

'Of course, there is Auntie Elsie...' I ventured. But that just got a very firm 'no' from her.

Of course Jo-Ann came and she liked what she saw of the cottage, with all its renovation work done. Mum slept with Auntie Peggy in Grandad's big double bed and I had to put up with Jo-Ann in one of the single beds in mine. She grumbled the whole time. She didn't like sharing a bedroom, there wasn't enough space for all her clothes, she'd said the bed was uncomfortable and she was cold.

The 11th of September dawned with a slight heat mist that foretold of a beautiful autumn day to come. Auntie Peggy looked lovely in her pale lemon silk dress with its matching jacket and cream straw hat with a little netting veil and two flowers on the rim, one a daffodil yellow the other in brilliant red.

I'd taken her into Darlington to get our outfits. We'd tramped the streets until we came across a little shop down a side road and Auntie Peggy's dress was in the window. 'That's it.' She'd said. 'I like that.' It was at a very good price. The woman who owned the shop (a one woman show) had made it especially for someone else who had never turned up to collect it. This was not a bad omen for Auntie Peggy. In fact, she said it must be her lucky day. The shoes were a problem. She didn't want any with a high heel, as she would be in them all day and needed to be comfortable.

We were foot sore and weary, when she spotted them, again in a side street. They were very pale yellow with a fairly low heel. A perfect fit. She was really pleased with her purchases.

We went to the biggest (then) department store, called Binns, for lunch and browsed through the women's department. And that is where I found my dress. It was in palest lilac with tiny flowers all over it. My hat was also straw, with a lilac bow on one side of it. My shoes were high-heeled sandals. I tried it all on and was very pleased with the effect.

But Auntie Pegs was going to knock Reg's socks off. She looked lovely when she was dressed and ready to go.

Jo-Ann was simply beautiful. Beside her, I felt quite drab and frumpish. But nothing was going to spoil Auntie Peggy's day.

The four of us were in the sitting room at Crofters Cottage having a drink of champagne to celebrate. Reg had sent it down the day before. At great expense, too, he had organised a taxi to take us all the way to Darlington.

'To Auntie Peggy,' I said, lifting up my glass and clinking it with the others. 'And may she be very happy with her Reggie.'

My mother, looking lovely in cornflower blue, said 'To Peggy and Reg and may they be so happy, this is going to be such a memorable day.'

Jo-Ann just looked bored and downed her drink in one. When Auntie Peggy went off to the bathroom I hissed at Jo-Ann 'At least look as though you're happy, even if you're not. You're mouth has such a downward turn you would frighten a gargoyle.' She looked startled and said, 'Mum... did you hear what she said?'

'Need Mumsy to defend you? By the way, that lie you told Auntie Peggy about me has worked against you.'

'What do you mean?'

'Work it out for yourself, you dimwit.'

'Be quiet you girls. I don't want your aunt's day spoiled by you two arguing and Jo-Ann, a smile makes you so much more beautiful.'

It worked a treat; she was so vain. One simple comment about her beauty and she always brightened up. But she was going to get her own back on me big time.

'My last day in this cottage,' said Auntie Peggy, when she joined us again 'that I have lived in for the past 18 years.' She sounded quite forlorn.

'But you will be coming back at odd times, as a married woman.' I enthused.

'So I will,' she said happily, her mood changing, 'so I will. I'm so glad that Reg wants to keep the cottage as our retreat.'

'I hear the taxi tooting its horn, let's go and get this show on the road!' Mum said brightly.

'I have your powder compact in my bag, together with your lippy if you want some minor repairs, during the day.' I grabbed her arm. 'Time to go Auntie Pegs. You okay?'

She nodded. She looked so happy, if a touch nervous. 'Yes, lets go.'

Reg was bowled over by Auntie Peggy. I have never seen her look so pretty or so happy as she was on that day.

They said their vows in clear voices and suddenly they were man and wife. 'You may kiss your wife, Mr Boulting.' He took her in his arms and gave her a bear hug and a sweet kiss.

It was a simply wonderful day, one that will stick in my memory for ever.

They were staying for the weekend in the hotel where they had their small reception. Reg couldn't spare the time (the hotel was really busy) but he had promised Auntie Pegs he would take her to sunnier climes and a longer honeymoon in the winter. I gave her a huge emotional hug when it was time for us to go. She was starting out on a new chapter in her life and I wished her so much happiness and health. I got a bear hug from Reg that knocked my hat askew.

'Thanks lass, for all you have done.' He was quite emotional himself.

'I've done nothing.' I didn't think I had done anything to be thanked for.

'Ah but if it wasn't for you, I would never have met the light of my life, would I?'

There was no denying that but I said, 'If it was meant to be, you would have met somehow.'

'And thank you, too, for these two nights here. A grand present.' Mum, Jo-Ann (I assumed) and I had clubbed together to pay for the weekend. What do you get a couple who seem to have everything.

'I'll see you at 8.30 sharp on Monday,' I said, to lighten the mood.

Reg, whose eyes sparkled so much I thought he must be connected to the National Grid, said, 'Cheeky young hussy! Go and give your aunt and I a bit of peace and quiet.'

In a final flurry of goodbyes, we left.

I felt drained and emotional as I waved to them until I couldn't see them anymore.

But it wasn't Monday that I got to see them again.

Mum and Jo-Ann were staying on for another five days. I didn't know how I was going to cope until the following Tuesday when they would be returning home. Jo-Ann's behaviour was increasingly appalling and she was constantly rude to Mum. Even Mum got tired of it and was perpetually telling her off, to no avail. Me, she simply ignored as though I wasn't there. It was about the only thing that kept me sane! I could almost enjoy that!

At about 4 am on Sunday morning I woke up suddenly. I don't know what it was that woke me up but I couldn't seem to settle again so decided to make myself a hot drink and use the loo downstairs. I had to pass Jo-Ann's bed to get to the door. It was empty. Maybe she hadn't been able to sleep either. I crept downstairs as I didn't want to wake Mum up in Auntie Peggy's room. The door at the bottom of the stairs was open and from the glow, Grandad's lamp that stands on his desk must have been on. I could hear a lot of shuffling going on and the sound of drawers opening and closing.

In a flash of intuition I knew what Jo-Ann was looking for. I missed out the third squeaky step and silently pushed the door open a bit more, just enough for me to get through and peep out. Grandad had a very imposing desk. It was antique and highly polished. It had stood in his room from the time he had lived there. After he died I had persuaded Auntie Pegs to have his bedroom, pointing out that we couldn't share her room for ever, so we'd had the desk moved downstairs. It now stood across the corner under the stairs. And there was Jo-Ann, going through the drawers. My anger was almost uncontrollable but I stood and watched her for a full minute. She was concentrating so hard on her task that she didn't see or hear me. I crept back upstairs again. My mother had to see this or she wouldn't believe me. I hoped Jo-Ann would be so intent on what she was doing that she wouldn't hear anything. My mother, bless her, was fast asleep. But I was so angry. I shook her gently, whispering. ' Mum, Mum, wake up.'

'What...?' I put my hand gently over her mouth and put a finger up to my own lips.

'What's up?' she whispered.

'Come with me please but be as quiet as you can and remember the third step up creaks.' More awake, she climbed out of bed and together both of us crept down the stairs.

Jo-Ann was still sifting through the papers. Less than five minutes had elapsed since I had first seen her.

Poor Mother was shocked and stood open-mouthed, watching her eldest daughter. I quietly walked to stand about five feet from the fireplace. No creaking floorboards here, just carpet over cement. Still Jo-Ann hadn't seen us or was even aware she was being watched. She was getting annoyed at not finding what she was looking for and snapped shut the last but one drawer. She looked up, listening for any noise. It was then that Mother made her presence known.

'Jo-Ann, what do you think you are doing?'

She turned sideways, so still didn't see me. Her hand went to her throat as she saw Mum. Guilt showed clearly on her face.

'I... I was... No. I was clearing the desk out. After all it does belong to you.'

'So you were clearing it out in the dead of night... and what then? Are we supposed to take it on the train with us when we go home?'

'Well, no. We could get furniture removers in.'

'And where in the hotel do you suggest we put it? Your father already has a desk.'

'It would look lovely in the main drawing room.'

'To get spoiled and scratched by the guests? Be honest for a change Jo-Ann. You were going through the papers. What were you looking for?'

'Look, Mum. Lucy wanted me to clear it out as she found it up-setting to do so.'

'Lucy wouldn't have had the job of clearing it out, that was for your Auntie Peggy to do.'

This is where I made my presence known. I took two-steps forward and said, 'You are such a bloody liar!' She spun fully round, shock again registering on her face and her lip curled.

'You!' She spat out.

'Yes me. I saw you 5 minutes ago. I got Mum down to see you. I knew she wouldn't believe me unless she saw you for herself, going through private papers. Just like your lies in telling Auntie Peggy I wanted this house left to me when she died. I know exactly what you are looking for. Her Will.'

'Rubbish! What would I want that for?'

'To see who she has left the cottage to. It wasn't good enough for you to stay in at Grandad's funeral but now it's all spruced up you want it. Only you're too dim to know that her will is now invalid, since she has married. Who do you think paid for all of this?' I waved an arm around. 'Reg and I. Auntie Peggy has little money of her own. Reg wants it for his holiday retreat. I work, we share and I'll let you into a little secret. The cottage is being left to me.'

You wouldn't think such a beautiful face could turn so ugly but it did. She flew at me in a terrible rage and hit my face hard and gave me a push and I fell to the floor, hitting my head on the brass fender that surrounded the fireplace. I didn't black out but I certainly saw stars. She started kicking me. My legs, stomach and arms when I lifted them to try to shield my face. My poor mother stood rooted to the spot in total shock and disbelief. But suddenly she moved and grabbed Jo-Ann and pulled her away from me.

'I hate you!' She screamed.

'The feeling's mutual, I can assure you,' I muttered. A sudden memory came to mind: the laundry room at the hotel, being left unconscious and bleeding. I pulled myself into a sitting position. 'It was you, wasn't it? To put us off the scent, it was you who put the full basket of linen away and started both washing machines going?'

'What? Putting towels away and starting washing machines? That's hardly my style.'

'Then how did you know it was towels that the basket was full of?'

Mother was watching us, first Jo-Ann and then me. She knew what incident we were talking about.

'Yes, Jo-Ann how did you know it was towels?' She asked.

'Lucy just said.'

'No she didn't, she said linen.'

' I'll tell you how.' Her voice was rising. 'Because I hoped you'd die!' She yelled at me. She struggled out of Mum's grip and went for me again. 'I'm bloody going to kill you!' She screamed, dashed to the fireplace, picked up the poker and held it high to get a good swing at my head. My head was bleeding and I was feeling very odd indeed and couldn't move away. Mum grabbed Jo-Ann and pulled her away. The poker missed me but caught Mum on her arm. Mum went a terrible colour and I thought she was going to pass out. With the look on Mum's face Jo-Ann dropped the poker and burst into tears.

'That's right, Jo-Ann. True to form, when all else fails, cry. That always brings the men running. But there aren't any here to come to your aid.' I said from the floor. I think that's what I said. Mum said later that I was mumbling. I tried to get up but didn't make it.

'What are you doing, Lucy?' she asked.

'Someone has to phone for the police. I want her taught a lesson.' I managed to say fairly distinctly.

'No, I'll go. You need an ambulance and you certainly won't make it to the phone box in the state you're in.'

'Your arm... it may be broken.'

'That's possible but I have to do this.'

Jo-Ann just cried louder.

Mother turned to her and shouted. 'Shut up, you lazy, selfish, bully and would-be murderer. You're no daughter of mine. Get to your room now.'

Meekly Jo-Ann turned to go, glared at me, then went upstairs.

There are no locks on the bedroom door. Mum went into the scullery, came back with the broom and went upstairs with it. She put it through the door handle and rested each end on the door-frame, so that Jo-Ann couldn't get out of her room while she was away to ring for an ambulance and the police. The phone box was about 100 yards up the road from Crofters Cottage.

'I've locked her in her room, I won't be long,' she said.

'But Mum, your arm...'

'I have to do this Lucy, for you, for me and even for her upstairs.' She raised her eyes ceiling-wards, as if she could see Jo-Ann through the floor. 'Yes, I have to do this,' she repeated.

She had come down in her dressing gown and slippers, clutching some change in her hand and holding her damaged arm with the other. She seemed to be gone for such a long time.

I began to feel really groggy, sick, cold and really odd and my head hurt. I refused to let myself go to sleep or lose consciousness. I knew Jo-Ann was locked in her room even so I had to keep awake just in case she got out. Though what I was going to do to defend myself was anyone's guess.

The squeaky third step gave her away. She'd kill me now while Mum was away. I felt too groggy and faint to do anything. I saw her evil face swimming before my eyes. I saw the poker raised up in both of her hands and then descend. I awoke in my terror to find I had been dreaming. Relief flooded through me, then I passed out.

My mother, on returning, woke me again.

'I've rung for an ambulance and the police. Lucy, Lucy! What's wrong?'

I remember nothing else.

XVI.   1964

I awoke with a splitting headache and found myself in hospital. My mother was on one side of my bed, with her arm in plaster, and Auntie Peggy was on the other.

'Oh, thank God,' My mother said, 'You've finally come back to us. We have been so worried.' Mum started crying softly.

'You've been unconscious for three days. They found a clot on your brain and they had to remove it quickly or you would have died. We are lucky to have you.' Auntie Peggy looked terribly upset and was trying hard not to cry herself.

'Jo-Ann...' I muttered, my mouth was so dry I could hardly form the words.

My mother managed to say through her tears. 'The police are holding her.'

Auntie Peggy carried on with, 'She appeared before a Magistrate yesterday. She pleaded guilty to G.B.H. on the grounds of diminished responsibility.'

My mother took up the story. 'The attempted murder charge was dropped because you hit your head on the fender and that was deemed an accident, even though she pushed you and was going to hit you with a poker. Her solicitor assured us that it wouldn't stand up in court because in actual fact she didn't connect with your head and in the event could have missed anyway, though to me that's rubbish. She is still in jail. Your father will stand bail for her. I refused. I am just so sorry Lucy, so very sorry. For the first time I have seen Jo-Ann for what she is and what she is capable of. I'm just trying to come to terms with it all.'

Auntie Peggy bent forward. 'When they let you out, Reggie and I will look after you at Crofters Cottage. You always said that it worked some magic on you and Reg is having a telephone installed. When your mother rang the Pub on Monday morning to tell us what had happened, we were so shocked.'

I heard the words but really didn't take it all in. I tried to smile and form the words 'Sorry to cause you worry.' but nothing came out but a groan.

A nurse came in not long after.

'Hello, glad to have you back with us.' She said looking at me. 'I expect you have a nasty headache? I'm here to give you something for that.'

My mother and Aunt Peggy in turn, bent over to kiss me goodbye and went down the ward, both of them were dabbing at their eyes. The nurse moved forward to see to me and gave me an injection and soon oblivion overtook me and I went to sleep.

They had dispersed the clot by going up through my nose, both of my eyes went black and the whites of them were very bloody. They had also sewn up the gash at the back of my head, which necessitated in a lot of my hair being shaved off. I was in intensive care for six days but remained in hospital for another ten. I was only allowed home because Auntie Peggy and Mum, who was going to stay on for some time, were going to be there to look after me.

I thought it would be easier back at Crofters Cottage but in truth it wasn't. They did think of bringing my bed downstairs but that was impractical, the sitting room was too small for that. I refused a commode, or worse, a potty. A trip downstairs to use the bathroom was a bit like climbing Mount Everest. I'd have to sit on a step halfway down, to catch my breath and twice when coming upstairs again. Poor Auntie Peggy and Mum spent their time popping up and down the stairs. They would take it in turns, day by day to see to my needs. After all, Auntie Peggy was a newly-married woman, the last thing she would want to do is to look after an invalid. So Mum slept every night in Grandad's room.

I didn't see much of Reg. The hotel was quite busy and I didn't expect him to do the sick visiting bit and he wasn't keen to leave Mavis on her own but he found Mum's help invaluable but then she had experience and was an old hand at running a hotel. He did come down once or twice just to see how I was getting on.

The first time he came to visit me he said, 'I'm going to give you a rise when you come back, lass. I didn't realise you did so much. Things don't run so smoothly when you're not there. Mavis does her best but she's just not you. The staff are always asking how you are. You're very popular.'

I did get my rise when I went back to work. But I did find that I got tired very easily. Reg gave me one of the spare bedrooms in the Red Lion itself, so they would be on hand if ever I needed one of them during the night. I never did but it was such a kind thought. When I went to bed, I slept the sleep of the dead. It wouldn't have surprised me if one of them hadn't peeped in on me during the night to check that I was okay. Mavis had done a great job and hadn't made any really bad mistakes. The staff were so sweet and each one came up to reception during my first day back, to say how glad they were that I had returned. Two of the kitchen staff said that they hoped Reg would be better tempered now! It made me smile.

My mother had gone back, which saddened me, but of course I had known that she would have to go eventually. Jo-Ann was also back home but had to report to the police station each week. Conditional Discharge didn't seem enough to me for what she had done.

Auntie Peggy bloomed and seemed so happy with her 'Reggie'. He was inordinately proud of her and was a different man. The three of us went back to Crofters Cottage as often as possible as winter approached. Now we were on the telephone, Mavis only had to ring through if any problems arose. It would take Reg or me 15 minutes to get back. We knew it was possible that we wouldn't be able to stop at the Cottage when the snows arrived, as Redmire could get cut off, so we made the most of the time we had.

Working in reception one spring morning, a young man walked in. 'I've found you.' He announced. I vaguely recognised him but just couldn't place him. 'Let me give you a clue. Ice creams.'

'Sorry,' I said. 'This is so embarrassing. It means nothing to me, except I do like ice cream.'

'I'll give you another clue.' He put his head on one side, as though thinking. 'I know... trains.'

Suddenly, I smiled. 'Yes, I remember. You were the rude young man who stared at me when I walked back into my compartment but redeemed yourself by buying me an ice cream.'

'That's right. Did I really stare? How rude of me. I was off to my first interview.' He held out his hand to shake mine.

'I'll even tell you your name, It's Martin, no...Mathew but I can't remember your surname.'

'Mathew Howard, Ma'am, at your service.' He did a funny little salute I was to come to know so well.'

'It's nice to see you again,' he said.

'And you. Are you staying here?' I asked.

'In Leyburn yes but not in this posh place, I can't afford these prices. I came into the Red Lion for a mid-morning drink. I asked this nice chap behind the bar if he knew of a Miss Lucy Bradley. He said not only did he know you but you were his niece and you worked in the hotel, so here I am.'

'That would be Reg, a lovely man. He gave me my first job and I have been here ever since.'

'Reg said you'd had a bit of a bad time lately. How are you? You look bonny enough to me.'

'Thank you kind sir. My, it's a long time since I've heard the word bonny but yes, I'm fine now.'

'When are you off duty?' He asked.

'At six tonight.'

'Come out for a meal with me, at the Sandpipers?'

'Now that's an offer I can't resist. It's my favourite place. That would be very nice, thank you.'

'Seven alright?'

'That will be great,' I affirmed.

'That's settled then. Where do I collect you from?'

'Here would be fine. I live here mostly in the winter.'

'Useful to be related to the landlord,' he commented and we both laughed. Just then Reg appeared, via the connecting door to the Red Lion.

'You remembered him then?' Reg asked.

'Eventually. He had to give me a few clues at first. This is Mathew Howard, Reg, I met him on a train about six or seven years ago. Mathew, this is Reg Boulting, my boss; he's married to my aunt.' Both men shook hands.

'Pleased to meet you, Sir,' Mathew said.

'He's asked me out to the Sandpipers for a meal.'

'Nice place. Got somewhere to stay lad?' Reg asked Mathew.

'Yes, across the road, at the Magpie Guest House.'

'Oh, Aye, Maggie runs a clean place and can cook too. You'll be comfortable enough there. When we're full here, I send people over to her. Not late mind, the lass has been ill.'

'Reg!' I burst out. 'I'm nearly 23.'

'Aye, maybe so but you have been very ill.'

There was no point in arguing. 'Oh well, yes, maybe so. I won't be late.'

But I was. Mathew proved to be an affable host. We found that we had a lot in common. We liked the same music and had seen a lot of the same films. I liked musicals as he did. We just chatted like we were old friends and had known each other for ages. He told me he worked in a bank and had just been promoted. He had worked in Crewe as a bank teller then Darlington and now in Richmond as a cashier. The meal I don't remember but over coffee, our heads close together, we just talked and talked.

He asked me about my illness but I sketched over that. I didn't think he'd really want to know that my sister had nearly killed me.

'It was back in September. Nearly seven months ago. But still they worry.'

'It must have been bad, then, if they still worry.'

I hesitated. 'They tell me I nearly died.' I forced a smile on my face. 'But I'm fine now and they have to let it go.'

'Well I think we had better get you home, as it's coming up for midnight.'

He held my hand all the way back to the Red lion, then asked politely if he could kiss me goodnight. I had butterflies in my stomach but I said that he could. He was gentle but firm. He put his hands on my shoulders and gently pushed me away, then gave me a smackeroonie of a kiss on my forehead. He gave me his funny little salute, smiled, turned smartly and strode away.

When I let myself in, I was met by an anxious Auntie Peggy and a furious Reg. 'What time do you call this?' He demanded. I must have looked a bit surprised. Auntie Peggy said, 'We were getting a bit worried, Lucy.'

'Why?' I asked. 'Mathew is a perfectly respectable bank cashier and you knew where I was. I'm nearly 23 and I should be out, living it up, painting the town red and coming home late every night. We got talking and just forgot the time. I'm only back now because the owner was getting restless.' This was perfectly true. The owner had cleared the tables, taken off the dirty tablecloths and put on clean ones, then had set the tables again for breakfast as he had a few guests staying. The waitresses had gone and he was the only person left, apart from us. There was a lot of shuffling of papers and a cough or two to remind us he was still there and wanted to lock up.

'It's just after midnight,' Reg said. 'Late enough.'

'That maybe so, Reg, but I don't think that's too late and how often do I get asked out?' I stalked off, up the stairs to their private flat and went to bed in a sulk. Before I nodded off, though, I went over the evening in my mind and went to sleep with a smile on my face. I saw a lot of Mathew after that and I was always back late. I wasn't in love with him but I liked him a lot.

Lewis blew into my life in late summer. Tall, dark and incredibly handsome. His sports car had skidded to a halt outside the entrance to the hotel, sending gravel shooting out in all directions like shrapnel. He made a beeline for me, lent his elbows on the reception desk and said, 'I see a beautiful face before me. A vision in blue!' I actually blushed.

I smiled and said. 'Can I help you?'

'I'm sure you can but later.' His eyes crinkled up at the corners when he smiled.

'I need a bed for a couple of nights.' He took off his leather driving gloves and slapped them on the counter. He had long fingers and short, clean nails.

'When do you get off? And what is your name.'

'At six and my name is Lucy, Lucy Bradley.' I knew I sounded breathless and my voice had gone up a note.

'Well Lucy Lucy Bradley, I'm Lewis Alexicon. I'll pick you up at seven precisely, here.'

I handed him his key; he didn't appear to have any luggage with him so I didn't ring the bell for Tommy.

Tommy had never fully recovered from the beating he got from Robert. He went from a damaged boy to a damaged young man. Reg had taken him on as a porter. He did whatever he was asked but had terrible fits of depression. Carol, his mother, had never got over it either. She had had to sell her flat and she now lived in a warden controlled flat in Richmond, as Tommy was no longer able to look after her. It was all very sad.

I escorted Lewis Alexicon myself to his room. Once there he turned and gave me a drop dead gorgeous smile.

'Tonight at seven then,' he said softly.

He was an exciting man to be with. Mathew, sweet, dependable and nice, was no match for Lewis. He threw money around like confetti, without boasting about it. It wasn't the Sandpipers this time but the smartest restaurant in Richmond. I found Lewis intriguing, sexy and exciting. Poor Mathew, to my eternal regret, didn't stand a chance.

XVII.   1964-1965

When I had known Lewis for six weeks he asked me to marry him. My heart missed a beat and surprise must have registered on my face, because he said, 'I've asked you too soon but I fell in love with you as soon as I entered this hotel and saw you working behind the desk. I vowed then, that I would marry you one day.' He took my hand and twisted his fingers into mine. He then kissed each finger, without taking his eyes off my face.

'I won't ask you again, Lucy. You tell me when you're ready.'

My heart was beating so loud, I thought he must hear it.

'Of course I'll marry you, Lewis,' I said softly.

He came round my desk and dragged me into the stationary storeroom that was situated behind my desk. He picked me up, twirled me round and said, 'Fantastic! Oh, I am so pleased.' He kissed me on my lips, firmly and passionately.

'Lucy, we will be so happy, you'll see.'

'We hardly know each other,' I said, rather breathlessly.

'Six weeks is long enough for me to know that I have found the right girl and what fun we will have in getting to know each other and finding out all our little secrets.'

'I would so like to meet your family,' I sounded quite breathless.

'That should be easy. There is just my mother and myself. My father died long ago. Come and have dinner at the family home and meet my mother. She's a darling and will love you, because I do. When is your next day off?'

Swept up by his excitement, I said I would love to but he would have to wait a week, as I had just had my two days off.

He said. 'I can't wait that long.' And seemed almost annoyed. To placate him I said I would ask Reg if I could have another day off. At that, he was full of smiles again.

Reg said that would be alright as we had been very busy with a convention, a wedding and a 21st birthday party, all in quick succession and anyway, if he was going to have to manage without me in future, it would either be the making of Mavis or the breaking of her.

I knew that between now and the engagement announcement I would have to tell Mathew – and that wasn't going to be easy. To me, he was more than just a good friend. But did I mean the same to him because when we had come back from a day or evening out, another date was never arranged, he would simply ring a day or two after and ask me out again and he always kissed me goodnight and they were getting very passionate.

I hadn't seen him for three months. He'd had to go to Bristol on secondment. He'd rung once a week and said he was missing me like crazy and working hard and in truth I had missed him also. I really thought I was falling in love with him.

Once I knew he was back, I rang to ask him if he could meet me on Friday evening, at the hotel. It was now a Wednesday and I had butterflies in my stomach already, thinking of Friday's meeting.

Mathew came into the hotel at 6.30. My duty finished for the day.

'Come into Reg's office, I need to have a private word with you.' He followed me in.

'Mathew...' I started and stopped. After a few seconds, I said again, 'Mathew... oh dear, this is so difficult to say.'

'Take your time,' he said quietly. 'You know you can tell me anything.'

I cleared my throat 'I don't know if you have heard any rumours...' I hesitated 'Umm... Do you know, or have you heard of the Alexicons?'

'I do know of them, they bank with us. They are a wealthy family who live north of Darlington, in a village called Loxton. Why?'

'Oh.' That had come as a bit of a shock. I hadn't known that they were wealthy. 'Well, Lewis Alexicon... has asked me to marry him.'

If I had hit Mathew, he couldn't have looked more shocked. He said nothing but stood, looking at me. He had gone very pale. I had to look away; I couldn't bear the look of pain in his eyes.

'I'm so sorry,' I mumbled.

He reached into the pocket of his jacket, took out a tiny box and placed it on Reg's desk.

'This is no good to me now,' was all he said, then he turned and walked away. I didn't see him again for six years.

I knew what the little box would contain. I picked it up and opened the lid. Inside was a lovely engagement ring. It had three diamonds in a row, in a very pretty setting on a gold band.

Reg came in just then. 'Was that young Mathew I saw leaving?'

'He gave me this when I said I was going to marry Lewis.'

'Oh dear, took it badly, did he?'

'I think so. I can't keep it, what would Lewis think?'

He gave me one of his bear hugs, then said, 'Well, lass, he should have made his feelings known to you before this time, then he wouldn't be the loser.' Reg took the little box with the ring in it. 'I'm going to put it into the safe and that's where it'll stay until such time as you want it back.'

I thought, later, that was an odd thing to say.

My meeting with Lewis's mother was awkward, to say the least. We didn't meet in her house, after all, but at the Alexander Hotel in Richmond. The reason for not going to her house was given as some decorating work was taking place. 'The dust just gets everywhere,' she said.

Mrs Alexicon was a tall, elegant lady, who at one time must have been very beautiful. I felt that life, perhaps, had not been too good to her. She was dressed in a very well tailored suit in sky blue, a bit old fashioned but gorgeous material. She was older than I thought she would be, maybe, middle sixties.'

For a start, I didn't think she approved of me as a bride for her darling son. Talk was somewhat stilted and cold. I put it down to simple nerves on my part. I felt that I had to get on with her, there were too many stories about dreadful mother's-in-law and Lewis obviously adored her. I was to get to know Mrs Alexicon very well and got to like her very much.

Before we had gone off to dinner, Lewis had presented me with a stunning ruby ring. It had diamonds circling the ruby, all set on a gold shank. It fitted perfectly. I don't know what I ate, I was too nervous to take it in.

The wedding was a big affair. Whereas Auntie Peggy's had been small and simple, this was big and brash in comparison. All of Darlington and Richmond seemed to be there. There were over 180 people. Most I didn't know from Adam. Reg had put the large conference hall at my disposal but it wasn't good enough for Lewis. He wanted the Alexander Hotel in Richmond. I pointed out that as Reg had offered to pay for it, he wouldn't be able to afford that. Lewis merely swept me off my feet, whirled me around and said that only the best was good enough for me and he was paying for it. I think Reg was a bit hurt by this when I told him.

'I'm so sorry Reg. I don't want to upset either you or Auntie Pegs, but seriously, you shouldn't have to pay for it anyway.'

'I doubt that your father will,' he said gravely. This was undoubtedly true. He wasn't even coming. He had refused after I'd given Mum the message that he was welcome to come but then Reg was giving me away, as Reg had been more of a father to me that he had ever been. Reg was very touched that I had asked him.

My dress was a beautiful creation in pure silk, with hundreds of little pearls and sequins sewn onto it. The bodice was heart-shaped and the skirt was very full, ending in a three-foot train. It was stunning. My veil had tiny lover's knots embroidered down each side. It was seven feet long. I had Sylvia as my bridesmaid. She was now a pretty 14-year-old. I had just her as Lewis didn't seem to have any young relations. In fact, he didn't seem to have any relations at all.

Peggy said I looked stunningly beautiful. There were tears in her eyes. I begged her not to cry or she would set me off. We hugged tightly. 'Be happy, my dearest girl,' she whispered.

Mum came, as did Jo-Ann, which surprised me. I really didn't think she would be interested enough, as she wouldn't be the centre of attention. I thought too, that after what she had done to me, she would feel guilty and not be able to face me. But not a bit of it. She behaved towards me as she always had, with contempt and as though nothing had happened.

She had arrived looking beautiful, as ever, and appeared to charm Lewis although he reassuringly said, 'beautiful, she may be... but she isn't my type at all.'

It rained the entire day but with hundreds of umbrellas available I arrived at the church dry and seemingly composed. At the reception, my mother took Mrs Alexicon aside and introduced her to distant relations of ours. Sir Leonard Stephenson (my remembered Uncle Teddy) and his wife, Lady Barbara. He'd had a brother called Grayson but he had been killed in the war. They had a huge estate in Scotland, breeding Aberdeen Angus cattle. The family were incredibly wealthy. Mother had kept in contact over the years with Lady Barbara. I never did work out the relationship between them and us. Mrs Alexicon, seemed to warm to me after that! I obviously wasn't the gold-digging commoner she thought I was!

There were pointers that should have warned me of the disaster to come. Where was Lewis at the reception and where was Jo-Ann, who seemed to be missing at the same time? When he came in he said he had been 'caught in the gents by some old fart, who wanted to talk business on my wedding day!' Jo-Ann came in later, looking very dewy eyed, hanging onto the arm of Lewis's best man. I thought nothing of it.

Lewis lost his temper when some wine got spilled onto his morning suit (not a Moss Bros special but his own). He just seemed irritated all the time. I put it down to nervous energy, the expense of it all, wanting everything to be just right, with excitement thrown in.

My mother and Auntie Peggy helped me change into my going away outfit, a lovely pearl grey wool dress, with a fur trimmed colour on the matching jacket. We said a very emotional goodbye. I'd said I would still ring Mum on a weekly basis. And keep in touch with Auntie Peggy and Reg. I was only going to the other side of Darlington, after all, not the other side of the world but I may as well have been. I'd had to give up working. Mavis, my understudy was as competent as she was ever going to be. Reg had taken on another village girl, called Kathy, who was very eager to learn. I'd worked with them both in my last month, trying to teach them how to welcome people properly, know what room they were in, write everything down if need be, never show they were getting into a flap and how to be confident, unflappable, competent, receptionists. 'One golden rule,' I said, 'if you are going to be busy with people coming in the next day, do your homework. Check that you know their names and which rooms they will be in the night before they are due to arrive. The rest of your duties will just come naturally. The job is varied and interesting. If you like people, it's a lovely job.' Now it was up to them.

Suddenly Lewis and I were on our own, on our way to our holiday destination. One night in London – at the Hilton Hotel, no less – then up and away to St Kitts in the Caribbean for two whole weeks. I had a wonderful honeymoon and loved almost every minute of it. If Lewis didn't seem able to relax, then that was his problem. Usually I could charm him out of any tantrum or upset. The things that made him cross were often silly. Like losing his luggage keys. I found them in the darkest recesses of his jacket pocket. Because I'd found them, he said, I must have put them there for a joke, because he swore he had looked there. I got him out of that sulk by simply taking him to bed and telling him how wonderful he was! There was an uncomfortable moment when he got very angry when his steak wasn't done to his liking; he swore at the waiter and told the chef to get some cooking lessons as he was hopeless. He caused an uproar in the dining room. I didn't solve the problem of his overdone steak. I just suggested that it would be far more romantic to have room service and eat on our own private balcony, thereby making sure it didn't happen again. I thought he just wanted everything to be perfect and was disappointed if they were not. Once home, I thought things would settle down and everything would be alright. How wrong could I be?

The house was mansion sized. It was called The Priory. It was a ten bedroom (not counting the attic rooms) mausoleum of a place that I found was cold, dark and dingy. I was shocked when I saw it for the first time when we came back from our honeymoon.

Mrs Alexicon welcomed us home and a Mrs Ebson, her daily, helped us in with our mountain of luggage.

'Tea is in the drawing room but first I thought you would like to freshen up. I have moved your things, Lewis, into the master bedroom.'

'Thank you Mother, that was good of you.' He said. We hefted our luggage upstairs, helped again by Mrs Ebson.

The bedroom was massive. It was situated above the entrance hall. At the top of the stairs corridors went to the right and the left. I was itching to see where they all went to.

'Your job,' Lewis said, as we came down the stairs later, 'is to decorate this place.' He threw his arms out, encompassing the whole house.

'That will take a lot of money and a lot of time,' I said, rather shocked but also secretly pleased that I could have the chance to cheer the place up and keep myself busy.

'Well,' he said shortly. 'I have the money and you will have the time.' At the bottom of the stairs he opened the second door on the left. 'This is my study; it is my domain. This room I don't want touched. But it must be kept clean at all times. I hate dust.'

I felt that he was giving me his orders.

'Discuss wallpaper, paint and any decorating ideas with Mother.'

'Does she live here too?' My heart sank.

'She does. Have you a problem with that?'

'No, No,' I stammered, 'it's just that you never told me.'

'Did I have to?' He demanded.

'I think you could have mentioned it,' I tentatively said.

'Well, now you know... and so you can't accuse me of not telling you anything, we have a live-in cook, a daily cleaner and a gardener, so I expect everything to be spick and span at all times.'

'I take it that they are your orders?' I asked, happily enough. I thought it was all a bit of fun and a bit of a joke.

'They are. What were the vows about? Obey?'

'So I have no say in anything? Is that what this is all about?'

'Right again,' he snapped. Then, in a softer tone, he said, 'I'm very exacting, I know.'

'I take it that I can employ someone to actually *do* the decorating?'

'Yes, you goose. I would hardly expect you to climb ladders. Strip wallpaper and hang the damn stuff.'

'Just so as I know,' I said.

We had been standing in the hall. He reached for my hand and we walked into the drawing room to have afternoon tea with his mother.

Mrs Alexicon played bridge twice a week and had theatre trips and dinners with friends. It was difficult to pin her down but I did discuss all aspects of decorating with her. I found that she had her own suite of rooms. They were at the end of one of the passages. It comprised a bedroom and her bathroom next door and across the hall was her sitting room and a galley kitchen. She had a doorway created across the passageway leading to her quarters so that it was completely private.

Mrs Ebson, found me wandering around and asked if she could help me. 'Yes I hope so. I need to speak to Mrs Alexicon but I can't seem to find her. I know she's in as her car is in the garage.'

'Just go along to her rooms and knock on her door.'

'I didn't like to disturb her in her private domain.'

'She got her rooms arranged about three months ago. Once she knew Mr Lewis was getting married, she said to me. "The newly-weds won't want me hanging around them all the time," so got her rooms organised.'

'How considerate of her,' I said, surprised.

'Oh, she is a lovely lady. You'll find that out for yourself in time.'

And I did.

'Do what you like dear. It's really up to you,' she said, when I at last got to see her.

'Lewis said I was to discuss all aspects of decorating with you.'

'Did he, dear? Then that's what we will do. Where are you going to start?'

'I thought the hall, to brighten it up.' I was immediately embarrassed – it was like telling her that her house was dingy – but she immediately put me at my ease.

'Yes. Lovely. A coat of paint will work wonders.'

'I was hoping to do a bit more than that, Mrs Alexicon.'

'No dear, you must call me "Mother". Lewis would like that. And, do what you like with the hall. It's so dark. Just remember that neither of us likes too much dust and dirt hanging around in the air. It affects my sinuses. Did he give you the name of the people who did my small conversion?'

'No, he didn't.'

She tutted. 'Men are all the same. He wants you to see to the decorating but doesn't furnish you with the information you need.' She got up from her chair and walked to the escritoire in the corner, opened the top of the desk and took out her address book. She leafed through it until she found what she wanted, wrote their name and number on a scrap of paper and handed it to me.

'They are really good and clear up after themselves.'

'That's useful to know, thank you.' I said.

'Now dear, how about a cup of tea?'

I didn't really want one but I thought it better not to say that so instead I said 'that will be lovely.' We chatted away quite happily. I stayed for about an hour and found her easy to talk to and not as cold as I had first thought.

XVIII.   1964-1966

I had the hall stripped of its frightful paper. The men I had hired were very good and tried to keep the dust down to a minimum. They put dustsheets down everywhere. The wallpaper had been up for years and was dirty, dusty and crumbled rather than came off in long strips. Lewis, who usually worked from home, went out in the morning and when he came back in the evening, after the decorators had gone, he was not a happy man.

He surveyed the mess after the first day and strode across the hall and into his study, slamming the door behind him. It opened almost immediately.

'Lucy!' He called. 'Come here please.'

I walked into his study. 'Look at this,' he said and swept a finger across his desk. His finger came away with a light covering of dust on it.

'I thought I said to keep everything clean at all times.'

'Darling Lewis,' I said, surprised. 'We are decorating and Mrs Ebson cleaned this room today. I asked her especially.'

'Well, you have no right to. She does different rooms on certain days. She has her routine, so don't interfere.'

'But Lewis, if she hadn't done this room today, it would be even more dusty.'

'Don't argue. What is the matter with *you* doing it?'

'If that's what you want me to do, that's fine. I'm not afraid of hard work.'

'Perhaps I should dismiss Mrs Ebson and you can do all the cleaning, instead.'

I looked at Lewis in complete astonishment. 'As I obviously have no rights in this house whatsoever and can't even ask our, sorry, *your* cleaner to change her routine slightly, then it's a pretty sorry state of affairs. You must do what you feel is right.' I stalked out of the study. I was furious.

I learned very quickly that retribution always came later and at unexpected moments. That evening, while changing for dinner, I had been wearing an old pair of dungarees and a shirt that had seen better days and needed a shower. Lewis charged into the bedroom, grabbing my right arm, pulled me round to face him, then slapped me hard across my face. I must have looked totally stunned. Maybe that annoyed him too, because he slapped me on the other side.

'Don't answer me back in future and never walk out of my study when I am talking to you,' he snarled. 'You do as your bloody told.' Then he punched me in the stomach. This folded me up and his knee came up and I hit my chin on it. 'Keep this place bloody clean!' I collapsed on the floor. I was shocked beyond belief that my beautiful man, whom I loved so much, could treat me like this.

I lay on the bed doubled over with pain and crying.

In those three and a half years of our marriage, his viciousness put me in hospital five times. Black eyes or broken bones were the norm.

I'd call Mum, as usual and Auntie Peggy, once a week if I could. The first time he caught me on the phone I got a beating. It seemed as though he wanted me to lose contact with all of the people I loved. Reg and Auntie Peggy must have been very hurt, as they were never asked over. Lewis wouldn't have it and I never visited them, how could I? With my swollen face or cracked cheekbone, or split eyebrow, or broken arms and the appalling bruises. I felt trapped. After a beating he would be so nice to me, just as though nothing had happened. He would present me with a piece of jewellery. I believe it was his form of apology, although he never said he was sorry, not once. Always it was a gold bangle, with earrings or a necklace, as well, depending on the severity of the beating. My first gold bangle, had tiny diamonds going round the outside, it was very pretty. I finished up with a drawer full of them.

Two months after our return from our honeymoon, he started to go away mid-week. He would go early on a Wednesday morning and be late back on Thursday evening. He said he was going to conferences and meetings. I don't know where they were being held and I never asked. Sometimes, though not often, he would go away for a weekend as well.

My days alone, when he went away, I learned to treasure and value, free from his awful behaviour and evil presence. I could relax. I'd go into town, if I was fit enough. He had given me a Hillman Minx as a wedding present. He also opened a bank account for me and put in £40 a month (a lot of money then) but anything purchased had to have a receipt and every penny had to be accounted for or there was trouble. I used my money from the rent of my house in Leyburn. I'd cash one pound and use it to ring Auntie Peggy and Mum when I was in town. I didn't mean to deceive Lewis about it, it just never cropped up in conversation. The longer I left it to tell him about that account, the more difficult it got to mention it. I knew I'd get a beating if he ever found out. I kept the chequebook in one of the attic rooms.

One day I had come back, having visited a hairdressing salon. I wore my hair loose and it was long, Lewis liked it that way. They had done well with it and it did look nice when they had finished. It cascaded just beyond my shoulders and ended in a mass of curls. I was really pleased with the result. As usual, I handed him the receipt. It was for a moderate amount of money. He turned on me there and then. He screwed my hair round his hands and hacked my hair off with a pair of scissors, until my beautiful curls lay on the carpet. I looked a mess. 'That will teach you,' he said, 'to spend so much on your vanity.' The next day I visited another hairdresser. I could hardly go back to the one I had visited yesterday. I said my younger brother had cut my hair off in spite. Whether they believed me or not, I don't know and really didn't care. Some hair was off from the scalp, so there was little they could do. I suggested they shave it all off. They were a bit dubious about this but did as I asked.

'I know what we can do,' one of the girls said. 'Wait a minute...' and she disappeared.

Her mother had a milliners shop and she came back with a turban. This I wore home with the receipt for both the hair removal and the turban. Both together, they cost more than the original hairdo. I placed both receipts in front of him at dinner that night. He looked up to remonstrate with me, about the cost, I think. I simply removed my turban. I'm glad to say it gave him quite a shock. I got another gold bangle!

Another time, he'd asked me what I had done in town. I asked him how had he known I had gone to town. He said he checked my mileage on the car! I couldn't believe he would do that.

'Just an outing for a bit of shopping. Milly Franks (our cook) wanted a few things. Check with her if you don't believe me.'

'I'm not doubting that,' he snapped. 'Who do you meet?'

'Meet?' I asked stupidly. 'Meet whom? I don't see anybody, neither do I make arrangements to meet anyone. What are you getting at?'

We were in his office at the time, him in his chair, I was standing the other side of his desk. He stood up and came round to my side.

'Men,' he snarled. 'Who you meet in town.'

I stared at him. 'What makes you think I'm meeting a man or anyone? Why would I want to? I swear to you, I have not met anyone in town, now, nor would I ever in the future.'

He obviously didn't believe me. He put his hand up to the side of my face. It was quite a slow and gentle movement but, with terrible force, he slammed my face down onto the top of his desk. There was a sickening crunch and excruciating pain and I passed out.

I woke up in hospital in an awful lot of discomfort. My face was bandaged and I could only look out of one eye, the left one. The other side of my face had taken the full force of the blow. Lewis would visit and played the loving husband well. Mrs Alexicon came to see me, bearing flowers. Lewis must have told her that I had gone up a ladder and fallen off, because she said, 'we have the workmen in to do that. What were you thinking of, going up a ladder, you poor, poor girl?' I had cracked my cheekbone and jaw (not the same side when Robert attacked me), I had whiplash on my neck, I was in a neck brace and my shoulder had taken a battering too. My arm and over the shoulder blade were in plaster. I was in hospital for three weeks. I was in an awful lot of pain and once more could only eat soups and soft foods, mostly through a straw, as my jaw was wired up and my cheek bones had to be put back together again. They promised that the scarring would be minimal. A plastic surgeon was called in to do the stitching up. When it was fully healed, it looked just like a small, unobtrusive wrinkle, that could only be seen in a certain light. By the time I got home, Lewis, for some reason of his own, had moved all my things out of the marital bedroom and into another room at the end of the right passageway. Across the hall was another door that opened on to the stairs to the attics that had six more bedrooms and two more bathrooms. This time I got another bangle and a very pretty necklace for my trouble.

Lewis told me I could decorate the bedroom how I liked. When I was well on the way to recovery, that is what I did. It was at the corner of the house so it had two side windows and a large window that looked over the front garden. It was a large room so I had it partitioned off to make an en-suite I put myself in another room until the decorators had finished. I loved my room and it became my sanctuary. It was bright and airy. I had huge scatter cushions and another settee. I had found it in the attic and had it re-covered. The room was painted in a matt white. The wallpaper had tiny flowers scattered over it. The material for the settee and the curtains carried on the same theme of pink and white. It was a pretty girlie room.

Lewis still visited me for sex but any love on my part had simply gone.

I used to visit Mrs Alexicon, in her private quarters quite often, she always welcomed me in. One day she almost dragged me in to show me her latest acquisition. She had bought herself a little dog. He wasn't a puppy but about 18 months old. He was sweet. He was a little white Cairn. His name was Caesar. She asked me if I would be prepared to exercise him during her bridge afternoons and theatre trips. I gladly agreed. I became devoted to the little dog and as I recuperated he and I used to go for long walks in the afternoons. I'd walk through our woods and stroll by the lake and go all the way round it. The lake was positioned behind the parish church. By the churchyard's entrance there was a door set into the wall. Mrs Alexicon and I would use it on the occasions we went to church. We always went to the candlelight carol services at Christmas time. Even Lewis would come with us occasionally. There is a path skirting our high boundary wall from that door and this kinks in at the end to allow for our own little road that leads to our drive. Our short private road is in a half moon shape which allows you to use it from either end. It was once the main road to Darlington before they built the by-pass. I got very attached to that little dog. Lewis was unimpressed. But as it was his mother's, he didn't stop me from walking him.

Another time she said, 'it could do with a bit of cheering up in my apartment. With your flair for interior design and colour we could make these rooms very cosy.' I enjoyed the time we had together. Armed with swatches for drapes, colour charts and wallpaper books, we would pour over them in the afternoons when she was home. During that time we got very close. She told me she'd had a daughter. She had been drowned in a boating accident.

'It took Lewis a long time to recover from the shock. He always blamed himself, you see. He is a strong swimmer. Elaine was not but could swim. A breeze had got up during the afternoon and it made the water in the lake quite choppy. He said the boat overturned. He wasn't too worried, as he knew Elaine could swim but she never came up. He said he'd dived down many times but couldn't find her. We had police frogmen in to drag the lake. They found her, of course. Her feet had got tangled in the weeds at the bottom of the lake. Poor child, she must have been terrified. Lewis was 14 at the time, Elaine was 10.'

'How terribly sad,' I said. 'It must have been a dreadful time for you.'

'Yes,' she murmured, 'you never get over losing a child.' There was a long pause, then she shocked me by saying. 'I've been married before, you know. The first time I was just twenty years of age. He was called Thomas Buckingham. He was such a nice man. We had a baby quite quickly but she died when she was just eight months old. I was devastated, of course. Then, two years later, Thomas got cancer and he died as well. It was an appalling time for me. I was widowed by the time I was 24.'

'Oh no,' I breathed. 'How shocking, how awful. Life hasn't treated you very well.'

'In one way, no, it hasn't. I married again at 32, having vowed I'd never marry again but Alex was very like Lewis in looks and could charm the birds off the trees, as the old saying goes. I had Lewis at 36 and Elaine four years later.'

'What was Elaine like?' I dared to ask.

Mrs Alexicon settled herself more comfortably in her easy chair.

'Oh, she was a very pretty child and loved by everyone. She had such a sunny disposition. She could make you laugh if she thought you were down. Sibling rivalry between Lewis and Elaine was only to be expected. He was very jealous at first but she looked up to him and copied everything he did and he loved her. Lewis is so like his father; Elaine was very like me. But her father adored her.'

She drew me out too. I told her many things about my life, with my father and Jo-Ann.

'I noticed at the wedding how unlike you are,' she said.

'The beautiful one.' I murmured. 'I was made to feel like the ugly duckling.'

'Oh no dear. You have far better qualities than she has. What will she have when her looks go?'

Yes, we got to know each other well and I liked her very much.

I offered her my newly-decorated bedroom while her apartment was being done. She was charmed with it and accepted my offer.

'This is delightful,' she said, after I showed her my room. 'I can't wait for my rooms to be done. If they are anything like this, I shall be thrilled. When can the men start?'

'Next week, they said.' I replied.

'I'll move all my knick-knacks off the walls and move out most of my clothes. I don't want to see my rooms until they are finished, then I shall have a wonderful surprise.'

'But you've chosen all your fabrics, paint and wallpaper.'

'Yes dear, but seeing it up and completed will make all the difference.'

'No pressure then,' I said, and we laughed.

Four weeks later she moved back in again.

She'd chosen linen look wallpaper with a tiny gold thread running through it. It had been very expensive but it was what she wanted. Long linen drapes hung at her windows, these also had a gold threat running through them, with heavy gold tassels that held them back. She walked round her sitting room, touching things. She pulled the cords to close her drapes, then, opened them again. She felt the wallpaper. I watched her with bated breath. She then crossed her hall and went into her bedroom.

The wallpaper here was in the palest mint green, with tiny pink roses scattered all over it, with matching curtains. It did look pretty.

'Lovely.' She said quietly. 'Oh yes. I love it. Thank you dear, so much.' I thought her eyes glittered a little. I looked away, to give her time to compose herself.

'I got the men to paint the kitchen and your bathroom. I hope that was right.'

'Yes, yes. Really lovely.' She was alright again.

'I'll help you to bring your things back, if you like.'

'No dear, you have done enough. I'll get Ebby to help me back with it all tomorrow.

But if you bring me my breakfast tray and some fresh milk from downstairs, I would be grateful, because I want to sleep here tonight.'

'I'm sure if Lewis can't bang a nail in for you for your knick-knack's I can do it for you.'

'Oh no, dear. I had them to brighten my rooms up. Such clean lines shouldn't be broken up with my rubbish. I just want my pictures back from the attic's and my big mirror for my drawing room.'

'I can get the men to do that tomorrow.'

'That will be wonderful and you can have your room back.'

'You're right. But there is no hurry. Some people can't abide a new paint smell.'

'Oh but I love it. So don't worry about that. What is your next project going to be?'

'Probably the spare room that I have been using, if that's alright with you?'

'Yes, good idea,' she said, nodding her head with enthusiasm.

'I'll discuss it with Lewis tonight,' I said.

'I think you have done enough for now. You've certainly made hefty in-roads into my bank balance,' he growled, when we met up at dinner.

'I'm only doing what you ordered me to do, Lewis.'

I should have known better than to answer him back.

The next beating came that afternoon and very nearly killed me. We were in his study. I thought, stupidly, he was coming round his desk to kiss me, as he had a smile on his face. He grabbed my right arm, swung me towards him and smashed his fist into my stomach. He then threw me backwards, my lower back hitting the corner of his desk as I collapsed onto the floor.

'Don't answer me back, you bitch!' he spat at me, then stalked out of his study. I lay there in tears and in terrible pain. My stomach ached intolerably as did my lower back and my right arm was beginning to swell after his vicious grip on it.

I lay there for what seemed hours but eventually I wearily got up but couldn't straighten up. I staggered up the stairs to my bedroom. Gingerly and with great care I lay on my bed and curled myself up. I ached and hurt all over. I lay there crying and thinking how could this terrible situation ever get resolved and how was it, if ever, going to end.

Cook was banging the gong for dinner, I tried to get up but moving caused intolerable pain to knife through my stomach. I simply couldn't make it for dinner and anyway I didn't want any, as I was beginning to feel sick.

Shortly there was a tap on my door. Mrs Ebson pocked her head round. 'Are you alright, dearie?' She asked, adding, 'Not feeling too well? By but you don't look too good.'

'A headache,' I muttered. It was true, I did have one, but everything else ached too.

'Would you like Cook to heat you up some homemade soup? It's tomato, your favourite.'

I didn't like to offend. 'That would be lovely,' I managed to say. In truth, I didn't want anything.

Mrs Ebson said, 'I'll bring it up on a tray for you. I won't be long.' She disappeared.

Shortly afterwards, another knock sounded, only louder. My heart fell. Lewis came in, bearing a tray. 'I believe you don't feel well?' He sounded quite concerned.

'Is it surprising?' I answered. 'If you continue beating me up and using me like a rag doll to be shaken an abused, I'll...'

'You'll what? Leave me? I don't think so. Where would you go? I doubt your precious aunt or Reg would have you back, not after the letter I sent them. Didn't know about that did you? You could always go back down south to your parents but if you did I would simply drag you back again.'

'What for? To continue abusing me, beating me up and humiliating me?'

He shrugged. 'I can do the caring husband bit very well.' He sounded quite satisfied with himself. 'No one knows or cares about what goes on behind closed doors.'

'Do you really think the staff don't know?'

'As long as they get paid, why should they care?'

I didn't answer, because I was beginning to think that Mrs Ebson suspected that he was mistreating me. If she thought so, then Milly (our cook) would know as well.

Delicious as the soup was, I only got two spoonfuls down me. I had to move the tray quickly away from me and despite the pain I was in, I raced for the bathroom where I was violently sick and with a sudden whoosh, blood started to pour out of me.

'Lewis!' I screamed. 'Oh God...'

He must have called for the ambulance, as Mrs Ebson sat with me on the bathroom floor, trying to stem the blood from between my legs with an arm full of towels. Mrs Alexicon was out at her Bridge Club.

I remember hearing an ambulance bell blaring but not much else as I drifted into unconsciousness.

XIX.   1966-1967

I was in intensive care for two weeks. I wasn't expected to live. I died on the operating table but they managed to revive me again. Because Lewis had punched me there before, it had caused a weakness in my stomach wall. What he had done, when he punched me that second time, caused my stomach to bleed internally and split open. I was in the operating theatre for five hours. They had to open me up to find out where the tear was. A nurse was in my room, with me, constantly. I was in terrible pain and each time I woke up they would give me an injection to make me sleep again. I was hooked up to a drip for five days, to replace the blood I had lost. It was a highly toxic mix as it had antibiotics and other drugs in it.

If Lewis ever thought that maybe he had gone too far in his beating this time, he gave no sign and played the loving husband well. He still went off for his conferences and meetings midweek. At those times Mrs Alexicon would visit me. I had no idea what excuse Lewis told her to account for my injuries, nor did I care. I was so ill and in so much pain that if she had asked me I think I would have told her.

I was in hospital for almost two months. I was allowed home only because there was someone at home to look after me, as I was very weak, had lost an awful amount of weight and looked frightful.

On my last day, packed and ready for Lewis to collect me. The doctor who had attended me, came and sat on my bed. He took my hands and held them between his own.

'Don't insult me or my colleagues intelligence by telling us this was an accident. Going by your injuries, they are the hallmarks of an abusive husband. Going by your records to date, you have been here five times, always with something serious but never as serious as this last time. Lucy, he will end up killing you. He nearly did this time. There are women's refuges. Would you like me to get you into one?'

I shook my head. 'He would find me and drag me back again. He has already said that.'

'I see. I'll just have to have a talk with your husband.'

'No, no, please don't do that.' I begged. 'You'll make it worse.'

'Trust me,' he said. He stood up and walked away.

He was young and enthusiastic and wanted to help the world. He really thought that speaking to Lewis would stop him from beating me up and would help my situation.

I don't know what he said to Lewis but he was late in collecting me. If he had had a dressing down by the doctor, there was no hint of it in his demeanour. He grinned at me as he came into my room.

'Ready to go darling?' He said brightly.

I stood up, rather unsteadily. Lewis took my case and my handbag in one hand and took my arm with his other.

'Slowly does it,' he said, as we walked out of my private room. I thanked the nursing staff for all they had done for me and Lewis passed an envelope to the Ward Sister.

'A little something to show you my appreciation for what you have done for my wife. It's to go towards the baby unit that you are trying to raise funds for.'

'Thank you, Mr Alexicon, that is very kind of you.' The Ward Sister took it, shook his hand and smiled at me.

'Be careful, my dear,' she said. 'We don't want to see you back here again. We will contact you when we open the baby unit as I'm sure we would love to have you at our opening ceremony. Maybe even Mr Alexicon would open it for us,' she simpered.

'I would love to,' Lewis said, and sounded so sincere.

I hobbled along to the lifts, Lewis's arm was still steadying me.

Down in the foyer, he sat me in a chair. 'Stay here, dear, while I go and get the car.' He strode off and left me there. I mean, he left me there. He didn't come back to pick me up. When it dawned on me what he had done, I realised that this was my punishment for the doctor's stern lecture.

I grew weaker and weaker and more and more tired. Eventually I got up and staggered over to a pay phone to call for a taxi. Luckily, some enterprising firm had installed a free phone service, which was just as well, Lewis had my bag with my purse in it, so I wouldn't have been able to pay to use the phone.

Within five minutes a cab arrived to take me home.

Once there, and with no key, I had to ask the taxi driver to ring the bell for me. Mrs Alexicon answered the ring. Surprise registered on her face and then she frowned. She bent down to look through the now opened cab door.

'Lucy? Lewis went off for you, where is he?'

'Search me,' I muttered, 'I don't know.'

'Oh you poor child.' She helped me out of the cab and into the hall, where I sat rather heavily on a chair.

'You'll have to pay for the cab, I'm afraid, I have no money on me,' I mumbled.

She got a few notes out of her handbag and stuffed them into the cab driver's outstretched hand. It must have been more than the fare with a healthy tip, for he touched his cap and said 'Thank you, madam.'

She closed the door and called for Mrs Ebson. She came to the head of the stairs, saw me and hastened down them.

'Oh, my God,' she gasped, 'you look terrible. I thought Mr Lewis was collecting you?' Without waiting for a reply, which was just as well, as I was beyond answering, she continued, 'with my help dearie, can you make it to your room?' Slowly, I stood up but swayed. Mrs Alexicon grabbed hold of me.

'She should never have been discharged from the hospital in this condition. It's a proper disgrace, it is really. I'll get cook to help.' Mrs Ebson turned to go.

'No no, I'll help you. You take one arm and I'll take the other.' My mother-in-law said.

Somehow we made it up the stairs. Our progress was painfully slow. I had to keep stopping along the way to catch my breath. I felt dreadfully unwell and my legs were shaking so much by the time we reached the top, that I had to sit for some minutes on a chair to gather what strength I had to continue to my room at the end of the corridor. Once there, Mrs Alexicon and Mrs Ebson helped me undress and get into bed. I fell into an exhausted sleep almost immediately.

Mrs Alexicon stayed with me to make sure I was alright. In the early hours of the afternoon Mrs Ebson came in to allow Mrs Alexicon to have her lunch and have a break. The sofa in my room is very comfortable, it was made up into a bed and Mrs Ebson slept there for three nights.

It was early evening when Lewis returned. He was allowed up to see me. His mother wanted him to see how ill I was, I think. I was asleep and unaware of his presence. Mrs Ebson told me later, as she was present at the time that he looked very worried.

I disturbed her once during the night, it was about 3.00 am. I wanted to use the loo. She was out of bed in a trice and helped me into the bathroom. She then waited outside until I had finished. She helped me back into bed again and tucked me in like you would a young child.

We both slept once more until Mrs Alexicon came in the following morning with a tray with my breakfast on it and a cup of tea for Mrs Ebson. I was grateful for the tea but simply played with the toast. Both ladies were kindness themselves during that very trying time and couldn't do enough for me. I was so very grateful to them both. Lewis's excuse for leaving me at the hospital was that he had a slight accident and bumped another car. 'The fool' (the other man) 'insisted on calling the police and I was kept at the police station, being asked stupid questions, all day.' I didn't believe him, because he would have been allowed to make a phone call to let his mother know where he was. I'm not sure that his mother believed him either.

A district nurse called that first morning and was very concerned about my condition. She said, 'I'm detailed to come here every day for a week. I shall consult with your doctor, who may or may not call later today but I am a bit surprised that you were discharged. Anyway, I shall see you tomorrow, if you are still here.' I found her last comment a bit disconcerting but I think she meant if I was not back in hospital again!

The doctor did call later in the day and was all for sending me back once more. But Mrs Alexicon and Mrs Ebson assured him that I would have round the clock care and if they had any cause for concern, they would call him immediately. He harrumphed his approval and left.

Again Mrs Ebson stayed overnight on my sofa and after a good night's rest with no disturbances I felt heaps better as long as I kept still. Even the dour nurse said I looked better when she called.

After Lewis's pathetic excuse for leaving me at the hospital, I didn't see him for a week. He still went away on his Wednesday to Thursday jaunts. I began to think that he was having an affair. I wondered why he didn't just divorce me and have done with it. But he had more in store for me, as I was soon to find out.

After two weeks of bed rest and when I was able to walk without it being too uncomfortable (it was easier if I clutched a cushion to my stomach), Mrs Alexicon would collect me late morning and, holding my arm in hers, we would wander along to her apartment. Mrs Ebson would bring us up our lunch on trays. The first time she said, 'I just thought you'd like to see different scenery for a change.' I thought it was very sweet of her. Caesar, her little Cairn was pleased to see me too. After our lunch she would walk me back to my bedroom, she'd make sure I was comfortably settled, then go back to her own apartment for her own afternoon rest, unless she was going out.

Even when I was back to full health we would often have lunch together in her apartment, leaving Lewis to have his own meal in isolated splendour in the dining room.

He never hit me again but what he did when he became angry was almost worse. He'd put his hands round my neck and squeeze.

I never lost consciousness but just when I thought I was about to, he'd throw me away from him. I usually collapsed on the floor in a heaving heap. I took to wearing Hermes scarves round my neck to hide the bruises.

One day, I had just had lunch with Mrs Alexicon. I was looking after Caesar as she was off to her Bridge Club. I had taken over the morning room that was at the bottom of the stairs next to Lewis's study as my own sitting room. I used that whenever I had Caesar to look after. I had joined Lewis in the dining room for coffee. Mrs Alexicon couldn't abide it, even the smell of it would turn her stomach, but I loved it, as it was the real stuff. He asked me if I wanted another cup and I said yes, I would love one. He got up from the table and with his back to me, poured out two more cups from the coffee pot on the sideboard. He looked at my reflection in the mirror above the sideboard and smiled at me. He suggested that we take our coffees in to my sitting room. Caesar, who had come downstairs with me, followed in my wake, all he was interested in was his walk. Lewis and I could always talk, communication between us had never been a problem. When I yawned suddenly, Lewis suggested that I have a rest before taking the dog for a walk. This seemed a good idea to me. He even took the used coffee cups out of my sitting room. I got comfortable on the sofa by lying full length. Caesar curled up on the floor by the settee and we both went to sleep.

I don't know what it was that woke me up, the closing of a door maybe, I'm not sure, even now. I swung my legs off the sofa, making sure I missed Caesar but he wasn't there. I called him but no sound was heard. I got up and walked round the room, looking for him and calling for him. I looked out of the window as I passed it and saw Lewis walking towards the wood with Caesar on his lead. My immediate thought was that was unusually kind of Lewis to take the dog for a walk. It must have been him coming into the room to see me about something and seeing me asleep thought that he would take the dog for a walk. But that thought went almost immediately and a more sinister thought rose in my mind. With no thought of my own safety, I ran for the front door. I swung it open and ran again, for the wood. I was so unfit I had to stop to catch my breath and then got a stitch in my side and had to stop again. I continued, just walking quickly. I headed for the clearing.

Just before the lake there was a little sandy area. I stood there, looking around, but couldn't see Lewis or Caesar. I heard a splash that seemed to come from the disused boathouse. I think I knew then what had happened. I went back into the wood to hide, crouching low, so that Lewis wouldn't see me. I peeped through the bushes I was hiding behind. I saw Lewis come out of the boathouse without the dog. He was wiping his hands on his handkerchief and was walking back to the path through the wood. He passed within four yards of me but didn't see me. I waited until he was out of sight, then ran for the boathouse. I quietly swung one of the double doors open. I couldn't see anything for a few moments, then my eyes became accustomed to the dim interior but I couldn't see anything untoward.

'Think.' I said to myself. 'You heard a splash.'

I looked into the lake and saw a rope. It was attached to a wooden stave sticking out of the water about 20 feet away from me. I am not a strong swimmer, nor did I know how deep the water was. I had to take a look to see what was hanging off the end of the rope. I took off my outer clothes, so that I would have something dry to get into when I got out of the lake but keeping my bra and pants on. I slipped into the water and gasped at the coldness of it. I was out of my depth immediately. I pushed myself away from the side and swam out into the lake. Once I reached the stave, I allowed myself a moment to catch my breath, then, realized that the rope was just resting on the wood. I tugged at it and the rope came into my hand with no effort. With the rope in one hand I had great difficulty in getting back to the side of the lake, there was something heavy on the end of it. I had to swim a little way, then tread water and pull the rope towards me, swim a little way again and repeat the movement. I was exhausted by the time I got to the edge of the lake. I heaved myself out and pulled the rope up from the water. On the end was a sack, it was tied tightly and I broke my fingernails in my frantic attempt to undo the knot. I opened the sack top and looked inside. I was almost sick.

Before throwing Caesar into the water he had beaten the little dog to a pulp; he must have been dead before he hit the water.

Lewis had put him into a sack, weighted the sack down with stones, then had tied the neck of the sack with rope. Having no knife with him to cut off a length of rope, he had to use it all, and in throwing it into the water, the long end must have snagged on the stave.

What was I to do? How could I tell Mrs Alexicon that her beloved little dog was dead, beaten to death by her evil son, the man I was married to. I wept bitter, angry tears.

I dressed in a hurry, shivering with cold. I carried the sack into the wood. I moved leaves and stones and tried to move some earth with my hands. I laid Caesar in his shallow grave and covered him with what earth I had been able to move, the leaves and the stones. I'd come back tomorrow and dig a deeper grave for him.

Still crying and using a different path back through the wood, I made my way weary way back home. Looking back on that incident, when Lewis poured me a second cup of coffee I think he slipped a sleeping drug into it. When I'm fit, sleeping in the afternoon is not something I usually do. The death of Caesar was premeditated.

Mrs Ebson and Milly Franks were in the kitchen, having their afternoon cup of tea when I walked in the back door.

'Miss Lucy, what have you been doing? You look as though you have been pulled through a hedge backwards.' Milly said, as she poured me out a cup of tea.

I told a half truth. 'Caesar is missing. I've looked all over the house and I've looked in the woods and gardens and just can't find him. I've called and called. I don't know where he's got to. I don't know where else to look.'

'Madam will be that upset if he can't be found,' Mrs Ebson breathed. 'Oh dear.'

'What do you think happened?' Asked Milly.

'He missed his walk this afternoon. I fell asleep in my sitting room, maybe Lewis just let him out.'

'Does he know,' asked Mrs Ebson, 'that the dog is missing?'

'I'd better go and tell him. I'll have another cup of tea and take one up to him, please.'

Milly got a tray and put the filled tea cups on it 'Do you want me to take it upstairs for you? You look a bit shaken.'

'No, it's okay, I can manage,' I said and went out of the kitchen.

I knocked on Lewis's study door, as I always did before entering, walked in and put the tray on an occasional table by the window.

'Caesar is missing. I can't find him,' I said. I couldn't let Lewis know that I knew what had happened to the dog.

'He'll probably come back on his own when he's hungry,' Lewis said. 'Don't worry.'

'I think something has happened to him.'

'Like what?' Lewis asked impatiently.

'Well, there are foxes in the wood. He wouldn't stand a chance against one of them.'

'If the little chap has gone, Mother will be very upset,' Lewis said, as though I was to blame.

'I thought I'd go out looking for him again.'

'Not now Lucy, leave it until morning; it will be dark in a few minutes.'

The following morning I rose early and, with a spade from the garden shed, I went back into the wood to dig a better burial place for Caesar.

XX.   1967-1968

Mrs Alexicon always blamed me for the loss of little Caesar. If only I could tell her – but of course I never did. It's true to say, she was very upset and maybe needed someone to blame. It was a long time before I was allowed into her inner sanctum again. And I did blame myself, too. If I hadn't fallen asleep and taken Caesar out for his walk, it would never have happened. I had to wait up for her to come back and tell her, because she would wonder why her little dog wasn't in her apartment to welcome her back when she returned from her evening out.

She kept to her rooms and even Lewis didn't get to see her. I was at a loss to know what to do. Getting another dog, I thought, would be heartless. No other dog would take Caesar's place and anyway, if she grew too fond of that, would he not end in the same way as Caesar had, beaten to death and thrown into a watery grave?

Her standoff ended in a fantastic discovery. I found I was pregnant. I was over the moon. I told Lewis over dinner one night. Surely, this would be a turning point in our relationship. What man wouldn't want his line to continue? He took the news very well and seemed as thrilled as me. We went up that evening to see Mrs Alexicon to tell her. We tapped on her door she took some time to answer it. She barely looked at me.

'Can we come in Mother?' Lewis asked. 'We have something to tell you.'

She stepped back from her door. 'Come in,' was all she said.

We followed her into her sitting room. She turned when she got to her fireplace to look at us.

'Mother, we are going to have a baby,' Lewis said.

The look of incredulity on her face was a joy to behold. Her stern face broke into a smile again and she hugged Lewis and kissed me.

'I could not have had better news,' she said, 'to get me out of the doldrums.'

My joy was short-lived. When I was 20 weeks gone, I fell from the top of the stairs to the bottom and broke my left arm and right ankle. I was waiting at the top of the stairs for Lewis to join me. He came running along the passageway and came up so quickly behind me that he said he couldn't stop. But I felt his hand and the push in the middle of my back. I'm certain I was pushed on purpose. I lost my baby that night but had to go through the trauma of giving birth. He eventually had to be pulled from my body with forceps. Although perfectly formed, he was too tiny and too damaged and frail to survive. Try as they did, they could not repair the damage done to me internally. They told me that having any more children was so slim a chance as to be almost non-existent. I cried bitter and angry tears once more. No matter what Lewis did, I never let him into my bed again. My love for him was as dead as my baby. My injuries healed in time but my heart wasn't so easily mended.

The next time he tried to throttle me was about three month later. I was just out of the plaster on my arm and ankle. I had been really depressed since I lost the baby. He told me to 'snap out of it as you're becoming a bore.'

I answered back by saying he was lacking in compassion, as it had been OUR baby that I was mourning. He barged into my sitting room that evening and put his hands round my neck, squeezing until I almost lost consciousness. He was yelling and swearing at me, calling me a 'bitch' and 'a pain in the arse'. As he threw me away from him, I collapsed on the floor again, taking in great gulps of air, as he stalked out, slamming the door behind him.

The following day, was his midweek jaunt. I found a message on my plate. It said to take one of his suits to the cleaners. I went through his pockets as usual, he was terrible at leaving things in his pockets, even bundles of cash. I always put his cash on his desk and anything else I found in his pockets. I never took any of the money. After all, after his revelation of checking the mileage on my car, how did I know it wasn't a trick to see if I would take any of it?

I got all the proof I wanted that he was having an affair. I found a receipt in his inside pocket. Maybe he wanted me to find out, who knows how his mind worked. It was for a night's stay for two at the most prestigious of hotels called the Harrington Hay Hotel just outside Birmingham. He hadn't even given a fictitious name and it was for a Mr and Mrs Lewis Alexicon. I sat and looked at the receipt for ages. That night I rang the number given on top of the receipt. An ultra-polite voice said, 'Good Evening, The Harrington Hay Hotel. How may I help you?'

'Could you tell me, please, if a Mr and Mrs Lewis Alexicon are staying with you tonight.'

'Who is calling?' Said the disembodied voice.

I said the first thing that came into my head. 'His mother.' I could hardly say his wife.

'Hold on a minute, I just need to check the register.'

A minute or two later she came back and said. 'Yes, Madam, they are here, would you like me to put you through to their room.'

'No. Don't even tell them I rang. He gets so cross if he thinks that I am checking up on him. I just rang to see if they had arrived safely.'

'I do so understand that. I won't say a word.'

'Thank you so much,' I said, and hung up.

I sat heavily in Lewis's chair behind his desk. I was overwhelmed with anger, misery and despair and a great numbing sadness. He'd called me terrible names and yet all the time he was carrying on behind my back. He'd hit and abused me so often and I wasn't going to stand for it any longer. I had to stand up for myself, there was no-one else to do it for me.

Up in my bedroom, I rehearsed what I was going to say to him when he got back. I went over and over it in my head, I even wrote it down, until I was word perfect. But when I saw him again, he was so angry that the words got stuck in my throat and I couldn't say anything.

'You'll be pleased to know,' he snarled, 'that my two days away were a complete disaster. A total waste of time.'

'Why should I be pleased Lewis? I'm really sorry. Would it help to talk about it?'

'Not to you, no,' he snapped.

For weeks I walked on eggshells, trying not to displease him.

The last time he tried to throttled me was on another Wednesday. He came into my sitting room. 'My study... *now!*' He roared.

I walked with trepidation into his study. He pointed to his desk. On it was my cheque book, that I had been hiding in the attic rooms. My heart fell.

'What is this? You dishonest bitch.'

I completely lost it. All my pent up anger welled up inside me. It was as though a switch had come on in my head.

'How can you call me dishonest Lewis?' I spat at him. 'When you have been carrying on behind my back for years.'

He looked startled but only for a moment. I continued with, 'I found a receipt in the pocket of your suit that I took to the cleaners. I also know you killed your mother's dog, because I saw you. I also know that you pushed me downstairs on purpose. So don't call ME dishonest!' I leant over his desk. 'And if you want to kill me, go ahead. What have I got to live for?'

'You little fucking tart.'

'And that's another thing,' I said, as I straightened up behind his desk. 'I have never looked at another man, not once, since we were married. My vows meant something to me but obviously they meant nothing to you.' They were the last words I was to say to him.

He advanced towards me. I stood straight and tall waiting for whatever punishment he meant to deal out. 'You sanctimonious cow, how dare you judge me?'

He flew at me and grabbed me round the neck, this time I really thought he was going to kill me. He screamed abuse at me and called me all the names under the sun, while his grip round my neck got tighter and tighter, then he threw me away from him just before I was about to lose consciousness. I landed heavily on the floor, hitting my forehead on the little occasional table by the window. He gave me a vicious kick on my right leg.

'It will give me the greatest pleasure this mid-week outing, to work out how to get my revenge on you.' With that he stormed out of his study. I heard the front door slam behind him. He'd gone off to see his lover.

I lay where I was, heaving great gulps of air into my lungs. I ached all over and my leg was throbbing and my neck was so sore I had difficulty in swallowing. The bump that appeared on my forehead from connecting with the little table ached too and my eyes were going black. I made my way up to my bedroom eventually and remained there for the rest of the day.

Mrs Ebson came up to my bedroom the next day to see me and asked if I was alright. I showed her the bruises and the dark marks on my neck. She was horrified. 'I couldn't help but overhear your argument with Mr Lewis yesterday.'

'I'm surprised the whole neighbourhood didn't hear.' I said, tiredly.

'You sit there, lovie and I'll get you a nice cup of tea.'

'Thank you, that will be lovely,' I croaked.

She went away and returned with my tea on a tray with a few biscuits. I thanked her.

She smiled at me. 'That's alright, madam. You look as though you have done a round with Mike Tyson, your eyes are so black. Do you want Cook to send up a couple of steaks for you? They say that's what you should use for black eyes.'

'Does it work?' I asked

'Never had to try,' she answered.

'Seems a waste of good steak to me. They're not painful, so we will leave it for now.'

'Alright, Madam.' And she left the room

It was painful sipping the tea but I felt a bit better after finishing it. I didn't touch the biscuits. I couldn't settle. I walked down to my sitting room, sat down, got up again and wandered into Lewis's study and sat at his desk. My hands brushed lightly over it. It was highly polished and a lovely piece of furniture. It had carvings on each drawer and the grab handles on the drawers were in the shape of a lion's head. I had enjoyed polishing it.

I don't know what made me do it. I'm not usually nosey but I opened each drawer in turn. I don't know what I was looking for, or even if I was looking for anything in particular.

Suddenly, an envelope caught my eye. The writing was familiar to me. My heart skipped a beat. I reached for it and held it in my hands for ages. I just stared at it. It still retained its lavender smell. Slowly, so slowly I took the letter out of its envelope, unfolded it and started to read...

'Darling Lewis,

I miss you like crazy when we are apart. Our time together is so short, which makes it all the sweeter when we do meet up. I almost wet myself when I think of our love making. It's sooo good. You are a wonderful lover. When are you going to leave 'The Bitch' and come to me? Our life would be fantastic but I think we would spend most of it in bed!

You should see me now. I'm wearing next to nothing and I'm remembering the times when you couldn't wait to have me and you'd rip my clothes off and I'd rip yours off.

My nipples are like hard little bullets just thinking of you. I am longing to have you inside me again.

Hurry to me my darling. I want you so badly.

All my love as always,

Jo-Ann

My hand went to my mouth. I felt sick and dizzy. In that moment I decided that I would have to go. He would kill me one day if I didn't. But this... this was the final humiliation and the most hurtful thing he could do.

Mrs Ebson found me sitting at Lewis's desk an hour later.

'Cook wants to know... What's the matter, dearie? You look quite grey'.

I looked up at her. 'He's been abusing me almost since we were married. I now find he is having an affair...' I whispered.

'No, no. How could he?'

'With my sister.'

Mrs Ebson gazed at me, disgust written on her face.

'You poor, poor girl. Does Madam know?'

'I don't know. I think she suspects that things have not gone well since I lost the baby. I have been so depressed I know. Anyway, I have to get away, so would you be good enough to get my cases down from the attic and have them placed in my bedroom?'

'Yes. I'll do that now before I do anything else.'

'Get Milly to make a few sandwiches. I'll have them in my room while I pack.'

I got up from the chair and limped to the door.

'Why are you limping? Miss Lucy.'

I pulled my skirt up to show her the bruise that had formed on my left thigh.

'The beast!' She blurted out.

'A few kicks for good measure.'

'Oh you dear girl, what you have been through. Do you need some help?'

'Yes, I'll choose what to take, if you could pack them for me.'

Really I didn't need help, I just thought she would like to be involved.

'I'll get your sandwiches and meet you in your room.' She scuttled off.

When she had gone, I went back to Lewis's desk and spread Jo-Ann's letter in the centre of his red leather blotting pad. I placed my engagement and wedding ring on the letter, I thought that would tell him that I had left and that our marriage was over.

When we had finished the packing, I gave Mrs Ebson the keys to my car and said I was going to take a shower. She went taking a couple of cases with her. Then I went to my escritoire and wrote a letter to Mrs Alexicon.

> My dearest Mother,
>
> I'm so sorry but I have to go. You must be aware that Lewis and I have not been getting on too well since I lost the baby. I now find that he is having an affair with Jo-Ann. I can no longer tolerate his behaviour.
>
> I hate to hurt you, as I believe we have become very close.
>
> I will be in touch with you,
>
> All my love,
>
> Lucy.

I left it on her mantelpiece in her sitting room. But she was never to get to read it.

In my bedroom I left all the bangles he had given me, in a heap on the cut glass tray that stood in the middle of my dressing table If he found me – and I was sure he would, no matter where I went – I was sure he would kill me but I was beyond caring.

After my shower I changed into a pair of black trousers and a red polo neck sweater (to hide the bruising) and wore my black high heeled boots. I said a tearful goodbye to Milly Franks and Mrs Ebson and she waved me off until I could see her no longer in my rear view mirror.

I drove to the petrol service station on the road to Scotch Corner, where I had my car serviced. I was now driving a Jaguar; a saloon in powder blue, last year's Christmas present from Lewis. He always got himself the latest Mercedes Benz, a Roadster that he was very proud of.

I simply gave my keys to a young petrol pump attendant and said. 'fill her up, check the oil, check the tyre pressure and wash the windscreen down for me please. I shall be in the café.' I had a cup of hot coffee. It could have been tea, it could have been anything, it was grey in colour but it was hot and wet. While there, I decided where to go. Lewis knew nothing about Auntie Elsie or where she lived. She had been coming to our wedding but had had a bad dose of flu and had decided that she had better not come as it had left her feeling rather weak.

I paid for the coffee and the petrol at the same cash desk and still waited for the receipt (old habits die hard) that I stuffed into my bag. I tipped the young man who had seen to the car for me and left. It was 6.30. I had some time to kill. If Auntie Elsie was on a late duty at her receptionist job at Sutton Bank she wouldn't be back until 9.00. I drove out of the petrol station and headed towards Scotch Corner.

At 9.00 pm I staggered up her short path and rang her bell. Poor Auntie Elsie, she got such a shock when she answered her doorbell to find me in a near collapsed state on her doorstep. She took in my lank hair and black eyes. I was so thin and the bruising round my neck stood out starkly against my colourless skin. She ushered me into her pretty sitting room. She sat me down and poured me a stiff drink. I don't like brandy at the best of times but it was what I needed.

'You ring your Auntie Peggy. I know she has been worried to death about you. I'll be in the kitchen making us something to eat while you do that, then we will have a good gossip. I have all night to listen to you.'

I rang the Red Lion Hotel. Mavis answered. 'Red Lion Hotel. How may I help you?'

'I would like to speak to Mr or Mrs Boulting.'

'Who should I say is calling?'

'It's personal, Mavis.'

'Very good, Madam, just hold on, please.'

'Reg here.' Said a familiar voice.

'It's... It's Lucy, Reg.'

'My dear girl, are you alright? Pegs will be so glad to hear from you.'

'I've left Lewis, Reg. He's been abusing me and I now find he is having an affair with... with... Jo-Ann.'

He said he'd come and fetch me home.

'No Reg, leave me here for a few days. Lewis always said, if I left him he would find me and drag me back. He doesn't know Auntie Elsie or where she lives. The Red Lion Hotel and Crofters Cottage is the first place he would look.'

'Although that is true, he isn't going to hurt you or take you home while you are with us. I know Pegs would want you home.'

'Reg, please, please leave it for now.' I started to cry. Auntie Elsie must have heard, because she came in just then and took the receiver from me.

'Reg dear, she is in a terrible state and very distressed. You may of course come over and see her for yourself at any time but I do think she would be safer here. You can't guard her all the time and that man (she couldn't bring herself to even say Lewis's name) has never been here and doesn't know that I even exist.'

'Okay Elsie, we will go with what you say. But we will be over to see her tomorrow. Give her mine and Peggy's love.'

Auntie Peggy and Reg arrived the following day. I totally broke down when Auntie Peggy walked into the room. She and I cried in each other's arms. They too, were terribly shocked at my condition and appalled by the bruising. Reg and Auntie Pegs booked into a nearby Bed and Breakfast place in Gilling West, just round the corner from where Auntie Elsie lived.

Over the next few days it all came out, sometimes with sobs, sometimes in control of myself, but more often not. But I could not bring myself to talk about my lost baby.

'Why did you stay with him for so long?' Auntie Peggy asked.

'I loved him. Lewis could charm the birds off the trees. But then lately, I've been asking myself that same question. I guess I would still be with him if I hadn't found that letter from Jo-Ann. That was the last straw for me.'

'The little tart!' Auntie Peggy said. 'Jo-Ann looks as though butter wouldn't melt in her mouth.'

'Little whore more like,' expostulated Reg.

'I never did like her,' Auntie Elsie said.

They stayed close to me in those first few days. At each knock on the front door, I jumped like a startled rabbit. At night it was worse; each creak, as the house settled down for the night, terrified me and I clung to Auntie Elsie, sobbing and shaking.

Poor Auntie Elsie, she would arrive at work the following morning shattered. Auntie Peggy and Reg stayed with me during the day. I wouldn't venture outside the house, not even into the back garden. Reg rang Lewis but could get no answer. He decided to go and visit him. He was gone for about five hours and we were getting worried. In my head I could see Reg lying injured somewhere having had a car smash. He eventually arrived back at Auntie Elsie's house, looking grey.

'Lucy, my dear, you must sit down, I have some disturbing news for you.'

I sat as he asked me to and looked intently at him.

'What is it? You're making me nervous.'

'When I got there the place was crawling with police. Lucy Lass, Lewis is dead.'

'Dead?' I repeated stupidly. 'Dead?'

'The police stopped me entering the house. They asked me who I was. Of course, I had to tell him, I saw no reason not to. A young constable told me that they needed urgently to see the younger Mrs Alexicon and did I know where she was. I said I did.

I demanded to see someone in charge. I said I've come to see Mr Alexicon. The Inspector, who the young constable called, came out of the house and said, 'I'm terribly sorry, Mr Boulting, but he's dead. He's been battered to death.'

'Battered to death?' I repeated. 'What about Mrs Alexicon?'

'You mean your mother-in-law?'

'Yes.'

'She found Lewis's body and is in intensive care after suffering a heart attack.'

At this news I just went numb.

'That poor woman has suffered so much,' I murmured. I sat in Auntie Elsie's house, shaking. Both Auntie Peggy and Reg tried their best to comfort me but nothing they did or said helped me, I was too distraught. I'd sit and cry with my hands across my tummy as though I was protecting my lost baby.

XXI.   1968

The next day the police arrived to take a statement from me. After that, I was escorted to the mortuary by them. There was no-one else who could identify Lewis's body. Reg came with me for moral support, which I needed badly. I kept having nightmares, where he would jump up off the gurney and grab me and say, "I said I'd find you wherever you were and drag you back!"

Lewis's handsome face was unmarked but the back of his head, so the mortuary attendant told me, was all but gone.

I cried such angry and sad tears. All that love I'd had for him wasted, gone, as dead as he was.

The police kept coming to Auntie Elsie's house to interview me. I got to thinking that they suspected me.

'Don't worry so much,' Auntie Elsie kept saying. 'You could never have killed Lewis and then arrived here when you did. You wouldn't have had the time. They know that. They have probably done the drive to see how long it takes'.

'It's all very odd,' I kept saying, over and over again.

I visited Mrs Alexicon in hospital. That was another reason I stayed with Auntie Elsie. Her place was nearer to Darlington. I told the staff at the hospital who I was and I was allowed to sit by her bed and hold her hand for as long as I wanted to. I whispered to her that despite everything, I had loved him. She seemed to understand, as I'm sure I felt her hand squeeze mine.

That night the hospital called. 'We wouldn't bother you at this time of night but Mrs Alexicon is asking for you.'

'I'll come immediately,' I said.

Auntie Elsie came out of her bedroom. 'Who was that, at this time of night?'

'The hospital Night Sister says that Mrs Alexicon is asking for me and is getting very distressed and agitated.'

'Wait and I'll come with you. With those vultures outside you won't get a moment's peace.'

The vultures Auntie Elsie referred to were the Press, who had stationed themselves outside her gates and were hanging around outside The Priory and the hospital. Every time I emerged from either one, they converged on me, firing questions. I had been told either to say nothing or say 'no comment'.

We threw on whatever clothes that came to hand and, breaking the speed limit, we raced to the hospital in Darlington, doing it in about one and a half hours, followed, of course, by the vultures. We were escorted to her private room by a policewoman. They were waiting for Mrs Alexicon to recover enough to get a statement from her.

She seemed to have shrunk in size. The dim nightlights made her look worse than when I had seen her earlier in the day. Her face was in deep shadow but her eyes seemed to glitter. A noise escaped her mouth. I bent nearer. 'What is it you are trying to say?'

She licked her dry lips. 'Your sister,' she whispered. I think my heart must have stopped for a moment.

'Jo-Ann!' I exclaimed in amazement.

She closed her eyes and nodded her head. 'She was there.' She managed to say.

'You mean she came to the house to see Lewis?' I asked.

Again she nodded her head. 'I saw her running out of the house, after he was dead, just before I found him.' She whispered.

'You think... she killed Lewis?' I was very hesitant in my question.

'Yes.' She murmured.

I looked back at the policewoman standing at the door.

'Did you hear what she's just said?' I asked her.

'No madam, I didn't.'

I looked at Auntie Elsie. 'Did you hear...?' I could tell by her expression that she had. She looked as shocked as I felt.

'You must tell the police, Lucy, you must.'

The young policewoman walked towards the bed. 'Did you hear what your mother-in-law said?' She asked.

I hesitated. 'She said, my sister killed Lewis.'

'Who is...?'

'Jo-Ann McCauley Bradley,' I said.

She disappeared out of the room, presumably to call the police station and let them know.

We stayed with Mrs Alexicon until she went to sleep.

I visited her every day and every day she got worse. I think she had just given up. All her children had been taken away from her by death and her longed for grandchild was now not a possibility.

I was deeply saddened but not surprised when I got a call from the hospital one morning to say that my mother-in-Law had passed away.

The police and the forensic people had done a thorough search of The Priory and had found other letters from Jo-Ann and my own letter to Mrs Alexicon that she would never see. They also found my wedding ring but not my engagement ring. The poker by the fireplace had Jo-Ann's fingerprints on it at the sooty end as she had used the heavy knob end to hit Lewis with. I really didn't understand but knew from personal experience that she was quite capable of killing someone. But I thought she was supposed to love him, so what had gone wrong? She was arrested for murder. She appeared before the local Magistrate the next day in Darlington.

Jo-Ann gave her name, address and pleaded 'not guilty'. Try as he would, my father could not get bail for her, she already had a record for GBH and had to stay in prison until her High Court trial was heard, a full year later.

The police had made a thorough search of her bedroom at my parents' hotel down south in Clevedon and had found my engagement ring. This didn't surprise me. It just seemed to incriminate her more.

There was so much for me to do in those few weeks after Lewis and Mrs Alexicon death's. I wasn't given time to brood, which was probably a good thing. I wasn't allowed to have his body for burial for about a month but I could hold Mrs Alexicon's funeral whenever it could be arranged.

Old Sam the gardener had been found dead in bed one morning. I went to his funeral to pay my respects. I had liked him. 84 years old, he might have been, but he had been a good worker and thorough. His grandson Joseph said he would try and fit Mrs Alexicon's garden into his busy day. I asked if he knew of anyone who could take his grandfather's place. He screwed his eyes up and said he would like the chance of extra work and do it himself, as he wanted to save up for a motorbike. I pointed out that it was a big garden to maintain, as he had the responsibility of looking after the wood, as well as the lake. He said would it be alright if he got in some help. One of the farm labourers would welcome a bit of extra cash, as he had a wife and five children. I had so much to do that I just told him to arrange it and we would see how it worked out.

The family solicitors had written to me to ask for a meeting and I got another shock. Mr Alexicon, who I thought had been killed in the war, was still alive but in a private mental institution – and I was expected to pay for his upkeep! I explained to the solicitors that I had no money of my own, so they would have to continue to pay for him to remain there from the proceeds of the estate. I rang the hospital to ask if he was allowed visitors.

'Yes,' they said. 'Mrs Alexicon visited him once a month.'

I decided that I would have to take on that job too.

The visit didn't go too well. Mr Alexicon lay on his bed, staring into space. The male nurse with him explained that he had to be kept sedated, as he could become very violent. Lewis was the spitting image of him. I found it all very disconcerting. I didn't stay with him for long but had a talk with the Charge Nurse. He told me that Mr Alexicon had come to them after the war, a very disturbed man. He didn't think that he would ever go home, as he didn't even recognise his wife, Mrs Alexicon. But he was strong and as healthy as he could be under the circumstances and could go on for a few years yet. But the Charge Nurse didn't think I had a duty to visit him.

'After Mrs Alexicon's visits he is very difficult to handle for some time.'

'So are you saying that I am not helping by visiting him?'

'Frankly, Mrs Alexicon, you're not.'

So I didn't go again. They kept me informed of Mr Alexicon's progress in a monthly newsletter.

Mrs Alexicon's funeral was held the following week. Her Bridge Club friends came to pay their last respects, as did the Theatre Group she belonged too. There must have been 50 or so people and, of course, reporters milled around, getting in the way, though the police tried to keep them at bay.

Milly Franks put on a very good buffet for the wake at The Priory.

The really silly thing was that I had to go cap in hand to the solicitors for some money to give Mrs Alexicon a decent send off, pay the general household bills and pay my two loyal staff their wages. I couldn't dismiss them; they came with The Priory and they were now my responsibility. The solicitors weren't overly pleased with this. I think they thought I was a just a gold-digger. I didn't really care what they thought. They weren't prepared to give me any money but told me to send all the bills to them and they would pay them. Which is what I did. They also wanted to know what I was going to do about the house.

I had no idea. My first thought was to sell it. It hadn't been a happy house for me and the death duties were high.

A month later I got a call from the police saying that they were releasing Lewis's body. I arranged another funeral. There was hardly anyone there. Auntie Peggy with Reg came, but only to support me. Auntie Elsie didn't want to come. She hadn't met Lewis and said she would be a hypocrite if she came. I could see her point. The family solicitors were there and a few people I recognised but didn't know well. The Press made their presence felt but I could easily blank them. I'd had enough practise, after all.

Again, Milly put on a nice buffet for the few people who came back to The Priory afterwards. But I was glad when it was all over.

Auntie Peggy offered to come with me to help clear The Priory of all Mrs Alexicon's and Lewis's things. We stayed there for two weeks. We would fall into bed exhausted at the end of each day. I found hundreds of photographs to sort through. I didn't want to throw them away but I didn't know whom they were of and no-one to help me. I put them all in a shoebox. I'd decide another day what to do with them. Mrs Alexicon had some fabulous jewels and a vast amount of really good quality clothes but quite old fashioned. I bagged it all up, intending to send it to a charity shop, then asked Auntie Elsie and Auntie Peggy if they would like to go through it first to see if there was anything they liked. Auntie Elsie took a lot of things, merely for the material, she had a dressmaker who was an excellent needlewoman and would be able to remodel all the suits and dresses for her. Auntie Peggy took her choice to the woman whom she had got her wedding dress from, to make up for her.

Then I was hit by the inheritance tax. I contacted Sotheby's and they sent a representative down to inspect Mrs Alexicon's jewels and pronounced them beautiful pieces and yes, they would take them to auction and also her valuable pictures. She had a Constable and a very good copy of a Monet and some others of only slightly less value, together with Lewis's Rolex and his own vast array of expensive personal items, half of which I had never seen before. They took it all. I was able to clear the tax without selling the house. Why I did that, I really couldn't say. What was I going to do with a house that big? It stood in its own land, had its own private lake and wood and the house was done up to my taste. Compared to the dark dingy place I had come to as a bride, it was now a tastefully transformed grand house. Why did I not just sell it? I couldn't have said why. There was something holding me back from making that last break.

Reg said it had the makings of a fine hotel. It did but did I want to run it? I thought of a nursing home but what did I know about nursing? Nothing.

I was now living back at Crofters Cottage and it had worked its usual magic on me. I'd put on some weight, thanks, in part, to Auntie Peggy's cooking! I realised, too, that I felt more relaxed and that feeling of dread had lifted and gone. All the bruises had vanished with not another one to take its place and I felt altogether better in myself, although I still had nightmares. But they were diminishing.

I walked through The Priory one late summer's day, just checking that all was tidy once more. All Mrs Alexicon's and Lewis's things had been sorted through and either given away to a charity or sold at auction. My own personal items were back at Crofters Cottage and I was just seeing that there was nothing else to do before locking up the house and heading for home. I wasn't thinking of anything in particular when the thought came into my head, like a voice saying, 'What are you waiting for? You know what you want to do.' I said aloud: 'Tell me, because I don't know.' Suddenly it hit me. I stood absolutely still. 'Of course,' I murmured to myself. The more I thought of the idea, the more I liked it. Lewis would have hated it!

I walked around the house again with new eyes. Yes, I thought, caught up with my idea. It would work, I'm sure. I'd have a word with Reg and Auntie Peggy tomorrow and speak to Simon Frobisher, the solicitor I had always used in Leyburn. I'd make an appointment to speak to him as soon as possible...

Mrs Ebson and Milly Franks had gone away for a break; Milly to her sister's in Bournemouth and Mrs Ebson, with her husband, had gone to Cornwall. They were on full pay still, until I decided what I wanted to do with the house. They were like family retainers. Mrs Ebson had worked there since she was 24 years old. Milly was the 'newcomer'; she'd only worked at The Priory for 10 years! I had contact numbers for them both.

I went back to Redmire, had a bath and returned to Leyburn. I poked my head round Reg's door at the hotel. 'Just to let you know I'm back. Reg.'

'I wish,' he said, morosely. I went into his office and closed the door behind me.

'What's up?' I asked.

'Don't want a job do you?'

'Reg, Mavis is perfectly good at her job and Ruth is too.'

'But they aren't you. I have to check behind them all the time. I never had to do that with you. You just knew what to do.'

'I'd take on a few hours, if you wanted me to.'

Auntie Pegs came in just then. 'Certainly not,' she said, having heard my reply to Reg's question. 'The girls are perfectly alright Reggie, you just fuss too much.'

'You didn't say that when we came back from seeing Lucy at Elsie's. A right old muddle they had got into.'

'Well, the offer is there if you want me to do a few hours but Mavis has to be in overall charge. I'm not intending to take her job from her.'

'I'll think on,' was all he said on the matter.

'You back here for the night lovie?' Auntie Pegs asked.

'No. I just popped in to ask if you could spare me a few hours tomorrow for lunch.'

'Stay here for the night. I've cooked Reggie's favourite, it's yours too.'

'Not steak and kidney pudding?' I said. She nodded her head.

'My mouth is watering already.'

'Well you can't say no to that,' Reg rumbled a laugh.

'No I can't!'

I stayed.

The next day I booked a table at my newly found favourite place, just across the square from the Red Lion. It served homemade fare and was clean and always full. I sat in the reception area of the Red Lion Hotel, at the table where Reg and I used to sit when Auntie Peggy used to visit us. It was like I had never been away. Mavis was working behind the desk. I felt that it should have been me standing there.

Reg came bustling in and a few seconds later Auntie Peggy joined us. We walked out of the swing doors, after Reg fired all sorts of orders to Mavis and telling her where we would be if there were any problems. We strolled over to 'The Cabin', got our seats and ordered our meal. Auntie Peggy and I had their delicious homemade salmon fish cakes with a cucumber sauce and Reg ordered a steak medium rare.

'Right Lass, you had something to say to us,' Reg said as he made inroads into his steak.

'Well, as you know I went to The Priory yesterday. I was walking through the rooms and I suddenly had this idea. Although your idea of turning it into a hotel was good, Reg, I'm not experienced enough in running one...'

'Not experienced enough?' Reg interrupted. 'Good God, you could run a hotel with one hand tied behind your back.'

'As I was saying,' I glared at Reg, 'I thought of turning it into a charity run place for battered wives.'

They both stopped eating 'My Lass,' Reg said, finding his voice first. 'What a grand gesture.'

'How would you go about that?' Auntie Peggy queried.

'I wouldn't have anything to do with the running of the place. I want it run by a charity that is up and running already.'

'That's a good idea. You'd need a good solicitor to find it for you. Simon is the best in town but you might need someone with more clout,' Reg commented.

'Yes, I'd thought of him and I will start with him. He might be able to point me in the right direction, I just wanted to speak to you two first, to see what your thoughts were on the matter.'

'I certainly think it's a lovely idea but it will take some time to sort out,' Auntie Peggy said.

'Gives someone battered like me, somewhere to go.'

'Except you did have somewhere to go.'

'Yes, okay but others don't.' There was silence as we returned to our meal.

'I don't understand why you didn't tell us Lucy.' I knew what Auntie Peggy was referring to.

'Not now Pegs,' Reg said. 'All in good time.'

'If it's been bothering her, Reg, I can talk about it.'

'Aye, it's been bothering us both.'

'The truth is, I don't really know. Pride, maybe. I felt a failure. Married less than six months and he was already beating me up. I got to believe that somehow I was to blame. They say you marry someone like your father. Lewis was a clone of him. I didn't want to heap worries onto you both. You were still fairly newly married and what could you do? It had to be me to decide that enough was enough.'

'I was always surprised that there were no children.' Auntie Peggy ventured, adding, 'A blessing, I suppose in the event.'

I said nothing but looked down at my now, empty plate. I had told no-one about the baby. It was my closely guarded secret. I still found it too painful to talk about.

'What is it, Lucy?' Reg asked. Very astute he was at times.

'Nothing.' I said. 'Should we have a sweet or just coffee?'

'Just coffee,' Reg said, 'and we'll have that at the hotel.'

I paid for the meal, with difficulty, Reg wanted to pay for it.

'My treat, remember?' I said.

We wandered back across the square.

'I'm just going off to make an appointment with Simon for tomorrow,' I said, going off on a tangent.

Reg grabbed my arm. 'No you're not. Coffee at home, remember?' He said, using my word. 'You can do that later.'

Auntie Peggy looked at him in puzzlement but said nothing.

As we entered the hotel, Reg said. 'Coffee for three in my office please, Mavis. Any problems?'

'No, Mr Boulting.' She sounded far less nervous than she used to be.

Once coffee had arrived, Reg said, 'Come on Lucy, out with it. Your aunt touched a sore point back there.'

Reg has lots of different voices. Soft, loving and gentle, nearly always, with Auntie Peggy, always nice with me too but totally different when talking with the staff. And a voice that says .'No joshing, No getting away with it. You tell me the truth.' This was one of those times.

I thought, perhaps, now was the time to let it go. I gave a sigh.

'I got pregnant in our third year of marriage. I thought Lewis would be so pleased. I even thought that this would, maybe, be the turning point in our relationship. He pretended to be pleased. We were heading for the stairs one day. He was running at full pelt along the corridor to catch up with me. He said he was running too fast to stop. He said it was an accident. He pushed me downstairs. I fell from the top to the bottom and miscarried that night.' Tears were running unchecked down my face. 'I was almost five months pregnant at the time. I know he pushed me. Mrs Ebson was the first on the scene, she said she looked upstairs for Lewis but he wasn't there but I felt the flat of his hand against my back. When I fell, I broke my right ankle and my left arm.'

Auntie Peggy's hand went to her mouth. 'Oh God no.' She got up and came to my side to give me a cuddle. My tear stained face looked up at her. 'He was perfectly formed but badly damaged and too tiny and fragile to survive.' I sobbed in Auntie Peggy's arms. When I looked up, Reg had gone out of the room. He came back in again with a brandy. 'Drink that up lass, make you feel better.' I sipped at it.

'You never said, I mean, even lately...' Auntie Peggy murmured.

'I couldn't. This happens when I talk about it.' I pointed to my tear streaked face. 'Afterwards I was put on strict bed rest but I have never really got over it. When I thought of ringing you, it would just start me crying again, then I could only ring when I went shopping. Lewis would beat me if I used the house phone to call you or Mum. It was as if he wanted me to lose all contact with the people I loved. Anyway, Lewis told me to "snap out of it." I was depressed for weeks.

It was partly to blame for the last beating he gave me. The next day I left and went to Auntie Elsie's. He told me if I left him there was nowhere for me to go as you wouldn't want me, at the time it made perfect sense, because there were times when I physically couldn't make a phone call. I thought you'd think I had just forgotten you. Mrs Alexicon kept me going. She was very sweet to me. We got on well.'

'Did she know?' Asked Reg.

'I don't think so. He always had a plausible excuse for my injuries.'

'The bastard!' Reg angrily got to his feet and in his agitation he walked to and fro in his office.

'I really loved that man,' I said sadly. 'If I hadn't found that letter from Jo-Ann, I sometimes think I would still be with him. Except I got to thinking that he would end up killing me.'

'My dearest girl,' Auntie Peggy said. 'And you are, Lucy. You're like a daughter to me.'

'Thank you Auntie Pegs.' Then, as we were all so emotional, I joked, 'I think you should just adopt me!'

Reg made us laugh by saying, 'My but we could do worse.'

But for me it could so easily have been tears again.

XXII.   1968-1969

I made an appointment with Simon Frobisher, my solicitor. I met him on Friday. He was very good but thought it would take a few months to organise it. He suggested he'd start by drawing up a contract for a Charitable Trust, so that it would be ready to sign when one was found. This seemed a good idea. He had a friend who could start hunting around for a suitable charity for victims of domestic violence. But he would always speak to me first, before any offer was made. I would hold the lease and take a small rent on the property. Making money was not my concern. I had that. If it all went wrong for whatever reason, I would still retain the house. I left him to get on with it.

He would let me know of any developments.

It was a few months later that Simon found a charity that seemed interested and interesting. I met a Mrs Taylor from the charity in Simon's office two days after he rang. It was arranged that the next afternoon we would meet at The Priory. She was quite bowled over when she saw the house. I think she was expecting something smaller and not quite so grand.

We sat in the drawing room after she had seen round the house. Milly Franks came in with a trolley set with tea things and one of her lovely cakes.

'We wouldn't want staff. The women have to look after themselves,' she said, after Milly had left the room.

'The staff – and there are only two of them, plus Joseph the gardener – come with the deal, Mrs Taylor. No staff, no house.' I was quite pleasant in my manner but firm. 'They are the family retainers. Their jobs end when they choose to go. Doubtless the women will need help keeping the house clean, to say nothing of the cooking.'

'But with the rent you'd want for this beautiful house, we couldn't afford to keep the staff and pay their wages.'

'I'm willing to rent this house to your charity for a peppercorn amount and I will pay the staff wages and I'm sure Joseph would want to stay on, with his friend who also works here at odd times.'

'That's very kind of you, Mrs Alexicon. Could you come to our next board meeting? We need to discuss it.'

'You tell me when it is and I'll fit it into my schedule.' I looked at Simon.

'I would want to be there too, Mrs Taylor,' he said. 'I would want to speak to your solicitor. He will need to read through the papers and go over them with your board of governors to see that all is quite clear and satisfactory to you. They have been ready for some time. I would also expect your Trust Chairman to be there.'

'I will be in touch with a date that hopefully will suit us all. But Sir Albert Peasebody is a very busy man.'

'Mrs Taylor, Mrs Alexicon is busy, as I am. Surely on an occasion like this, when Mrs Alexicon is making such a generous and outstanding offer, it should be marked by his presence?'

Mrs Taylor was slightly flustered and blushed. ' I'll see what I can do with dates and let you know.' She finished her cup of tea, refused another slice of Milly's cake and she rose to go. I showed her out to her car. We shook hands and she said, 'I'll be in touch.'

I merely smiled, said goodbye to her and went back into the house. As I came into the drawing room, Simon was pouring another cup of tea for himself.

'Do you want another cup?' He asked.

'Yes please, as you're up. What do you think?'

'I'm annoyed that she didn't appreciate that such an offer as you are making wasn't worthy of Sir Whatsit's presence.'

'Peasebody.' I reminded him. 'Mrs Taylor is hardly an envoy to send to someone in the hope of impressing them, is she?'

'You can always pull out.' Simon said.

'Yes, the thought had crossed my mind. But I will go to that board meeting she is arranging just to see what happens and to see what the others are like.'

Sir Albert Peasebody was a pompous prat who had been asked to head the trust just for his name only. He knew not the first thing about the trust. Mrs Taylor was there. She appeared to be more of a secretary than a manager. Major Hugh Towers, on the other hand, was fantastic. He was head of finances and organised charity fundraising events. I liked him and the rest of the board. But Hugh Towers, with his energy, was the one who made up my mind that this charity was for me. Simon liked him too.

It was arranged that all of them should come to see The Priory.

To say they were stunned was putting it lightly. Simon didn't insist that Sir Albert Peasebody should be present. He seemed a waste of time and space. Simon wasn't impressed at all.

In the drawing room afterwards we had tea. They had been down to the cellars and up to the attics and all places in between. Milly had really gone to town with little sandwiches and home-made biscuits, scones, with cream and jam and cakes. They were an enthusiastic bunch. I liked Betty Towers, Major Towers' wife. She walked with the aid of the stick but even she managed the full tour.

'How can you bear to let this beautiful house go?' she asked.

'It wasn't a very happy house for me. I could go somewhere when things got bad but some women have nowhere to go and no-one to help.'

'You weren't...?'

'A battered wife?' I finished for her. 'Yes, Mrs Towers I was.'

'Oh my dear, I'm so sorry. So dreadfully sorry.'

'It's all in the past now. I just wanted to give something to those less fortunate than myself. And if that sounds pompous, I don't mean it to be. What would I do with a big house like this on my own?'

The Major came in just then, he had been out in the hall with the others. I could hear him talking animatedly about his ideas. Mrs Towers was tired and had elected to sit with me.

'Fantastic offer, Mrs Alexicon.' He said enthusiastically. 'We will never be able to thank you enough.'

'Just to have it full of happy and safe families is payment enough, Major Towers.'

'I am thrilled with this great house. It should take at least ten families. The children could have the attic rooms. They will love it.' He was planning already.

'There is a boating lake, it's through the wood beyond the side gardens on the left.'

'Can I go and explore?' he asked, like an excited child.

'Of course you can!' I laughed, caught up by his enthusiasm.

'You go with the others dear,' Mrs Towers said. 'I've done enough walking for today.'

'You stay here then, dear. I'll see if the others want a walk. We'll have to walk off that lovely tea.' And off he strolled, telling the others he was off to see the boating lake.

Mrs Towers and I were left on our own.

'I'd rather it was kept between you and me that I was a battered wife, Mrs Towers.'

'Of course, Mrs Alexicon, if that's how you want it. I won't say a word, not even to Hugh. They say women can gossip but he can talk to anyone and get them to give more money than they want to. He's worth his weight in gold.'

'And charming with it.' I smiled.

When it was time for them to go, Major Towers came over to thank me, well they all did. He touched my arm and asked me to step out into the garden.

'We were wondering, Mrs Alexicon, if you would like to be on the Board of Trustees?'

'That is a lovely offer but I do need to think it over. To start with, once it was up and running, I was going to walk away. Let me sleep on it Major and I'll let you know.'

'I understand, we'll leave it like that then. Goodbye, dear lady.'

But as things turned out, I had to turn the offer down.

I hadn't intended to go to Jo-Ann's trial. Even now I don't know why I did. It was heard at Durham Crown Court. I sat in the public gallery, Auntie Peggy was with me for moral support. I sat hunched in a corner, trying to be invisible. My father was also there. I could feel his eyes boring into the back of my head. He still thought that I had killed Lewis. His darling Jo-Ann wouldn't hurt a fly. There were a lot of reporters around but they were far more interested in the beautiful woman being tried for murder than for the bystander I hoped to be mistaken for. We all stood when the judge arrived.

The first look at Jo-Ann as she came up from the downstairs cells was a shock to me. She looked stunning and beautiful; a little harder in the face and a slight plumpness had crept in but it simply made her more appealing. She presented a pathetic, sad innocence that would doubtless catch at the heartstrings of the jury.

After a lot of witnesses had come and gone it was Mrs Ebson's turn to take the stand on the second morning.

'Now Mrs Ebson, what time did Mrs Lewis Alexicon go?'

'About 5.30. Sir.'

'Could she have come back without you knowing?'

'No Sir, me and Milly Franks, the cook, were getting good at knowing the different sounds the cars make.'

'So you know when Mr Lewis Alexicon arrived home?'

'Yes, because his car sounded so powerful. It would be about eight.'

'So you heard Miss Jo-Ann Bradley arrive.'

'Yes Sir, but we didn't recognise the sound of the car.'

'When did she arrive?'

'About 8.20, Sir.'

'What other car did you hear?'

'Mrs Alex Alexicon came back via the back lane. She said two cars were in the drive. The one behind her sons she didn't recognise either. So she wouldn't have to move her car to let the visitor out, she drove down the back lane and straight into the garage.'

'What time was that?'

'She had been out to her Bridge Club, so she would be home at about 8.25, give or take a minute.'

'What happened then?'

'She came in the back door, Sir. She'd left her wet shoes just inside the back door and came into the kitchen in her stockinged feet'

'Did you tell her that Mrs Alexicon the younger had left?'

'No sir, it wasn't my place to. Miss Lucy had left her a note in her room.'

'How do you know that?'

'It was cold, Sir. I slipped a hot water bottle in her bed and saw it on her mantelshelf.'

'Did she speak to you on her way in?'

Mrs Ebson sounded affronted. 'Of course she did. She would never pass through the kitchen without having a word or two with us. She was a real lady. Milly Franks would always have a tray ready for her with a few sandwiches on it and a glass of milk, or make her a cup of tea or cocoa in the winter when she came in shramed.'

'Shramed?' The Q.C. asked.

'Sorry, I mean cold.'

'Why were you there?' He asked.

'I often stayed on for an evening. Me and Milly Franks are good friends see. The kitchen was always warm as it had an Aga. I'd wait for my husband to collect me.'

'What time did he collect you that night?'

'I don't rightly know the time he come for me. I had gone to the hospital with Mrs Alex Alexicon. He was unusually late, so Milly said.'

'In your own words, can you tell me what happened when Mrs Alexicon went out of the kitchen?'

'She picked up her tray and I opened the door for her at the bottom of the stairs. They lead up to the ground floor. As she passed she said, 'Thank you and goodnight.' We then heard Miss Bradley's car go, skidding all over the place, sending gravel out onto the lawns. I looked at the cook and said, 'That will cause grief with Sam when he comes to mow the lawns next.'

We went on chatting for a while, then Milly Franks went upstairs to check that the front door was locked. She found it open, so closed and locked it. As she came back, she noticed Mrs Alex Alexicon's tray on a side table. She saw the study door open and the light still on. She knocked, got no reply, so she peeped inside...'

Mrs Ebson couldn't go on.

'I realize this must be upsetting for you. Take your time. Would you like some water?' The judge asked kindly. 'It would be helpful if you could continue.'

'Thank you, that would be nice,' she whispered.

The judge asked a court usher to get some water for Mrs Ebson. After she took a sip she cleared her throat, dabbed at her eyes and continued. 'Milly called for me to come up. I could tell by her voice that something terrible had happened. When I got to the study I found Milly bending over Mrs Alexicon, who was on the floor. We got a terrible fright. I used the phone on Mr Lewis Alexicon's desk to call an ambulance for Mrs Alex Alexicon and the police. I realized that an ambulance was too late for Mr Lewis. The back of his head was... stoved in.' Mrs Ebson was now quietly crying and from where I was sitting I could see her shaking.

The judge called for an adjournment for lunch.

At 2.00 the trial started again. Milly Franks herself was interviewed. She gave more or less the same story as Mrs Ebson; it just differed slightly because she had found Mrs Alex Alexicon and Mr Lewis's body.

Auntie Elsie came next, looking very dashing in an elegant coat and skirt, with one of my turbans on her head. She was asked what time I had arrived at her house.

'She arrived at just after 9.00pm,' she answered in a confident voice.

That cleared me once and for all, as Lewis's death had been estimated at between 8 and 9 pm. It takes 1½ hours to drive from The Priory to where Auntie Elsie lived.

'Thank you Mrs Robbins, you may step down, unless my learned friend wants a word with you.'

'No questions your Honour.'

Auntie Elsie looked up at the gallery and she smiled at me. She had been quite nervous about appearing in court. That surprised me. I thought she would love the attention. So whether it was a smile to say "thank goodness that's over" or just a smile to encourage me, I never asked. When Jo-Ann looked up to see who Auntie Elsie was smiling at and saw me, her whole demeanour changed. She jumped up from her chair and started to scream and shout at me. 'You! If you had been there, I would have killed you for sure, you bastard!' There was an unholy commotion. It took some time to calm her down. The judge kept hammering at his gavel until quiet was restored in the court. Jo-Ann was then taken back down to the cells.

The trial ended that day. There was no point in carrying on, she had all but admitted her guilt. The jury were out for no more than 20 minutes. Jo-Ann was brought up from the cells again to hear the verdict. She was found guilty of manslaughter and given 21 years.

She looked shocked beyond reason and started crying hysterically. My father was ejected from the court for disturbance. He kept screaming, "No! No! It isn't true! It isn't true!" That left Auntie Peggy and me to deal with the reporters, who now realized who I was. They surged around us, shouting questions and taking photographs. We were rescued by two of the ushers, who guided us into the judge's private quarters. We were taken to a side exit and escorted into a taxi.

Even Auntie Peggy and I were shocked at her 21-year jail sentence.

XXIII.   1969-1970

Life is odd, you think that it will continue more or less along the lines of your present life. But something was about to happen that completely changed my life forever.

My mother arrived unannounced at Crofters Cottage one day. She had come down by train and had hired a car at Darlington.

'You look so tired. If you had let me know I would have collected you from Darlington.' I said. She seemed harassed and on edge.

'I need to speak to you; is Peggy here?'

'She's here Mum, so what's up?'

I called Auntie Pegs, she was in the scullery washing the floor down. I'd just finished washing up, she said she felt as though she hadn't done anything and pushed me out of the scullery and asked me to make a pot of tea for us both in the kitchen. This is what I had been doing when Mum had arrived. I had seen something pass the kitchen window out of the corner of my eye, but had taken no notice of it. When I became aware that it was Mum, I made tea for the three of us and took down from the cupboard a freshly-baked cake that Auntie Peggy had made that morning. We gathered in the sitting room by the fire. Spring it may have been, but it was still cold. Mum gratefully took a cup from me and cradled it in her hands to sip it.

'Bear with me,' she said, 'because this is going to be so difficult and some things I should have told you ages ago.'

I was now getting worried.

'You don't know, so prepare yourself for a shock Lucy. It never hit the papers and it was the best kept secret of all time. Jo-Ann had a baby while in prison. I'm so sorry, Lucy dear, however I say it, it's going to be hard on you.'

I felt I had gone white and felt weak and sick. Auntie Peggy got up and sat on the arm of my chair and put an arm over my shoulders. 'Take deep breaths Lucy, you've gone very white. I don't want you to faint on me.'

My mother continued. 'It was a difficult birth and Jo-Ann wouldn't even look at her baby when she eventually arrived, just turned her back on her. I said I would look after her, thinking that Jo-Ann would change her mind, but she hasn't as yet and I don't think she ever will. She is now three months old and I simply can't manage. She has me up every night and your father won't have anything to do with her. Jo-Ann just doesn't want to know. She isn't an easy baby and I'm exhausted.'

I looked at my mother, or rather, stared at her. There was a shocked silence, then I said in total astonishment, 'You want me to look after her don't you? That's what this visit is all about!'

'Lucy, she will have to go to an orphanage. I really can't cope. Your father... It's so difficult.'

'Barbara!' Auntie Peggy sounded appalled. 'You can't expect Lucy to look after Lewis's bastard after all he put her through and after what that dratted Jo-Ann has done. You don't know what you are asking of her.'

'But she didn't ask to be born. None of it is her fault. Everything that happened went on before she arrived,' my mother said, in a pleading voice.

Lewis and Jo-Ann. A child? I couldn't believe it. The two people I hated most in the world could still hurt me; Lewis from his grave and Jo-Ann from her prison cell. Here I was, widowed, wealthy and childless because of Lewis and Jo-Ann's indirect involvement.

'And what am I supposed to tell her when she grows up? That her mother killed her father in a fit of pique?'

'Jo-Ann killed Lewis because he wouldn't leave you to marry her. He treated her like scum that evening when she told him she was pregnant. He said he wouldn't marry a selfish tart and left earlier than usual, without paying the bill.'

'A selfish tart,' I gave a mirthless laugh. 'Well at least he got that right. So Jo-Ann killed Lewis and justified her actions by saying he wouldn't marry her and that's alright, that makes it all okay?'

'No Lucy, of course it wasn't right, it wasn't right at all what they, she did and I know it's asking a lot...'

I stood up. 'Asking a lot!' I said angrily. 'Well let me tell you something. I also got pregnant but when I was about five months gone, Lewis pushed me down the stairs. I lost my baby and probably won't be able to have any more because of the internal damage done. Three and a half years of abuse I suffered. I nearly lost my life at one point. My jaw is wired up and my arms and legs have been badly bruised and broken so often I've lost count. He stopped hitting me after my fifth stay in hospital, from then until I left he'd latched on to putting his hands round my neck and squeezing until I almost lost consciousness....' I stopped. My mother new nothing of this and looked totally horrified. 'You must think I come from another planet,' I spat out. I sighed and wiped my eyes. Talking of my baby always made me cry. In the deathly silence that followed, Auntie Pegs broke in to ask, 'Where is she now?'

'In the car, which is why it's parked just outside the front door. Believe me, if she cried we'd hear. I'll have to fetch her in soon, as she needs feeding.' She looked at Auntie Peggy. 'Can I stay here for a few days. I'm really so tired.'

I hiccupped and took a deep breath. 'I'll stay in the hotel tonight; you can have my room.'

'There is no need for that lovie,' Mother said. 'I don't like to think I've had you move out of your room.'

'Well, Reg won't be best pleased to share his bed with you and Auntie Peggy,' I said.

'Oh, I don't know,' said Auntie Peggy, trying to lighten the atmosphere, 'he might enjoy that!'

'Auntie Peggy!' I'm not sure if my laugh sounded genuine or not, 'I'm shocked.'

'You and I, Lucy, can share your room and the baby can sleep in her carrycot, though she is getting a bit big for it now.' I had to agree, it seemed churlish not to. She was my mother after all.

'I'll see if Reg can spare a cot,' Auntie Peggy said.

'A cot would be great.' Mother got up from the settee where she had been sitting. 'I'd better get her, it's got really chilly again.'

I had little to do with the baby then and didn't even look into the carrycot when Mum carried her in. I sat gazing into the fire. She took her upstairs and dealt with her there.

Auntie Peggy and I stayed downstairs. We stayed off the subject off babies; she, because she didn't want me to get upset again and me because I was seething with anger and incredible hurt and just didn't want to speak of it or I would cry again.

Reg arrived, laden with baby paraphernalia. He didn't seem at all put out by his unexpected guests but then he wouldn't and technically Crofters Cottage was still Auntie Peggy's house.

None of us slept much that night. The baby screamed solidly from 2 to 5 am! Peggy and a tired-looking Reg moved back to the Red Lion the next day. Not because of the baby; as it happened they would have gone anyway as they had only come down for a short weekend. Auntie Pegs had come the night before, Friday, so that she could spend some time with me.

This left Mother me and the baby there on our own. My mother was indeed very tired. She looked strained and had dark circles under her eyes. I suggested she go off for a rest after the baby's 2pm feed and nappy change. She agreed readily to this suggestion and leaving the baby downstairs, went up to lie on her bed.

The baby started to whimper. I didn't want to take her for a walk, as it had started to rain quite heavily but no amount of rocking the carrycot to and fro on its wheels would stop her. I had no option but to pick her up. Her whimpering stopped almost immediately and two big blue eyes looked at me and one tiny thumb entered her pretty mouth, her other hand grasped my little finger. Within minutes she was fast asleep.

That's when my love affair with my niece started.

I sat with her in my arms and just stared at her and tried to work out how I would manage if I took her on. Maybe this would make up, in some small way, for the baby I had lost. The probability of me having one of my own was very slim. But nothing, nor anything could take the place of my baby, he would always dwell in a small corner of my heart. Above all though, I argued with myself, this small scrap of humanity needed a stable and happy home life and I felt able to give her that. I would be 28 in November and getting stronger all the time. With no beatings and my body healed, I felt able to cope.

I looked at the sleeping baby and could see no likeness to Jo-Ann or Lewis in her. I bent my head over the baby and cried. I think it was for my lost baby, my failed marriage, for Lewis's appalling cruelty and Jo-Ann's deceit. It all just came to a head but I vowed never to cry again over those past events.

I cradled the baby all afternoon, it was only the squeak of the third step that alerted me to the fact that my mother was up. I dashed a hand across my face to wipe my tears away.

She entered the sitting room.

'I've had a lovely... Why Lucy, you've been crying. Look lovie, if this is what it's doing to you, I'll take her home and have her adopted.'

'No,' I gulped. 'I'll have her. I'm doing this for her and for no-one else. I can't see Jo-Ann in her or Lewis and that helps. I'll have her on one condition, that is I adopt her, legally and when Jo-Ann gets out of prison she has nothing to do with her. Ever.'

My mother looked surprise but smiled. 'I think we can agree on that. Jo-Ann really does not seem to be interested in her own baby and I'm so appalled by that.'

'What's her name?' I asked.

'I suppose you can call her what you like. I called her Chloe when I registered her, just because I liked it.'

'That suits me. I like it too,' I replied. 'Chloe, my adopted daughter. Has a nice ring to it. What surname did you register her as?'

'Alexicon,' my mother answered. 'Your father again, wouldn't have her registered in our surname. "She's Lewis Alexicon's bastard," he'd said, "and I don't want it talked about ever again."'

'Poor little girl,' I murmured.

'I'm so pleased, Lucy, I really am.'

'What else could I do for my own flesh and blood?'

The air seemed to crackle in a sudden change in the atmosphere.

'She isn't,' my mother said.

'I beg your pardon. What did you say?' I asked, puzzled.

'If you remember, I said yesterday that there were things I should have told you about ages ago.'

'Go on...' I said, levelly.

My mother put her head on one side slightly and a frown appeared on her still pretty face. 'It's difficult...'

'Start at the beginning,' I ventured, at a complete loss as to what she was going to say.

'During the war your father got wounded very badly. He was taken in by a French family who had a farm. The Resistance knew of the farm; it was at the back of beyond, miles away from anywhere. He was taken there by them. The family were really good to him. They could have been shot for harbouring a British soldier. He was kept in a hayloft. On the few occasions when Germans came to the farm for food, the family pretended to hate the British. We were already married at the time but he wrote to me saying he had fallen in love with the farmer's daughter and wanted a divorce.

I couldn't believe it. I had been worried sick about him and here he was, alive and well and asking for a divorce. The Resistance had smuggled his letter out of France. I was devastated and so angry. But... I started to see a man called Grayson. He was the younger brother of Sir Terence Stephenson. You know him as Uncle Teddy and his wife as Auntie Barbara. We fell in love and I became pregnant... with you. Lucy, lovie, Ray is not your father.'

'Go on...' I mumbled, too stunned to say much more.

'In the meantime, Sylvia Fleur, as your father's girlfriend was called, had died giving birth to Jo-Ann and Grayson was killed in that terrible war. After the war you would be two. Ray came back with Jo-Ann in tow. We talked far into the night and decided because of you two girls, to make the marriage work. We'd both been lonely and foolish but, looking back, if Fleur had lived and Jo-Ann had been a boy, I don't think your father would have come back. The farm was very big, you see, and prosperous and on his better days Ray would work on the farm. As the baby was a girl he was allowed to take her out of the country. Boys were needed to work and carry on with the farm, girls were not. That is why your father and Jo-Ann would disappear for two weeks of the year, for her French grandparents to see her. I tried not to make a difference or preference to you but I did grow to love Jo-Ann, she was such a sweet child. Unfortunately it was almost instant dislike between you and Jo-Ann from the start. Ray made no bones about his preference to Jo-Ann. At first he did try to get to know you and love you as I did but you would go all quiet on him and not speak. I spoke up for you often and told him off for using you the way he did when we got the hotel. I'm so sorry. Forgive me Lucy.'

I was lost for words on getting this news. Dumbfounded. Dazed. It was only Chloe moving in my arm that brought me back to reality.

'Why did you not tell me sooner?' I asked, once I had found my voice.

'It never seemed the right time.'

'So why now?'

'Your Uncle Teddy's father, old man Stephenson, has died and left you a small sum of money in his will. I liked him and his family and I always remained in contact. They excused my pregnancy on account of the war and were quite pleased, I think, that Grayson had been able to father a child before he was so tragically killed.'

'That's big of them,' I said, sarcastically.

'Don't be like that Lucy, they are good folk. They could have turned me out of their house without a second's thought but they looked after me until you were born and after. You have such a good memory, you must remember running around their huge garden.'

And I did. Suddenly memories came flooding back and I nodded my head.

'I remember a photograph. Me in someone's arms with Elena crying, we were having our photograph taken in a garden by Auntie Betty.'

Mother knew the photograph I was referring to.

'That was Grayson, your real Dad. You were very tiny then. He adored you. He was on leave but had to go back the day after. I never saw him again.'

'How sad that I never got to know him, that I never knew who it was who had held me in his arms. I always thought it was Ray.' I sighed. 'We lived in Redmire, though?'

'Oh yes, far safer here for the rest of the war years but we went to see them, especially when your father, sorry, Ray was away with Jo-Ann in France. You must remember my namesake Barbara. I still write to her. Our visits stopped when you were six. Ray wouldn't have it. He stopped taking Jo-Ann to France as well. He always maintained that the farm in France is where Jo-Ann picked up pleurisy and pneumonia.'

'Uncle Teddy and Auntie Barbara were there at my wedding,' I mused.

'Yes, they were.'

'Mrs Alexicon talked to them. I don't even feel so bad about Ray not being my father. Sometimes I did wonder why he didn't seem to even like me; now I understand. It must have been difficult for you.'

'Yes. He was aware that if Grayson had lived I would have happily given Ray a divorce. It wasn't easy. I really thought, at the time, that I was doing what I thought was for the best for you and me.'

'And now?' I ventured.

'I would have told Ray "no, go back to your French farm". I would have helped on the Stephenson's farm. They even offered me a cottage on the Estate. But in retrospect you always know what you should have done.'

I understood that 'in retrospect' perfectly.

'How different our lives would have been...' Mother mused. She gave a little shrug.

'While I feed Chloe I would really like you to tell me what your life has been like with Lewis. I need to know. I'm hurt and confused that Peggy and Reg seem to know more about your life than I do.'

'I'm sorry Mum. After all those years with Ray, I had to get away.'

'I do understand that. I always blamed Ray for you going. He was going to come down here and drag you back. I simply said, 'to use her as you have been doing? She would just go again.' It pained me to say it but I told him to leave you be.'

With no holds barred, keeping nothing back, I told her everything. At the end we were both in tears.

So much for my vow never to cry again over past events.

XXIV.   1969-1972

I called in on Auntie Peggy and Reg the next day. I hoped to catch them at Reg's coffee time, as I wanted to speak to both of them to tell them of my decision concerning Chloe.

Reg clumped upstairs ten minutes after Auntie Peggy called him on the intercom. We were on our second cup of coffee when he eventually arrived.

'What's up lass?' He asked.

They both remained quiet while I told them what I had in mind.

Reg was the first one to speak. 'At first I was appalled at your mother's cheek to bring down a baby in the hope that you would look after it, after all Lewis and your sister did to you, but I have had time to think on it and you're right, that child is totally innocent of its parent's crimes. You have a big and forgiving heart, Lucy. Given the circumstances, I couldn't do the same. But if you are certain, then I take my hat off to you and you will have whatever support I can offer you. What about you Pegs?'

'It's such a huge responsibility, Lucy. But if it's what you want and you want it for the right reasons, then go ahead and we will be behind you all the way.'

'The right reasons?' I queried.

'Lewis and Jo-Ann did you a great wrong.'

'Yes. But I'm not about to take it out on a defenceless baby. And it gives me a moment's pleasure to know Lewis would be furious that I have his baby to care for after all. And Chloe may be the only baby I can have. She is a lovely child – even though she screamed for most of last night!'

'I just want you to be sure, Pet, that's all. It will be grand to have a baby around us again.'

Reg harrumphed. 'Not if it screams all night.' But he was grinning when he said it.

Next, I sought out my friendly solicitor, Simon Frobisher. Simon didn't show horror or even mild surprise at what I was doing and I liked that. He said he would drawer up papers for Jo-Ann to sign. I wanted it to stipulate that Jo-Ann was to have no contact with Chloe whatsoever. He mentioned that I should contact Social Services. He said that they may have a problem with me legally adopting my ex-husbands baby.

He also asked me if Chloe had a legal guardian. I said my mother was but in truth I didn't know if she was legal or not.

He bent forward. 'On a personal subject, Lucy, and it's nothing to do with me, I know but I feel I should voice my doubt. I know this must have given you a dreadful shock on top of all the other knocks you have had. You will say that you have given this an awful lot of thought but have you?' I nodded my head. He continued. 'What you see now is a tiny, defenceless baby but what happens when she grows into a difficult and angry teenager, what then?'

'As if she was my own child I will deal with it. I shall have to. I will take it day by day and seek what guidance I can, if necessary. Reg and Peggy will be a tower of strength to me.'

'But they may not be.' Simon said. 'They may be gone.'

'True, but I do feel able to cope and with many years to live, hopefully, I hope to learn in that time how to break the news of her birth to her.'

'I've had my say. Good luck to you Lucy, my dear, what you are doing is such a kind thing to do. You're a force to be reckoned with.' He smiled. 'I'll be in touch about the papers.'

'Thank you, Simon.' I stood up, we shook hands and I walked out of his office.

Social Services didn't really want to know but did say it was a better idea for me to bring Chloe up rather than she be bought up in prison. It was a transaction that was about to be taken, with participants agreeing to the plan and she was my ex-husbands child, which helped. It was out of their boundaries. As long as the house was clean, big enough for her to have her own room and wasn't damp, they saw no problem, so things could go along as planned. Jo-Ann was the only loose cannon, as she could change her mind at any time.

My mother stayed on with me for another month and in that time she saw Jo-Ann in prison with all the documents. I think she thought my mother was going to adopt her. The papers were pushed across the table. Two jailers were present and a Justice of the Peace. He started to read his copy out to her so that she understood but she wasn't listening. Jo-Ann grabbed the papers that were on the table in front of her and signed them quickly. The two guards signed as witnesses, as did the Justice of the Peace. Jo-Ann merely said, 'The brat's gone then.' A statement not a question.

'Don't you want to know who is having her?' Mum asked.

Jo-Ann shrugged her shoulders. 'I assumed you were having her, or give her to Lucy, if it's what she wants. I don't really care.'

'I can't believe that you are so uncaring about your own baby.'

'She gave me a terrible time when she was born. Why should I want her?'

'Well, that was hardly her fault, was it?' Mum had snapped at her.

Jo-Ann just looked at her. 'You don't know the half of it.'

'Fortunately, I don't want to.' Mum answered. 'I'll go then, if the business is completed.' Jo-Ann got up from her chair, leaned forward to give Mum a kiss on the cheek, then turned smartly and with her jailers following in her wake, she stalked out.

Mum recounted it all to me and added, 'I thought I saw tears in her eyes.'

I found that hard to believe.

Jo-Ann had three months to change her mind before the final papers were signed. They were difficult months for me. In that time Jo-Ann could demand Chloe back and I would have to hand her over.

Chloe screamed for three hours every night. I thought it must be my fault because I was so jittery in case I got a phone call to say that Jo-Ann had changed her mind. But nothing happened. In those months, whenever Auntie Peggy and Reg came down to the cottage I would go to their flat above the Red Lion so that they wouldn't be disturbed by Chloe's crying. It wasn't fair that their treasured weekend should be ruined by a yelling baby. A cot was always up and ready for Chloe in a tiny bedroom (not much bigger than a box room) and I would have their other spare bedroom.

At least no-one in the hotel would hear her, although she had a powerful pair of lungs, The flat above the Red Lion Pub was far away from the guest rooms of the hotel.

On Sunday, I would join them for lunch and we could spend the day together. Sometimes Auntie Peggy would stay on to give me a break but I would still hear Chloe yelling at night.

As I had said that Mum was the baby's guardian, she had to return to see Jo-Ann again, to do the completion on my adopting Chloe. This time Simon Frobisher drove her in to Durham Jail to give her moral support. The same JP attended and the original two guards.

Mum reported that, like before, Jo-Ann just grabbed the papers and signed them without hesitation, then each of the others signed the documents, including Simon.

'I hope she gives Lucy heaps of trouble.'

'You're so nasty Jo-Ann. Right to the end,' Mum said and strode to the door. Simon bent forward to pick up the papers and gave Jo-Ann a hard stare that made her look away, then followed Mother to open the door for her and the JP.

Apparently, Jo-Ann called after her 'Mum...'

Mother said she looked back and said, 'You're no daughter of mine Jo-Ann, remember that.'

Jo-Ann had given a sort of shrug, muttered 'sorry' and turned to her jailers, who escorted her out.

Mum said Simon was very professional and a really nice man. He had left his professional hat behind when he suggested a cup of tea before heading back. Mum had gratefully agreed but first she said that she must ring me to let me know the news. She simply said, 'Chloe is yours. I'll tell you all when I get back. Simon and I are having a cup of tea first.' Auntie Peggy was with me and I burst into tears with relief. We held each other, the odd sniffle coming from her too. Then she said she must ring Reg to let him know the wonderful news. I heard his familiar voice yell down the phone, 'Congratulations! We need to celebrate.'

Mum and Simon Frobisher had chatted quite happily in the café he had taken her to. She admits she told him quite a lot about me and Jo-Ann. He seemed interested and attentive. I certainly didn't mind that. He wasn't going to make it public knowledge; that would be against his principles.

Once Jo-Ann had signed the final papers, I suppose I became more relaxed. Again I was in the Red Lion flat and woke up one morning to find it was six o'clock and realized that Chloe had slept through the night. This was a great turning point. It wasn't every night from then on that she stopped waking and screaming but in two months it had stopped altogether. She had started to smile as well when I went to get her. She became a happy and contented little girl, so pretty and sweet. I adored her.

I went up to Richmond to see Carol, who I hadn't seen for ages. She was totally confined to her chair now and Tommy was around too; it was his day off. He was a changed man. From his porters job at the Red Lion Hotel he had been promoted to bar staff. This gave him more wages. He could take orders and pour the drinks but adding them up was a problem, so he got himself a small calculator that he had with him at all times and rarely made a mistake. He still had his bad days but he was a whole lot better. Carol was very proud of him. She had Chloe on her lap for a while and thought her very sweet. Chloe recognised Tommy, who had always picked her up to give her a cuddle whenever he had been around if I called in at the hotel. I didn't stay long, as I didn't want to tire Carol out. I was sad to see her looking so poorly.

I had to refuse Major Hugh Towers' offer of being a trustee on the board of the Charity for Abused Wives at The Priory, as now I had the responsibility of Chloe. I hadn't been able to visit as often as I would have liked but I took Chloe with me when I did.

From its start, the house was full of abused wives and lots of kids, some who had been abused too. But on the whole it was a happy place. Lewis's study had been turned into a 'quiet room' (which had a certain irony to it) where the women could go who wanted some peace and alone time. His study was lined with bookshelves on two sides. An awkward woman called Grace took it over and turned it into a library. It was open for two days a week for two hours. As each book was taken out, it would have a number put into it and then its number was put into an exercise book with the title, the author's name and who had borrowed it. She got them eventually in alphabetical order. It had taken her weeks to sort through all the books.

Grace taking over the library had come about because squabbles were taking place. Mrs Ebson was treated no better than a skivvy and Milly, the cook, found herself detailed to prepare the vegetables and keep the kitchen clean. The entire house was beginning to look a bit grubby and uncared for. I felt very let down. One of the things they argued about was not being able to get to use one the of the six washing machines when they wanted to, as they were constantly in use. Kitty Mason, one of the three managers who took it in turns to stay at the house for a day, said could I have a word with them.

'Me! Speak to them? What on earth can I say to grown women?'

'Whatever comes to mind; it just might help.'

I was very unsure about this but said I would have a word. It was arranged for me to give them a 'talk' one day at ten o'clock I would have to ask Auntie Peggy to have Chloe for that day. She was always so excited about having her to look after.

I arranged to see them all in the drawing room. They wandered in, some arrived late and some were obviously cross and others just lost and unhappy with their lot. I was introduced as 'Mrs Alexicon (most knew but there was a couple of newcomers), the person who owns this lovely house.' I stood up, feeling apprehensive and nervous. I had never spoken in public before, not even to a small group of people.

'I do understand that things are difficult for you,' I began, 'but I think it's very sad that ten women can't agree on a few basic things. If you don't find a washing machine vacant, then start a rota. Washing doesn't have to be done on a Monday. Mrs Ebson is threatening to leave as she is treated no better than a skivvy. She is here to help you, not do all the cleaning work herself. I'm disappointed, as the place looks decidedly grubby and uncared for. I thought the idea was that you would not just keep your rooms clean and tidy but the common rooms as well. Those of you who don't like cleaning – and who really does? – could help Joseph in the garden, perhaps, or do something else. The children don't seem too happy either. They have come from one abusive household to another with their mothers arguing between themselves. I thought, my romantic idea, silly really, was the thought that you'd always help each other, be there for each other, help newcomers through the frightening first few days. Milly Franks isn't happy either. She's almost been shoved out of her kitchen. You've no idea how these two women were looking forward to starting their new jobs. Frankly, I'm disappointed. Having all been through the mill, I thought that would form a bond between you all...'

I paused to take a breath. This is when Grace stood up.

'And what would you know? You're nothing but a rich bitch.' It went very quiet. I even heard Kitty Mason's sudden indrawn breath. Other women were nodding and agreeing with Grace.

I didn't sit down defeated. I stood my ground and said, 'I'm a battered wife too, Grace.'

There was a sudden hush. 'What? Just a few scratches makes you a battered wife?' She mocked.

'Come with me, all of you,' I said, and marched out of the room. I didn't look back to see if anyone was following me. I knew they would; they would be too curious not to.

I stood at the bottom of the stairs. The women grouped around me, expectantly.

'Grace, humour me. Go up to the top of the stairs.'

She looked daggers at me.

'Go on Grace!' Someone said. She gave me another filthy look but climbed to the top of the stairs and turning, said, 'What now?' in a bored voice.

'Just come down one step, would you please?' She did this and looked at me again with an insolent look on her face. 'And...?'

'Fling yourself downstairs,' I said.

She looked aghast. 'Don't be daft. It's a long way down and there's tiles on the floor. I'd kill myself. What do you take me for?'

'*Scratches* you say. I fell from where your standing, Grace, right to the bottom. My husband pushed me down those stairs when I was almost five months pregnant. I lost my baby, of course. He couldn't bear the thought that I might love the baby more than I loved him. I was married to him for no more than three and a half years. He put me in hospital six times. My jaw is wired up and I have sustained such injuries as broken arms and legs so often I have lost count. Once I very nearly lost my life and I have such internal injuries that I may never have a baby of my own. And in case you are all wondering, the lovely Chloe is adopted. And that's "scratches" is it Grace? I suggest you come down the stairs carefully. I wouldn't want you to fall.'

There was dead silence amongst the women, most looked embarrassed and awkward, they shuffled back into the drawing room to await my return.

Grace looked chastened when she came down the stairs. 'Eighteen steps from top to bottom,' she said, and sat on the second step up. Her feet were wide apart and she rested her elbows on her knees and put her head in her hands.

'Me and my big gob.' She sighed and stood up. 'Mrs Alexicon, I'm so sorry. I... my mouth gets going before my brains are in gear. I'd die without my kids. They were my reason for staying with my husband. Then he started on my oldest and I couldn't stand for that.'

'Join us in the drawing room, if you feel like it.' I said. Then I turned on my heel and headed back into the sitting room. As I entered, each women stood up and started clapping and cheering. Someone was giving loud, piercing whistles. Emotional as I was, it was almost my undoing but I managed to stay tear free and in control of myself.

A month later, I visited again, taking Chloe with me. She was made such a fuss of. The house was spick and span with not a spot of dust anywhere. I found that one woman loved polishing brass and silver. Another approached me, asking if she could make jams and pickles and yet someone else asked if they could start a small playgroup for the youngsters. Grace spoke to me about her burning desire to sort the library out. Mrs Ebson's round face was smiling as she came to greet me and Milly Franks was at the helm again in her kitchen.

What I think helped was not my talk but that I was 'one of them', being a battered wife too. Someone had devised a rota for the use of the washing machines and three women were helping Joseph in the garden. They showed me what they intended to do.

To the side of the garages, beyond the back drive, there was quite a large area of land, it was newly dug, as they wanted to start a vegetable and a soft fruit garden. 'We can't afford all the fresh fruit for Edith to make her jams so we thought we'd grow it.' They said. They had been sensible enough to ask Joseph for his advice; they didn't want him to feel left out.

'Green fingers, they women, they can grow anything.' He'd said to me, when I had sought him out to ask how things were going.

'Great, smashing.' His friend had said.

Everyone seemed a lot happier. A sweet 'mumsy' woman had been voted in to help any newcomers settle in, who was also happy to have the other women just talk to her.

I kept in regular contact by going once a month and I used to come back with baskets of fruit, vegetables and then even eggs. The hens were kept in a wired compound at the end of the garden just beyond the vegetable patch. Life for these women had improved tenfold and the children seemed happier too. What really put a smile on their faces was when I hired two security guards after an incident occurred. Mandy's husband (Mandy was the woman who liked polishing brass and silver) had tried to enter the house. Joseph's friend, Eddie, had rugby-tackled him, then had sat his considerable weight on top of him until the police arrived. All they could do was hustle him out of the grounds, take him to the local police station, caution him with trespassing on private land and tell him if he did it again he would be prosecuted.

One guard was a black guy called Bill Sandy the other was a retired ex-policeman; his name was Greg Watson. Bill didn't seem to have a home to go to and on his time off he used to organise the kids into two teams, one team would go off into the woods to hide, the other team, once 100 was counted would try to find them or he would get them playing football; he'd include the girls in this as well. No-one was allowed near the lake unless they were accompanied by an adult. Bill would help get the kids to make rafts and they would have races across the lake. He taught some of them to swim. He'd take them on route marches around the perimeter of the grounds. With pieces of cloth picked up from market stalls he made them wigwams and make-do tents. They were quite scared of him at first but soon the children learned to trust him and look forward to his days off. They had fun and learned to laugh again.

I heard about him and promoted him to entertainments manager. He was well chuffed. He used to go off one day a week for a few hours and when he came back he would look a bit down for a while, or so the women told me; they wondered where he went.

But he was marvellous with those kids.

Life progressed for me. We went through a trying teething time with Chloe but I had no regrets about adopting her. I loved dressing her up in pretty little dresses, little white socks and white sandals, not that she stayed clean for long as she was a bit of a tomboy. Auntie Peggy and Reg adored her. Her first step, her first word and I'd be on the phone to Auntie Peggy to tell her. Chloe was my joy, as she was theirs. She was as pretty as a picture and had big blue eyes that seemed to have an inner sparkle and her hair was more my colour, blonde, not Jo-Ann's red.

At two years of age, I booked Chloe into a playgroup. Just two mornings a week at first, but this progressed to three as she loved it so much, then, when she was three, I booked her in for a full day midweek, to see how she would cope with that. Although tired after her first full day, she thrived on it and liked the food. But food was no problem with Chloe, she would eat almost anything I put before her.

Then one day I had a visitor...

XXV. 1972

I had just collected Chloe from Infants school. She had been skipping along ahead and suddenly started limping.

'I think I have a thtone in my thandal Mummy.'

'We'll be at the hotel in a jiffy Sweetheart. I'll sort it out then.' She waited until I got to her and, half carrying her, we walked into the Red Lion Hotel.

I sat in the reception area on the seat where Grandad and Auntie Peggy had sat on many occasions. I'd undone her left sandal and found a small stone lodged inside by the seam. I shook it out onto my hand and put it in the ashtray on the table next to me. As I bent down to put her sandal back on again, someone came through the swing doors. I didn't look up, busy as I was doing Chloe's sandal up. A pair of highly-polished shoes came into my view and a familiar voice said. 'I'll give you a clue... ice creams.'

I smiled. I didn't look up but only looked at Chloe's feet.

'Well here is another one... trains.'

I peeped up at him. 'Matt, how lovely to see you again.' I was slightly shaken at his reappearance.

'Reg said you were here. He sent me through to see you.'

'I didn't think you would want to see me again after the way I treated you.' My heart seemed to miss a beat.

He stooped down on to his hunkers and took Chloe's hand.

'How do you do,' he said, most politely. 'And what is your name?'

'Chloe.' She whispered. With strangers she is a little shy at first.

'That's a very pretty name for a very pretty girl and very like Mummy.'

'Far nicer.' I said.

He stood up and looked me in the eyes. 'Not here but later, we need to talk. Just talk. Come out to dinner with me?'

'At the Sandpipers?' I asked.

Matt lifted an eyebrow and threw his hands out slightly. 'Where else?'

'I can't give you an answer right now. I need to ask my aunt to see if she would have Chloe for the night.'

'I understand.' He said. He looked older, more mature but then so was I. My affection for Matt was still there. By the look in his eyes I could see that, despite all, he still loved me.

Auntie Peggy said she would love to have Chloe for the night and I could either sleep in their flat or go back to Crofters Cottage. She picked Chloe up. 'My little McCarthy Michaelmas Daisy.' And she cuddled her.

'Thath not my name, Auntie Peggy. Ith Chloe.' She lisped.

'Well to me, your just McCarthy Michaelmas Daisy.' Auntie Peggy started to make little chomping noises round her neck. 'I could eat you.' This was almost a ritual between them and it always made Chloe giggle and wriggle.

'I'll give her supper, get her bathed and ready for bed, if you could read her a story?' I asked.

'That will be lovely. You choose the book.' She was looking at Chloe, then looked at me 'I love having her, you know I do.'

'I know Auntie Pegs, I just don't want you to think that I'm taking advantage of you.'

Reg came puffing upstairs. 'Matt's downstairs and wants to know if it's alright for tonight?'

I ran downstairs and arrived breathless in the Reception area.

'Yes, Matt, they will be happy to have Chloe.'

'I'll pick you up about 7.30 if that's alright?'

'Perfect.' I said, smiling happily. 'I'll see you later.'

I ran back upstairs again. Auntie Peggy was just saying to Reg, 'We've got Chloe for the night, Reggie, isn't that grand?'

'Bags I read her a bedtime story. Just call when it's time.' And he clumped off downstairs again.

I made enough bubble and squeak to feed a small army. It was one of Reg's favourite suppers. He could have had any fancy meal he wanted from the kitchens downstairs but that was still his favourite. He'd even had it added to the menu as a side dish. Auntie Pegs and I were surprised at how often it was chosen. He and Auntie Pegs would have theirs later when Chloe was in bed. He liked his with pickles and cold meat. I made an indent in Chloe's little portion and put in a poached egg. It was a good way to get vegetables into her, especially if I was able to get it golden brown and crisp on the outside.

I sat with her and told her a little story. She'd heard it before but liked this tale, as it involved her.

'There was once a pretty little girl called McCarthy Michaelmas Daisy.' Chloe squealed her delight. 'Ith me and I'm called Chloe!'

'Well in this story you are called McCarthy Michaelmas Daisy and eat up or it will get cold. McCarthy Michaelmas Daisy had two Mummies but one Mummy was a naughty girl and the other...' I pointed at myself. 'Was a lovely, lovely Mummy.' I pretended to preen myself.'

Chloe grinned, 'But thometimth you get croth.'

'I need to get cross when you won't eat your tea and will you stop interrupting and eat up those peas? I know you like them. Now where was I? Oh yes but sometimes she would get cross if McCarthy Michaelmas Daisy was naughty or wouldn't eat up her tea. When she was a tiny, tiny baby her naughty Mummy couldn't look after her and that's how you came to live with me.'

When she had munched on her last forkful of peas, I passed her the biscuit plate. She had a good appetite but talked too much, causing her food to get cold and her to be slow, which is why I told her stories at mealtimes. I poured her a glass of milk. 'Now half an hour of T.V. while I have a bath, then I will tuck you up in bed.'

'Excuth me, may I get down?'

'You may.' I answered. The story forgotten, television being far more interesting, she sat on the sofa, tight up to Auntie Peggy. They watched a children's programme together. I'm sure Auntie Pegs was enthralled with it! I wanted my evening with Matt to be really special. I took great care with my appearance that night. I wore a new silk dress, it was in blue, with matching high heeled sandals. I wore the only piece of jewellery I owned. It had once belonged to Mrs Alexicon. She had given it to me as she said that the beads matched the colour of my eyes. I'd kept it back when I had auctioned everything else off at Christies. It was its colour that I liked rather than its monetary value. It matched the colour of my dress perfectly. I felt good and was on a high with expectation. I bathed Chloe in my dressing gown. I was running a bit late but Chloe was my main concern and Matt would have to wait. I was sure he wouldn't mind.

I left Chloe in bed, having a story read to her by Reg. He did all the different voices and I could hear her laughing. I popped in to say goodnight. 'My lass, you do look nice.' Reg said. Matt's downstairs waiting.'

Auntie Peggy was sitting on a chair on the other side of the bed; she looked happy and relaxed. 'You look lovely,' she said. 'Have a good time.'

'Be a good girl Chloe and I'll see you all tomorrow,' I said. I kissed all three goodnight and hastened out.

Matt looked at me when I met him in reception area and gave me such a sweet smile and did the slightest nod of his head, as if in approval. Once out of the hotel and down the hotel's drive, he took my arm.

'Because,' he said, 'in those shoes and these cobbles, you might trip up.'

The Sandpipers was no more than 100 hundred yards down the street. We dawdled, not saying anything, just happy to be in each other's company. Once we were sitting down I said, 'Matt...' savouring his name on my tongue. 'I just want to apologise to you for behaving towards you the way I did. I made totally the wrong decision and believe me I paid for it.'

'You were bowled over by a wealthy, good-looking man.'

'The wealthy part I really didn't know about, not to the full extent, otherwise, yes, maybe I was but then I didn't know what your intentions were. You never said. When we came back from being out you never made another date or even mentioned how you felt.'

'And how I regret that. Tell me what it was like for you being married to Lewis Alexicon?'

'I can't. I'd really rather not just yet. I tend to get rather emotional about it all. But one day in the future I'll tell you all you want to know. That is if there is going to be a future for us.'

'You can bet your boots on that. I ain't gonna let another guy walk off with my gal again. But let's eat, I'm starving. I've not eaten all day.'

I had salmon steaks in a lovely creamy sauce, with buttered and minted new potatoes and carrots. Matt had the old favourite steak and kidney pie. We both opted to have the lemon meringue pie. After our meal we took our drinks outside. We sat on benches facing each other. He took my hand and started talking.

'I was deeply hurt and told myself that I hated you. But out of the blue your face would come to mind and I knew I still loved you. Then I realized that it was partly my fault I'd had that ring in my pocket for ages without the courage to ask you to marry me.'

'It must have been a shock when I told you I was marrying Lewis.'

'Yes!' He nodded his head 'It was but that's behind me now, it's gone and a lesson to be learned. Don't hang around. I threw myself into work and took out just about every girl I came into contact with. But none seemed to grab my attention for long. I would take each one out just three times but I'd quickly find out that they weren't the girl for me. Just one black-haired girl I had a fancy for but realized I couldn't ask her to marry me when I still loved another, even though I thought she was lost to me by marrying someone else.'

'I'm sorry Matt, so sorry.'

He turned my right hand over and started to trace my lifeline with his finger. 'You have to stop saying you're sorry, Lucy. I love you. I always have and always will. I'm a one woman guy. I feel that maybe, I have been given another chance but that is up to you and if you are prepared to give me that chance...'

'Shouldn't it be me saying that?' I asked. 'I would certainly like to go out with you again. But I need to ask you to give me time. I've been to hell and back and don't want to rush headlong into another affair, no matter how permanent it might become.

Then there is Chloe and she has to be my first concern. This may sound brutal, I know but you need to understand the position I'm in and do you want to take me on again, when things have changed slightly.'

'By a little girl, who is sweet and pretty, just like her Mum.' He said softly. 'I don't think that changes anything. I'd accept a herd of baboons living with us if I thought I had a chance to be with you.'

I let that go about him thinking that I was Chloe's mother. I'd tell him that at a more appropriate time.

'I still have your ring. It's in Reg's safe.'

Matt looked surprised. 'I thought it would have been thrown out a long time ago.'

'Oh Matt, I could never have done that.'

'Well then wear it to tell me your ready.'

'Ready for what?' I asked.

'When you are ready to be my wife. I knew when I met you on that train, that one day you would mean a great deal to me. I was struck by your eyes.'

I was silent for a moment, then I whispered, 'Was there really that little girl with such high hopes and dreams?'

Suddenly, I started to cry. Matt looked concerned. He got up to sit next to me and put an arm round me.

'What is it, Lucy? What have I said to upset you? I know, I know, I've rushed you.'

I was unable to tell him, I hardly knew myself. Eventually I hiccupped to a stop.

'S... Sorry. I can't even give you a straight answer as to why I should cry, because I don't know. I think I've just found it so emotional.'

Matt slipped away, back into the Sandpipers and came back again with a brandy.

'Sip it slowly, it will make you feel better.' He said gently. When I reached for the brandy my hand was shaking. I don't really like it neat but I did as he told me and sat sipping it, saying nothing until it was gone. His arm was around me again shielding my messed up face and red eyes from the world. I felt safe and comfortable. I sighed and lent into him.

'I promise you, that if you give me this chance, I'll make every effort to make you very happy. Now, I think I should get you home.'

I could only nod my head.

He walked me slowly back to the Red Lion Hotel, holding my hand all the way.

The next day I asked Reg if Matt's ring was still in the safe.

'Aye lass, it's not been moved. Do you want it?'

'I'd just like to see it, again.' I had been waiting in the office for him to come downstairs to collect the post, just to ask him to open the safe for me. He fetched it for me.

'It'd slipped down to the bottom of the safe, I thought for a moment it had gone.'

The little box looked so small as I held it in my hand. I pressed the button to spring the lid open and there it lay in its velvet nest. It sparkled in the morning sun.

'You alright, lass?' Reg asked.

I smiled. 'I'm fine Reg. Truly fine. I haven't felt better.'

He touched my shoulder as he went by.

'Join Pegs, Chloe and me for breakfast. I left her making it, I just came down for the post.'

'Thank you, I'll be up in a minute.' Reg dropped the safe keys on the desk. 'For you to put back if you want to.' Then he turned and I could hear him clump upstairs to his flat.

I touched the sparkling ring and took it out of its little box, I put it on my ring finger.

If anything it was slightly too big. I admired it greatly. Three diamond in a row set on a gold shank. Nothing like the big brash one I'd got from Lewis. I preferred this one but then, I could be biased of course. Truthfully I didn't want to take it off but I did and put it back in its box. I held it to my lips for a moment then snapped the lid closed and put it back into the safe. I locked the safe and went upstairs to join Auntie Pegs, Reg and my darling daughter for breakfast.

XXVI.　1972

My relationship with Matt went from strength to strength. Chloe nearly always came with us wherever we went. I took him down to Crofters Cottage. Matt was charmed with it. We walked down to the river and took a picnic with us another day. I took them beyond the falls, it's a bit of a climb but Chloe is like a mountain goat, very sure on her feet. Matt was a bit winded by the time we got there. The water is much deeper and we were able to have a swim. Chloe had her rubber ring with her and just splashed about in the shallows. On another day we walked to the tiny church along a very narrow lane. I got Reg to drive us to Aysgarth, a village up beyond Redmire, to see the magnificent falls there, then do the riverside walk back to Redmire. Chloe ran on ahead but ran out of steam. Matt picked her up and she sat on his shoulders. He hung on to her red wellies. She liked that. It's a seven mile walk back to Redmire and our picnic area and a further mile to the cottage. We had supper and I settled Chloe off for the night without any trouble, she was deadbeat. Matt and I remained downstairs. I went to bed once he had gone home but it was getting harder to let him go, to be apart and with the long lingering kisses, I knew he felt the same.

We went away for the weekend for me to meet his mother. Auntie Peggy offered to have Chloe. She was given the choice, she chose to stay with Auntie Pegs and Reg. If she had come with us she knew she would have to be on her best behaviour. Matt's mother was a sweet, white-haired lady, fiercely proud of her son. His father had been killed in the war and she had never remarried. We were put in separate bedrooms to meet again at breakfast the following morning. It was a lovely weekend; she made me feel very welcome.

Matt courted me, in the true sense of the word. Gradually, I relaxed and one day took the ring out of the safe for good. I didn't wear it but asked Matt down to Crofters Cottage for a meal. Chloe again was given the choice to come with me or have a more exciting time with Auntie Pegs and Reg. She loved staying with them simply because they spoilt her and that's what her choice was; for once I was pleased with her decision.

I spent a lot of time preparing the meal. I did avocado pears with the centres filled with prawns and pink dressing set on a little green salad. Then roast lamb with a garlic and breadcrumb topping. I chose carrots (for colour) peas and cauliflower as the vegetables. I made my own cheesecake for a sweet and a selection of cheeses to go with the biscuits. Coffee, I hoped to have later in the sitting room. I got candles and used Auntie Peggy's best linen with matching serviettes. When I was satisfied with the end result, I went along the passageway beyond the sitting room to have a bath, then upstairs I chose my deep blue sheath dress that is mid-calf length, in silk. I brushed my hair and pinned it up and wore my favourite necklace, the one Mrs Alexicon had given me. I surveyed myself in a full-length mirror in my bedroom and was pleased with how I looked. I had a bit of colour in my cheeks and I did look well.

Matt arrived promptly at seven. He was enchanted with everything. The old range was alight and sparkled as I had black leaded it that day and a fire was laid in the sitting room for later.

It was such a romantic evening. Matt carved the lamb for me and ate all I put in front of him with relish. I don't think he noticed that I didn't eat much. I was too filled with nervous anticipation.

Afterwards we cleared away and washed up together in the scullery. He lit the fire in the sitting room while I made the coffee and put all the dishes away. There I joined him with a tray of coffee. We sat one each side of the fire, like any married couple. Talk was easy but then it always had been. But he was no fool.

'That meal was fabulous,' he said, 'but I noticed you didn't eat much.'

'I cooked it and didn't feel hungry.' I said.

He leaned forward. 'What's worrying you?'

I smiled lazily at him and got up from my chair. I picked the ring up, still in its box from the mantelpiece and knelt down in front of him.

'Matt, do you love me?'

He looked serious and surprised. 'You know I do Lucy, so much. What's this all about?' I opened my hand and the little ring box sat on the flat of my palm. He stared at it, then looked at my smiling face.

'Humour me Matt. I so much want to marry you. But I want you to ask me properly.'

He did that funny little salute that he does. 'Yes ma'am.' He said. He took the little box from my outstretched hand and pushed the little button to make the box open. He stood up and I sat in the chair he had just vacated. He took the ring out of the box, went down on one knee and said simply. 'Will you marry me?' said a little unsteadily, I thought. I bent forward and took his face between my hands. I looked him in the eyes. 'I would love to, my darling.'

'Oh Lucy,' he murmured. He took my left hand in his and slipped the ring onto my ring finger. He kissed the finger with the ring on it. He stood up and pulled me up from my chair. He put his hands on my shoulders and pulled me to him. He bent his head slowly and took possession of my mouth in one beautiful heart stopping kiss. His hands slid round me and he crushed me to him.

'I love you so much,' he said, before kissing me again. Eventually he said, 'I can't wait too long for this marriage to take place.'

'Too much time has already been wasted,' I murmured.

'Can you manage it in three weeks' time?' He asked.

I laughed gently, looking up at him. 'Silly,' I said, 'the banns have to be read and that takes care of three weeks and that's only if we can see the vicar as soon as possible.

But after that... oh yes please!'

We kissed again. We were getting carried away with our emotions. I could feel his hardness pressing against my thigh. I pushed him away and put my fingers on his mouth.

'Matt, my darling, listen. I am no virgin, as you know, but despite that I would like to wait for our wedding night. Do you mind? Do you understand?'

'Yes Lucy. I do understand and I'll do what you ask. Although I really want you, now, here, this minute but I'll wait my darling, I'll wait.'

'Just a few weeks, Matt, that's all. Let's go back to Leyburn and tell Auntie Peggy and Reg, that's what they did to me when they got engaged and it was 2.30 in the morning. This is payback time!' I laughed. 'Come on.'

Matt smiled. 'Good idea. If we stay here it's putting temptation in my way.'

'Put the fireguard in front of the fire while I fetch a jacket.'

I raced up the stairs to get it. I was so excited.

Auntie Peggy was already in bed. Reg was just locking up. He saw our smiling faces through the clear glass of the side door to the hotel. He smiled back and unlocked the door again.

'What time do you call this?' He grumbled good naturedly.

'Where's Auntie Peggy?' I asked.

'Where you should be, young lady, in bed. Go on up Lucy. Matt, a word please.'

I ran upstairs, along the passageway to Auntie Peggy and Reg's room and knocked on the door.

'Come in,' she called. I went in. she had been reading but put her book down and took in my smiling face.

'About time! Reg and I have been expecting this for weeks!' She took my left hand to look at the ring. 'It's so pretty and it's very like mine.'

'We want to get married as soon as possible.'

'You're not...?'

'Pregnant?' I finished for her. 'No I'm not.'

'How soon is 'as soon as possible'?' Auntie Peggy asked.

'Once the banns have been read.'

'Heavens! That doesn't give us much time to organise things.'

'I just want a small wedding like you and Reg had. I'm officially a widow and it's Matt's first time, so we can marry in Redmires church, unless he wants a big affair.'

'Where are the menfolk anyway?'

'Reg wanted to have a word with Matt.'

'Oh no! He's not asking him what his intentions are and what his prospects are, is he?' We both laughed. Just then Reg and Matt came in. Matt was carrying champagne flutes and Reg was carrying the bubbly.

It was just like the other occasion when they had announced their engagement to me in the middle of the night. I looked at Auntie Peggy and she gave me a slight nod of her head, she was remembering too. Then we all sat on the bed, drinking champagne and talking. They drank to our health and happiness and we drank to theirs.

'What's the timescale, lass?' Asked Reg.

'As soon as the banns are read,' I replied.

'You're not...?'

'Don't you start. I've just had that from Auntie Peggy!'

'Chance would be a fine thing,' Matt said morosely, which made us all laugh.

My laugh turned into a yawn that set us all off.

'Time for bed.' Said Reg. 'You can sleep in bedroom three if you want to Matt.'

'Thank you, that's kind of you, Sir but I think I'll push off home and tell the news to Mum.' He looked at me. 'She will be so pleased.'

'Before you go, we have some news too. We're selling up. I want to be able to spend more time with Pegs. We should get a tidy sum for this place and we would like to travel a bit before we get too old to want to. We'll keep Crofters Cottage as our permanent home, where we can come back to between times.'

'Wow Reg, you certainly choose your moments. How far have you got with selling up?'

'Nowhere as yet. We wanted to tell you first, give you first refusal if you're interested?'

'Reg! I could never run this place on my own.' I protested.

'You almost did seven or eight years ago,' he argued.

'Reg, I didn't. I never did the books, the wages, the ordering, you did that and that took you all your time. I can organise, I make a good receptionist but that's all.'

'Matt?' Reg turned to him.

'I'm a banker, Sir, a financier.'

'Well I couldn't think of anything better, put the two of you together and you've got a working team.'

'We could never afford it,' Matt said.

Reg looked at me. 'Haven't you told Matt anything?'

'We talk all the time,' I replied, deliberately missing the point.

'You know what I mean,' Reg said in 'his' voice.

'I will Reg, I promise. But not tonight. I don't want anything to spoil tonight.'

'Aye, well, think on,' Reg growled.

'I'm sorry about the hotel.' I looked at Matt. 'My first and only job was here. I'll miss it. Reg believed in me, even more than I did myself,' I sighed. 'I'll bid you both goodnight. If I take the keys, Reg, I'll lock up after Matt's gone.'

He passed me the keys. I kissed both of them goodnight and escorted Matt out. We passed Chloe's bedroom and both crept in. She lay fast asleep, looking like an angel. I bent forward and gently kissed her. Matt simply stroked her cheek with his index finger. 'Such a lovely little girl,' he whispered. I closed the door very quietly and we headed downstairs.

'I'm missing something here.' He said. 'What is it you have to tell me?'

'I'm frightened it might make you change your mind.'

'Nothing will make me change my mind about marrying you and you'd better believe that. Anyway, I can't imagine you've done something so terrible.'

'It just changes things. I will tell you, but not tonight Matt, I don't want to spoil this lovely night.'

'Now you have me worried.'

'If you love me enough, we will overcome it.' I kissed him on his lips and put my arms round him. 'Just remember I love you.'

He held me tightly. 'That's the first time that you have said that.'

'How remiss of me. I'll just have to tell you all the time then, won't I?'

'Yes please.' We kissed again and had to drag ourselves apart. Could I keep this 'no sex' going until we were married? I doubted it then.

'Drive carefully.' I begged.

'Don't worry, if you noticed I didn't have much to drink tonight. My happiness will keep me awake. I only have to drive to Richmond; it's not far.'

He didn't kiss me again, it was better that he didn't, he went out of the door and I locked it behind him, we blew kisses to each other and I watched him drive away.

He was back again the following day. It was a Wednesday and he had the whole day off. I'd stayed at the flat overnight but had gone back to Crofters Cottage earlier. Chloe, at three-and-a-half was doing her midweek full day and I had taken her there before heading back to the cottage. Auntie Peggy or Reg must have told Matt where I was. When I opened the door to him, he smiled and threw his arms out. I dragged him in the front door and let him enfold me in a bear hug and a passionate kiss. 'I didn't know you had today off, you never said.'

'I've taken a lieu day. I've worked over a few Saturday mornings, this is in exchange for them.'

'I was just clearing up bits and pieces from last night and I've just washed the tablecloth and the napkins we used. Then I was going to put the fire on and settle down with a good book and probably nod off.'

'Oh well, if you'd rather do that, I can just start back again.'

'Not on your life!' I said, laughing up at him.

'You put the kettle on and I'll start the fire.'

'Okay, good idea. You get your fires to go first time. It would take me ages to get it going.'

Within half an hour we had a blazing fire going and were into our second cup of tea. Matt was tucking into a cake I had made a day or two before. 'What did your Mum say?'

'She is delighted, she really is. She likes you. She thought that you were just a bit skinny. I went to sleep with a smile on my face.'

He munched on his second slice of cake. 'I think we have to decide where we are going to live. Richmond would be my first choice. What about you?'

I leaned back in my armchair. 'I've been so happy here. But this is Auntie Peggy's house and this is the place they will come back to between their travels. Would this area be too far away for you to go to work?'

'It depends on the traffic, of course. It takes, what, half an hour to get from Leyburn to Richmond? Then another 20 minutes to get here. Under an hour travelling time isn't bad.'

'But it does get cut off in bad weather. So maybe we should think again.' I mused. 'I wouldn't mind living in Leyburn. Anywhere, really, as long as I'm with you. You are all I want.' I looked at him and smiled lazily. 'I'm so lucky in having you.'

'I thought I was the lucky one and don't look at me like that, it gives me naughty thoughts.'

He bent forward and picked up the poker to stir the coals with. I had a sudden flashback and shivered.

He noticed 'Are you cold?' He asked.

'No, no.' I said. 'Reg said last night that we need to talk, or rather I need to and I suppose this is a good a time as any.' I paused, collecting my thoughts. I started way back to what happened after Auntie Peggy's wedding. He didn't interrupt but looked horrified.

'I really think that if Mum hadn't been there Jo-Ann would have killed me. Mum took the blow from that same poker that you're holding that broke her arm. Anyway Jo-Ann is now in prison for 21 years. But you probably know that from the reports in the papers. Reporters were round us like a rash after Lewis was killed. It was a bad marriage from the start. The beatings, his nasty habit of getting his revenge at unexpected moments, sometimes for nothing more than a comment he took as a slight. The punching me in my stomach. The terrible bruises on my arms, legs and body, the black eyes, the broken arms and legs and one terrible time when I nearly lost my life; five times in hospital and always for something major. My right jaw is wired up, he smashed my face down onto his desktop. He pushed me downstairs when I was pregnant and I lost my baby that night. I was nearly five months pregnant at the time. Then he told me to 'snap out of it' when I was depressed. The last straw was finding out that he was having a torrid affair with Jo-Ann. He'd meet her at the Harrington Hey Hotel, Birmingham way. I packed my bags that afternoon and left. I stayed with an Auntie Elsie because he didn't know where she lived. Here or at the Red Lion would be the first place he'd look to find me and he always said that if I left him he'd find me and drag me back. For two days I feared every knock on the door, then finding out he was dead and the police thinking that I had done it. I had the motive and had disappeared. Mrs Alexicon found Lewis when she came back from her Bridge Club and had a heart attack from the shock. Before she died she told me Jo-Ann had killed Lewis. Auntie Elsie was there with me and heard what she said. The police had already found her fingerprints on the sooty end of a poker that had a very heavy knob on the holding end; she'd used that to kill him, they didn't tell me that they had found those prints they just wanted to see what I would do.' I looked at Matt, his face was shocked and chalk white, I continued. 'Mrs Alexicon was very wealthy. They lived in a huge house the other side of Darlington, about three hours' drive from here.

Everything was left to Lewis. There is a father who Mrs Alexicon said was killed in the war but he lives in a mental institution. I have to pay for his upkeep. Lewis hadn't made a will, so it all had to go to probate. Mr Alexicon can't have the money as he is incapable of seeing to it, so it all came to me. The house, I have leased out to a charity for Domestic Violence. The inheritance tax I was able to pay by selling all of Mrs Alexicon's jewels, a few very good paintings a small collection of art objects and Lewis's Rolex watch and a ring, given to him by his father and loads of other things I didn't even know Lewis had. I'm worth about a million and a half. Because of all the internal damage, the chances of me getting pregnant again are so slim as to be non-existent and lastly, Chloe isn't mine, she is the product of Jo-Ann and Lewis's affair.

Jo-Ann turned her back on Chloe when she was born and wanted nothing to do with her. I adopted her at three months old because she was a sweet, innocent child who shouldn't be made to suffer the sins of her parents. And I'm a bastard from an affair my mother had during the war, when she thought that Ray had left her for a French tart who bore Jo-Ann, then died. Jo-Ann and Ray are no relatives of mine.' I paused, thinking if I had left anything out. 'That's it Matt, all of it; I have left nothing out.'

Matt stared at me and seemed unable to say anything.

He got up and pulled me to my feet. He cuddled me to him and said, 'My poor, poor darling. You must have been to hell and back.'

'Yes, I have.' I said into his shoulder. 'But you may think differently about me now because of my background.'

Immediately the reply came back that my birth made no difference to how he felt about me. 'I love you for you. It's not about where you come from or how you came to be. I love you.'

'Sod the promise about waiting until we are married.' I said against his searching mouth. 'I want you now. I need you to prove to me that, despite all, you still want me.' I could feel his hardness pressing against my inner thighs, I knew he was ready by the look in his eyes. There, by the fire, we made love. My need was bordering on hysteria. Our urgency made it all the more powerful and passionate. We didn't hold back, we each gave our all.

Later, in my bedroom, in the double bed, we were able to take our time over it. Matt outmatched Lewis many times over. With Lewis, lovemaking had always lacked that special something that Matt had in abundance. He was an ardent, amorous and sensual lover.

Much later, Matt went downstairs to make us both a cup of tea – in my dressing gown! It was now about two. We'd missed out on lunch but a lot we cared! Over our tea we snuggled up in bed again, to drink it. I asked, 'Does the money cause a problem?'

'Only in as much as I should be the main breadwinner.'

'And children?'

'We have each other, Lucy. Yes, it would be lovely to have children but we have the delightful Chloe. I'm amazed that you took her on given her birth circumstances but I feel that it's very like you to be so forgiving. After all, it happened before she was born and she mustn't ever suffer for her parentage. As far as I can see, she's got a super Mum and you have done so well with her. She is a delightful little girl and very well behaved. My Mum will love her. And your birth is of no consequence. I have told you that but it would be interesting to know more about your family.'

'I'm a grandchild of Lord Stephenson. My uncle is Sir Leonard Stephenson.'

He spilt his tea as he chocked. 'Crumbs! I'm in bed with the landed gentry!'

Once I stopped laughing, I said, 'So you still want to marry me?'

'Don't be daft, of course I do, especially after what you have just told me. No, that came out wrong, it sounds as though I'm just after your money and I'm not. I just want to look after you, keep you safe, surround you with love and show you what a good solid marriage is all about. We'll be a great team. It's all I ever wanted and the most important thing is that we will be together for always.

You've had a rotten deal so far. I can't wait. What an exciting prospect.'

He put his teacup down and turned to me. I think he wanted to make love again.

'This is one thing you will have to get used to, I need to go to collect Chloe from kindergarten and to be on time. I need to go now, so go away.'

Matt said he would stay behind and clear up and get the sitting room fire going again.

I had a quick shower and I got to Leyburn in time to get Chloe from kindergarten. Once back at Crofters Cottage, Matt had found a few things in the fridge and was singing at the top of his voice while cooking all of us a 'high tea' (a Yorkshire term, meaning bigger than tea but smaller than dinner). 'My culinary expertise doesn't get much better than a fry up.'

I laughed gently at him and said it was good of him to do it.

'I have an ulterior motive.' He said. 'It means I get to stay a bit longer with you and Chloe.' Chloe was quiet, as usual, after her full day at kindergarten. 'It's nice to see you.' I commented. 'Isn't it Chloe?'

She just said 'Yeth', carried on eating, then said, 'Ith he thtaying over?'

'No, darling, he's just visiting,' I said, trying not to laugh.

'Can I get down pleath?'

'Is there anything you would like to do this evening?'

'I want to get my colouring book out.'

'Lovely idea. You look tired Sweetheart, are you alright?' I said, and started to clear the table.

'Yeth.'

Matt and I washed up together. 'I hope she isn't starting with a cold or something. She's extra quiet today.'

'I'll get going soon and leave you to have an evening together.'

'No, stay on for a while. After all, she is going to have get used to having you around.'

He smiled and said, 'I don't need to be encouraged to stay on. Do you live here permanently?'

'Yes. Chloe and I sleep in the same room when Auntie Pegs and Reg come down for the weekend, which is most weekends. When

Chloe was a baby, I'd move myself into their flat when they came down. She had a powerful pair of lungs and would scream solidly from two to five most nights.'

'Can I ask you something?' He poked his head out of the scullery to see where Chloe was. 'Have you ever regretted your decision to adopt Chloe?'

'I don't deny it was a difficult three months but, no, never. I adore her. I took over from Mum when she was three months old. Mum had had enough; she looked dead on her feet when she came here with her. I wanted nothing to do with her at first and couldn't believe that Mum was suggesting that I look after her. I'd suggested that Mum go up for a sleep the second afternoon they were here. Chloe had just been fed and was a bit restless. I didn't want Mum to be disturbed so I lifted Chloe out of her carry cot to quieten her and that was it, she stopped crying and looked at me, stuck her thumb into her mouth and went to sleep. I just knew I'd have her but with stringent conditions that Jo-Ann had nothing to do with her, ever. She hadn't wanted her from the start. Mum said she thought Jo-Ann would jump at the chance to be rid of her baby and she was.'

'How heartless.' Matt said, quite shocked.

I shrugged my shoulders and sighed. 'I was wealthy, childless and my biological clock was ticking away and she possibly would be the only chance of having a baby I would ever have. She didn't make up for my lost baby, nothing could do that, he's tucked away in a corner of my heart but I thought how lucky I was to have this second chance of having a child and I took it. It doesn't mean I love her any less, it's just a different love.' Matt took me in his arms then and just rocked me. I hadn't cried but he knew I was upset.

We pulled apart when we heard Chloe coming down the passageway to the scullery.

'Mummy, I'm tired.' She whimpered.

'Tell you what, I'll run your bath and we'll see if we can blow some soapy bubbles.'

She was sound asleep by seven.

Matt stayed on for a cup of coffee and after a passionate kiss and a cuddle he left, with promises to come down tomorrow.

He tried to make it down each evening to see me after work. As he said, work at the bank didn't finish when they closed at 3.30. They had things to do, balance the books and check and double lock each money drawers and sort out cheques etc...

One of those evenings we spent at the vicarage, with the vicar giving us a pep-talk on the sanctity of marriage. He knew who I was; who didn't? The press were at it again. 'Murdered Husband's Widow to Marry Again.' At least it was only in the local papers.

We let it be known that we were marrying in Darlington Registry Office. We both wanted a quiet wedding. We certainly didn't want to be invaded by the press. So few people were coming it was quite easy to keep the little Redmire parish church ceremony a secret.

Matt often stayed for an evening meal and at the weekend, when Auntie Peggy and Reg were down, he seemed to get on well with them. It would be Friday or Saturday that Auntie Peggy said that, as they would be there anyway, why didn't we go out for an evening, as she would be there to babysit. We'd go to Richmond and see a film or go and see his Mum. She had met Chloe and thought she was adorable and would shower her with sweets.

I made a trip to Darlington and visited the little shop were Auntie Peggy got her wedding outfit from. I explained what I wanted. She took me into her back room that was crammed with material and I found exactly what I wanted. I told her my time scale (that Sunday was the first time the banns would be read). She raised her eyebrows. 'Wow, that doesn't give me much time but I can do it. I have outworkers who stitch for me now. Come for your first fitting in a week's time,' she said.

It was my turn to say wow. She let me have a snippet of material so that I could get matching shoes, bag and hat. I found all that I wanted that afternoon. The hat was one of those once in a lifetime creations. It had a huge brim and every square inch of it was crammed with multi coloured silk flowers, it sounds hideous but it was lovely. My dress was quite plain. Mid-calf length in a pearly white silk, it had a swirly skirt with a fitted bodice and a long sleeved bolero to go with it. The shoes were also in the same colour, the clutch bag matched the hat. It would give me a bit of colour.

When I returned to Leyburn, where we were staying for the night, as Auntie Pegs had collected Chloe from School, she was in a sulk and wouldn't eat her tea. It was because I hadn't taken her with me. I gently reminded her that she was now at kindergarten and she couldn't just take a day off when she felt like it. I'd taken her into her room, sat her on her bed and sat myself on a chair. 'Now, what's up? I won't have you being rude to Auntie Peggy. She loves you and you hurt her when you're rude. It's the same for Grandad Reg and me when you're being naughty. We hurt as well.'

'Don't you love me anymore?' She asked in a tiny voice.

I was shocked. 'Of course I love you. I always have and that will never change. You know I love you. What has brought this on?'

'You thpend a lot of time with Mathew.'

'Chloe, you surprise me. Today I was on my own. I had things to do in Darlington. Yes, he comes down most evenings and I see a bit more of him at weekends but you are often with us. In fact, I can't count the times when the three of us have been out together and you are often given the choice of who you want to stay with and you chose Auntie Peggy quite often.'

'I don't like Mathew.'

'Chloe! That's a dreadful thing to say and I know you don't mean it. Look at all he does with you? Look at all the fun you two have and he can always make you laugh and he loves you too.' Chloe looked down, her damp eyelashes sweeping her cheek.

'You are a much loved little girl. You have Auntie Peggy and Grandad Reg, who also loves you.' She started to cry in earnest. All I could do was take her on to my knee and cuddle her until she stopped.

I talked it over with Auntie Peggy. She suggested that Chloe might be jealous at the obvious chemistry between Matt and I but would not be able to put into words, so came out with not liking him as her childish explanation. It being her only way of explaining her feelings.

I took Chloe to Darlington on Saturday. I asked Auntie Pegs if she would like to come as well but she said that Chloe and I should have a day on our own, just the two of us. We chose a pretty silk dress for her from the Bridal Department at Binns. It really cheered her up. The previous night I had told her that I wanted her to be my bridesmaid at my wedding. I had explained what a wedding was all about and that Matt would be living with us forever. She seemed to accept that but was far more interested and excited about being dressed up and looking pretty in an especially lovely dress. It was in the 'little Bo- peep' style and in the palest pink. I also got her a pair of ballet shoes. She loved it all. I told her it was a secret and she wasn't to tell anyone. Once home we put it all away in her bedroom cupboard and said no-one was to see it until the day of the wedding. She was a happier little girl than she had been on the Wednesday night.

I had let Matt know that we were staying at the Red Lion Flat for the night as Auntie Peggy and Reg were not going down to Crofters Cottage that weekend as Reg couldn't afford the time. He'd had people interested in purchasing the hotel and wanted to keep 'on the ball', as he said.

When Matt arrived she was just having her tea. We would all eat later.

'Had a nice day?' He asked cheerfully. I left Chloe to answer that.

'We've been buying thecrets.' She lisped.

'Wow! I didn't know you could buy secrets. Can I see these secrets?'

'Thilly, it wouldn't be a thecret if I told you.'

'That's true. But I like secrets too.' He replied, then said. 'Anyway, I have a thecret too.'

'What ith it?'

'Can't tell you, It's a thecret.'

Poor Chloe, she'd fallen straight into his trap.

She laughed though, then looked at me for help. 'Well our secret is better than yours and all will be revealed rather sooner than later but until then it's to stay Chloe's and my secret. Isn't that right Sweetheart?'

'Yeth.' She said stoutly.

Chloe surprises me sometimes. She got off her chair, went to stand by Matt and said, 'I'm thorry.'

Matt looked surprised and said, 'why are you saying sorry, Chloe?'

'I told Mummy that I didn't like you.'

'Oh, I see. Well that's a pity because I have come to really like you, very much. Now it's my turn to say sorry. I didn't know you didn't like me.'

'But I *do* like you, tho' I shouldn't have thaid I didn't.'

He lifted her on to his knee. 'It's like this, Chloe. I love your Mummy and you and I thought we could be a proper little family in our own house. Does that seem alright to you? Because we have to discuss big things like that with you to see if you like the idea?'

She thought about this for some time. I almost held my breath, waiting to see what she would say.

'Thath all right.' She said eventually and ended with, 'Would you be my Daddy?'

Matt was visibly moved and there was a slight break in his voice. 'So that's alright with you, is it? You agree on us being a proper family with me as a... a Daddy?'

She nodded her head and lifted it to give him a kiss on his cheek. Matt gave her a tight cuddle.

'Can I watch some television before I have to go to bed? And can Matt read me a thtory but Grandad Reg has to be there to help him with the big wordth.' I stifled a laugh behind my hand and chose that moment to clear the table. When she had hopped off his knee she scampered into the sitting room. I said to Matt, 'Are you alright, darling?'

'Whew! What a little sweetheart. No wonder that's your pet name for her.' He took out a large handkerchief and blew his nose.

When Reg came in later, Chloe got up to greet him and said. 'Grandad, Matt's going to be my new Daddy.' She nearly started us all snivelling.

Matt did get to read Chloe her bedtime story, and Reg was there to listen as asked to.

Every now and then, Matt, with a perfectly straight face, would ask Reg what a word was. I was listening by the door and I had to turn away as I was laughing so much.

XXVII.   1972-1973

Our Wedding Day dawned bright and clear. It was a glorious September day. The wedding was set for two o'clock. Matt had agreed with my wish to have a quiet wedding, although I think if I had wanted a big white wedding with all the trimmings he would have agreed to that as well. He was such a love. He had stayed at the Red Lion Hotel at Reg's invitation the night before, with his best man with him, a banker friend called Peter who I had never met before. I should imagine a few drinks were downed that evening.

I went from Crofters Cottage to the village church in Reg's car with him driving with Auntie Peggy and Chloe. It's not a very big church but it would take all the guests that we wanted. A wedding car had already been dispatched to take Matt and his best man. Matt, I was told was sitting in the front pew looking very nervous indeed! Chloe looked adorable in her Bo-peep dress; she carried a little basket of rose petals to throw at us after the ceremony. I held a small bouquet of pale roses, freesias and gypsophila, that I wanted after the ceremony to put onto Grandad's grave. Auntie Peggy said I looked stunning. Reg said, 'Smashing, by God you do lass,' then had to take a speck of dust out of his eye! I have to say it but Chloe was as good as gold all day. She loved the fuss people made of her.

David came with his cross-eyed wife. Their daughter Sylvia looked lovely and was now a very grown up 18-year-old. Michael was away at university and couldn't come. Tommy and Carol came; she looked very frail and ill. Matt's mother came with a family friend. Auntie Elsie was there, looking very glamorous on the arm of her gentleman friend. Mrs Ebson came with Milly Franks and my mother and, much to my surprise, Ray (I could no longer call him my father) was there. Counting me, there were 19 people in all. The little church was crowded. The service was lovely and, all of a sudden, or so it seemed, I was Mrs Mathew Howard.

We held our reception in the Red Lion Hotel conference room. All the staff were asked to come to that and the guests staying in the hotel at the time, so Mavis had little to do but answer the phone. It was a truly memorable day. Even Ray's dark, brooding looks couldn't dampen my happiness. The only unpleasantness was when I excused myself to go to the ladies room. I reached the door and suddenly Ray was in front of me.

'I shall never forgive you.' He snarled.

I must have looked surprised. 'Why is that?' I was totally bewildered.

'For framing Jo-Ann.' He fumed.

'I didn't.' I gasped. 'You know I didn't. She almost admitted it in court and may I remind you, that she was having an affair with my husband.'

'Exactly, that's why you killed him.' He grated out.

'Grow up Ray and face the facts. She killed him because he wouldn't divorce me to marry her when she was pregnant with his child.'

'How much did you pay them?'

I was even more perplexed by this remark. 'What on earth do you mean. Pay who?'

'The police, of course, you always were dim.' He growled. 'To make them say the fingerprints were Jo-Ann's and not yours.'

'No money changed hands, or sexual favours, for that matter. I left The Priory before Lewis came back. Mrs Ebson said I'd left before Lewis came home. Now enough of this and let me pass.'

'I hate you.' He said with feeling.

'Well, the feeling is mutual, so that's okay isn't it?' I spoke very pleasantly.

'Lucy, is this fellow bothering you?' Reg asked.

'Yes, he is.'

Reg stepped in front of me, facing Ray. 'I would have thought you'd done enough damage to Lucy, Ray. Leave her alone. You can't let it go, can you? Jo-Ann was found guilty and with her past record for GBH you surprise me that you could even think it was Lucy.'

Reg turned to me and said, 'Come on lass it's nearly time for you to go.'

I gave Ray a look of pure loathing and turned away. I never saw him again after that.

'Are you alright, lass?' Reg asked.

I was shaking. 'Please don't mention this to Matt, there is no need for him to know.'

'Aye lass, alright, I won't.'

Apart from that unpleasantness, I really had a lovely day and I wasn't going to let Ray spoil it. But it left a sour taste in my mouth for quite a long time.

I told Matt I was going upstairs to change into my going away outfit. Auntie Peggy came with me, as did Mum and Auntie Elsie, to help, they said but it was just for a good gossip. I told Mum what Ray had said.

'It doesn't matter that all the facts were against Jo-Ann. He just can't take it on board that she is a killer.'

'He's desperate to blame me for Lewis's death, as he has blamed me for just about everything that happened at the hotel. I'm surprised he wanted to come.'

Mum looked guilty. 'I'm so sorry lovie. I suggested it. He'd said you never come home. I said 'Can you blame her?' He said to show no hard feelings he'd come.'

'He came only to upset me.'

'Yes Lucy, unfortunately you could be right. I wasn't going to tell you today but now I think I will. We are divorcing. I can't stand it any more. On and on he goes about Jo-Ann and I've had enough.'

'What about the hotel?' I asked. 'That has my blood and tears in it.'

'It's sold, subject to contract. We had to take a loss on it. He'd drunk most of the proceeds and wasn't helping and the hotel was beginning to look a bit dowdy and uncared for. It needs a lot of TLC to get it back to how it was when you were there.'

'I'm sorry,' I said, 'it must have been hard for you.'

'Yes, it has. I should never have taken him back.'

Auntie Elsie pricked up her ears. 'Taken him back? What do you mean?'

'I'll tell you another day Elsie, not today. It's my daughter's wedding day and she needs to get off with her Mathew.'

'Don't let that horrible Ray get to you. He isn't worth it. Sorry Barbara but I never liked him very much.' Auntie Peggy said, who could be quite blunt at times.

'Here-here,' Auntie Elsie put in. 'By the way, I loved that hat you wore.' And she pointed to the large blue creation that Auntie Peggy had just picked up to put back into its hatbox. 'I might borrow it one day.' She was changing the subject. 'That suit looks good on you, just your colour.'

My suit was a sky blue wool two-piece with a fake fur colour, over a cream blouse. I had on my feet high heeled dark blue shoes and to keep my hands warm matching gloves. On my head I had two big silk flower heads sewn onto a blue net. I knew I looked good, because I felt good.

'My favourite colour Auntie Elsie. Most of my clothes seem to be in blue.'

'Well, you certainly look really lovely and I do so like your Matt.'

'My lass,' Auntie Peggy said, 'you look so bonny.'

Mum couldn't say anything as she was trying hard not to cry.

'Mum.' I said, now almost in tears myself.

'Oh Lucy, I have missed you so much. Always it was "Jo-Ann looks beautiful" but you could knock spots of her today.' I gave her a hug. It must have been very hard on her. 'Good luck, my darling daughter and tell that Matt to look after you.'

There was a loud knock on the door.

'If that's Matt, you can tell himself yourself.' I said, smiling. Auntie Peggy opened the door and there stood Matt, holding Chloe in his arms.

'Lucy darling, you look lovely. We need to get off and this little girl is dead tired.' He put her gently down. Auntie Peggy held out her arms and Chloe flew into them.

I said a tearful goodbye to everyone and when I hugged Auntie Peggy I thanked her for everything she had done for me. I don't think my mother heard because she was speaking to Chloe at the time. I bent down to enfold Chloe. 'I'm only going away for a week Chloe and you will have a wonderful time with Auntie Peggy, Grandad Reg and Grandma Barbara and when I come back, you, Matt and me are going house hunting and that will be so much fun. You'll get to choose your own bedroom.'

She started crying. This is what I had been dreading, leaving my little girl crying.

'Why can't I come with you?' She sobbed.

'Not this time Sweetheart, but after this week we won't ever have to be parted again.'

Auntie Peggy said, 'Just go Lucy, she will be fine.'

'Look what I have in my bag for you,' Mum said, and tipped her bag upside down onto one of the beds. 'See if you can find it amongst all this rubbish.' From the door I looked back and Chloe seemed engrossed in searching through Mums 'rubbish' on the bed. I looked at my family one final time and my heart was bursting with love for them. Matt grabbed my hand and we walked away to start our new life together.

In a shower of confetti, blown kisses and shouts of 'good luck' I stepped into the car that was to take us to Darlington Station to catch a train that would take us to London, where we would spend one night before catching our plane to Southern Ireland at two the next afternoon. Matt had relatives there who we would call on while we were there but we were not staying with them. Matt had always said how beautiful Southern Ireland was and we were really looking forward to our honeymoon; just to be on our own was good enough for me.

He looked at me when we were in the train. 'How does it feel to be Mrs Howard, my darling?'

'Fabulously, amazingly wonderful,' I said, rather breathlessly. He hadn't let go of my hand once, except to carry the luggage and heft it onto the racks above our heads. We were sitting thigh to thigh; we couldn't have been nearer to each other. I looked at his hand clutching mine, they were strong, capable hands that I knew could be sweet and gentle. I squeezed it as it lay on my lap.

He lent nearer, close to my ear. 'I can't wait.' He stated. 'I just don't know how I am going to contain myself until we get to London. We have hours to go.'

'It will be all the sweeter and better for the wait.'

He gave a longing groan. 'I'll keep you to that promise.'

We had a meal on the train. Neither of us had eaten much at our reception, having been too full of happiness and too busy chatting to our guests to bother with food.

We alighted from our train and hailed a taxi to take us to the Dorchester and fell exhausted into bed – although neither of us slept much! He was as impatient to make love as I was. That taste of things to come three weeks ago on the sitting room floor at Crofters Cottage and later in my double bed had done nothing to slake our thirst for each other. We revelled in each other's bodies and couldn't get enough.

Our honeymoon was a glorious week of romantic days and passionate nights. We met his relatives who had organised a huge party for us and an Irish party is something else. We enjoyed it so much and got on so well with his aunt and uncle and got them to promise to come to see us sometime in England.

By the end of our week I was more in love with Matt than ever.

We spent another night in the Dorchester on our return and caught the mid-morning train back to Darlington. Reg again was there to meet us. 'Chloe was fine, by the way and we loved having her.'

'Spoilt rotten, I expect.' Was my caustic reply.

'Aye well, she deserved to be. Your Dad, no Ray, was sent home with a flea in his ear by your Mum who is still with us and staying in your room at the pub. So you will be living for a time at Crofters Cottage; we hope that meets with your approval.'

I was delighted of course, as I love that place.

'We've left a meal for you and the range is on, so the house should be warmed through for you. Chloe, who has been an angel, is out for the day with your Mum so that Peggy could get down there without her knowing. Rightly or wrongly, she thinks you're coming home tomorrow, because your Mum packed your room up and it's all in carrier bags and boxes for you to put away, so you have a night to sort yourselves out.'

'Thank you so much, Reg. You are a star.'

'Hey,' a voice said from the back of the car. 'I thought I was.' We laughed. We had had a wonderful holiday but it was good to be back home. Reg wouldn't come in, he just dropped us outside Crofters Cottage.

It took us most of the remaining evening to get my things put away and get ourselves unpacked and get the first load of washing on the go. The meal Auntie Peggy had left us was consumed with gusto. I was looking forward to the next day when I'd see Chloe again. It was arranged for us to come up to The Red Lion Hotel whenever we were ready, around lunchtime Reg had suggested.

Matt had a further week off and we spent it house hunting but we didn't have far to go. I'd taken Matt up to see my little house and we found that old Mr Randall's place was up for sale. Matt was very taken with the area and liked the thought of renovating an old place. He was very good at DIY. But even he realised that he would need some help. The obvious choice was David but he wouldn't be able to start until the following year because he was so busy. He wouldn't start renovating an old place in the winter anyway.

'But there are things you can start on, the house and barn need clearing. You need an architect to draw your plans for the extension to the house and for whatever you need to alter in the barn. Then it will need to go to the planners for them to pass it. By spring you might have completed that part, before you can start on the renovation work.'

He spoke sense but we were a bit disappointed that work wouldn't go ahead until then.

We showed Chloe what we wanted to buy. I think she was a bit disenchanted when she first saw the building. 'But it'th tumbled down,' she said.

'We aren't going to live in it as it is. I'm going to renovate it, do it up, make it into a proper house for us,' Matt explained to her. 'With Uncle David to help, I promise it will be lovely when it's finished.'

Chloe just looked at him as though he was mad.

When the architect's plans were drawn up, we showed her them. We were excited and maybe it was infectious, as she seemed to make some sense of all the lines on the architect drawings.

Mr Randall's house was a two-up, two-down. The front room was a nice size. I think he must have lived and slept there. The kitchen was a disgrace and upstairs there were two bedrooms and no bathroom. The roof was sagging and leaked and clearly had done for years. The floorboards would have to be taken up as they had got too damp to use and the roof taken off completely, as there was woodworm in the rafters. Matt could see it in his mind's eye, completed and finished. At the back of the house he wanted a dining room extension, above which would be Chloe's bedroom.

There was a problem with the house plans but those for the barn were passed in the first Planning meeting so we started on them first. I'd go there from dropping off Chloe at school; I could get far more done without her with me. Auntie Peggy came up to help most days. We moved many barrow-loads of soil and musty hay into a corner of the garden from those outbuildings. Matt wanted to keep all the farm implements and tools we found in the tool-shed where the chickens had lived. Obviously the birds had gone but the mess was quite sickening.

I'd go to the school to collect Chloe in whatever I had been wearing that day and must have looked a sight, filthy and smelly. I'd remain in the car so no-one would see me! She would come to me, then we would head back to Crofters Cottage. Winter was fast approaching and it soon got dark. I'd have a bath, then start on our evening meal.

At the weekends Matt would be up early to carry on where I had left off. I'd go up with Chloe at midday with a picnic that we would have in the old man's sitting room. Chloe was in her element, as it had a huge garden. It was safe for her and she could amuse herself by 'playing house'. They were exciting and enchanting days but hard work and tiring.

We started on the barn first. We cleared out the disgusting old outside loo and made it into our front entrance, which went straight into the cow byre. Half was made into a living room-cum-kitchen and the other half was the bedroom. From there we made a door into the tack/work room that became the second bedroom for Chloe and the pigsty was reconstructed to make a bathroom.

As Matt said, at least we would be on site when the building started on the main house.

Half way through the work on the barns, the house plans were passed but we decided to continue with the barns anyway. We needed to vacate Crofters Cottage because Reg and Peggy had now sold the hotel. Completion would be in three months and they would then want the cottage back, although they never said so.

That winter was a very wet one, with little snow, so at least Matt was able to get to work every day and the sand and salt lorries were out early, so he was always able to get through and I was able to drive Chloe to school.

We were greatly excited when the barn conversion was completed. With Matt's help, I packed up all our personal things from the cottage and transferred them to the barn. A lot of things had to be left in boxes but at least we were in. I went back to Crofters Cottage to give it a good clean and to say goodbye to it. I had been a resident on and off for many years and mostly happy ones. I left the key with Auntie Peggy at the hotel. They would be moving out in two weeks' time and into Crofters Cottage to plan their first holiday together.

XXVIII.   1973

The only tragedy to mar our first year of married life was when Tommy rang to say that Carol was failing fast and she wanted to see me. I went to see her that afternoon. Carol was very weak but I understood that she was asking me to keep an eye on Tommy for her. I promised that I would but wondered if he would want me to; after all, he was the same age as I was. But if it gave her comfort I promised I would do what I could.

He was still working in the Red Lion Hotel and the new owners had said that when they took over they would be keeping most of the staff. Tommy was one of those kept on; after all, he knew his job inside out and now was the Bar Manager with the job of ordering stock, hiring and firing bar staff and many other duties that seemed to have slowly crept onto his shoulders but which he seemed to thrive on.

Tommy rang a few days later to say that Carol had died. I went to her funeral but Matt didn't; after all, he hardly knew her. It was such a sad occasion but at least she had lasted longer than her doctors had predicted. Tommy visited her resting place once a week to put flowers on her grave and do a bit of tidying up.

Once in our newly-renovated cottage, I offered the barn conversion to Tommy on a proper rent-paying basis. He wasn't going to accept charity. He was thrilled. It meant that he could vacate one of the hotel staff rooms where he had lived for quite a few years when on duty. On Sundays, if he wasn't working, he would come over the courtyard that divided the barn from our cottage to have dinner with us. He and Chloe were old friends and got on very well. He was so grateful that he offered to try and tidy the garden up. I had mentioned how lovely the garden had once been. Nearly all his time off was spent in the garden, doing what he could. He worked hard and eventually it began to look as good as it used to. Matt and I were very impressed.

Then two great things happened. The people who had brought Inspector Wright's house next door put the house on the market. They were emigrating to Australia to be with their daughter and granddaughter. I believe her husband had left her. I spoke to Matt about buying it.

'I have all that money in the bank and apart from paying the staff wages at The Priory and Mr Alexicon's bills, the money just sits there and I would love to buy next door.'

Matt pursed his lips. 'Do you really want it?' He asked.

'Well, with Tommy in the barn conversion we have nowhere for guests to stay.'

'We've managed this past year, darling.' Matt said.

'Cos' no-one has wanted to stay with us Matt. I really want to buy next door... please.'

He really hated using my money. We had tried living on his salary and managed fairly well but I was beginning to feel that the cottage was just a bit small. 'Please...' I wheedled. I could usually twist him round my little finger.

'I'll agree, but on one condition,' he eventually said.

'What's that?' I asked.

'That it's in your name only.'

'No, I can't agree to that. It's silly. It has to be in both of our names.'

'In Chloe's then.'

'Matt no, when she reaches 21 she is going to inherit a large amount of money that I put into a trust for her as soon as the adoption came through. After all, you will be doing the work and renovating and knocking down walls to make doorways and anything else we need to get done.'

He heaved a sigh. 'Let me think it over.'

'Please don't take too long thinking about it Matt, I'd hate to lose the opportunity.'

His mind was made up a week later. In that week I realized that I had missed a period. I said nothing to Matt. I didn't want to get his hopes up, only to have them dashed when my results came back negative. But they came back positive! I was over the moon. I had the telephone receiver in my hand to ring him at the bank and tell him the good news, then I put it back into its cradle. I had a better idea. I would prepare a romantic meal for Matt for that night and tell him over coffee.

I prepared his favourite meal of roast lamb with a garlic and breadcrumb topping, then left out the garlic, as he was working the following day and his breath would be awful. Garlic does tend to hang around for a day or two. I made my own concoction of a cheesecake. I took time with the table. I got some candles and got out my best china and linen. I closed the door to the dining room, before going off to collect Chloe from school. I thought of telling her and then decided that Matt had a right to know first. We could tell her tomorrow. The kitchen was the warmest place in the house, so it was doubtful that she would go into the dining room and see the table and start asking questions. If that happened, I wouldn't be able to keep the news to myself.

Wednesday was a late night for Matt. The bank always held a meeting after work on that day, to iron out any problems if there were any, or had discussions on certain financial matters. It had thought to be a better time or else the tellers, cashiers and managers were going home only to come back again later on in the evening for the meetings and some lived some distance away.

Chloe was already in bed when he came home that day. She'd had her tea in the warmth of the kitchen and I had heard her read from her school reading book. I'd said to her, 'Soon you'll be able to read me a bedtime story.' She had laughed.

'Send Daddy in to say goodnight when he comes home.'

'I won't have to ask him sweetheart, he'll do it anyway.'

'He doesn't always.' She argued.

'He always does Chloe but he'd tell me you were asleep and he always gave you a goodnight kiss. He never forgets.'

'Oh well, if I am asleep, say goodnight from me anyway, won't you?'

'Of course sweetheart, I'll give him a kiss from you as well. Now go to sleep.'

'Night, Mummy,' a sleepy voice said.

When Matt came in I was in the kitchen. He always came in the back way, as he would have parked the car in the courtyard. I welcomed him with a big kiss.

'What's this all about?' He asked when I eventually let him go.

'It's none of your business.' Then I stopped and said, 'Well, it is your business and it's all your fault! Don't go into the dining room and your bath is ready, sir.'

'But it's not my bath night tonight,' he teased and grinned like a naughty schoolboy.

'Upstairs,' I said, pointing to them.

'Bossy women...' He grumbled to himself as he went up. I heard him walk into Chloe's room to kiss her goodnight. They seemed to have formed such a delightful bond. They adored each other.

In half an hour he was back down again looking very relaxed in a pair of chinos and a matching fawn shirt I'd given him for his last birthday. I'd had a chance to change as well and wore my favourite blue silk dress with Mrs Alexicon's matching necklace.

He swept me into his arms and nuzzled my neck.

'You look lovely as always,' he said, then, 'Have I forgotten something? It's not our wedding anniversary or a birthday is it?'

'All will be revealed shortly. Go into the sitting room and fix a drink for yourself and me please, though I do have some champagne on ice.' He turned smartly and came back into the kitchen.

'I'll open the bottle,' he said grinning.

He sniffed the air. 'Something smells delicious.'

I just smiled at him and opened the dining room door.

'Wow, that looks nice!' He said as he spotted the table.

Once seated, we clinked our champagne flutes together.

'To us.' I said, raising the glass and taking a sip. I got up and said, 'I'll just get the first course...'

It was home-made chicken liver pate with hot toast.

'Mmm...' he munched happily. 'This is good. So what's the occasion? Put me out of my misery. What have I done? Or, more to the point, what have *you* done?'

'I haven't done anything. How can you think I have done something awful just because I chose to give you a lovely meal?'

'I know you well enough, my darling, to know you are up to something.' Again I just smiled.

The roast was so tender and the vegetables were done just right, without becoming soggy. The cheesecake was so nice even I had two helpings. There was just enough left for Chloe to have tomorrow for her tea.

Later, we took the remaining champagne into the sitting room. He lit the fire and we snuggled up on the sofa together.

'So what is it that earns me a delicious meal on my return from the bank?'

'Matt darling, the love of my life… I'm going to have a baby.' I said softly.

His mouth dropped open in surprise. He was unable to say anything. I could see the glitter in his eyes in the firelight.

'Lucy darling.' He mumbled into my hair. 'This is wonderful news. Have you been to see the doctor? Have you had it confirmed? I can't believe it. It's fantastic. Oh God, what have I done to deserve such wonderful news? I'm happier to hear it than anything else I can think of.'

'I take it that you're pleased?' I teased him.

'I am delighted, far more than words can say. My dearest wife, how I love you. So that was the reason for that glorious meal. Come to bed Lucy… or shouldn't we make love in case it hurts the baby?'

'It won't hurt the baby, Matt and we don't have to go to bed. You've just lit the fire.' We looked at each other and both remembered the time at Crofters Cottage when we made love in front of the fire. He gathered me to him and we kissed deeply and passionately and together we rolled off the sofa and onto the floor…

The following day at teatime we told Chloe. All her friends at school had brothers or sisters, so she took it well and got quite excited. 'So when can we collect it?' She asked.

Matt and I tried hard not to laugh. 'Well, it has to grow in my tummy for a few months, Chloe.'

'We got so carried away last night, I didn't even ask when it was expected,' Matt said.

'The 22nd of April, next year. So we have a long way to go,' I replied.

'I've made a decision too,' Matt said. 'I was thinking about it at work yesterday.'

'What's that darling?' I asked.

'I think we should go for the house next door. But I decided that before I knew about a new baby. This wonderful news just proves to me that I made the right decision.'

'Oh, Matt! Matt, Oh, that's fantastic. Thank you.' I kissed him heartily. Chloe had often seen us kissing and took that show of affection as normal.

'Should we go and see it now?' I was so excited.

'It may not be convenient for them.'

'I'll go and ask them.' I dashed out of the cottage and went next door.

'Give us an hour.' Mrs Ashby said. 'We've just sat down for our tea.'

'We can leave it until tomorrow if you like.'

'No, it's fine for tonight. See you in an hour.'

I raced back to tell Matt and Chloe that we could go after they had finished their tea. We decided to have ours in the intervening time. At 6.40 we went next door. Mrs Ashby beamed at us and let us in. We knew her quite well, so she said, 'No guided tour dears, just wander around at will. Open doors and cupboards and poke into holes and corners. We have nothing to hide.'

It was odd for me going into that house again after all those years. Mr Ashby, though, had done enough alterations to the house for me to hardly recognise it. The pokey hall was gone. They had taken down the dividing wall to the dining room on the right; it was now a light and airy entrance foyer. On the back wall dividing their house from our cottage, they had built a downstairs cloak-room and on the left wall they had installed floor to ceiling cupboards for all their outdoor coats, etc. The sitting room on the left of the front door extended from the front to the back of the house and was a lovely room. The far end was their dining area and on the back wall they'd had French doors put in.

The kitchen, straight ahead from the front door, was the same size I remembered it to be but hardly recognisable as it had been stripped out and totally modernized. The stairs led up from the kitchen as they did in our cottage. On the first floor there were three good-sized bedrooms and a bathroom.

There was no hesitation on my part. I think Matt was smitten as well. After our tour of the house, we stayed for a coffee and said we were interested in buying. They were delighted. I didn't haggle over the price, as it was a very fair one. They had wanted to sell up as quickly as possible so had put the house on the market at slightly below its proper market value. We shook hands and agreed that night.

'It's nice to see the garden taking shape again.' Mr Ashby said. 'I did a bit but I am no great gardener. Your man seems to know what he is doing.'

'A nice young man, very polite.' Mrs Ashby commented.

Chloe's eyes were dropping. Matt took her home.

'Who is your solicitor Mr Ashby?'

'That nice Simon Frobisher.' He answered.

'Oh, this gets better and better. He's ours as well. I'll contact him tomorrow.' I said.

'This was meant to be.' Mrs Ashby said. 'I'm really pleased it's you and Mathew who are buying the house.'

I smiled. 'I'm thrilled. The cottage next door is a bit small. I didn't want to go to the bother of moving, which we would have to do as I'm expecting a baby so we will need the extra rooms. This will be so exciting.'

We met Auntie Peggy and Reg, back from their fortnight's holiday abroad, at Darlington station. I did for them what they had done for us when we had come back from our honeymoon. I'd got the old range going and had a meal ready for them to heat up when they returned. They both looked relaxed and blooming. We left them at the door. Matt just helped them into the cottage with their luggage. I arranged for them to come up to our cottage next Sunday for a meal, so that we could tell them of our news. Matt's Mum was coming too. Tommy didn't have the day off, so wouldn't be there.

Chloe was so excited about seeing them again. She ran to the end of the lane so that she could see them coming up the hill. She pelted back again, shouting 'They're coming! They're coming!' Matt had gone off earlier to collect his Mum.

I welcomed them both again; it was good to see them looking so well and simply good to see them.

'We have secrets to tell you,' Chloe said, jumping up and down.

We all sat in the kitchen, as it was cold for October. The sitting room fire had just been put on to warm the room through for us to relax in after lunch.

'My, it's nice and warm in here,' said Reg.

'I was so cold last night. I couldn't warm up. I had two hot water bottles in my bed,' said Peggy.

Poor Auntie Peggy, she did suffer from the cold.

'Did you enjoy yourselves?' I asked.

'We had a grand time, lass, we really did.' Reg seemed to be in a good mood.

'We'll show you the photographs when we get them developed.' Auntie Peggy chimed in. 'Now we want to hear your secrets, if they are for telling.'

'Chloe, do you want to tell them?' I asked.

'Which one?' She asked.

'You mean you have more than one?' Matt's Mum asked.

'We have two,' she said, looking at me for guidance. I touched my tummy.

'Hang on...' Said Matt and went to the fridge to get the chilled champagne out.

'Well this must be important if it calls for champagne,' Reg said, grinning.

'Right Chloe, fire away,' Matt said, starting to undo the cork.

'Mummy's got a baby growing in her tummy.'

The champagne cork popped into a silent room as the news sank in. Auntie Peg jumped up and gave me a cuddle. She couldn't say anything she was so choked up.

Reg beamed, 'Well done lad!' He said to Matt, as though he'd done it all on his own.

'My lass, I'm that pleased,' he said, turning to me.

Matt's Mum also looked very pleased. 'Lovely, lovely news. Congratulations to you both.'

'So the doctors were wrong in their assumption.' Auntie Pegs managed to say. 'I'm delighted for the both of you. When?'

'Not until April, so we have some way to go. I'm well over the three-month period though, so I wanted you three to be the first to know.'

'Don't tell your mother that we know before she does; she'll be very hurt.'

'Auntie Peggy, I never see her to tell her anything. She's either with Auntie Elsie, when her new husband is abroad on business, or she is out with her latest fancy man.' My mother had moved into a cottage in Harmby. Her divorce absolute had finally come through. She was busy living life to the full, well shot of Ray. When I had seen her last, weeks ago, she looked much more relaxed and far happier.

'Do tell. Who is it?' Auntie Pegs asked.

'I think it's Simon Frobisher.'

'The... Your...?'

'Solicitor.' I finished for her.

'She's never said.'

'Now come on, don't you get upset, you're not often home either,' Reg said.' Enough of this idle gossip, I want to make inroads into this champagne.'

'Absolutely,' Matt's Mum added.

'Ladies and gentlemen,' Reg said, raising his champagne flute and standing up. 'Here is to Lucy and Matt, not forgetting our Chloe.'

'I'll drink to that,' said Auntie Peggy.

I sipped mine and gave Matt a brilliant smile.

'I want to propose a toast.... to my lovely, lovely family... all of you.'

'Hear-hear,' cheered Matt.

'I'm starving,' Reg muttered.

'Let's eat then,' I said.

Over lunch, we told them about the house next door being up for sale and that we were going to buy it and make the cottage and the house into one dwelling.

'Well you're going to need more space with a baby on the way.' Matt's Mum said. 'So I think it's a grand idea.' I could have kissed her. That remark would set Matt's mind at rest about using my money to buy the house next door. I knew it had been worrying him since we'd decided to go ahead with it.

Later, after a cup of tea, Matt's mother suggested that he took her home. He happily agreed to that. Chloe asked if she could go with them; she had come to like 'Granny Howard'. She lived in Richmond, so they would be gone about an hour and a half. Auntie Peggy and I left Reg toasting his toes and dozing in the sitting room and we went back into the kitchen to clear up and get stuck into the washing up.

'I'm so pleased about your news Lucy, after what those doctors said about you probably not having your own children. It's fantastic news. Reggie, I know, is tickled pink.'

I turned a smiling face to Auntie Pegs. 'Isn't it just wonderful? Someone will have to pinch me to make sure I'm not dreaming. Chloe seems taken with the idea, too.'

'Any names thought of yet?'

'I like Clair, if it's a girl. For a boy, I like Simon, it's Matt's second name.'

'I like both of those. I knew a Simon once, he was very dishy.'

'Auntie Pegs, you shock me.'

'Oh, it was ages ago. Tell me about the house next door.'

'I'm so excited about that. Matt was against it at first, he hates me using my money. I think his mother saying what a good idea it was to get a bigger house has settled his mind a bit. Of course she doesn't know the circumstances concerning the money and that I will be paying for it but she doesn't need to know that.'

'What's it like inside?'

With a lot of gesticulating on my part and drawing on the old wooden kitchen table with my wet hands, she got the general floor plan.

'So what we want to do is knock down the dividing wall in our bedroom into their bedroom, which will give us a really big room. The baby's room will be just across the landing, which is above the big sitting room. Chloe wants the room next door that's above the dining area. But if this baby cries like she did I think she will be move back into her old room.'

Auntie Peggy laughed. 'Don't I remember those times?'

'Next to the room Chloe wants, is a small bedroom that's over the pantry, the main bathroom is next door over the kitchen. As you know Chloe's bedroom that she has now, is over the extension, that will become the guest room and our present bathroom will be separated from the main house, so that visitors can have their own bathroom.'

'Well, you certainly have it all planned out.'

'But won't it be lovely, when you come over for dinner, like today, Christmas, Birthdays and other celebrations you can stay over instead of going home.'

'What a lovely thought. What about the downstairs?' Auntie Peggy asked.

'That's another big change around. A doorway will have to be put into what was their dining room that is now their big hall, into our present sitting room and the wall dividing the two kitchens will be taken down completely, to give me a big kitchen. Unfortunately, we will have to make a new stairway, as neither is really suitable.'

'What about your present dining room?'

'Probably a playroom or, a place to pack their toys away in. Near me, so I can keep an eye on them but not under my feet in case I'm carrying hot trays.'

'And your present sitting room? I do like that room, it's so cosy.'

'I thought a den for the winter, you're so right, it is so cosy in there, or maybe a study as Matt often brings work home.'

'It sounds lovely.' Auntie Peggy said enthusiastically. 'I'm so looking forward to seeing it completed.'

'So am I Auntie Pegs, so am I.'

With the washing up done and another pot of tea 'mashing' we made way to our cosy sitting room to wait for Matt's arrival home with Chloe.

XXIX.   1974-1982

Right on cue baby Clair arrived at 10.00 on the morning of the 22nd of April 1974. I had been in labour for 2 days on the third day it was decided that I would have to have a caesarean section as the baby was showing signs of distress and I was exhausted. They gave me an epidural and told me I would feel nothing. On the operating table, they put a screen in front of me at chest level so that I couldn't see what was going on. Matt sat near me, looking white, strained and tired. He'd been with me throughout. Rubbing my back to try to ease the pain, he held my right hand as the other had a drip going into it and tried to encourage me. He was worried sick.

In truth, I felt nothing but a slight pulling sensation as the doctors eased her out.

'You have a girl and she is perfect.' The doctor said, grinning over the screen. 'Would you like to cut the cord Mr Howard?'

Matt looked as though he was going to be sick.

'Er no, I don't like the sight of blood. I can put a plaster on my daughter's leg or arm, anything else is beyond me.'

The doctor grinned again.

The baby was cleaned up and handed to Matt. I was in no condition to hold anything, I felt totally drained and so weak.

Matt was shamelessly crying. He sat next to me with this tiny baby in his arms. 'Look Lucy, she looks just like you. So sweet, so tiny and so gorgeous.'

In those days, after having a baby you had to stay in hospital for at least 10 days. Bored silly, I badgered the doctor to let me out after seven. I said my new house was ready for me to move into and I would have round the clock attention. He still said no but I could go once the stitches were out the next day. With the stitches removed and everything appearing to be healing as it should be, I could go home. I rang Matt, highly excited, and told him I could be collected that afternoon.

Simon Frobisher had really got a move on with the conveyancing on the house next door and in two months it belonged to us. No planning permission was needed, as it was all internal work that needed to be done. Matt and David had got on with the alterations, as we wanted to be in when I had the baby.

At six months gone, I'd showed little sign of being pregnant but had ballooned after that. I waddled like a duck. Matt and Chloe loved placing their hand on my tummy, especially when the baby was moving. I went from our cottage to hospital and back to the completed house. Auntie Peggy and my mother must have worked really hard to get the house cleaned up for my return. They had been allowed in to see me in hospital, Chloe hadn't, so hadn't seen her little sister.

When I arrived home, Matt stopped the car by the front entrance. The little porch had had a new coat of paint, as had the front door. The door was opened by my mother, who took me in her arms to welcome me back and guided me into the large sitting room. Auntie Peggy and Reg were there to greet me, as was Chloe, who was as excited to see me as I was to see her and the rest of my family and to see the completed house.

I sank into an easy chair as Chloe flew to me. 'Mummy, Mummy I have missed you so much.' I gathered her into my arms and eased her onto my knee to hug her tightly.

Auntie Peggy was next to greet me; she bent over the chair arm to kiss me, as did Reg. 'Welcome home lovie.' Auntie Peggy said. 'And many congratulations.'

'Aye, I second that.' Agreed Reg.

'It's so good to be home.' I smothered Chloe's face with kisses. 'Oh, I have missed you so much.'

'I've drawed a picture for you and Clair, Mummy, I hope you like it.'

'I will love it, so will Clair. She has brought you a gift.'

'Oh has she? Let's see, let's see.' She was so excited and she slid off my knee.

Matt came in just then, carrying Clair in her carrycot. He had just been parking the car in the courtyard. Clair's present to Chloe was sitting at her feet.

'Is this for me?' Chloe asked. I nodded my head. Inside was a cute baby doll.

'My own baby.' She gasped. 'Thank you Clair.' She looked at the sleeping baby.

'Hello Clair. Isn't she sweet? She's very small. Some of my dollies are bigger than she is. Daddy and me have been sorting out loads of my old toys for her to play with and we got her a hug teddy.'

'I think you mean a huge teddy, Chloe.'

'Oh no.' she said confidently, 'It's a hug teddy 'cause you hug them.'

I couldn't argue with that. I gave her another cuddle.

'You sweet child.' I said softly.

My mother came in carrying a tray set with tea things, that she put onto the dining room table.

'Your Aunts made some scones. They look really nice. I thought a cup of tea and a scone would go down rather well. Then I thought that maybe you should go back to bed again. After I had you, I was on bed rest for three weeks.

'Things have changed a bit since then Mum.'

'But you had such a tough time.'

'Ah but look what I got for it.' And I gazed at Clair. 'I'm feeling pretty fit, Mum, really I am. And I don't want to waste time staying in bed.'

'My lass but you had us worried.' Auntie Peggy said.

'You can say that again.' Said Matt from his easy chair. 'After a cuppa and one of AP's scones you're going on a guided tour of your new house.'

'I can't wait.' I was so excited. Chloe stuck to my side for the rest of the day. On my guided tour of the house, she held onto my hand. I was thrilled with it all. From the new entrance, with its cloakroom and cupboards, through to the kitchen and all places in between. 'It seems so big.' I said. 'Huge.' I ran my fingers along the new worktops. And looked at the new built in oven and hob. The Aga, the only thing I wanted to keep, looked as though it had been polished to within an inch of its life, as it gleamed on the end wall. Then up the stairs that came out to the right of the big bedroom. I walked in and spied the crib that stood at the bottom of the bed. 'What a lovely room.' I enthused.

'It's all so lovely.' I kept saying.

'Come and see my room Mummy.'

'Don't hassle Mummy. She'll get there in her own time Pet.' My mother said. I gave Chloe's hand a little squeeze of reassurance. 'Let's go.' I said.

I'd never seen her room look so clean and toy free.

'My Chloe, you have been busy.'

'Granny said I had to help you by keeping my room clean and tidy.'

'Well, you have certainly done that.' Another little surprise that I hadn't thought of in my original plan, the little room that sat over the big pantry down stair had been joined up to Chloe's as her playroom. Two new toy boxes stood each side of the window and a desk was between them. On the opposite wall was a bookcase that was full of her books, puzzles, painting books and crayons, paint box, felt tip pens everything a little girl would want. Hanging on the walls were paintings and drawings done by Chloe. From a few pegs, shaped like animals, hung her skipping rope, two hula hoops and a large linen bag with a pretty girls face sewn on it, as well as Chloe's name, this was her dirty clothes bag.

'The boxes were handmade and painted by David. The rest I asked him to make' Matt said who was just behind me.

'How nice. I am impressed.'

'He took a carpentry course once and likes to keep his hand in. It's his gift, because he didn't know what to give to a new baby. He reasoned that Clair would get presents showered on her so made this especially for Chloe.

'How sweet of him.'

'It was a devil of a job to persuade him not to call up tonight. I said to leave it as you would be too tired.'

'Yes, I just wanted to see my family, just wanted to get back home and sleep in my own bed.'

I walked along the hall to the side of the stairs to the guest room, what a surprise there. There was no passageway to Chloe's old bedroom, just another door, through which was the original bathroom on the right of the room that we had put in, opening out to a nice sized guest bedroom.

Chloe answered my unspoken question. 'Granny's sleeping in here.'

'I hope you don't mind, dear. I thought you might need a bit of help for the first couple of weeks.'

'Of course I don't mind, what a lovely idea, thank you.'

'I feel you should go back to bed, though, lovie.'

'Don't fuss Mum, There is little point as Clair will need feeding soon and I want to stay up for supper, to have my family around me. Where are Peggy and Reg?'

'Baby ogling, I think.' Matt sounded amused.

I settled in and was pleased to be home once more and what a home to come back to.

I marvelled at it each day. Clair was such a good baby and only cried when she was hungry or needed her nappy changing. Her restless time was in the evenings. Mum was a great help in those first two weeks, I was very grateful to have her there. Auntie Pegs called quite often to lend a hand but went out more with Chloe, thinking that she might feel left out.

We managed alright on our own, once Mum had gone. Matt would come home late on Thursday having done all the shopping for the week. He tried his hand at cooking and managed a few simple dishes but was happy to hand the reins over to me once the first month was up.

I watched Chloe, as no way did I want her to turn out like her mother. But she seemed charmed with her baby sister and 'shared' with her upbringing, like putting talcum powder on Clair after her bath. Changing nappies was beyond her but I'd get 'Mummy, Clair needs her nappy changing, she's smells awful' or 'I'll go and get her hat, you've forgotten it again.' when we were just about to go out. She loved feeding Clair and would sit well back on the sofa with Chloe half on her knee and half on a cushion. Chloe would talk to her all the time. I'm sure she thought that Clair understood all she said.

Chloe was a lot like me in many ways, my colouring and my temperament but could be quite stubborn. Clair, on the other hand was so like Matt; laid back and easy going but once her mind was made up nothing would make her change it and she did have the occasional temper tantrums and was a Daddy's girl. Her hair was jet black and her eyes went brown, a replica of Matt's.

Auntie Peggy and Reg adored them both and showed no favouritism between the two of them. They still went away on their extended holidays but were always home for Christmas.

Auntie Peggy, Reg, my mother, with Simon Frobisher would arrive mid-morning loaded down with gifts. Matt would go off to collect his Mum. Auntie Peggy would help me in the kitchen, while the two Grannies would amuse the children in the big sitting room. The three men would go off for a quick drink together. I didn't mind, as long as they weren't late for Christmas lunch. We'd have it late anyway, while listening to the Queens speech. After a cup of tea, Matt would take his Mum home again and my mother would go off with Simon, I assumed to his house. Auntie Peggy and Reg would stay over in the fourth bedroom. We'd just have a relaxing day on Boxing Day and eat cold turkey, cold pork with lots of pickles and picked onions, always Reg's favourite meal. Tommy usually joined us on Boxing Day, bringing his own gifts for the children.

Clair would be eight months that first Christmas and Chloe would be six years. Clair couldn't take it all in, wide eyed, they would dart all over the place. I'd puree whatever we were having and as usual Chloe fed her, She'd open her own mouth when Clair opened hers it looked so sweet. Like a little mother she was. It was the most magical Christmas ever. I enjoyed every moment of it.

Apart from Clair getting mumps, that Chloe didn't get, even though they played together, they both had measles and chicken pox they were relatively healthy children.

In 1977 Tommy surprised us all by marrying a Kathy Hill, one of the receptionists employed by the new hotel owners. She was a pretty, dark-haired girl. We went to their wedding, Chloe was 10 then and Clair was four. Tommy wanted them as bridesmaids with Kathy's younger sister, Emma as chief bridesmaid who was 14. They looked as pretty as pictures.

When two children arrived in quick succession, they were given a council house in Harmby. Carol, Tommy's mother, would have been so proud of him. He'd battled through his problems and was now the under manager of the hotel.

The barn conversion, named The Barn, was often used by Matt's mother when she came to visit us. It meant that Matt could have a drink as he didn't have to turn out in the cold to take her home. She was quite happy staying there. She liked her own space and I think maybe, the children became a bit too much for her as well.

At thirteen Chloe wanted to know the details of her mother's imprisonment. I told her the absolute truth. I could see no point in not telling her. She had a right to know and she could easily find out anyway.

'Why did you adopt me? I was no blood relation to you at all and you must have hated both Jo-Ann and Lewis for what they did.' She asked.

'That's easy to answer. I saw a tiny baby that needed a stable home, that needed love and attention and a secure life. I loved you almost from the moment I saw you. You couldn't be held responsible for the sins of your mother and father. I just hope I've done right by you.'

She smiled somewhat sadly. 'I must have a lucky star that shone on me the day you saw me. My life could have been so different. No regrets?'

'Chloe Sweetheart, never. Not for one moment. Not even as a tiny baby and you used to scream every night from 2am to 5am even then. I felt that I was the lucky one. I loved you and you brought such happiness into so many people's lives. Auntie Peggy and Reg adored you and still do.'

'The bad Mummy and the good Mummy. I remember those stories very well.' She mused.

'It was supposed to, sort of prepare you, make it easier for you, though I doubt that it has.'

'But you have Clair, now.'

'Clair is Clair. She isn't you. If you lose one child, no matter what you do, or however many children you might have, that one child can never be replaced. I'm doubly blessed by having you and Clair. Just remember that Daddy and I love you both so much.' She was quiet for a few days as though thinking it through. There were no temper tantrums, nor did she become difficult. It worried me that she seemed to have taken it so well.

I was happy in my personal life. Matt and I were still like young lovers. But there were no more babies. I hadn't thought there would be any. I was just so lucky to have had Clair. She was my little miracle.

My beautiful children were happy and settled. Chloe was doing very well at school. Reg and Auntie Pegs were still doing their travelling and I expected marriage announcements at any time between Mum and Simon; and I never tired of my lovely home.

But storm clouds were gathering that I was not prepared for and that ruined everything...

XXX.   1982-1984

My happy contented life came to an end when Jo-Ann came out of prison. She was on parole and had to report to any police station every Thursday. She had been let out early for good behaviour. She had served just 16 years of her 21-year sentence.

She had been to Bristol to see Ray, her father, but his tiny, one bedroomed flat in the Redland area was not up to the standard she wanted, so she had left. She got Mother's address from Ray's diary and came to see her. Mother was probably as shocked to see her as I was. Mother told me she had said to Jo-Ann that under no circumstances was she to contact me and wouldn't give her my address.

But addresses are quite easy to come by, from the Electoral Roll or just using a telephone and asking directory enquiries.

It was a Wednesday afternoon and Matt was working late. I had collected Clair from school but not Chloe; she always did gymnastics on that day, so had stayed on. Jo-Ann just rang the bell. She looked the 16 years older after that time in prison. Her hair, I suspected, was helped to be that colour by a bottle. She wasn't quite as beautiful but still very striking although rather hard-looking.

'Aren't you going to ask me in?' she said.

'No,' I said sharply, 'I'm not. I don't want you here. You'd taint everything, so just go away.'

'I want to see my daughter.' She demanded.

'She isn't here.' I said through gritted teeth. 'So you've had a wasted journey. Now go away. You gave up all rights to her and turned your back on her when she was born. I adopted her legally and one of the conditions was that you didn't try to see her, ever.'

'Who's that?' She asked, catching sight of Clair, who had come into the hall to see who I was talking to.

'Clair is just 10 and you can leave her well alone. She is nothing to do with you, so clear off or I will call the police.' I was so angry.

She turned away. She couldn't afford to get in trouble with the police.

'You'll be hearing from me.' She tossed over her shoulder as she walked away.

I told Matt that night that Jo-Ann was out of prison and had just turned up. 'Like a bad penny.'

He said, 'Well if she becomes a nuisance we can get an injunction against her, forbidding her to come within five miles of us.'

'That's a bit drastic; she may not call again, although she did say I would be hearing from her.'

I really think sometimes that I am quite stupid. She did worse than that. She got a judge to grant her visiting rights. Social Services appointed a Social Worker to work with her. Before a judge, in his private chambers, I said, 'she had shown herself to be an uncaring mother. When she gave her baby to my mother after she was born she referred to her as "The Brat" and simply didn't want her.'

Jo-Ann, looking dashing and beautiful, dabbed with a hanky at her nose and said, it had hurt her so much to give her daughter away but she had thought it to be for the best, as she didn't want her baby to be brought up in prison.

This was complete rubbish, as Simon Frobisher testified. Then my mother put her spoke in and said she thought Jo-Ann had tears in her eyes when she had handed the signed papers over.

The Social Worker intervened and had her say. The judge took a recess to think it over and Jo-Ann got her visiting rights. I never forgave my mother for making the remark about seeing tears in Jo-Ann's eyes. Nobody else did either. Simon was furious and broke off his relationship with her.

My mother had come to Crofters Cottage and told Auntie Peggy what Simon had said. 'I asked him yesterday, what I should say and he said, "Just tell the truth."'

'And what did he say today to change that opinion?' My aunt asked frostily.

'He said, "I didn't realise you were going to tell the judge that you thought you saw tears in her eyes. I stared at her that day I picked the papers up from in front of her and she looked perfectly alright to me." What am I going to do?'

'Beg forgiveness from Lucy, I should think.' Auntie Peggy replied shortly.

She was telling me all this at my house the following day.

'She needn't bother to come here.' I said. 'I can't ever forgive her. That could just have swung the judge's opinion. Did Mother stay with you last night?'

'No. Reg refused to have her.' Auntie Peggy said. 'I have never known him so angry and really upset for you. Neither of us slept last night.'

'Nor did Matt or me. I don't understand anyone giving a convicted murderess visiting rights. When she signed those papers, I specified that Jo-Ann was never to see Chloe again or get in touch when she came out of prison. They obviously mean sod all.'

Mother came to see me not long after Auntie Peggy had left. I showed her into the big sitting room.

'What can I say?' She asked.

'I think you've probably said enough, don't you?' I snapped back.

'Maybe she'll get bored and just go away.'

'Don't be obtuse Mother. Every time Chloe blinks Jo-Ann will see pound signs.'

'You think she is after Chloe's money?'

'She's not stupid. Jo-Ann will know that I have settled money on Chloe. She may not realise that Chloe can't touch it until she's twenty-one. I'm confident that's what she's after.'

'What can I do?' My mother sounded pathetic.

'You, who have always stuck up for Jo-Ann, can go to hell. This is going to have far reaching effects.'

How right I was proved to be.

My mother flinched as though I had hit her. 'I'm so sorry, I do apologise.'

'I don't accept it Mother,' I said ungraciously, 'and I would be grateful if you would go.' I turned my back on her and walked into the kitchen. I heard the front door close quietly as she went, then I sat on a kitchen stool and howled until I had no-more tears left.

Every Friday after school, Jo-Ann called round with her Social Worker. I only offered them a cup of tea with a few biscuits that we always had in the kitchen. Her visits lasted an hour to start with.

Only I know how totally charming Jo-Ann can be when she wants to be. She turned this charm onto Chloe to the exclusion of everyone else. She would be gone by the time Matt came home from the bank. She would bring expensive gifts for Chloe but nothing for Clair. Eventually, I asked Auntie Peggy to have Clair every Friday, I couldn't bear to see her upset and hurt. Chloe became greedy with her gifts and wouldn't share them with Clair. She would take whatever the gift was up to her room and wouldn't even show them to Matt or me.

'I can see you're very smitten with your birth mother,' I said to Chloe.

'And why shouldn't I be? She is very generous and very pretty.'

'You're too young to see it but she is a very dangerous lady. And just remember, she murdered your father,' I shot back.

There came a day when the Social Worker and Jo-Ann arrived to take Chloe out for the day and then it got to once a week. Chloe always came back with glowing accounts of where she had been taken and what they had done. Chloe started to call me Lucy, saying that I wasn't her mother. I was so hurt by this.

'I may not have given birth to you, Chloe, but I have looked after you since you were three months old. I have been a mother to you in every other way since and I adored you.'

'I notice it's in the past tense,' she answered back.

'Love is unconditional Chloe. No matter what you do, I shall always love you.'

She became surly, rude and uncooperative, Matt would get so cross with her. I knew what Jo-Ann was doing, she no more wanted Chloe than before, she was just getting back at me and wanted to hurt me as much as possible.

When Chloe went upstairs to get an expensive jacket that Jo-Ann had given her, Jo-Ann had said, 'You have such a lot of money; surely you could share some of your good fortune with me?'

'You must be joking,' I shot back. 'You took my husband and then killed him. Why would I want to give you anything?'

'Because he was going to dump you and marry me.'

'No!' I said, 'He refused to 'dump' me as you put it, when he found out you were pregnant and he certainly wouldn't want you then. What was it Mother said he called you? "A selfish tart" comes to mind. About the only thing we agreed on.'

I looked at the Social Worker, who was standing nearby.

'You're really taken in by her, aren't you? The only reason she wants Chloe back is because she knows that that will hurt me more than anything else and she wants to get her greedy hands on Chloe's money, that she thinks I have put by for her. Chloe has become naughty, cheeky and calls me Lucy. God alone knows what lies Jo-Ann's been filling Chloe's head with.'

'I wouldn't know. I leave them to be together for a while.' The Social Worker said.

This really shook me. I hadn't realized that they had been left alone.

'I blame you and a stupid judge for giving visiting rights to a murderess and upsetting a perfectly innocent, impressionable girl who is going through a difficult time anyway with her hormones all over the place and your interference is making it more difficult for her to cope. And it's all in the name of doing what's best for her.

What piffle and utter rubbish. She was like any other 15-year-old teenager. Now she is muddled and confused and doesn't know where she's at. Surely you can see that? If Jo-Ann really loved her daughter she would have let her be, knowing she was well, happy, loved and secure.'

'I'm just doing my job.' The Social Worker said.

'Well, all I can say is, God help those who have to have a Social Worker and I hope I never need your services. Social Workers make me want to puke!'

Chloe came back into the kitchen just then, which ended the conversation.

I remember the day the Social Worker came on her own to collect Chloe and take her to Darlington to stay with Jo-Ann for the weekend. She had rented a charming two-bedroomed flat there. Chloe was as excited as she was nervous. I felt betrayed and devastated when she walked out the door with hardly a backward glance. I had Auntie Peggy with me at the time; we turned to each other and hugged tight. We were both crying. Clair was with Reg. I had thought it better for her not to see her sister going. There was no telephone call that night as she had promised. I could imagine Jo-Ann telling her not to bother.

I lay in Matt's arms that night, shedding bitter and angry tears once more. But nothing was going to lessen the hurt.

Chloe had changed again when she came back on Sunday night. She had a huge amount of make up on. She was aloof and barely spoke unless she was spoken to. She ignored Clair as though she wasn't there. It upset me so much to see Clair so hurt by her adored sister's attitude towards her.

Matt, whom she had always got on well with, tried to reason with her but got 'You're not my father, just as she...' and she nodded in my direction, 'isn't my mother, so what would you two know?' She stormed out of the kitchen and locked herself in her room.

Another time he had said. 'Look Chloe, your mother and I can take your rudeness. We don't like it but we are strong enough to take it. What about Clair? She is a lot younger than you are and she is hurting badly. She doesn't understand why you are being so nasty to her when you have been so close in the past, so if you can't speak pleasantly to us, at least lay off Clair, she has done nothing to hurt you. You have been closer than sisters.'

All Chloe said was, 'But she isn't my sister, is she?' And flung out of the kitchen again.

Chloe stayed away two weeks with Jo-Ann and came back a nasty, troubled teenager. She wouldn't do anything she was asked to do, was lazy, stayed up late most nights watching TV and smoking. She was just 16. Her grades at school fell, she got behind with her schoolwork and never did her homework. I was constantly asked to go to school and talk it over to see what was happening. I could hardly tell them that my murdering sister, Chloe's real mother had turned up and that was the effect it was having on her. I told them I was trying to deal with an angry teenager and was sure it would turn out all right eventually, given time. Of course, it didn't, she just announced that she was leaving school and left with no grades.

When she was asked whom she would prefer to live with and chose Jo-Ann, I was stunned, dumbfounded and shocked. I felt as though a ton of bricks had fallen on top of me and I couldn't breathe. I felt that Jo-Ann had won the battle and that this was what she'd had in mind all along.

Of course, we had to let her go. Matt and I saw her off from our front door. The car she went in was driven by the Social Worker. Chloe had packed only the clothes that Jo-Ann had given her and had left her room in a chaotic mess. I said to the Social Worker as we stood in the hall waiting for Chloe to come downstairs with the last of her things, 'I hope you're satisfied with a job well done and I hope to never see you again.'

She had the grace to look embarrassed. 'This wasn't meant to happen. I never thought...'

'That's the trouble,' I said, 'you never thought. Jo-Ann has you reeled in good and hard.' It was only my anger that stopped me from crying when Chloe went out of the front door. Once the car had gone out of sight, Matt led me into the little sitting room. I was shaking, then I started sobbing. This was my worst nightmare.

But it wasn't; worse was to come...

XXXI.   1984-1987

Mathew and I immersed ourselves in decorating and gardening, just to keep busy. I got more involved in The Priory, the Sanctuary for abused women, and Matt often worked late at the bank instead of bringing work home. He was now Manager at the bank in Richmond. I was always home to collect Clair from School, also in Richmond.

Between us, we gave her lots of time and attention. After all, she was grieving as well, she was just 11 years old, I'd often come across her crying. All I could do was take her into my arms and cuddle her.

One day, about six months after Chloe had gone, I went to collect Clair from school. I arrived at the gates in good time as I always did. I'd spent the afternoon with Matt's mother, who lives not far from the school. I waited in the car, expecting Clair to turn up at any minute and I went on waiting and started to worry at her non-arrival. I walked into the school and to the staff room and was met by Mrs Watson, the headmistress, coming out to go home.

'Hello Mrs Howard, can I help you? I'm in a bit of a hurry as I have a meeting to go to.'

'Where's Clair, Mrs Watson?'

'She went out with all the other children.' She replied.

'But she hasn't come to the car.'

'Would she have gone off to play with her friends?'

'She'd never do that; she would ask first.'

She pointedly looked at her watch.

'I can see you're in a hurry and not really interested in a missing child!' I snapped.

'Mrs Howard, of course I'm interested. I'm sure there is a simple explanation. Her form teacher is still here, let's ask her.' She turned and went back into the staff room and I followed.

Clair's form teacher, Irene Barnes, was marking some books. She looked up with a smile, which vanished when she saw the look on my face.

'Have you seen Clair Howard, Irene? She hasn't turned up to meet her mother.'

Clair's form teacher looked puzzled, 'Why yes, a red-haired woman called to collect her, about...' she looked at her watch, '...an hour ago.'

'Didn't you think to ring and check that it was alright for her to be picked up by someone else?' I asked, scared suddenly and fuming.

'But Clair knew her and went quite willingly. The woman said that Chloe was in the car outside and wanted to see her.'

I went forward and picked up the phone that was on a desk and dialled Matt's bank.

'Put me through to the Manager, at once,' I barked, as soon as the phone was picked up at the other end.

'Who's speaking?'

'It's personal.'

'Wait a minute, please Madam.'

A second or two went by; I was tapping the desk with my nails in my agitation.

I could hear his voice, giving a message to the girl who had answered the phone.

'Matt!' I screamed down the phone. I heard his voice break off mid-sentence.

'What is it, darling?' He asked.

'Jo-Ann's got Clair.'

'Where are you?'

'At her school.'

'Stay put. I'll be with you in minutes.'

I was in a state by the time Matt arrived, although, as he had said, he was only a few minutes. The headmistress had used the phone after me to give her apologies, as she was going to arrive late for her meeting. 'An incident.' She gave as her excuse. I could have hit her. A missing child is hardly an incident, for the parents it's a major catastrophe.

As Matt walked in I was sipping a cup of tea made for me by Irene Barnes.

'I haven't the time to talk about it now but you will be hearing from me.' He said. 'This is a disgrace, to allow just anyone to walk into a school and take a child.' He was obviously very angry and upset. The headmistress looked a bit taken aback. Matt grabbed my hand and we both ran out.

I knew Jo-Ann's address and that's where we were heading for but it's a two-hour drive away.

'The police will be quicker to pick her up than us,' Matt said. We stopped at the first telephone box we came to. He dialled 999 and explained in a few minutes what had happened.

Going as fast as we dared and breaking the speed limit, we raced to Darlington. I was frantic and so angry; we both were. What if Jo-Ann was going to hurt Clair? But would she with Chloe there?

'What the hell does she think she's doing?' Matt kept saying. 'Who does she think she is just to collect Clair from school? Isn't one of our children enough for her to have?'

I kept fairly quiet, with my own thoughts. She'd been convicted of murder once... I scolded myself, don't go down that road but the thought wouldn't go away. Maybe it was just a stupid prank that she was playing and we would find Clair talking quite happily to Chloe and pleased to see her again.

Maybe this is what she wanted; my two children. Get Clair on her side and tell her that she could see Chloe whenever she wanted to, then I would come out as the bad one if I refused to let Clair see Chloe. Thoughts kept flowing quickly through my head as we flew along to Scotch Corner.

When we reached the road where Jo-Ann lived in a block of flats, the police were all over the place. We were stopped from going down the road until we said who we were, then we were waved through. We stopped outside the flats and an Inspector came over to us. By then, I was past consoling; I suspected the worst. Matt held tightly on to my hand, it was obvious that he had the same thoughts.

The Inspector got into the car with us to fill us in on what had happened so far.

'There is no sign of Miss Bradley and the two girls. We are searching the flat now to see if there is any hint of where they may have gone left in side. There are no personal effects left at all. We have informed the landlord and he is in there, now, seeing if anything of his has been taken. So far he has said nothing is missing but that Miss Bradley owes him two months' rent. One of my constables is interviewing others who live in the block but so far no-one saw anything. A woman across the road...' he took out his notes and flicked back a page or two, '...ah yes, a Mrs Irvin came to say that a motorised caravan was parked here last night. She remembers that, because it was in the way and her husband couldn't swing his car into his garage. She says that four people got into it, a man and a woman and two children. One, a teenager who had been living with her and the other, a much younger girl. Mrs Irvin recognised the woman because she has seen her before and said she was a very pretty woman. Her red hair was covered with a head square; she also said that they went about three hours ago. Do you have any idea where they may have gone?'

We both said that we had no idea at all.

'Unfortunately Mrs Irvin didn't get the registration number and could only say it was in a cream colour.'

'There must be hundreds of those on the road.' Matt said morosely.

I was crying silently. Tears were coursing down my face.

'Try not to worry,' the Inspector said. 'Miss Bradley may have just taken them for a caravan holiday.'

'You don't believe that Inspector and nor do we,' Matt said in irritation. I was beyond saying anything.

'We are unable to do very much, Mr and Mrs Howard. Mrs Irvin has rung her husband at his office but he isn't in at the moment. We are hoping that he can give us more information on the motorised caravan. As she said, it was dark when he returned last night and still dark when he went this morning. I can only suggest that you go home, they may be there waiting for your return.'

I muttered, 'I don't believe that either.'

The Inspector said, 'Well you never know. We'll keep in close contact with you and if anything – anything at all – develops, we will be in touch'.

We took our homeward journey a bit slower.

I felt ill with worry. I couldn't eat or sleep and Matt was just the same. He took a week off sick so that we could be together. The house was so quiet it spooked us both. Auntie Peggy and Reg had been about to go on holiday to be back just before Christmas but they cancelled it. They lived in our house, looking after us, making sure we ate something. They were terribly upset too. We needed to be together. Of my mother, I saw nothing.

The police rang every day to report any developments. Mr Irvin hadn't got a good look at the motorised caravan, so was no help whatsoever. No motorised caravan of Mrs Irvin's description was seen. All of them were stopped and searched at every sea-port. All airports and motorways were watched. The newspapers carried photographs of Jo-Ann, Chloe and Clair. A warrant was now out for Jo-Ann's arrest as she had failed to report to any police station, thereby breaking her parole order and also for kidnapping a minor.

But it was as though they had vanished into thin air.

Christmas came and went but no-one in our immediate family celebrated. Matt and I both lost weight, had black shadows under our eyes and looked and felt awful. If it had not been for Auntie Peggy, neither of us would have eaten anything.

My mother arrived at my house one day. She looked pretty grim herself. 'It's just a thought, and I don't want you to get too excited about it, and I don't know how she did it, but I think she might be in the farmhouse in France.'

'What farmhouse?' asked Matt.

'She was born in France to a French mother, who died giving birth to her. Ray used to go back after the war and take Jo-Ann with him to visit her grandparents. When she was eight, he stopped doing it. He thinks that's where she picked up pneumonia and pleurisy that she nearly died of,' my mother told him.

'We must tell the police. They can get Interpol involved,' Matt said, showing enthusiasm for the first time in a long while. Even I was hopeful.

The police got on with it straight away once my mother had found the address. Jo-Ann was found at the farm and was arrested on sight but of the children, there was no sign. She hadn't even noticed that they were missing. She was hungover after a heavy night of drinking, tried to fight the Gendarmes off and giggled delightedly when she gave one a black eye. She wasn't laughing, however, when she was thrown into a French prison to await transportation back to England.

Two bedraggled girls turned up at the British Embassy in Paris. Without passports, it took them sometime to make the Embassy

Officials understand who they were. Clair was taken to hospital very poorly indeed but got so frantic without Chloe that Chloe was allowed to stay with her. Matt and I flew over to France that same evening and got to see them for the first time in three months. I unashamedly cried. Matt was near to tears as well. Clair was very unwell and looked dreadful, a lot of her hair had fallen out and what was left was a frightful yellow colour.

Chloe looked from one to the other of us and burst into tears and said what a cow she had been and how sorry she was. I had Clair on my knee in a hospital easy chair. I just kept kissing her. She clung to me tightly as though she would never let me go. I could only ease her into bed when she fell asleep.

Poor child, she did look very unwell.

XXXII.   CHLOE'S STORY

I didn't realise that Jo-Ann was going to abduct Clair. I had merely said that I missed her. The next thing I am at the school gates waiting for Jo-Ann to come out with Clair. I was surprised when she was bundled into the car. I said to Jo-Ann, "What are you doing? She said "It's all arranged. I've had a word with Clair's mother and she said it was alright for us to take Clair on a little holiday." You know how plausible she is and stupidly I believed her.

We went to a place I don't know and there we changed to a proper caravan and hitched it up to a car. The caravan was full to the brim with our possessions. I have no knowledge of when she packed it up. It must have been at night. The man we were with is no relation, just a friend who was doing Jo-Ann a favour. We went to Dover and just before the port, Clair and I were put into the caravan and hidden in the storage seats in the sitting room area. I think Clair was drugged to keep her quiet. I may have been too, as I seemed to be on a high and just agreed to this great adventure of being smuggled into France. Jo-Ann came down to the parking area with some food during the night but Clair was out for the count.

We stayed hidden and the next day, after we had reached France and had gone through customs, we were allowed out. It was a long journey but quite a simple one. Although I don't know how anyone is supposed to drive through Paris, the traffic is terrible. The farmhouse was huge, draughty and terribly cold. They had a generator for electricity. One of Jo-Ann's Aunts, Aunt Maria, was very good to us. We were made very welcome by the whole family. Clair, though, was most unhappy and cried every night and spoke to no-one. They spoke no English and my French is sketchy at best. I promised Clair that I would somehow get her home. Jo-Ann had bleached her hair and I think she used too much, or something, as it made Clair ill and her hair started to fall out.

Jo-Ann wasn't very kind to her. She'd tell her that you didn't want her anymore and that she had to live in France for the rest of her life, so she had better buck her ideas up. I also realized, rather late in the day, that Jo-Ann only wanted me for the money and to get back at you. She thought I had plenty and kept asking for some, when I kept telling her that I didn't have any, she lost her temper and then ignored us both. It was when she started lashing out at Clair that I decided the time had come when I had to get Clair out. It just happens that Fridays are always very busy. The milk lorry comes at 6.00 and stays for a continental breakfast. I think there is a thing going on between him and the nice aunt. The egg man comes too, at about the same time.

I had got used to driving the old Land Rover, because I drove it to take the farm workers their picnic lunches to them when they were working in one of the fields some way from the farm. They have acres of land, it's a huge farm.

Jo-Ann was drinking as though it was going out of fashion and this day she was asleep from a heavy night the evening before. Taking nothing with us, we nonchalantly walked out of the farm-house and I took the Land Rover. Unfortunately, I had to take their egg money as well. As I said, the journey to Paris is a very long way but quite simple. Just to get to a main road takes an hour. Clair slept for most of the way. Once in Paris, I parked the Land Rover and got a taxi to take us to the British Embassy. My driving is not good enough for me to get through Paris in one piece.

Well, that's it. You know the rest. I've left nothing out that I can think of. Now you're here, I can't imagine that you want me hanging around, so I'll head back to the farm. The Land Rover should be where I left it.'

'Don't you want to come back with us?' I asked hesitatingly.

'I didn't imagine you'd really want me. Apart from Jo-Ann's bad behaviour, I quite like the farm.'

'That's not answering the question,' I said.

'Well, yes, but I don't want to lose contact with the farm. Aunt Maria was really nice and I want to pay the money back and return the Land Rover.'

'I have an idea,' said Matt, who had remained quiet, like I had, throughout Chloe's monologue.

'Clair is going to be here in hospital for a little while, I think. Why don't you and I go to the farm tomorrow? I'll hire a car, take you to where the Land Rover is and follow you. Then we have a car to come back in and we can pay them back their egg money and return the Land Rover.'

It may have just slipped out but she said. 'That would be a lovely idea, Dad.' I said nothing, nor did Matt; he pretended that she always called him Dad.

'What do you think, Lucy?' Matt asked.

'Well, yes, I think that's a good idea,' I answered.

'They just accepted us in the family. They have no television or phone, it's possible that they don't know anything about us. I don't know what yarn Jo-Ann told them.'

'It's a pity you didn't stay on for a little longer. The Gendarmes called later in the day and arrested your mother for breaking her parole order and for the kidnap of a minor,' Matt said.

'Oh no! All that trouble for nothing.'

'No, not for nothing, Chloe; you were doing what you knew was the right thing to do for Clair and for my part I'll be eternally grateful to you,' I said gently.

'I second that,' Matt agreed.

They were appreciative at the farm the next day, so Matt told me later. The Gendarmes had cautioned them all and they were horrified and so apologetic once they knew the truth. Matt told the French police that he didn't want the French family prosecuted, as they simply didn't know that they were harbouring a kidnapped girl. We were willing to let any charges drop.

In her halting French, Chloe thanked them for having her to stay and said she would love to come back again someday. They nodded, smiling, and said they would be very pleased to see her again.

We arrived back in England with relief and were met by Auntie Peggy and Reg at the station. They were shocked at Clair's condition but she was loads better than she had been. We organised a party to celebrate the safe return of the Chloe and Clair. It was such a happy time.

We celebrated a late Christmas and even managed to get a tree. Matt and I were so thankful to have our two girls back. They were spoilt rotten by Auntie Peggy, Reg and Mum. It had been her idea to go to the farm to see if the children were there and I was so very grateful to her for that. I couldn't hold a grudge against her forever.

Chloe joined in the fun and seemed glad to be back home. She was a changed girl, very pleasant and she seemed happy and contented. She gave up smoking, stopped drinking and went back to school. She worked very hard to catch up and had extra tutoring in the evenings. Eventually she got nine O levels. I was so proud of her. She never mentioned her mother and started to call me 'Mum' again, as she used to.

Clair didn't fare quite so well. She had terrible nightmares for weeks after and couldn't bear me to be out of her sight. I used to leave her crying at school each morning, which upset me. She only became the bright, happy child she had been before the abduction about a year later, when she began to do better at school again and settle down. She and Chloe became very close again.

Jo-Ann resides in a high security prison once more. She has to do her full sentence, the remaining six years, with two years added on for kidnapping a minor, eight years in all and I didn't think it was long enough.

I don't know why I visited Jo-Ann in prison. She had completed about two years. I went just the once and then wished I hadn't, as she told me something that shook me to the core of my being and totally ruined my peace of mind. I will never forgive her.

XXXIII.   1987-1988

I have no recollection of driving home. I assume I gave all the right signals and caused no accidents. I don't even remember walking out of Durham prison. I 'came to' from my reverie and found myself sitting in the kitchen, clutching a hot cup of tea.

My head was in a whirl. Jo-Ann was a liar, a cheat and convicted of murder and child kidnapping and yet something in her voice made me think that she was telling me the truth although I clutched at the straw that what she had told me was a pack of lies. I only had to ask Matt and all would become clear but if it was true, it would be too painful to take in.

I wasn't collecting Clair from school anymore. She was fourteen, after all. She walked to the square in Richmond with three friends who lived in Leyburn and lots of other girls who caught their busses to different destinations, so I wasn't expecting her for another hour. All I could do was prepare dinner. I was on automatic pilot and did things by instinct whilst my head just went round and round. By the time Clair and Matt came home (Chloe was studying medicine and was away at medical school) my head was splitting. Matt showed his concern; he said I looked grey.

'How did the visit go with Jo-Ann? I would say badly, by the look of you. I did say that I didn't think it was a good idea.'

'So you did,' I said, rather sharper than I meant to. 'I'm sorry. I think I'll lie down for a while. I have a dreadful headache.'

'I'll bring you up a cup of tea and some pain killers,' Matt offered.

'Thank you, that will be nice.' And I walked out of the kitchen.

I pulled back the coverlet on our bed, took off just my outer clothes and got between the cool sheets. Matt came up with my tea and some painkillers.

'Come on Lucy, what did she say to upset you so much?'

I remained quiet while I sipped some tea and took two tablets.

'Are you sure you don't know?' I eventually asked.

He sat on the bed and looked at me with a slight frown on his face. 'What an odd question. Of course I don't know what she said.'

'According to her you do.'

'Well, you'd better say what it was, as I haven't a clue what you're talking about.'

'Look me in the eyes and tell me that you didn't know Chloe was yours.'

He looked shocked beyond words. 'Mine! Chloe's mine?' He stared at me. 'And you believe that lying cow?' Apart from confusion in his voice, he was also angry. 'How could Chloe be *my* child? As far as I know, I have never met Jo-Ann.'

'Did you never see her when she was collecting Chloe?'

'Never. I was always working.'

'Well, she knows you very well. You had an affair with Jo-Ann about six months before you met up with me again.'

'This is just ridiculous. I have never met or even seen her, other than her pictures in the papers and they weren't very clear.'

'She said if you were to deny that you have met her, I'm just to say 'your black beauty.' Jog your memory does it?' I said nastily.

'My black beaut...' Then he stopped and I could see from his face that he remembered and knew what I was talking about. He opened his mouth but no sound came out. He closed it again. He got up from the bed and went to the window and gazed out, unseeingly, I suspected.

'Yes, I knew a Black Beauty,' he said, very quietly. 'But her name was Josephine McCarthy and her hair was jet black. I told you about her. I swear on my life that I never realized she and your sister were one and the same person.'

'I don't know if I believe you,' I said from the bed. 'I want to believe you, I really do, otherwise I have been living a lie for the past 16 years. She said it was all planned out. You were to take up with me again, get married, then divorce me, take me for half my fortune and with Chloe you were to live happily ever after with her.'

'And you believed her?' He sounded amazed and hurt; he turned round from the window so that he could see me when he spoke.

'I don't know what to believe.' I was weeping quietly.

'Lucy, please. She said all that but, on my honour, I never connected you to her. She spoke of 'my wealthy, fucking sister'. I only half listened to her ridiculous plans. I told her that I loved someone else. I couldn't ever love her. She's a brash, selfish tart, who is a murderer, amongst her other crimes. As for Chloe being mine, yes it's possible, we did have sex – and that's all it was for her. She doesn't love anyone bar herself. But she never told me that she was pregnant when we split up. Nor did she ever say who her sister was.'

'But you came back, got in touch again and married me. Is this the part where you say it's over and you want a divorce, take half my money and go off into the sunset with Jo-Ann? You'll have a long time to wait; she has another six years to go and will be 50 years old by the time she comes out.'

I think he was coming over to sit on the bed again. I threw a hand out to him and said, 'Don't you dare come near me!' He stopped mid-stride and turned back to the window.

'I don't know what to say to you to get you to believe me. All the rubbish she spouted about you and her 'big plan' is what made me finish with her. It was Reg who got in touch with me by letter to say your marriage was over and I should just visit you and take it from there. I took heed of what he said, not what Jo-Ann said. By then I had forgotten what she had said, anyway.'

'But you would know my marriage was over it was splashed all over the papers, for God's sake, she'd killed him!' I cried at him.

'I think Reg meant that you weren't grieving any more and that you were fit and well. Ask him. I just hope he remembers. I walked into the Red Lion Pub that day and he said, 'good to see you lad, she's in the hall' when I went into the hall and saw you, all those feelings came tumbling back. On our wedding day, I thanked Reg for getting in touch and telling me you were free. If I wanted to go ahead with Jo-Ann's plan, why have I not asked for a divorce long ago, taken Chloe and toddled off to France to await my lover's release from prison and why wasn't I around when she visited Chloe here, just to get a glimpse of her?'

'What is it about her that men see? She's had both my husbands and tried to take Chloe and Clair away from me.'

'It's a sad fact, Lucy but unfortunately she hates you and is eaten up with jealousy. Why should you have so much when she has nothing, is how she thinks.'

I remained quiet.

After a few minutes I said, 'That's the most truthful thing you've said this evening.'

'What do you want me to do?'

'Go.'

'Lucy, darling, after all we've got between us?'

'But what is it we have?'

'A happy marriage, two adored children, both of whom are doing well. We should be enjoying life and happy with our lot. We have so much to be thankful for.'

I heard all he was saying but wasn't taking it in.

'I want you to contact Chloe and ask her to have a blood test and for you to tell her why and for you to have a blood test as well.'

'And then?'

'It depends on the answer you get from that.'

'And if she is my child, what then?'

'I think you can say that this 'happy marriage' is over.'

Matt was white faced and at that moment I felt nothing for him.

'You surely don't mean that?'

'Unfortunately, I do.'

'Lucy please. I have always loved you. I have never loved anyone else as I have loved you. On my honour.'

'What price your honour?'

'You mean the world to me. Our life together has been perfect from day one, other than the frightful time when Chloe went to live with Jo-Ann and the time when she kidnapped Clair, which was just so terrible. I don't want to lose you. You are far too precious to me.' Matt said sadly. 'I count my blessings, daily.'

I remained quiet; I was too angry and too confused with my own feelings to find an answer.

'You can sleep in the spare bedroom tonight and remain there until such times you can organise a blood test for yourself and Chloe and until Auntie Peggy and Reg come back from their latest holiday and I can check with Reg your claim that he wrote to you to tell you to come and see me, is true.'

'Why would I lie about that when it's so easy for you to check up on it? Anyway, they have only just gone.'

'Well that gives you plenty of time to organise your blood test and tell Chloe to get hers done, doesn't it?' I said angrily.

Hurt as he undoubtedly was, he walked out of the bedroom and went down to the kitchen. He must have tried to put on a brave face for Clair's sake and have their dinner, I didn't want anything, I stayed in the bedroom crying quietly.

It was difficult in those following days. I tried to be as normal as possible when Clair was around but when she was at school or out with friends, I barely spoke to or even looked at Matt.

His blood test done, we waited until Chloe rang to say she'd had hers done and was coming to see us with the phial of her blood that weekend, as she wanted an explanation. It was lovely to see her but I could see that she was worried. Clair threw herself into Chloe's arms.

'How smashing to see you.' She cried. 'I didn't know you had a holiday coming up.'

'I don't actually, just lots of free periods. I should be studying really. I just wanted to see my annoying little sister.' And she tickled Clair to show she was just kidding.

'And Mum and Dad as well, of course.' She added.

The next day, when Clair had gone off to school Chloe sat in the kitchen and looked at Matt and me. 'What's up? I can feel the tension in the air.'

'Have you got your blood phial with you?' Matt asked.

'Of course.'

'We need to make an appointment with the doctor and take the blood phials along for him to see them,' I explained.

'Why?'

I looked at Matt and remained quiet. He coughed nervously.

'Come on Mum, Dad, we've always been able to talk.'

'It's difficult Chloe... It appears... It appears that I might be your father.'

Chloe naturally looked dumbfounded and stared at Matt and said accusingly, 'but you always said that you had never met Jo-Ann.'

'A long time ago, before your mother and I married, I had an affair with... with Jo-Ann.' Chloe gasped and her hand flew to her mouth.

Matt continued with, 'in my defence I didn't know it was Jo-Ann. She called herself Josephine McCarthy and she'd either dyed her hair black or had on a black wig. I'm so sorry Chloe.'

'I see why the blood tests were needed. It's not conclusive. It will be a definite no or a possible yes.' She looked at the two of us and pursed her lips. 'For my part and selfishly, I'd rather have Dad as my natural father then the bastard Jo-Ann had an affair with and was Mum's first husband. But I do understand that it is obviously a huge problem to Mum. For that, I'm truly sorry.' She got up, came to my chair and then bent down to cuddle me. 'I do understand Mum, really I do. Jo-Ann is such a selfish bitch. I don't even think of her anymore and certainly not as my mother. You are that in every way. But you must be so hurt by this. First Lewis and then Matt. But please don't let this awful thing come between you two. I don't know a more loving couple. Your love for each other should be strong enough to get you both through this. Don't let her stories, true or otherwise, destroy you both. It will mean that, in a way, she has won.'

Oddly enough, her words did comfort me far more than anything Matt had said. I squeezed her hand that was on my shoulder.

'Whoever your father is, nothing changes between you and me Chloe. I shall always love you.' I said rather sadly.

'And Dad?'

'I don't know.' I hesitated, ' It's something... something I need to think through.'

'Don't let her win Mum, Please.' Chloe begged. 'That would please her so much.'

Our doctor said it would take a few days to test the blood but he would let us know as soon as possible. He understood the urgency.

There was no doubt, when the results came through, that Lewis was not Chloe's father – but Matt wasn't either!

Chloe was devastated. We went up to see her, to let her know. It's not something we could tell her by phone. 'So I'm a product of a one night stand,' is all she said, but I knew she was hurt and upset.

The news helped to start to heal the rift between Matt and me, especially as Reg remembered sending a letter to Matt to tell him I was free. It was just such a shame that the reason for our marriage to start healing should cause Chloe such heartache. She was no nearer to knowing who her father was.

It was Matt who went to see Jo-Ann in prison. He went with my blessing. He came back very upbeat. 'Chloe will be pleased that she isn't the product of a one night stand. Her father is a Charles Harvey, the man Jo-Ann was going to marry but who dumped her when the murder hit the papers.'

'How did you get all this information from her?' I queried.

'I asked the prison Governor if I could have a private word with Jo-Ann. I was shown into a side room, with just the Governor as a witness. I simply asked her who Chloe's father was. She prevaricated for a while, until the Governor said if she couldn't answer truthfully, if she knew what truth was, she could have her stay in prison extended. Once she started talking, she couldn't stop. She eventually was led away, crying.'

We did a bit of sleuthing to find out more about Charles Harvey. He was in publishing and was, by all accounts, well thought of. He was happily married with three children. We told Chloe that we wouldn't stand in her way if she wanted to meet up with him but she never did. She said that it was more than likely that he knew nothing about her and she didn't want to be the cause of any upset between him and his wife. She also said, 'Why, when I have got the nicest Mum and Dad in the whole world, would I want to muddle my life up even more by meeting yet another man who is supposed to be my father? And anyway, all that could be a pack of Jo-Ann's lies.'

We had to agree with her.

I have been staying at Crofters Cottage while Auntie Peggy and Reg are away yet again. I needed to be on my own. Clair is loving having her father to herself for a while. I imagine that late nights are the order of the day and her being thoroughly spoilt while I am away. So much has happened, I needed time to reflect and with the healing properties that the cottage seems to have, I feel loads better, so much so that I have a 'date' for tonight. Matt is calling for me at 7.30 and we are going to the Sandpipers for a quiet, romantic dinner.

XXXIV.   1988-2008

Chloe went on to great things. She passed her medical exams with flying colours. Matt and I are so proud of her. With her big inheritance that she got when she was 21, she could have taken life easy, done a lot of exciting things, gone on fabulous holidays and bought expensive jewels and become a 'follower of fashion' But she did none of these things. Once she had finished her exams and with her medical degree, she got together a team of doctors and nurses and flew to Africa to help the poor and starving. She has two clinics built and is about to start on her third, just red tape is holding her up. People will walk for more than two days with their ill relatives, just to get to see her in the hope that she, or one of her team, can help them. She writes as often as possible but her time is short. She comes home once a year for three months, as with the others she needs time to regroup and re-charge her batteries. Poor girl is exhausted when she returns home. Chloe married a French doctor; his name is Phillip Lafarge. By design, they have no children; she says she couldn't bear it if her children turned out to be like Jo-Ann and in her view it was better if the Bradley line died out, because future generations with Jo-Ann's evil in them could come out in some way and devastate someone else's life. She couldn't put innocent people through being tainted by her blood and anyway she has hundreds of children in the bush although her 'home' is still with us.

Chloe and Phillip will go for one month to France to see his family and spend a week with her Aunts Maria, Teresa and Francis. They are charmed to have her stay and are fiercely proud of her too. Her French, of course, is now word perfect!

Clair, also still lives at home. To be exact, she lives in the Barn conversion with her husband Oliver, who is a computer expert. She has two children, both boys. Before her marriage she went to university to study law and now works for Simon Frobisher. She loves her work. My job was to look after my two grandchildren when she was working; this I loved. Clair adores Simon, who should retire but can't let go of the reins! She is reluctant to leave home. I put that down to her being kidnapped by Jo-Ann all those years ago, the fear of maybe never getting home again has stayed with her and may never go. She is also wealthy in her own right but, unlike Chloe, she enjoys the good things in life. Her delight is to take me to Darlington and go on a spending spree. I'm happy to oblige.

Matt no longer works at the bank. He had a cancer scare two years ago and prefers to potter in the garden. He calls himself 'Tommy's labourer'. Tommy also still works in the garden. Both of his girls are married now and 'off his hands'. He still works at the Red Lion Hotel but is Manager of the whole outfit. His mother Carol would be so proud of him. We talk of her often. Matt and Tommy became firm friends and David is included in that friendship. They meet down at the Red Lion Inn once or twice a week for a drink and a chat. David and Tommy come for lunch sometimes, especially if Tommy's wife is working.

My biggest sadness was the day Reg rang to say he couldn't wake Peggy. (We dropped the 'Auntie' tag a long time ago). I knew what had happened. I was as devastated as Reg was. Matt had to make all the funeral arrangements. Reg and I spent a lot of time together. They had got a little dog as they had stopped going on long lengthy holidays and we would walk down to the river. It reminded me of my walks with Grandad and Honey. Reg couldn't conduct his life without his Pegs and died just a year later. We took over the little dog; his name was Jack. I was so upset at Reg's going but felt at least he was with his beloved Pegs again. I feel they are close to me in times of need. David is on his own. Shirley left him once he found out how she had behaved with the children; I think he threatened her, so she left. I imagine his boot helped her out of the door. Only Sylvia is married and also works with Simon Frobisher as a clerk. Tim never married. I truly believe Shirley scarred him for life and he is gay.

My mother and Simon Frobisher finally got it together, although they never married, they seemed happy enough. I believe that was her choice. 'Once bitten twice shy,' she used to say to me. I saw her quite often and miss her now. She died 10 years ago. I cannot say I was as devastated as when Peggy died.

And Jo-Ann? I gave her a handsome sum of money when she came out of prison to get out of our lives and as an extra precaution, we took out an injunction against her to stop her from coming within five miles of where we live. She moved to France. I send a monthly check to her and she knows that if she bothers us in any way, they will stop. She got herself a small apartment on the Left Bank in Paris. I am told she drinks most of the money. Her looks have gone and she is almost unrecognisable as the beauty she once was. She sleeps around with all sorts.

The gendarmes rang yesterday, saying that she had been found dead in a gutter. She had syphilis.

The same morning I found a lump in my breast.

XXXV.   2009 ~ MATT'S STORY

I killed Lucy, as surely as if I put a gun to her head and pulled the trigger. When she found the lump in her breast and the resulting tests came back positive, we were both devastated but we were strong in our desire to beat this horrid thing that had invaded her body. She went through chemotherapy. The lump refused to go away but grew smaller over time. It was when a tumour was found in her head that we began to worry; apparently the lump in her breast was secondary to the tumour in her head. After vigorous chemotherapy and radiotherapy, all the tumours became pinpricks in size but wouldn't go away.

Lucy was overcome with sadness when she lost her hair. It seemed more important to her than the tumours. It wasn't that, of course, it was just the final straw.

The chemo made her so ill that sometimes she could not even get out of bed, she was constantly sick and became very weak and thin. It was her decision to stop both treatments. She wanted to die with some dignity and with whatever time she had left she wanted to be able to enjoy without feeling so ill all the time. I didn't agree with her but I had to go along with her wishes.

I took her away on holiday to Australia and we had a really wonderful time. She looked so much better being off those invasive drugs that, to begin with, you wouldn't know that she was so ill.

In those final months, although terrible, we forged a new and altogether more beautiful relationship, a time that I will treasure forever. At night, which was her worst time, I'd hold her in my arms and we would tell each other lovely stories that always began with 'Do you remember...' I called Chloe to say she should come back as soon as possible. She was very shocked and dreadfully upset.

Clair was such a help; she would sit with her Mum for hours. She took it upon herself to do all the shopping, cleaning and cooking. I took the time she sat with Lucy to catch up on some sleep, although I could cope as long as I got four hours a night.

I'm sure the doctor gave me more morphine phials than I needed but I gave her the recommended dose. We didn't need a district nurse to attend us, we saw to ourselves. Lucy was hooked up in her last week to a drip as she was eating nothing and not drinking enough and was getting dehydrated.

Lucy became so ill that I could no longer see her suffer so much. One night, after holding her close and telling her how much I loved her, I slipped a double amount of morphine into her drip. I then called the girls in to tell them I thought Lucy was slipping away. They wouldn't know what I had done but the doctor knew; my understanding of the situation was that that was the reason for the extra morphine phials being given to me. He seemed satisfied with what I had done, although it was never spoken of.

There were so many people at Lucy's funeral. All the women from The Priory arrived *en masse*. Just the newer women stayed behind to look after the children. A few of the members on the board of Governors arrived and Greg Watson, formerly one of the security guards, came, as did Bill Sandy, now voted onto the board as entertainments manager after Major Towers' death. Friends of Lucy's came, including her greatest friend, Wendy. Some of Clair's friends came too.

Tommy and David were towers of strength to me. I left all the arranging of Lucy's funeral to them. There must have been close to 60 people there. Afterwards we went to the Red Lion Hotel for the buffet, the hotel that had been so much a part of Lucy's life. I couldn't imagine holding her wake anywhere else.

Afterwards, I simply went to pieces. I missed Lucy so much. I loved her to distraction. Her presence is everywhere in the house. The double bed is cold and lonely without her to cuddle up to. Only now, eight months after her death, can I talk about her without breaking down. I rattle about the house, feeling lost and lonely. I have closed down the big sitting room and three bedrooms. I live in the snug, kitchen and bedroom. This brought me to the decision that I should live in the barn conversion and Clair could have the house. The house needs children. Clair has two sons, Simon is 12 years old (he was named after Simon Frobisher, who died suddenly last year) and Michael is 10. There is another late arrival on the way. Clair is 36 and would dearly love a girl this time around. She asked me that if it was a girl could she name her Lucy. I am having to think deeply about this. For me there is only one Lucy.

Sorting through Lucy's personal effects was very painful for me. Chloe and Clair offered to do it for me but I must do this myself; I owe Lucy that. It took me ages to pluck up the courage to do it and more time in actually doing it as almost each item I touched brought back so many happy memories. Her perfume still hangs in the air. I sprinkled some on my tearstained pillows. I believed it would help me sleep but halfway between sleep and wakefulness, I'd forget but only for a moment, it was like a hammer blow to my senses when I remembered that she was gone from me forever and sleep would evade me once more.

Chloe has only just gone back to Africa but she is coming home soon for good. She has forged her name in hard graft, now there are younger people to take over from her. Her French husband Phillip is also taking early retirement. Except retiring is not what they have in mind. They are thinking seriously of opening an orphanage and running it between them. They really are a delightful couple.

Some of the children who came to the clinics for help are now adults and are trained as doctors and nurses and have returned to their villages to carry on with what Chloe started.

Most of the colleagues who went out with her, have gone back to where they came from, all for different reasons, the heat was one reason and Malaria was another but all will have memories to treasure. Now, others will have to manage the clinics without Chloe and Phillip. She intends to visit them once or twice a year to see how they are managing. Chloe has assured them that she will not be checking up on them.

Sorting through Lucy's things is when I came across her journal, not that she kept it hidden or locked away, and her letter to us was with it. It was in her escritoire that she had brought over from The Priory. I often came across her scribbling away in it. I could have read it at any time if I had wanted to but I hadn't thought I should.

But here she was, asking me to read it. I put it to one side, intending to read it once I was settled in The Barn.

I lit the log fire in the barn conversion and sat myself down, with a whisky at my side, I stated to read her journal and couldn't put it down.

When I had finished reading it, I was appalled. I stared into the fire. She had kept that terrible secret to herself for all these years. I felt as though I didn't know Lucy at all. But thinking about it, the next day, I understood perfectly why she had done it, all that pain that she had gone through while being married to that monster, Lewis. I could even understand why she had let Jo-Ann take the blame, what I couldn't understand was why she had never told me.

'My darling girl.' I murmured to myself. 'Why could you not have told me?'

Tomorrow I should go to the police with her journal. Is that what she wanted me to do? I reasoned with myself, but for them to do what? All those involved were dead; what did it matter now? She had wanted her daughters to know but they wouldn't believe it and I wanted them to remember their mother as the wonderful woman she was, a warm, loving, fabulous person and a great homemaker and so kind and generous and to remember her with love. To me she was the greatest love of my life.

I placed the journal on the fire and watched it turn to ashes.

XXXVI.   LUCY'S JOURNAL

It was quite easy to kill Lewis. Everything just fell into place for me. As a battered wife, who had nearly been killed once, I absolutely felt that it was either him or me. After he found my cheque book in the attic, he would beat the hell out of me and probably end up killing me. I felt it was a bit futile to run away as I was sure he would find me, he'd said he would. He then would drag me back and kill me, this I was sure of.

I left The Priory at 4.30. Mrs Ebson had waved me off (bless her). I drove to a service station on the other side of Darlington that I had used often. Lewis and I had our cars serviced there, as they would loan us a car, although Lewis would never have driven me there for my car to be seen to. I was expected to make my own arrangements for getting home and for collecting my car later.

I wore a polo neck sweater (to hide the bruises on my neck) in bright red, black trousers and a pair of black high-heeled boots and a pair of dark sunglasses to hide my black eyes; at least I was colour co-ordinated! I must have cut quite a dashing figure in the drab and cold petrol station. I parked by a pump and left the car (a Jaguar 420 saloon, last year's Christmas present from Lewis). Telling an attendant to fill her up, check the oil and wash the windscreen, I said I'd wait in the cafeteria and have a coffee and would he tell me when the car was ready please. He smiled pleasantly and took the keys from me.

I sat trying to clear my brain enough to think were to go. Auntie Elsie, although nearer, seemed to be the obvious choice as Lewis didn't know her, since the Red Lion and Crofters Cottage would be the first places Lewis would look to find me. If Auntie Elsie was still working at Sutton Bank Hotel, she could be working this evening. I would have to wait somewhere until she would be back. I needed to kill some time. And that word 'kill' reverberated in my brain. That's when I decided that I would have to kill Lewis. I had really had enough of his cruelty and couldn't take anymore.

A young lad came into the cafeteria about 10 minutes later to say the car was ready; he said he had parked it just outside and that it had needed no oil. I thanked him and gave him a handsome tip, something I had never been able to do before. Lewis didn't believe in tipping. I paid for the coffee and the fuel at the same cash desk; she handed me my receipt that I stashed in my bag. Old habits die hard; I had religiously saved all my receipts for three and a half years for Lewis to check through. I drove out of the station and headed towards Scotch Corner.

About a mile further on, I turned right onto the old Darlington road. I passed a sleepy hamlet. After the village green, I noticed a left turn that said *Gilling West 20 miles* – the village where Auntie Elsie lived – a nice shortcut that I hadn't known about before. I went over a narrow bridge, turned the next right and then left back onto the Scotch Corner Road again. To my right, in the distance, I could just make out the lights of the service station where I had filled up with petrol. I headed back to Darlington and went through the town at a snail's pace. There must be a football game on or something important; I had never seen so many cars. This would seriously hold me up on my return and I wondered if the bypass was finished yet. A notice had said 'Closed' when I had passed the turning earlier on.

I drove into the churchyard next door to The Priory and parked in a coppice. It was a proper parking place but not often used, as people preferred to park nearer the church. I remembered that choir practise was on a Monday, Wednesday and Friday but this was Thursday, so no-one would be around. I donned the brown overall housecoat. I had my wellingtons sitting on a carrier bag in the foot-well behind the passenger seat. I leant back to pick them up; stuffed inside were a pair of thick woolly socks. I put these on, and the wellingtons, which were about two sizes too big for me. They were all Lewis's things. He had given them to me as though they were the crown jewels and said, 'keep these things with you at all times, in case you have a puncture and have to change a wheel.' I had never changed a wheel in my life, so they had never been used. In the pocket of the overall was a pair of rubber gloves; I put these on as well.

I stepped out of my car and listened. All was quiet, not a sound could be heard. I hurried across the church drive and into the little path that leads to the door let into our boundary wall. Above the door is a wooden lintel with a deep indent in the top of it where the large key is kept. I reached up for it. Having located the key, I took it down, inserted it into the keyhole and turned it. The click it made as it unlocked the door sounded loud in the silent surroundings. I stepped into our garden and, taking the key out, closed the door, reinserting the key on the inside of the door and locking it again but leaving the key in the lock.

There is a rough path, kept clear by old Sam, that runs along the boundary wall, the other side of which is the main road to Darlington. It's quite straight, the path, until it curves in to take account of our private road that leads to our main front gates. The path is maybe 200 yards long from the door in the wall to the bottom of our drive.

All along the drive and on each side are mature rhododendron bushes. I kept close to these, so that I was in deep shadow, even though it was quite dark and little light reached here from the lamp-post lining the main road. I had known Lewis wouldn't be home and, anyway, his Mercedes wasn't in the drive, nor was Mrs Alexicon's car.

I hugged the sides of the porch so as not to put the security light on, then entered the porch, took my boots off and left them behind the still open outer door. They would not be detected, that door was never closed until Lewis went to bed. It was his last job to close the door and lock it. The door into the hall wasn't locked either. I silently opened it, stepped inside and closed it just as softly and padded across the hall to Lewis's study and entered it. The curtains were open; it had been one of my jobs to close them when it got dark. Mrs Ebson wouldn't think of it and anyway, although she would be still here, talking to Milly in the kitchen, she was now off duty and waiting for her husband to collect her.

Lewis's desk is in front of the French doors that lead into the front garden at the side of the porch, making a little patio area. Slightly behind his desk but to the right of the French doors is a large cupboard; between that and the side wall was a small space I could hide in. The space was left to accommodate the floor to ceiling curtains when opened, as they were now.

I looked round the room and shuddered. It was a large imposing room but to me it was a torture chamber, where a lot of the beatings had taken place and where he had smashed my face on his desk. I felt my cheek where the wiring was still in place, it would ache sometimes even now, especially in the cold.

I walked towards the fireplace and picked up the poker; it's very heavy as it is made out of cast iron and has a brass knob at one end. With this in my hand, I hid to the side of the cupboard and waited.

I must have waited for about an hour.

Lewis was early. He usually comes home on a Thursday at about 10.00 or later. The grandfather clock just outside Lewis's study door struck eight as his car entered the driveway. His car lights flickered through the rhododendron bushes, lighting up the study intermittently. I stood stock still, gripping the poker with both hands, so hard that my knuckles turned white.

'This is the time to go,' I said to myself, 'slip out of the French doors while there is still time...' but I couldn't move. I heard Lewis slam his car door, walk towards the porch, cross it, open the inner door and close it behind him. I heard his footfall as he came across the hall and then the study door opened. He left it open to give himself enough light to see his way to his desk light and switched it on. I heard the squeak of his leather chair as he sat down in it.

There was complete silence for moments only, then he started swearing. I wondered if he had spotted my rings and Jo-Ann's letter in the middle of his blotting pad. He was getting angry as I could hear his chair squeaking loudly and his swearing got louder and more vulgar. It was then I crept out of my hiding place and stood quietly behind him. I raised the poker above my head and brought it down onto the back of his head. Blood spurted out onto the overalls. I doubt that he felt anything, certainly not the pain he had inflicted on me over the past three and a half years. He fell forward over his desk. I didn't check to see if he was dead, I was sure he was. I left the dirty blood-stained poker on his desk as the final indignity, he would have hated to have a dirty poker left on his gleaming desk.

It was time to go. There was no-one in the hall as I sped across it in my stockinged feet. I opened the front door and stepped through it, then closed it quietly behind me. I dragged on the Wellingtons and once again hugged the porch walls so the light wouldn't go on. I had just regained the rhododendron shadows when I thought I heard footsteps on the steps to the porch but the security light didn't go on; maybe it hadn't been switched on in the hall. I'd have to hurry now. If Lewis had a visitor and the visitor found Lewis dead in his study, police would be crawling all over the place in minutes. I tried to run but kept slipping out of the Wellingtons. At the bottom of the drive I stopped to get my breath and looked back but couldn't see the study window. I could have if I stepped out of the cover of the rhododendrons but I didn't want to do that.

I hugged the boundary wall and quickly walked on. I hadn't gone far when a car turned into the drive. I didn't stop to see who it was but hurried on. Nothing seemed to happen back at the house, no screaming sirens. A police car raced towards the house but went past at breakneck speed towards Darlington just as I reached the gate in the wall. I peeped through the greenery but could see nobody. All was quiet, just as it had been when I had arrived.

Still no police cars arrived at The Priory. Maybe the visitor was Mr Ebson, in which case he was early. Maybe there had been no-one going up the steps I had come down 15 minutes or so earlier. Maybe I had imagined it, or the wind was playing tricks on me. It had also started to rain in a steady downpour.

I unlocked the door set in the wall and stepped out, took the key out of the lock and reinserted it on the outside, then, pulling the door closed behind me, I locked it again and returned the key to its hiding place in the lintel. Once at the car, I sat sideways on the driver's seat to remove the wellingtons, socks, gloves and overalls. The socks and the gloves I shoved into the wellington boots and once again placed them on the carrier bag in the well behind the passenger seat. The blood-stained overalls I put on the seat beside me. I put my own boots back on, started the car up and drove slowly out of the churchyard. I didn't put my lights on until I had gone about 50 yards and only then because in the far distance I could see another car's lights approaching me.

I only just touched the outskirts of Darlington before turning right and using the new bypass that would connect me with the Scotch Corner road. It still had a NO ENTRY notice up but it was a chance I had to take that it went right through to the other end, which I could not see. If there were road works at the Scotch Corner end that I could not get through, I'd have to come all the way back again.

Surprisingly it was clear, so I couldn't understand why it was still marked as closed. I joined the main road to Scotch Corner with no problems. Before reaching the service station, I turned right once more onto the old Darlington road and drove like the clappers, like a maniac, knowing that I would see the lights of any approaching vehicle and be able to slow down. I stopped on the little bridge and dragged the Wellington boots out, still with the gloves and socks stuffed inside and threw them into the fast-flowing river below, followed by the overalls. I drove fast again to the hamlet, where I slowed down; I didn't want to miss the right turning that would lead me to Gilling West. Twenty miles to go. The lane connected eventually to the road I would have come in by if I had gone to

Scotch Corner and taken a right there. This way I missed out 15 or so miles. I turned right and, trusting to luck that there were no police around, I drove swiftly again until I came to the road that led to Gilling West. There is a very steep hill there that goes down and down and also goes on and on until it reaches the village, ending in a gentle slope at the village green. I drove down to the end of the green and took a tight right turn to go half way back up the other side, another left turn and there was Auntie Elsie's pretty cottage, just a little way along the road on the left.

I had done it! I was safe but reaction was setting in and I started to shake. I staggered up her garden path and rang her bell.

XXXVII.   SAM'S STORY

Old Sam could tell a few stories about Mr Lewis Alexicon, Oh, aye, that he could and he didn't like him, one little bit.

On this day he took a crowbar and a screw driver from the garden shed down at the bottom of the garden, on the left of the house, it was placed hard up against the bushes at the back of which was the lane to the garages. He had already said goodnight to the ladies, Mrs Ebson and Miss Franks, having enjoyed a cup of tea with them. He was off to the back gate, the one that led to the church. He wanted to lift the gate up slightly, which was where the crowbar would come in handy and tighten the hinges.

Mrs Alexicon, senior, had said it was difficult to open as it seemed to have fallen slightly, or maybe the wood had swollen because of all the rain. He worked diligently but he was very cross. The younger Mrs Alexicon had gone over two hours ago, run away so Mrs Ebson had said, couldn't take the beatings any longer she had supposed.

They all knew what a bastard Mr Lewis was. For all his la-de-da way's he was no better than he should be. Old Sam kept his thoughts to himself, though. But no-one knew Mr Lewis like Sam did. Oh no.

Finished with what he was doing and satisfied that the gate was now working alright, he had tested it by opening it using the key on top of the lintel to unlock it and had swing the gate backwards and forward a few times, just to make sure. He relocked the gate and returned the key. He walked down the long path bordering the boundary wall, coming eventually to the drive which he crossed, intending to take the crowbar and screwdriver back to the shed but although it was very dark other things had caught his attention that needed sorting. The latch on the front gate was loose and Mrs Alexicon Senior had asked him to cut the Ivy back from the side window of the porch. He was at the door of the shed to get the shears, when he heard Mr Lewis's powerful car turn into the drive; it must have been about eight o clock by then.

Old Sam had worked himself up into a rage by this time and had decided to teach Mr Lewis a lesson he wouldn't forget. Slowly, he made his way back to the main house.

Suddenly as plain as day, he saw Miss Lucy come out by the front door. She was dressed in very odd clothes and looked like a shop-keeper. He watched as she slid round the side of the front porch. Quietly, Sam entered the porch, slipped out of his Wellington boots and entered the house silently by the hall door. Mrs Alexicon Senior was out, he knew that, as her car wasn't in the drive or in the garages he'd looked in as he had passed them by. He padded across the hall in his stockinged feet. Mr Lewis's study door stood open but his light wasn't on. Sam slipped through the open door. Mr Lewis was lying half over his desk. Sam could see that quite clearly without the light on. He edged over to the desk and poked Mr Lewis in the ribs with the crow bar. Mr Lewis groaned. Sam had a few words to say to Mr Bloody Lewis.

For instance he had seen Mr Lewis rock the boat and little Miss Elaine fall in the lake. He had seen Miss Elaine get to the surface and cry out. He's seen the young Mr Lewis break the surface of the water close beside her, then, they had both gone under again.

Only Mr Lewis had come to the surface once more. He hadn't thought at the time that anything was amiss. The young Miss Elaine could swim, he had seen her. He had thought that she would be out of his view on the other side of the upturned rowing boat. Mr Lewis hadn't seemed at all worried and had swum slowly to the side of the lake and climbed out and walked without hurrying up the little grassy bank to the path through the wood. Only when Sam heard the tale Mr Lewis had told about diving down repeatedly to try and get his sister did Sam have alarm bells ringing in his head. He was positive that 'Master Lewis', as he was then called, had drowned his little sister.

But if he told his story, who was going to believe him? Sam had been around but too far away to help the day Mr Lewis killed Mrs Alexicon's little dog. It had been so unexpected. The first blow to the dog's head had been enough to kill the little fellow; he hadn't needed to keep hitting him. Sam had seen Miss Lucy swim out to the rope that held the sack that Mr Lewis had used to put the dog's body in. He hadn't gone to help her because he realised that Miss Lucy just had her 'undergarments' on. He didn't want to embarrass her and anyway she seemed to be coping very well on her own, so he had stayed away.

Sam had found the dog's grave a few days later. It had a single white rose on it and, after that, one every week until Miss Lucy was injured again.

Mr Lewis was an evil man. Just like his father to look at but totally different in character. Mr Alexicon senior was a true gentleman but had come back from the First World War a very disturbed man. He had been getting better but the death of little Elaine, whom he had adored, seemed to tip him over the edge. Mr Alexicon, Sam thought, suspected his son of misdoings but seemed afraid of him. Anyway, now he lived in a loony bin. Mrs Alexicon visited nearly every week.

Sam wasn't afraid of anyone or anything. He put the desk light on for a second only and gazed at the injured man. Sam had always pretended that he was a bit stupid and slow; it had suited his purpose. His father had said, 'Never seem to be cleverer than the landed gentry, lad.' But Sam had put two and two together, seeing Miss Lucy in her getup and now Mr Lewis injured and the poker lying on the desk. It took little time to work it out. No way was he going to let Miss Lucy take the blame for this. He, Sam, would. Anyroad, he thought, Mr Lewis deserved all he got. He lifted the crowbar that he still had in his hand and brought it down onto Lewis's head. It made a satisfying crunching sound.

'That'll teach yer a lesson an' no mistake, yer bastard. Now that nice Miss Lucy, who has always treated me with respect, can come back 'ome again.'

He turned and walked out the way he had come in, put on his Wellington boots, which he had left in the porch, and started for home. Just as he got to the garages, another car came into the drive. He didn't recognise it but it was no concern of his. He put the screwdriver back where it belonged in the shed but took the crowbar with him, walked to the five bar gate, opened it just enough for him to slip out, then closed it behind him. He crossed the lane and had gone through the stile into the field to go home when lights appeared in the lane. He looked behind and saw Mrs Alexicon senior get out of her car. He almost went back to help her but by the time he was nearing the stile again she had already driven through the gate and was getting out to close it again. Sam turned away and trudged across the field. He was going to be soaking wet by the time he got home as it was raining and had got very windy.

Home to Sam was one of the little cottages that belonged to Mr Gilmore, who farmed the land behind The Priory. He had worked there and had taken on the job of gardener for Mrs Alexicon to supplement his income and keep his family going. His sons had worked on the farm as well but they had all moved away to better paid jobs in factories and got married. His grandson, Joseph, lived with him now and worked on the farm. He could turn his hand to anything to do with agriculture. Sam didn't do farm work any longer, his first love was gardening, with the occasional odd job thrown in.

He went to the back door of his cottage and leant the crowbar against the outside wall. Sam opened the door and stepped inside, the wind was so contrary that it whipped the door out of his hand and it closed with a bang, causing the crowbar to jump and fall into the bushes that were by the side of the back door, never to be seen again. Sam took his Wellingtons off just inside, then stripped off to wash in the old stone sink in the cold scullery. The cottage was barely updated. It did have hot and cold running water but no bathroom, just a privy outside. But it was home to Sam and his grandson. The rent on the cottage was minimal, thanks to Joseph, who still worked at the farm.

Old Sam was cold; the quicker he got to his bed the better, he'd warm up in there. He climbed wearily up the stairs, went into his bedroom and got into his big double bed. He'd hand himself in to the police tomorrow and tell them what he had done to Mr Lewis and what he knew about him. My, he was tired, but after a good night's sleep he'd feel fine in the morning...

When called on the next morning to sign Sam's death certificate, the doctor said he was a good age, at 84, still to be working.

Joseph was heartbroken.

~ End ~